As Snow Before a Summer Sun

DEBORAH HOWARD

Lewis Publications

Contents

PART FOUR

Copyright

Copyright © 2023

Lewis Publications

This is a work of fiction. Names, characters, places and incidents are either the product of the author's imagination or are used fictitiously, and any resemblance to actual persons, living or dead, business establishments, events or locales is entirely coincidental.

Dedication

Dedicated to my loving husband, Theron,
who has the wisdom and self-confidence
to allow me the time and the freedom
to follow my imagination wherever it leads.

Thank you for your patience,
support, and enthusiasm for my work.

Acknowledgments

I'd like to thank Dee Brown for writing *Bury My Heart at Wounded Knee,* which changed my life and my heart forever. When I read this paragraph in Brown's book, I could not get it off my mind – and, from my imaginings, this book sprang forth:

"In response to this, Sheridan and Custer moved on to Fort Cobb, and from there sent out runners to the four tribes in the area, warning them to come in and make peace or else they would be hunted down and killed. Custer himself went out in search of friendly Indians. For this field operation he requisitioned one of the more attractive young women from his Cheyenne prisoners to go with him. She was listed as an interpreter, although she knew no English."

Bury My Heart at Wounded Knee, Dee Brown, Henry Holt, and Company, ©1970, p.170.

I'd also like to thank my friends, Julie Burch, BettyAnn Canney, Judy Howe, and Curtis Thomas for their input, intelligence, and imaginative suggestions for this project.

I can't speak highly enough of the museums and forts I visited while researching this book. I'd especially like to recommend visits to Anadarko, Oklahoma where I was given the opportunity to tour Indian City USA (where Black Kettle's great-grandson led our tour), The National Hall of Fame for Famous American Indians and The Southern Plains Indian Museum and Craft Center. My congratulations to Oklahoma for providing excellent statewide museums, parks, and opportunities to learn about Indian history and culture. Very well done!

Many thanks to Kass Nickles at Coyote Hills Guest Ranch in Cheyenne, Oklahoma where I had the privilege to ride across the Black Kettle National Grasslands on horseback, making it possible to visualize the countryside and to transport myself via the imagination to that same location in 1868.

Last but not least, my thanks to Fort Larned in Kansas— the restored fort on which I patterned Fort Cobb. It provided the framework on which I built my own "set design" for this book.

Part One

One

November 18, 1868

Indians!

Cordelia Lawson hopped onto the boardwalk, partially hiding herself behind a post. For a moment, she thought her heart might beat out of her chest as she stared, breathless with excitement.

Her first wild Indians! How delightful. They rode into the fort towards headquarters. Her skin tingled with excitement—or the below freezing temperatures. She couldn't tell which.

Pulling her thick, woolen shawl tightly around her shoulders, and leaning into the numbing wind, she continued toward the trader's store, her eyes riveted upon the strange visitors to Fort Cobb. She took in every movement, every texture, every color of the scene.

The six men rode up to General Hazen's office. The older man threw his leg across his horse's neck and slid to the ground. The others followed suit. Contrary to her expectation, their skin was not red but a deep burnished bronze.

Cordelia studied the older one the best she could from across the grounds and wished for a closer look. Even at this distance she found him spectacular, though not at all handsome. This, she reasoned, must be their chief. She only saw his leathered face for a moment as he spoke to one of the other men. This wasn't the savage beast she expected. This was a king, a chief.

Yes, she could see what Robert meant about this being a poor and tired race. Their buckskin leggings and tunics seemed stained and bedraggled. One wore boots that looked suspiciously similar to Army issue. The others wore moccasins—some were plain buckskin, others painted with fading colors. Poor? Yes, certainly poor, she thought. But tired? Perhaps. There was something old about all of them—something in their manner that told a story of . . . what was it? She struggled for the right word. Resignation. That was it.

As they strode toward the door of the headquarters, Cordelia noted the way they moved—different from the heavy thudding of the soldiers' boots. Their steps made no noise. Instead, they moved with a quiet self-assurance, especially the older one.

The Indians' hair was the blackest she'd ever seen, but with a sheen clearly reflecting the sunlight. Two feathers were worked into the hair of the old one. Two of the other men wore their hair loose around their shoulders. The rest wore long braids trailing almost to the colorful beaded straps around their waists.

All but one glanced her way and turned their attention to the headquarters. The other one turned toward her, his eyes squinting into the sun, studying her with the same scrutiny with which she observed him—mirror reflections of each other. Apparently, he was as curious about her as she was about him.

He was splendid—the feather tied into his hair, the beads around his neck, a breast piece of bone and leather hanging from his shoulders. The moment was broken when he turned to follow the others into the headquarters.

Once inside the trader's store, Cordelia rushed to the grimy window, staring across the parade grounds at the horses tied in front of the general's office. Chewing her lip, she desperately wanted to know what was going on over there.

She was here to post a letter to her mother. Still distracted, she handed the letter to grumpy Bill "Griff" Griffinstein, the post trader. She spotted the bolt of heavy cinnamon-colored wool fabric she'd seen on her last excursion to the store. She'd decided to take Bess up on her offer to make her a new riding skirt and jacket out of the material—"to go with that copper hair of yours," Bess had said. Cordelia usually chose to wear shades of green to accentuate her red hair and green eyes, but she had to admit that the warm, lustrous hue of this fabric would look nice with her coloring.

But right now, she couldn't quite keep her mind on what she was doing. The door of General Hazen's office was like a magnet to her eyes—and her attention. Whatever was going on over there, she didn't want to miss a thing. She ordered the material and Griff cut and packaged it with his usual surly scowl. She was too distracted to care. This wasn't the first time she'd felt he resented her presence at Fort Cobb.

From behind her, she heard him growl, "Can't fer the life of me figger out why a lady like you would come out here like 'is. No place fer a lady, if you ask me."

Without turning, she responded, "You know why I came here—to be with my husband. That's all I want. All I've ever wanted."

The door of the headquarters opened. Cordelia's head bolted upward like deer on alert. An enlisted man walked briskly from the headquarters to the trader's store. When he opened the heavy door, the icy fingers of the wind whirled around the store, causing Cordelia to shudder as she wrapped her shawl around her. The temperature outside was dropping fast.

"Ma'am," he said, acknowledging her. She nodded in response.

To Griff, he said, "General Hazen says you wanted to know when them Cheyennes came in."

"Yep. I need you to give this to them," he said, lifting a large parcel onto the counter. "Jennie's belongings. She wanted me to give them to her people so they could divvy them up."

Cordelia was surprised to see Griff's eyes tear up. She knew he'd just lost his Indian wife—a woman they called Cheyenne Jennie. Maybe he wasn't as gruff as his exterior would indicate.

"General Hazen givin' them their rations?" Griff wanted to know.

"Nope. Says he can't do that."

Griff shifted his eyes to stare out the icy window, then grunted, "Wait."

He put together a pouch carrying tobacco, crackers, coffee and sugar—delicacies for the Cheyenne. "Here, give 'em this, too."

Another icy blast assaulted Cordelia as the soldier sprinted from the store to deliver the supplies to headquarters.

"Why, Mr. Griffenstein, that was very generous of you," she said.

Eyeing her suspiciously, he turned his back to her without saying a word.

Her attention again was on the headquarters as she watched the Indians exit the building, carrying the few bundles, and mount their horses in one spectacular leap. The one looked around as if he were searching for her again, then nudged his horse onward. They rode slowly out the gate and down the path leading to their village in the Antelope Hills. Finally, she felt she could breathe again. Had she been holding her breath?

As she was about to collect her package, Robert walked out of the headquarters and watched the retreating Indians for several moments. With his hands on his hips and his brown hair blowing in the gusty chill, he looked down and moved towards the store.

She met him at the door. "Robert! I saw them! They were extraordinary! What happened in there?" Sensing his worry, she asked, "What's wrong?"

"Cordelia, what are you doing here?" Her husband's voice sounded tired, old and somehow far away.

"I had to post a letter and do a little shopping. Running into you is a pleasant surprise, I must say," she said, flashing him her most disarming smile. It didn't work. Gloom still encircled him like a black wreath.

"Tell me what's going on in that brilliant head of yours. What happened with the Indians, Robert?"

He glanced at the trader, who served at the post as a civilian, and drew Cordelia closer to him. "We'll talk about it tonight," he whispered to her. "I really can't tell you anything now." In a normal tone, he continued, "As for now, I believe I'll have a brandy in the officer's club. Have a pleasant afternoon, Cordelia. I'll see you at supper tonight."

She watched as he lifted the hinged countertop, passed through, and made his way into the back room of the store, which served as an officer's club. Griff followed him to serve as bartender, she guessed. Since he'd already listed her purchase and put it on their account, she picked up her package and, bracing herself against the bone-chilling cold, made her way at a brisk clip to the officers' quarters for a visit with her friend, Ela.

~*~

Arriving only a month ago, Cordelia was still settling in to her new surroundings. Raised in Baltimore, she was experienced with cold, but the force of this bitter, driving wind seemed to send icy tentacles deep inside her bones. Here in Indian Territory the wind took on a character of its own, imposing itself on almost every aspect of daily life.

If she ever questioned her decision to travel west, all she had to do was remember her reason for doing it. Robert. Being near him was worth any inconvenience. That's why she thanked God for this new fort where Robert, as a Captain in the Army, was awarded the privilege of living in the Married Officers' Quarters. It was the opportunity they'd waited for. When he sent for Cordelia there was no question but that she would go—even if that meant traveling for the best part of a week to get here.

She smiled, remembering the joy on his face as he helped her from the coach. The love flowing from the softest brown eyes she'd ever seen encompassed her even before his arms did.

Still smiling with the memory, she knocked at her friend's door.

Dr. Norman Anthony was the post surgeon, commissioned as a captain. His wife, Ela, arrived almost a year before Cordelia. She always greeted Cordelia as cheerfully as if she were in the luxurious estate from which she had come. Like Cordelia, Ela left everything to follow a soldier's life. In a way, these visits reminded Cordelia of home and her mother. Their visits were always so . . . civilized.

Though ten or twelve years her senior, Ela Anthony's warmth and hospitality gave Cordelia a sense of belonging at the fort. Living here was not easy. But Ela remained somehow separate from it.

Cordelia also enjoyed Dr. Anthony, or "Doc," as everyone called him. Gentle and soft-spoken, he was a man with a quick wit and easy-going temperament. He and Cordelia struck up an immediate friendship.

Seated across from Ela, her teacup filled for the second time, Cordelia heard the front door open and close and was delighted to see Doc Anthony tromp into the parlor, rubbing his hands together for warmth.

"Mrs. Lawson! So happy you could make it this afternoon, my dear. My wife told me she invited you for a visit. I hoped to have the chance to see you, too."

"Thank you, Doc. How are you?" Cordelia offered him her hand, while holding a teacup in the other. As he pressed her hand to his lips, she continued, "I brought some of Bess's shortbreads for tea. Please have one."

"Thank you, my dear. I believe I will." He reached for the fragile china plate from which Ela served the treat and took one of the sugar-dusted shortbread biscuits. "Mm. It's delicious—absolutely melts in my mouth. Please thank Bess for me, will you?"

"I'd be happy to."

"So what are you two hens in here clucking about? Or should I even wonder? Not my numerous shortcomings, I hope." His eyes twinkled.

"No, you're safe, Norman," Ela laughed, passing him a hot cup of tea. "Mrs. Lawson informed me that she's seen her first Indians just now. And they intrigue her, it seems."

He took a seat next to his wife on the blue and white striped divan. "Yes, the Indians are something, aren't they? I've

9

treated a few of them in the hospital over the past months. Of course, you'll use that information with discretion, I hope. I can't have it known that Indians were treated in the same hospital we use for our own soldiers, now can I?"

"What difference does that make, Doc? They're people, aren't they?"

"That depends on whom you ask, my dear. The popular opinion in these parts is that they are not human beings at all, but some other strange and savage species. They're being slowly exterminated, I'm afraid. Treaties have been signed that will force them farther from their homeland and onto smaller and more remote reservations. And who can forget Sand Creek?"

"Sand Creek?"

Ela patted her hand and said, softly. "Well, it was a battle that took place a few years ago. Most of Black Kettle's tribe was wiped out in the slaughter. We don't talk about it much. It was much too horrible."

At the mention of Black Kettle's name, Cordelia straightened in her chair. "Black Kettle? Robert has mentioned him to me, I believe."

"He's the chief of the Southern Cheyenne. That was Black Kettle she saw today, wasn't it, Norman?" Ela asked.

"Most likely. And he's quite a chief. The story is that Colonel Greenwood gave him an American flag and told him that as long as that flag flew above him, no soldier would fire upon him. So Black Kettle flew the flag over his lodge at all times. During the Sand Creek Massacre, he took the flag and urged all his people to gather around him—told them they would be safe as long as they were under that flag. The Indians huddled under it like chicks under the wings of a mother hen. Well, obviously Colonel Chivington was not apprised of this arrangement because he ordered his men to cut down any and all Indians in the camp. Black Kettle and his wife managed to escape with only a handful of their tribe. Chivington and his men slaughtered the others, I'm afraid. It was a nasty business, my dear. Most distressing."

Cordelia covered her mouth with trembling fingers. "Oh, my," she managed. "That poor, poor man. And yet he was here today. He still trusts the soldiers?"

"What other choice has he? He's ordered to remain in his camping ground. He can't travel away from there without permission from General Hazen, unless he comes here for supplies. But General Hazen has promised him protection as long as he and his people obey the guidelines given them. Therefore, they can live in peace, for now."

"Thank God," Ela whispered.

"But their camp is so far away. Robert said it would take a couple of days to get there. How can we offer real protection from such a distance?"

"Good question, my dear," Doc answered, peering over his glasses. "They would have to send a messenger, I would think."

"Yes," Cordelia murmured softly, taking a sip of her tea. "I suppose so, but I don't see how the soldiers could help from this distance. I feel sorry for them. They seem so helpless."

"Humph!" Doc snorted. "Helpless at the moment, perhaps, but don't confuse helplessness with innocence. They can be fiendish in their torture of our people. General Hancock's companies have been on the prowl for hostile Indians for four months and have killed only two, by their last count. Hancock was superb in the war, you know, but there's a vast difference between fighting Confederate soldiers and coming face to face with the greatest of all cavalry fighters—the plains Indians. So, while Hancock and that feisty George Custer are coming up empty, the hostile Indians they're searching for have butchered better than two hundred white settlers in Kansas alone."

"I thought General Custer was supposed to be some kind of big Indian fighter—at least that's what *he* implies," Cordelia said, cynically, "so why is he coming up empty?"

Doc laughed. "I'm told his strategies have been lacking. From what I've heard, the illustrious general's main gifts seem to be relentless courage and a limitless supply of energy. It seems he never tires, which is why he pushes his men sometimes beyond their abilities. Where fighting Indians is concerned, I'm afraid he's more actor than playwright, if you catch my drift. He follows orders better than he devises strategy," Doc said, with a wink and a chuckle. "On the other hand, this is not a white man's war anymore. Fighting Indians is very different and this country is their home."

"Tell her about that woman in Abilene, Norman," Ela coaxed.

"Well, story is that the Indians have a quaint little method of torturing white women they find unprotected on the prairie. They strip them down naked and stake them spread-eagle on the ground."

"Norman, you don't have to tell everything!" came Ela's mortified cry.

"Woman, you asked me to tell this story, and I'm telling it!"

"Well, don't be so indelicate, dear. You'll shock poor Mrs. Lawson to tears. She's hardly more than a girl."

Cordelia lowered her eyes to her saucer, trying not to smile at Ela's discomfort. Curious as a child, she was hungry to hear the rest of Doc's story.

"Please, go on, Doc," she urged.

After clearing his throat and giving his wife a cautionary glance, he continued, "Anyway, with a woman in this helpless position, they'd build a fire right on her belly. Of course, the woman would die a horrible death. They did this with a woman they captured near Abilene. What they didn't know is that she was both deaf and mute. She couldn't have screamed out, you see. But they interpreted her silence as bravery. And that is a thing all Indians respect. So they brushed the fire off her belly, took her back to their village and cured her wounds. Story has it that they married her off to the chief's son. Five months later, she was rescued and taken back to Abilene."

"Tell her what she did! Tell her!" Ela chirped. Without waiting, she finished the story for him. "First chance she got, she ran back to her Indian husband. She wanted to be with him! Can you imagine?"

"Fascinating! Why, I don't know what to make of this. Are you certain it's true?"

"That's what we heard," Doc chuckled.

Two

Back in her own apartment on the opposite end of the Officers' Quarters, Cordelia anxiously watched for her husband's arrival as the dinner hour approached. The wind had turned bitterly cold and flakes of snow began their quick but silent descent to the ground.

The married officers' quarters were located in this large rough-hewn stone house, separated into several apartments. Robert's rank entitled them to one with a bedroom and a parlor that also served as their dining room. An identical captain's quarters occupied the other end of the house where Doc and Ela Anthony lived.

Four good-sized rooms separated the two larger living quarters. These rooms were designated for the married lieutenants on the fort. Their rooms were furnished with a bed, dresser, chair and a small dining table. They were to share the kitchen and the privy with the captain.

The room directly across the hall from the Lawsons' parlor belonged to Robert's best friend on the fort, 1st Lieutenant Todd Otis, who awaited the arrival of his wife, Nicole, any day now. They had a baby girl named Nora Alice, whom he'd never seen. Nicole was waiting until the baby was fit for travel before joining him at Fort Cobb.

The other lieutenant's room on this end of the house was vacant now. The last lieutenant was killed during a race with another officer when his horse stepped into a prairie dog burrow and flipped over onto her helpless rider, snapping the soldier's neck like a stick. His tearful wife left on the same stagecoach that brought Cordelia to the fort.

Since there was a connecting door between the lieutenants' rooms, Cordelia asked General Hazen if he would assign both rooms to Lieutenant Otis, since he was expecting his wife and baby soon. It made perfect sense to Cordelia to provide a more comfortable living arrangement for the young couple. He refused, saying that it wouldn't be fair to the other lieutenants, who lived on the other end of the house in their one-room quarters.

Cordelia decided to drop the subject until Nicole and the baby arrived. Then she would resurrect her appeal to General Hazen on their behalf, hoping for a change of heart. She usually ended up getting her way, so she was content to wait —for now.

Cordelia came from relative affluence. Her father owned a factory for the manufacture of fine leather boots and shoes; her grandfather owned land in Delaware where he raised rare game birds, as well as more common fowl. Few were the sportsmen back east whose blood didn't rush with excitement at the prospect of a pheasant hunt on a cool autumn morning. Part of her grandfather's income came from selling the gorgeous feathers he harvested from his birds.

As a little girl, Cordelia enjoyed watching the game birds and tried to give each one a suitable name. She especially adored the peacocks with arrogant plumes crowning their nervous heads and the glorious display of their tail feathers, a veritable palette of colors, which excited little Cordelia's imagination.

She'd never forgotten one magical morning walking through the fields with her tiny hand nestled comfortably inside her grandfather's. Stopping, he picked up a peacock feather from the frosty ground. As he lifted it, the light severed the morning mist and played along the azure sparkle of the feather.

"See this splotch of color up here at the tip?"

"Yes, Papa."

"It's the feather's eye, Delia. And do you know why the eye is so brilliantly green?"

"Tell me," she whispered, scarcely able to contain her curiosity.

"The peacocks have seen your eyes, sweet one, and they're trying with all their might to find a way to match their color. But alas, they have failed. They'll never be able to match the color of those eyes, child. So don't get too close to them. I think they're jealous of you, Delia."

She'd looked up into his kindly face and twinkling blue eyes and, blinking hard, tried to open her eyes as wide as she could so he could see them better. He laughed his hearty laugh and gave her the feather to keep forever.

Remembering that laugh, she thought about Lieutenant Otis. Perhaps that's why she'd taken to him so quickly. His laugh was reminiscent of her beloved Papa's. Todd had become like a brother to her in the short time she'd lived here.

But she wasn't the only one who enjoyed Lieutenant Otis's company. He was popular with officers and enlisted men alike. He had an easy wit, laughing bright blue eyes and a wide smile that lit his whole face—the kind of irresistible smile that left one helpless to do anything but smile back in return. Loose-

limbed and agile, he towered over most of the men at the fort—
six feet, two inches tall.

She'd never known anyone named Todd before, but he'd
explained that his mother's maiden name was Todd and that's
why they called him by that name. Michael Todd Otis.

Like a keen-eyed eagle searching for a morsel of food,
Cordelia scrutinized the parade grounds for a sign of her
husband's return. Come to think of it, she hadn't heard Lieutenant Otis come in for the evening, either. She pulled her
shawl tighter around her shoulders, as cold draughts came in
from around the window.

Meanwhile, a warm fire blazed in the fireplace and the delicious aroma of beef stew hung heavily in the air. Bess had
brought the steaming bowl in a few minutes ago and placed it
on the table. A serving plate covered with biscuits, hot from the
oven, was draped with a towel to keep them warm.

Finally, Cordelia spied the shape of a lone soldier leaning
into the wind, tramping through the snow toward their house.
It was Robert, home at last, holding his cape tightly around
him as he fought the onslaught of the cold. Since there'd been
no hint of a winter storm this morning, he'd left his heavy
cloak hanging on its hook in the parlor.

The door opened and he stood stamping the snow off his
boots before entering the room. The worn and distant expression she'd seen earlier was still there. He warmed himself by the
fireside without saying a word, the warm glow illuminating his
handsome face and deep, brown eyes.

"Robert," she began.

"No, Cordelia. Not now. We'll talk later. Let's have a
pleasant dinner first. You're not going to like the news I'm
bringing home tonight."

"Well, you simply cannot expect me to ignore a statement

like that, can you? Now, I really *must* know what you have to tell me. I won't eat a bite until you do."

"Very well." Slowly unbuttoning the first three buttons of his uniform, he took her hand, bent to kiss her proffered cheek, and took his seat at the table.

While she served the thick, rich stew and hot, buttered biscuits, Cordelia searched her husband's face and waited for him to speak. He blessed the food, as usual, but also asked the Lord to give their military leaders wisdom and restraint.

"Amen."

After taking two slow bites of the thick stew, Robert shook his head in appreciation. "It's delicious. We're so blessed to have Bess here with us, aren't we?" He took another spoonful of stew before continuing.

"You know, I always feel a little guilty when I come home to a meal like this. The enlisted men only get coffee and a left-over loaf of bread for supper, you know. In the bakery, they bake one loaf of bread per soldier, per day. What they don't eat for the noon meal, they eat for supper. Even so, it keeps the baker pretty busy—273 loaves of bread every day, right now."

"That's very interesting, Robert, and I wish there was something we could do about it, but don't we have other things to discuss this evening?" Her restraint was wearing thin.

After taking a swallow of his milk, he added, "My mother used to say that dinnertime should be a time to discuss pleasantries. Discussing disturbing things could cause all sorts of problems with the digestion."

"Robert! That's a wives' tale. I'm dying of curiosity!" She pounded the table with her fist. "Now tell me this instant."

"All right. I hate to tell you this, my dear, but I'm afraid we'll be sharing our humble abode with visitors soon."

"Our house?"

"Well, not exactly. They've asked Todd to move into the

bachelor officer's quarters for a while. General Custer and General Sheridan are expected to arrive next week and will be staying here at the fort for an undisclosed period of time."

"Custer! Robert, really. Why spoil such a nice dinner by speaking that man's name?" Cordelia placed her spoon on the table with a clang and wiped the corners of her mouth with the napkin.

"Cordelia, stop pouting. I told you this news would be unpleasant, didn't I?" Robert reminded her. "Yet, you wanted to know. So I told you. That's it. You should have trusted me. I knew you wouldn't want to hear it—now or ever."

"I'm sorry. You're right, darling. I begged you to tell me. But why are they coming here? And why can't they stay in General Hazen's house instead of booting poor Todd out? The general has an extra bedroom upstairs, you know. Besides, I heard that Custer was wintering at Camp Supply. What's happening, Robert?"

"I don't know for sure. But something is afoot. Of that, I'm certain. Custer wouldn't be coming here unless he had orders of some kind. But I don't know what they are. One thing's for sure, those two generally mean there's trouble coming. You've got Sheridan's icy reserve against Custer's eternal flame. It's an alliance that almost always entails danger of some kind. General Hazen hasn't taken me into his confidence about it. I'm certain he knows something, but he's certainly not talking. He behaved quite strangely today with Black Kettle and his warriors."

"How so?"

"Well, I've seen how he behaves with the Kiowa and Comanche leaders. He usually enjoys his companionship with them. He's always welcomed them, has always treated them with kindness and honesty. But when he met Black Kettle today, he was . . . different. Not exactly rude, but cold. They came because Griff had asked them to pick up Jennie's belongings. But Black Kettle also said he'd heard that soldiers were coming to destroy their camp. I'd swear that news travels faster among the Indians than it does to us by telegraph. They wanted permission to move their camp closer to the fort for added protection.

"You know the Kiowa and Comanche already have villages set up less than a mile from here. Hazen granted them permission weeks ago. But he was unusually gruff with Black Kettle today and immediately turned down his request. He told them to go back to their camp. He said since the Cheyenne are among those who have been attacking white settlers in Kansas, he could not allow them refuge and told them they'd just have to surrender if they found themselves under attack. Black Kettle swore that his people had not attacked anyone, that he and his people would always honor the treaty made at Medicine Lodge.

"But Hazen was immovable. I've not seen him act this way. He finally offered to allow Black Kettle and his wife to come live in the fort for protection, but refused to allow the village to move any closer.

"Black Kettle would have nothing to do with coming here for protection without his people. He asked for rations, but General Hazen refused those as well. Just sent them on their way. I think Black Kettle knew General Hazen was hiding something. I could see it in his eyes. Black Kettle has a way of somehow looking beyond things."

"What an odd way of putting it," Cordelia said.

"That's the only way I can describe it." For the first time, Robert looked straight into Cordelia's eyes and whispered to her as if the room had ears, "Some would think this most blasphemous, but I believe that old chief is very wise. He's been through a lot, Cordelia—more than you know."

"Yes, the Anthonys told me about Sand Creek this afternoon. The poor man."

Robert nodded. "And after all that, he's willing to live within our restrictions for the sake of peace. He wasn't happy today, though. That was obvious. When he left, I asked General Hazen what that was all about, why he was so abrupt with Black Kettle. He didn't answer me. I must confess that knowing Custer is coming adds a degree of concern to this whole affair."

"Oh, Robert, you don't think Custer will attack those Indians, do you? I mean, General Hazen has promised our protection, hasn't he?"

"Yes," Robert told her, "but you didn't see his face today. He knows something."

Almost under his breath he added, "The face of Judas with his thirty pieces of silver. Something like that. He told them that if they are attacked, they are to know it did not come from him, but from the great war chief in the north. That's Sheridan, I guess."

He seemed to be setting her mind at ease by saying, in a stronger tone, "Perhaps I'm imagining the worst, my love, but I fear for Black Kettle and his people."

They ate the remainder of their dinner in silence, lost in their own thoughts. After dinner, while Bess and Lucy cleared the table, they settled down to their separate pursuits as they tried to relax and think of other things.

Robert read by the light of the lantern on the table beside his big chair. Meanwhile, Cordelia attempted to sketch the Indians she'd seen that day, pausing here and there to remove a pin from her hair. One by one, the curls fell down around her shoulders as her hand deftly filled in the outlines of her drawing, then added layer upon layer of detail and shading until she had captured the allure of the unusual and striking people she'd beheld.

She looked up to find Robert watching her.

"You're not reading, darling. I find this studious gaze of yours a trifle unsettling."

"Ha! Now you know how I feel every morning when you watch every move *I* make."

Grinning, she said, "I suppose so. I'll have to do it with more discretion. I don't want to make you feel *too* uncomfortable." She returned his somber gaze for a moment before continuing. "You really are worried, aren't you?"

"Yes. I am. I've had this ominous feeling all day." He leaned forward for a peek at her work. "Show me what you've done there."

She raised the sketch so he could see.

"Amazing," he breathed. "You couldn't have seen them for more than a minute or two. And yet, you've captured them, Cordelia. I'm very proud of you."

"Thank you, my love. I've found a stopping place for tonight. Are you almost ready for bed?"

"Absolutely. I feel old and tired tonight."

"Not *too* old and tired, I hope," she teased.

"My darling, you are incorrigible," he told her with a smile as they walked slowly to their bedroom, his arm wrapped around her waist. "And that makes me a most fortunate man."

~*~

Later, in the dark, he spoke to her in a thick whisper.

"Are you still awake?"

"Yes."

"I need to ask you for a favor, my love."

"What favor? Anything you ask of me you know I'll do."

She turned toward him and stroked his shoulder, enjoying the masculine smell of him.

"Try to be civil to Custer when you see him."

"Ugh!" She flopped to her side with her back to her husband. "Please, Robert! Now I'm going to have nightmares!"

She could hear his soft chuckle as she closed her eyes and settled down for a long, restless night.

~*~

Except for the muted rose glow from the fireplace, the room was still black, and she knew it was too early to get out of bed. Shivering from the cold, she snuggled closer to Robert, protectively pulling the warm feather comforter over his exposed arm. He stirred, but didn't wake.

While she tried to go back to sleep, she heard it. So that's what woke her up.

The wind's long, plaintive howls hurled themselves against their sturdy rock quarters. Trying to muffle the sound with her covers, she scooted closer to her husband. She lay there listening to the wind until she realized she would not be successful returning to her dreams.

Carefully, so as not to wake Robert, Cordelia crept to the fireplace, her stocking feet feeling the cold emanating from the polished oak floor. As silently as possible, she stoked the fire, dressed hurriedly and wrapped herself in a thick blanket she'd brought from home.

Reveille hadn't sounded yet, so she knew it was still very early. From her bedroom window, she stared into the blackness as she listened to the wind, ever rising in intensity, in its maddening search across the prairie.

Soundlessly moving her lips, she prayed, careful to ask for Robert's protection. She thanked the Lord again for this opportunity to live here with Robert and asked for the blessing of feeling his arms around her for the rest of her life.

From behind her, she felt those arms encircle her as she leaned her head back onto his shoulder.

"I didn't hear you get up," she whispered.

"You seemed lost in thought. Why are you up so early?"

"I couldn't sleep. It's the wind. Listen."

They both paused.

In a hushed tone, she said, "It almost sounds like screaming, doesn't it?

"Yes, I suppose it does," he agreed.

Sighing, she turned to embrace him, pressing her face tightly against his neck. "I'm so happy."

"I'm glad. I was afraid you'd take one look at this place and jump on the next stage home," he chuckled.

"My place is here with you," she reassured him. "Besides, this place has a beauty all its own. I wouldn't have missed it for the world. I'm afraid you're stuck with me, Captain Lawson."

He kissed her tenderly, then pushed away from her. "I'd better get dressed. Reveille will sound any minute now."

"Yes, you go ahead, darling."

~*~

"Breakfast's almost ready, sir," Bess informed Robert, who stood straight and tall in his blue uniform in the middle of the kitchen. He accepted the cup of strong, hot coffee she passed him.

Bess was a treasure. As a housekeeper, she was efficient and pleasant, going about her work with energy and joy. But as a cook, she was superb. He remembered how stark life on the fort seemed before Cordelia, Bess and her daughter, Lucy, came out here. With Cordelia's arrival, life became instantly richer—

and more civilized. He enjoyed his life more than ever before—even if there were storm clouds on the horizon for the Indians.

"Thank you, Bess." He sipped his coffee and half-turned before noticing Lucy.

"What are you doing, Lucy?" he asked, walking a couple of steps toward her.

"Pouring vinegar over these new wicks for the lanterns, sir. It gives them a clearer flame when you burn them, Mama says," she said in a voice slightly above a whisper.

"They sure do. My mama taught me that when I was just a girl," Bess said.

"Hmm. Interesting. I've never heard that before."

~*~

Bess smiled after him as he strode confidently back into the house with a decided spring in his step. Bess looked after him and said, "He sure is feelin' good this mornin', ain't he?"

She winked at her thirteen-year-old daughter.

"I think he's happy almost all the time," Lucy replied. "He's got Miz Lawson here with him now." The love between Robert and Cordelia was a well-known fact to everyone. They made no secret of it, after all.

Although the kitchen was attached to the house, it had a separate entrance accessible only by opening the heavy exterior door at the end of the hallway and crossing the back porch. Bess and Lucy had their own tiny quarters above the large pantry adjoining the kitchen.

They packed breakfast on trays and delivered it to the room that served as a dining room and parlor. They heard Cordelia's soft singing from the bedroom.

Robert sat at the heavy oak table, sipping his coffee.

"Cordelia!" he called.

She entered the room, pulling her red curls behind her, tying them back with a sage green ribbon. Acknowledging Bess and Lucy, she asked, "How are you two today?"

Looking at each other, they responded in unison, "Just fine, ma'am."

"No need to make the bed. I already did it."

"Now you didn't hafta do that, Miz Lawson," Bess scolded.

"I don't see why not," she said, taking her seat opposite Robert. "Good morning again, darling," she said, giving him a flirtatious grin.

Once their plates were placed before them, Robert said grace as Bess and Lucy stood nearby. After the blessing, Cordelia looked at her small "staff" and said sweetly, "We'll be fine now, I think."

"Yes, ma'am." They began their retreat down the hall toward the kitchen.

~*~

Cordelia placed her coffee cup noisily in the saucer and carefully studied her husband. "You're so beautiful, Robert."

"Cordelia. Really. I've told you, men are not beautiful."

"You are." Her gaze caressed him as she memorized for the millionth time his thick, nut-brown hair—nearly shoulder-length now, his soft, smoldering brown eyes, the strong, squared line of his chin, the full lower lip under the dark moustache. Tall and thin, he was nicely shaped with well-defined muscle. She eyed him with undisguised adoration and breathed a heavy sigh.

Halfway through breakfast, they heard the bugle's muffled blast.

"You'll be late for roll-call," she volunteered. "Look, the

men are already scurrying into formation." She flashed him an impish smile.

Standing, Robert plopped half a biscuit into his mouth, placed his napkin on the table and removed his hat and cloak from the rack. He walked to her, knelt beside her on one knee and said, "I love you. You know that, don't you?"

"I do. And Robert, please don't worry about the Indians. I'm sure you'll think of something to ensure their safety. Please be careful and come back to me safely at the end of the day."

"By God's will, I shall." He planted a firm kiss on her waiting lips and stepped purposefully into the light of day and the noise of the fort coming to life.

Three

Fort Cobb wasn't as grand and well-appointed as some of the others. In fact, it was small and plain by comparison—but Robert and Cordelia Lawson found life pleasing here.

Having heard tales of the vast emptiness and monotony of the plains, Cordelia had not necessarily looked forward to coming out west. She had much rather have remained in Baltimore in their big house near the harbor. At times, she missed her parents, and her pretty linens and furnishings, her rich rugs and her piano. She had everything she needed there, except for the most priceless thing of all—her husband.

So she'd covered her furniture in sheets of white muslin, shut and locked the front door, said goodbye to her folks, and made her way out here to be with Robert. The only comforts she brought with her were some dresses, a few pieces of jewelry, linens, a couple of hats, a heavy cloak and shawl, a blanket, four books she'd yet to read and her drawing tablets, pencils and paints.

Expecting nothing but a flat expanse of wilderness, Cordelia was surprised by the rolling landscape of the prairie, the fluid motion of the tall grass in the unrelenting wind, and the brilliant bursts of color everywhere. The earth itself was the most remarkable shade of deep red-orange punctuated by the blues, greens, golds and browns of the wild grasses found in great abundance on the plains.

She found it odd that the scrubby trees, found mostly near creeks or riverbeds, all grew leaning to one side—living testaments to the sweeping strength of the ever-present wind. Overall, she found this remote land exciting and utterly lovely—even in winter.

Though they'd been married almost two years, she and Robert had been apart for much of that time. For one thing, Robert refused to marry her until the war was over. He didn't want to leave her a widow if he didn't survive. They married within two weeks of his return and lived for only ten months in the two-story home her parents gave them as a wedding gift.

Married life was blissful, for the most part, but even Cordelia had to admit that living together in the same house presented certain challenges. After all, being an only child, she was used to getting her way—*all* the time. Robert had his own ideas and sometimes insisted on his way, much to Cordelia's irritation.

Plus, she was a romantic, which he sometimes considered silly and childish. She didn't realize until they married that Robert was all business. It took considerable cajoling to break through his stiff, formal exterior, to make him laugh, to take his mind off of his daily responsibilities long enough to relax and try to have fun.

During their courtship, she knew she was the center of his world. But after they married, she didn't feel like that anymore. All he seemed interested in now were his daily routines and responsibilities, about which he was dead serious.

It was one thing for him to have that expectation for

himself. The trouble came when he'd comment that perhaps she could apply herself more productively to life rather than living in "a dream world," she remembered him saying.

How dare he try to change her? He may have changed, but certainly she vowed never to let life's responsibilities deprive her of that awareness of all things beautiful that she treasured. And when was it *her* turn to get her own way? She knew the Bible said the wife was to be submissive, but she found that principle particularly difficult to embrace.

So, though their love for each other was never in question, it was far from a perfect adjustment to married life. They were struggling with those very issues when he was assigned to Fort Hays.

In his letters, Cordelia rejoiced that, once again, she seemed the center of his universe. She made her love for him clear in hers, as well. Getting her own way again was nice, but she knew she'd trade that serenity immediately for a chance to reunite with him again.

Nine long months later, he transferred to this brand-new fort. It was then he was given his own living quarters and it became possible for his wife to join him.

Travel in 1868 was slow and ponderous—first by train, then boat and finally stagecoach. It had been a difficult, uncomfortable journey, but the three women arrived with hope and excitement abounding.

Bess had lived with Cordelia's family in Baltimore for thirteen years. Cordelia could still remember the night she came to them. Cordelia had been a child back then and was supposed to be asleep, but when she heard the quick-clip of voices downstairs, she sat upright in her pink-frilled bed. Creeping out to the top step, she watched and listened through the railing as the whispers grew faint, but more desperate. Pinpricks of excitement stabbed her senses as she strained to hear what was happening downstairs.

Then she heard it, the cry of a baby, quickly hushed—then nothing more. She desperately wanted to see that baby but knew she'd better not.

Cordelia had been nine years old then, but she remembered it like yesterday. She'd crept back to bed undetected only to wake to the baby's lusty cry once more.

She later found that fifteen-year-old Bess, great with child, had journeyed all the way to Baltimore from Georgia carrying a letter from the Maxwells, a well-to-do family in Savannah—friends of Cordelia's parents. Bess had been born into servitude, that's true. But the Maxwells were kind and treated their people well. Cordelia wasn't quite sure what made Bess leave the Maxwell place, but whatever it was must have been pretty bad, she gathered.

Cordelia remembered many black faces around their house in those early days—some smiling, some swollen and bruised, some even boldly flashing hatred her way. She didn't fully understand why her parents welcomed these reluctant strangers into their home, except that her mother had told her once it was to help them find their way, whatever that meant. Most only stayed a few days or even hours.

But they invited Bess to stay indefinitely. Raising baby Lucy became a family affair. Cordelia remembered her mother telling Bess it was a great blessing that she arrived when she did or else Lucy would have been born in the street.

Bess, only six years older than Cordelia, became one of her closest friends over the course of years since that first night. No one knew Cordelia better than she did—except maybe her mother.

Now Cordelia found herself gazing out the dusty dining room window as Fort Cobb unfolded before her. It had turned into a pretty day, after all. The sun shone brightly on the company of soldiers manning the fort. She enjoyed the sight of the busy soldiers in their dark blue uniforms purposefully striding across the snow-covered parade grounds.

Underneath that snow, the tall, bleached prairie grass inside the quadrangle was trampled to near-balding along the paths cutting through its center in both length and width, revealing the dusty red clay underneath. The many buildings that made up the fort framed the quadrangle.

In the center stood the wonder of the fort—a 100' flagpole, from which an American flag flew. But it was no ordinary flag. It measured twenty feet wide by thirty-six feet long—quite a handful for the soldiers whose job it was to raise it every morning and retrieve it at the end of the day, especially in these blustering prairie winds. That flag could be seen for miles. It was the first sight she spied as her stagecoach rounded the last bend past the rolling hills. It was still almost a half-hour's travel before they pulled into the fort.

As they approached the fort, Cordelia was surprised to see that there was no stockade around it; the buildings were openly accessible to the plains surrounding them. The only fencing was at the stable enclosure and behind the officers' quarters. Her husband later explained that there was no need for a stockade. The Indians living nearest them were friendly and besides, they rarely resorted to a full-frontal assault. Their most common style of warfare was picking off solitary riders to or from the fort, or the occasional ambush of travelers or homesteaders making their way west.

The stockade around the horses was a precaution against the intermittent raids of the Cheyenne, notorious for their adept skill at stealing horses. In Cheyenne society, this was considered not so much a crime as it was a much-admired and prized talent.

Cordelia, very curious about these ferocious people, had been anxious to see her first wild Indians. And now she'd seen them.

Robert had warned her that the wild breed of Indian was different from any people she'd ever known. Plus, she'd read the stories about the wild Indians in the west.

The Cheyenne camped many miles away on the Washita River amid the Antelope Hills. He'd told her about Black Kettle, that he was a fine old man—soft-spoken and polite. He frequently proclaimed his affections toward the white man and his country.

Cordelia frowned to think those remarkable people might be in danger from white soldiers. She wondered if there was anything she could do to keep them safe. But what could a woman do in this world of soldiers determined to wipe them out?

~*~

After a shampoo with her favorite mixture of one penny-worth of borax, half a pint of olive oil and one pint of boiling water shaken together, Cordelia allowed her hair to dry before the fire into its tight, natural curls. She only used a dab of the pomatum to leave it glossy.

Finally, with Lucy's help, Cordelia was able to capture all the long, red curls and pin them atop her head, leaving several fashionable wisps curling around her delicate, lightly freckled face.

"There!" Lucy stood back and examined her work, hairpins still loosely clamped between her teeth. "Miz Lawson, you look beautiful."

"Well, I don't know about that, but it's done anyway. Thanks so much, Lucy. It looks ever so much better when you do it than when I try to do it myself. Sometimes I'd like to cut it all off."

"Miz Lawson! Don't you even say such a thing. Your hair is the softest, prettiest hair I ever saw. Mama says it's the color of a copper teakettle in the sunlight. And it is. When the sun hits it, it almost glows."

"Thank you, Lucy. You're very sweet to say so. I suppose I like the color, too. I just wish I could wear it loose all the time, or simply tie it back, like I did as a child. It was so much easier then. You know I hate to spend time on things like hair and dresses and the like. I'd rather be painting or reading or taking a walk outside. Besides, that wind out there is going to mess my hair up no matter what I do. Even trying to use that worthless parasol is no use. I'm afraid that contraption has seen better days."

"Sometimes I think I seen better days myself," came Bess's velvet voice.

Startled, Lucy and Cordelia whirled to look at her smiling countenance.

"And just what are you smiling about, Bess?"

"I heard what you said about taking time on that mess of hair you got. You ought to be thankin' the good Lawd for that head of hair. I told you that plenty of times, Miz Lawson."

"Is that what's got that big smile on your face?"

"No, ma'am."

"Then what?"

Another sheepish grin flashed across Bess's plump face as she brought her hand from behind her back. In her hand was a note, which she held up provocatively.

"What's that? Tell me it's not from Mrs. Hazen. Please!"

"I'm not sayin' it is, or it ain't," Bess teased, waving the little note beyond Cordelia's reach.

"Isn't," Cordelia corrected, pretending indifference to the note.

"So, you don't even want to know who sent it?"

"Well, now that depends on who it's from," Cordelia said, a little smile playing at the corners of her mouth. "If it's from Mrs. Hazen, I believe you can keep it. I'm not in the mood for her criticism today."

"All right, then. Here you go. It's not from Mrs. Hazen. I was just teasin' you, ma'am. One of the privates brung it to you from Miz Anthony."

"Oh, good," she said, opening the note. Reading, she said, "She's thanking me for my visit yesterday, and for bringing your famous shortbreads, Bess. She didn't need to do that. I should have sent *her* a note, I suppose. I'm forgetting my manners, aren't I?"

Cordelia shuddered against the cold. "Lucy, will you put another log on the fire in the parlor? I sometimes wonder if I'll ever be truly warm again."

"Yes, ma'am."

Lucy placed two more sticks of wood in the fireplace, and poked them into place, sending the flames leaping only a little higher, as Cordelia wandered into the parlor. Wood, in this vast frontier, was a tough commodity to come by. It was usually far from dry and invariably was the type of wood that burned quickly but gave off little heat. One soldier had, as his full-time assignment, the task of locating and providing wood and kindling for all the fireplaces in the officers' quarters. Still, it was a constant struggle to keep warm.

Four

For almost two weeks now, Cordelia had wondered about the fate of the Indians in the Antelope Hills to the northwest on the Washita River—the Cheyenne tribe led by Black Kettle. She worried about how they had fared in the horrible blizzard that hit the plains a week ago but mostly, she worried about whatever plans involved General Custer. She'd been unable to forget Black Kettle's sage expression, or the curiosity in the eyes of the one who lagged behind the others.

In the bright sunshine of the afternoon of November 30, she heard a commotion outside. Looking through the thick glass window plate, Cordelia was able to see soldiers running in the direction of the front gate. Straining to see more clearly, she pressed her nose so close to the glass that she could smell the alcohol Bess used on the windowpanes to keep them from icing over.

Pulling her woolen shawl around her shoulders, Cordelia, following the clamor, traced her way across the parade grounds, checkered with melting snow. She suspected she knew what the fuss was about—Custer. But she was curious to see what kind of welcome he would receive from the frenzied troops around her.

Her mind flashed back to seven weeks ago. Having arrived a day or two before, she attended a ball held at the fort. That's the night she first met George Armstrong Custer.

Cordelia had looked lovely that evening, so everyone said. She'd worn the only "dress-up" gown she'd brought with her—a golden taffeta one layered with a soft creamy color of heavily embossed organza. This gave a frosty shimmer to the gold underneath. It provided a warm contrast to her emerald eyes, and copper red hair, braided and stacked on her head, tied with a golden bow. Her skin shone with a peachy radiance that reflected her health and vitality.

Cordelia noticed that Robert had not been able to keep his eyes off her all evening. She liked that. Once, when she knew he was looking, she'd raised her crystal glass to her lips and, watching him with eyes that drew him closer, lowered the glass slowly across her lower lip, momentarily touching the rim with the very tip of her tongue. Casting her eyes again in his direction, she could read the hunger in his eyes from across the room as he approached her.

Even in this crowded room full of drinking, darting, dancing people, it seemed they were the only two in the place. The din of music, clinking glasses and laughter seemed muffled, the swirling colors were hazy mists around them. Their eyes locked in shared anticipation. There was only Robert and her pounding heart. He quickened his steps as he made his way to her, politely excusing himself as he zigzagged through the crowd. She felt the color rising to her cheeks when
. . .

"Oh, Mrs. Lawson, dear!" Mrs. Hazen's piercing, high-pitched voice cut through Cordelia's muted dream-like apparition so sharply as to cause her to physically wince. The noise and motion of the hall came immediately into clarity, much to Cordelia's irritation.

"My dear, this is such a proud moment for us all. You really must meet this great gentleman. Mrs. Cordelia Lawson, may I introduce General George Armstrong Custer of the 7th Cavalry."

His grinning face loomed over hers for a moment too long and an inch too close before he bent to kiss her hand. "Madam, may I say that it is an honor to make your acquaintance? And if I may be so bold, I should like to tell you that you are the most ravishing creature in this room tonight."

Looking into his dancing ice-blue eyes, she took in the gaunt features, the heavy moustache, the curly reddish-blond hair falling across his much-decorated shoulders. He was thin, but the way he moved gave Cordelia an impression of underlying strength and agility.

Usually open and friendly to everyone, she was confused by her instant dislike of this man. Certainly she'd heard of him before, sometimes referred to as a hero and other times as a pompous fool. He'd certainly given ample evidence of both. She answered a polite, but cool, thank you and returned her gaze to her husband, who'd made his way to her.

"Ah, my love, I've had the privilege of meeting General Custer. I believe you know each other?" she greeted him.

"Yes. Hello, sir. Is Mrs. Custer here with you tonight?"

Still watching Cordelia's face, Custer answered, "No, I'm afraid not. My darling Libby decided to stay at Fort Riley until the Indian uprising has ended."

"Yes, dear," Robert told his wife, "General Custer has been summoned to handle the Indian situation. He is quite the Indian fighter."

"Yes, I'd heard." Turning to Custer, she asked, "And why do you fight them, General? Are they really such a threat?"

"Ah, yes, my dear Mrs. Lawson. They are but savages at best, attacking our peaceful settlements, laying waste our farms, besieging travelers upon the road to the west. They are quite horrid, really. I only hope you never have occasion to come face to face with the beasts. There is no telling what a savage would do to one as lovely as you," he said with a slight bow.

Cordelia pretended not to notice as he eyed her from head to toe. Listening to him, watching the slow, lascivious smile crawl across his face, she couldn't suppress the notion that perhaps *he* was the monster, not the "savage Indians." Though she'd missed much of what he had been telling her, she shivered slightly as he concluded, "therefore, they must be eliminated."

"So, you march into their villages and kill them. Is that what I am to understand?"

"Mrs. Lawson, surely you don't think I *enjoy* killing them! On the contrary, I would rather take them in and establish them in camps where they could be fed and exposed to our civilized culture and religion. But alas, none of them are truly willing to see the necessity of these changes to their society. Instead, they prefer to remain in their filthy lodges, running around half-clothed, frothing with desire to kill all white settlers in this area. I view my service only as a means to protect you and the other fine citizens of this great country, and to rid it of such stubborn and contemptible creatures."

"I see," Cordelia said. Then slipping into her sweetest and, for those who knew her well, her most sarcastic tone, she continued with a flutter of her lashes, "Well, I suppose we should all be thankful for your bravery then, sir. I know I shall sleep better just knowing you're here to protect me."

Turning to her husband, she flashed him a radiant smile and took his arm. "Now, darling, surely it's time for that dance you promised me. Is it not?"

"General, you'll excuse us, I hope? My wife can be very demanding at times, you see."

Custer leaned over her hand once again before saying, "Captain Lawson, I applaud your taste in women. You're a lucky man, sir. A very lucky man."

"Thank you, sir. Shall we, my dear?"

"Please," Cordelia smiled.

~*~

General Custer, grinding his teeth more than a wee bit, twisted his moustache as he watched them spin into the circle of dancers. He wasn't accustomed to such open hostility from women. In fact, they usually fawned over him in such a way that irritated him. This one was different, he thought, watching her dance with her tall husband. And there he was, left behind in Mrs. Hazen's worshipful grasp.

~*~

Remembering this meeting, Cordelia involuntarily shuddered. From outside the gates, she could make out the sound of ... what was it? Some kind of music? Yes, that was it.

Spotting her friend, Dr. Anthony, she joined him on the boardwalk in front of the headquarters. "Do you hear that music, Doc?"

"Yes. The strains of 'Garry Owen,' Custer's favorite marching tune. The perfect cadence for the advance of his troops, I've been told. Only George Armstrong Custer would travel with a sixteen-piece band with him—all mounted on white horses, I've heard. He brings them to every engagement."

"Well, I think that is chilling," Cordelia stated matter-of-factly. "Wait a moment. Doc, does that mean he's been to battle? Has he attacked Black Kettle's Indians at Washita?" Her frantic eyes searched her friend's face.

"I don't know, dear. We'll have to wait and see."

A platform had been hastily erected inside the gates where General Hazen stood at attention next to General Philip Sheridan, who had arrived the day before. It was the first time she'd seen him, though she'd heard about him for years.

He was referred to as "Little Phil" because of his short stature. Now she saw the name fit him. His piercing brown eyes seemed eagle-sharp as the procession of cavalry rode into the fort in review. Though his mouth was smiling, his eyes were deadly, she decided.

Cordelia stood on tiptoe on the boardwalk, directing her attention toward the fort's entrance as the scraggly Osage guides, dressed and painted for the occasion, led the column chanting their war songs and giving their war-whoops at intervals, followed by the scouts on mules. Next rode the ragtag remnant of the Cheyenne—the captives from the battle, mostly women and children—all under guard. The band, playing Custer's lively tune, rode in next—and yes, mounted on white horses. It was followed by none other than the great man himself, George Armstrong Custer, his officers and staff, and then came the troops by platoons.

Cordelia's heart raced as the procession passed her by. There was so much to see and so little time to take it all in. So much color and motion. She had to admit it was quite impressive—by far the grandest sight she'd seen since coming west.

Major General Sheridan returned Custer's salute, then applauded him, smiling broadly. Sheridan was the one who brought General Custer back into the military after he'd been court-martialed and sentenced to a year's suspension from the Army, Robert had told her. She could see that Philip Sheridan was proud of "his boy."

And General Custer reflected the excitement of a schoolboy let out for the holidays—a boyish exuberance and energy demonstrated his belief that, for a true cavalryman, life in the saddle on the free and open plain is the pinnacle of his existence—the best life has to offer. George Custer was born for this kind of occasion.

Gallantly, he sat upon his splendid thoroughbred, Dandy, who pranced for the crowd, painting an elegant picture. His saddle was black Morocco leather ornamented with silver studs. Instead of his dress uniform, the general was dressed in buckskins. A fur pillbox hat graced his head with his reddish-blond ringlets trailing beneath. Cordelia was surprised to see him wearing a full beard instead of his usual heavy moustache. Over a navy blue shirt, he wore a belted buckskin jacket, fringed at the shoulders, the pockets, the hem, and down each arm. Tucked into his black troop boots were buckskin pants, fringed down each leg. His signature red scarf draped his neck, its ends flying behind his shoulders. He was quite a sight.

Whether a person loved this man or hated him, Cordelia had to admit that it was hard to tear her eyes from him. She suspected he'd do well on the stage, as he seemed a natural-born actor.

The bright and ready smile on his weathered face changed his usual hang-dog expression to one of ultimate triumph. He tipped his hat to Cordelia as he passed before her, flashing his pearly-white teeth in a side-wise smirk. She glared back with a frown of annoyance.

In his gloved hand, he waved something in the air that Cordelia couldn't quite identify. It was a staff with some kind of black fur or hair attached to the end. The men cheered wildly.

"Oh, dear God," Dr. Anthony gasped.

"What is it? What?"

"Those are scalps, Mrs. Lawson. Avert your eyes, my dear." He gently tried to turn her, but she fought his protective arms and stood horrified as she saw the mass of black, shining hair held up for all to see.

"Oh, Doc."

Suddenly Robert was at her side. "Cordelia, please. You're white as a ghost. Let's go home. I'll take you right now."

"Robert, what's happened? Was it Black Kettle?"

"Yes, dear. It was."

Though distraught by the news and by what she saw, Cordelia nevertheless turned her attention to the captives, on their feet now, herded into the octagonal block guardhouse. Most were young women and children but there was one very old man, a young woman heavily with child, and a couple of older women—all holding fearfully to each other as they peered at the soldiers with terrified eyes, black as a raven's wings.

Cordelia's gaze settled on one woman in particular. She was a most attractive young woman, carefully supporting an older woman beside her. She was taller than the others, lithe, and graceful. Cordelia noticed the defiance in her dark eyes as she glared one way and then the other, helping her companion across the hard-packed earth toward the place of their imprisonment. Her skin was burnished satin, her fine curved nose ended in nostrils flared with unmasked anger and hatred.

"Robert, look at that woman. She's breathtaking, isn't she?"

"Which one do you mean?" he asked, and then, "Ah, yes, I see her. Quite . . . striking."

The end of the procession came near as the rear guard escorted the handful of wounded soldiers to the hospital.

"Duty calls," Doc growled, as he headed toward the two-room hospital with ten cots per room.

"Cordelia, let's go," Robert told her.

Lieutenant Otis made his way to them. "Have you heard?"

"Heard what?"

"Custer defeated Black Kettle's tribe on the morning of the 27th. Caught them sleeping. They killed Black Kettle and his wife, Medicine Woman Later."

"Dear God," Cordelia breathed. "I don't think I can stand to think about it. The very fact that I saw him here a few weeks ago and now . . ." Her voice broke as she felt the sting of tears at the back of her eyes, remembering Black Kettle's wise, gentle face.

"Where are the men? I didn't see them come in with the other captives."

Robert gently explained that the braves had either been killed or had fled to fight another day. "They generally stay behind and hold the soldiers' lines long enough to allow the women and children to escape. The number of women and children tell me that most of the warriors are dead. They probably died trying to save their families."

They edged closer to the platform in order to hear General Sheridan's address. He publicly congratulated Custer for "efficient and gallant services rendered." He boasted in the fact that this proud country had finally wiped out the worthless and worn out old Black Kettle and his band of ruthless, cutthroat Cheyenne.

Cordelia couldn't believe her ears as Sheridan explained how General Hazen had promised Black Kettle sanctuary if he would only come in to the fort before the military operations began, but the old fool refused the offer and preferred rather to fight, where he was finally vanquished by the bravery of these fine soldiers.

This was astonishing. What a bold-faced lie. How could anyone believe it? After carefully observing the crowd, she glared at Robert, who looked impassively at the ground. They both knew a different story.

"But that's not true! Can he get away with that, Robert? He's misleading the men. Look at them, Robert. Listen. They're cheering! They're treating Custer to a hero's welcome! How much valor does it take to attack a sleeping village of peaceful people and murder them there?"

At that, the heavy-set woman in front of them turned to face Cordelia. It was Mrs. Hazen, the general's wife. She curtly addressed Cordelia's remarks, her chin held high.

"Careful, my dear. You sound an awful lot like an Indian sympathizer. These savages don't know the meaning of the word 'peace.' You've no idea what a load of concern they've been to my poor husband. He's had nothing but trouble from them from the start. I won't truly feel safe until they're all dead and rotting in hell."

"Well, may God forgive you for that, Mrs. Hazen," Cordelia's eyes flashed over her startled expression, and she turned then to Lieutenant Otis, who had moved to take her other arm.

"Lieutenant, have they really asked you to vacate your room and move to the barracks with the enlisted men? I can't believe they'd ask you to do that to make way for the likes of George Custer."

"Humph!" snorted Eleanor Hazen. "You'd better caution your wife, Captain Lawson. She is going to jeopardize your reputation here if she continues to express such sentiments."

"I'm comfortable with my wife's attitudes, Mrs. Hazen. Thank you for your concern, though."

Robert and Todd gently but forcefully led Cordelia from the crowd. When they had advanced past the crowd of cheering soldiers, they released their hold on her.

After tramping in silence through the melting snow,

Cordelia pressed her new friend, Todd Otis about his moving. "Yes, it's true, I'm afraid. But General Hazen has promised that when Nicole arrives, I'll get my quarters back."

"Do you know yet when that will be?"

"No. Her last letter said, 'soon.' That was almost two weeks ago."

"Good. You know, I'll be happy to help out when she needs me, Lieutenant. I only wish they'd come today so Custer wouldn't have the occasion to step foot in our house. It will be a contagion of sorts in my way of thinking."

"Cordelia, please," Robert groaned. "Mrs. Hazen was wrong to reprimand you for your attitudes but she was right when she said that you must be more careful about speaking your mind. Other than Dr. and Mrs. Anthony, Todd and ourselves, the rest of the troops here are of the mind that the Indians are dangerous creatures who should be wiped off the face of the earth. I know you don't agree with that. Neither do I, and I really don't think General Hazen believes it either. But you simply must use more discretion, I think. And if you can't be more careful about speaking your mind, perhaps you could remain silent?"

"Robert, really!" Cordelia, feeling wounded, couldn't believe he was siding with Mrs. Hazen.

"I'm only encouraging you to be more careful. That's all."

Leaning toward her, Todd laughed, "I think you're wonderful, myself." Cordelia looked up into his laughing blue eyes and offered him a little smile. She trusted his big, open grin and felt comfortable with his easy-going style. She felt somehow grateful to him for taking up for her . . . even a little.

"No one understands the wonder that she is better than I," Robert reminded him. "I just want her to be careful. There is an appropriate time and place to discuss one's opinions. Doing it in public is never advisable. You must be more concerned about what people might think."

"Oh, Robert, really. I cannot believe you just said that."

"You're not an impulsive little girl anymore, my dear. You're a grown woman and my wife. I'm afraid that title comes with some degree of reservation before causing a stir."

She glared at him, but didn't respond.

Having reached the door of their home, she turned the knob to go in as the men turned back to the fort. "Aren't you coming in?" she asked.

"No. There will be a lot to do and a lot to talk about today, darling. You stay put, you hear? We'll talk more tonight. I mean it, Cordelia. Don't leave the house."

"Lieutenant, will you come for dinner?" Cordelia asked.

"I'd be delighted." Todd snapped his heels together and bowed low before her, coming up laughing, doffing his hat dramatically. "I wouldn't miss this for the world."

Five

Cordelia slowly made her way to the kitchen to speak to Bess and Lucy. Bess was cutting up a chicken, and Lucy was busy filling a crack in the stove with a mixture of wood-ash and salt, reduced to a paste with a little bit of water.

"Miz Lawson, what's wrong? You look just awful!" Lucy spouted.

"Thanks, Lucy. A woman always likes to hear things like that."

"Missy, sit in this here chair and rest a bit." Bess took her by the shoulders and pressed her down into the waiting chair. "Now, tell us all about it."

"Are we having chicken for dinner tonight?"

"Yes, ma'am, we is."

"We *are*," Cordelia gently corrected. "Well, I've just asked Lieutenant Otis for dinner. I hope we have enough. And if we don't, you may give him my portion. I don't have much of an appetite."

"We got plenty, ma'am. Now what's wrong?"

Cordelia looked into Bess's kind face. Touched by the concern she found there, she burst into tears.

"Oh, Bess! It's the Indians, *my* Indians! Custer's men butchered them. And now he's here waving their scalps around and all the soldiers are whooping it up out there and treating that . . . that arrogant . . ." Words failed her as she gave way to the sobs tearing at her throat.

Bess's warm, strong arms encircled her and held her, rocking to and fro. Her throaty bass voice crooned, "It's all right. Ever'thing's gonna be all right, Missy. Since the beginnings in the Bible times, men been finding folks to beat up on. Nothing different now, Miz Lawson, 'cept they found someone new to treat bad. That's just life, ma'am."

~*~

Cordelia spent the rest of the afternoon in the parlor working on her sketch of the Indians—turning the sketch into a painting. The soft light filtered through the window and Cordelia could hear the moaning of the cold wind blowing across the plains—moaning or mourning as it searched for its people, she thought. The sound of it grew steadily higher and higher in pitch until it shrieked dismally over the plains.

She worked on through the afternoon and her labor became a memorial to the Indians. She found herself wishing to have had the opportunity to see them in their village, watch them with their children, and laugh with them around their campfires. Then she could paint them living and vibrant instead of frozen in time, standing in the cold afternoon sun next to their ponies in front of the headquarters. Still, she worked with the colors, and the shading until it was finished to her satisfaction.

When it was done, she put her brush down, and gazed into

the eyes of the one who had regarded her with such scrutiny. She had captured the eagle-sharpness and blended into those eyes the curiosity she'd recognized—recognized because she'd returned that curiosity. The two of them were linked together for a moment—a moment that could never exist again. Slow tears tracked down her cheeks as she gazed into that face.

Lucy came into the parlor to stoke the logs in the fireplace. She carefully placed two more on the fire and threw in a tablespoon or so of salt to revive the flames. Though she worked quickly, she also observed Cordelia and without speaking, her presence provided solace to her friend nonetheless. She could see the sorrow in Cordelia's face.

"My heart is broken, Lucy."

"I sure am sorry about that, ma'am. Is there anything I can do to help?"

"No, but thank you. It helps just knowing you care." Cordelia reached for Lucy's hand and gave it a little squeeze.

"Mama said to tell you that supper will be ready in a half-hour."

"Thank you, Lucy." She turned her attention back to the painting and leaned forward to add her signature to the corner.

~*~

Hearing the sound of male voices coming from the porch, accompanied by much stomping of boots, Cordelia rose from the divan and opened the parlor door to greet them.

"It's nice to have you home. You both must be freezing! Robert, why don't you pour yourselves a brandy? I'll check on dinner."

Pausing to receive a little kiss on the cheek from Robert, she braced herself for the cold and ran the short distance from the back door of the hallway to the kitchen.

Bess was taking the chicken up and carefully placing it on the platter when she entered the room.

"Mmm. That smells wonderful. How did you prepare it?"

"I just split it open and cooked it a little while on one side and then the other, added some butter and seasonings and put it back on the coals for a little bit longer. Gets real tender like that."

"It sounds marvelous. What else are you serving?"

"Well, we found some mushrooms growin' over by the cavalry barracks. They's the good kind. So I steamed a mess of 'em for supper tonight. They'll go real good with my mashed potatoes and biscuits."

"That's lovely, Bess. Thank you. I don't know what I'd do without you." Her chin trembled slightly. "I really don't."

"Now, Missy, don't you go to cryin' agin. You look real pretty right now. Don't go messin' your eyes up. Captain Lawson ought to come home and see you smilin' at him like always. Don't you think so?"

"Yes, I do. You're exactly right."

She raced back into the hallway, breathless from the cold. Smoothing her hair and gathering her composure, she smiled as she made her entrance into the parlor.

"Hello, again," she said as she breezed into the room. She held her hand out to Todd and he brushed his lips across it in a casual but polished manner.

"Lieutenant Otis, what a pleasure it is to see you again."

"Why so formal? You called me 'Todd' today. Please feel free to do that."

"I will, thank you. Dinner is ready. They'll be serving it any moment now."

"Fine. Darling, let me help you with your chair." Robert held her chair for her as she took her place across from him. "Todd? You sit here."

Bess and Lucy brought in the trays of food and served them. Robert blessed the food and the staff retreated to the kitchen.

"I don't believe this," Todd said wonderingly. "It's the best meal I've had in months! I can't wait to taste it, especially these mashed potatoes. Look at all that butter," then, "mmmm. They're delicious and these biscuits fairly melt in my mouth."

In spite of her grief, Cordelia couldn't help but giggle at his obvious pleasure. She looked over at her husband with laughter in her eyes.

"We shall have you over more often, Todd," Cordelia chuckled.

"Well, it is delicious. He's right about that," Robert added.

Cordelia picked at her food, wanting to know what happened during the day but refusing to ruin the evening with questions. As if reading her mind, Robert offered, "Well, today was monumentally unproductive. People have done nothing but talk about the battle from this morning to now."

"You mean the *massacre*," Cordelia muttered, paying particular attention that her husband had used such a softer term for it.

"Yes. Well, Custer was under orders from General Sheridan, my dear. Sheridan was heard to say that the object at hand is to reduce the Indian tribes to such a state of submission and poverty as will cause a permanent peace. So it wasn't Custer's idea to attack. Of course, he carried his orders out with his usual enthusiastic flair. General Sheridan definitely picked the right man for the job."

"Yes, he is a man who certainly enjoys his work, isn't he?" Todd said, as he took another bite of chicken.

Robert continued, "Cordelia, you may not have heard but we lost a whole company of men, as well. Major Joel Elliott had a platoon of nineteen soldiers. Apparently, the Arapahos came down from their camp when they heard the gunfire and surrounded Major Elliott's troops. Custer's men never located Major Elliott or his men but they're fairly certain that all were lost."

Todd spoke up again. "I heard from one of Custer's men that they didn't look for the bodies for long. Nightfall was coming and he didn't want to waste time looking for dead bodies. Some of his men are pretty upset about it. Leaving their dead out there like that just doesn't sit well with them. They think he should have found and collected their bodies before moving on."

"Well, I should think so. And no, I hadn't heard that we had sustained any losses," Cordelia stated. "I'm so sorry. Did you know the major, darling?"

"I've never met him," Robert said. "Have you, Todd?"

"No sir. But he's been riding with General Custer for quite a while, I think. I've heard the stories all afternoon. I wish we didn't have to go to that reception tonight. I've heard enough stories for one day."

Immediately, he froze in mid-bite and looked anxiously at Robert and then at Cordelia, realizing too late that he'd said too much.

Cordelia stiffened in her chair and stared at her husband, who had a distinctively guilty look on his face. Her eyes narrowed as she asked, "Reception? Tonight? What's this all about?"

"Well, Cordelia," Robert began, as he cleared his throat and shot another accusing glance Todd's way, "the Hazens are hosting a spontaneous little reception in their quarters tonight for the officers and their wives. I was just about to inform you of this."

"Of course you were." Her brows knit together and her mouth formed a decided pout as she announced she had absolutely no intention of attending any such reception for that snake, Custer.

Robert and Todd shared an uneasy look and Robert continued, gently, "I wish you would reconsider, my love. I'm afraid your comments this morning have been the talk of the garrison today." He tried to chuckle a little to soften the message and then, clearing his throat again, he continued, "It will appear as though you have something personal against the general if you don't come tonight."

"Well, that's fine. Because I do. Besides, I still can't understand why everybody still calls him 'General'. I thought he was a lieutenant colonel. But no matter. Whatever he is, I detest him. I loathe him. I abhor him. Need I continue?"

"No, I think we both understand how you feel about him. And as I've explained to you before, we call him 'General' because he *was* a general in the war—and a good one! And at the age of twenty-three, he was the youngest general ever. After the war, he was given this command and made a lieutenant colonel. But we still call him 'General.'"

"I wouldn't be surprised if we have to call him 'President' pretty soon," Todd chuckled, with his mouth full. "This victory really put some feathers in his cap, if you know what I mean. He's, by far, the most popular military figure in all history!"

"Really, Todd," Cordelia replied, "I think you exaggerate his importance!"

"I don't think so," he argued.

Just as Cordelia opened her mouth to respond, Robert interjected, "It doesn't really matter, does it? It's a matter of opinion and it depends solely upon whom you ask."

Robert's eyes pleaded with hers. "Cordelia, I'd count it a personal favor to me if you'll reconsider and come with us tonight," he urged.

"I won't. I'm sorry, Robert. I cannot go to any such reception and even *pretend* to honor a man I detest. What he did to those people has forever changed any opportunity he had, however remote, to obtain my respect. So am I to assume that you and Lieutenant Otis will be in attendance?" She looked from one to the other with her arms crossed.

After exchanging careful glances, both nodded. Robert explained, "We're both expected to be there. We're officers. We have a certain duty to attend. However, we don't plan to stay there very long, though, do we, Todd?"

Todd shook his head emphatically.

Searching her face, Robert implored, "Cordelia, is there anything I can say to change your mind?"

"I suppose you could command me to go. You *are* my husband and it is my duty to submit to you." She stared at her plate, picking at her food.

"And if I commanded you, would you ever forgive me?"

"No! Never!" she teased. Becoming somber once more, she delicately dabbed the corners of her mouth, then dropped her napkin onto the table. "I'm sorry, Robert. If you insist I go, I shall. But I would rather not. That's just how I feel."

"All right, Cordelia. I won't ask you to go against your conscience. You don't have to go."

"Thank you, Robert."

As she rose from the table, the gentlemen stood as well— Todd looking sheepishly at his belt buckle and Robert watching her carefully.

"Now I'll say goodnight to you, Lieutenant."

"I thought it was going to be 'Todd' from now on."

"It's 'Lieutenant' tonight, I'm afraid." With that, she turned and walked stiffly to the comfort and solitude of her bedroom.

They watched her until they saw the doors close, and then

spent several silent, awkward moments before sitting to continue with dinner. It was, after all, most delicious.

~*~

After they'd left for the reception, Cordelia sat on the divan in the parlor reading a collected work of Alexandre Dumas. This particular story was "Isabella." Bess sat next to the window, her head bent to the work of her fingers on the cinnamon-colored fabric Cordelia had purchased. Lucy was up in her quarters over the pantry.

The soft light from the fireplace illumined the pages as Cordelia read, *"'Well,' added Isabella, 'but what say you to the military profession?'*

'It is,' answered Masaniello, 'a holy one, when it calls on you to deliver your country, but a cowardly one, when it merely serves to oppress it. The only profession which would have suited me,' continued the fisherman, 'is that of an artist. Twenty times has the celebrated painter, Salvator Ross, sketched before my eyes, in this very bark, the majestic views by which we are surrounded.'

'Why did you not become his pupil, then?' asked Isabella.

'I contented myself with being his friend,' replied . . ."

A loud rapping at the front door disturbed her reading. Cordelia and Bess exchanged anxious looks. In the time she'd been here, never had anyone called on her this late in the evening!

"You want I should answer that, ma'am?"

"I don't know. I suppose so." Then, "No, let me get it."

Cordelia carefully closed her book but rushed to the door after the pounding became more insistent. When she opened the door, she stared into the leering face of General George Armstrong Custer himself!

"Sir, I'm afraid it's quite late and my husband hasn't

arrived home from your reception yet. I believe you are to stay across the hallway in Lieutenant Otis's quarters," she said, pointing to the door across the hall. "The door should be open."

"I know where I am to stay, my dear. That is not the issue."

"It's not? What *is* the issue, General?"

Leaning toward her, he huskily whispered, "*You* are the issue. Or rather, my broken heart is the issue, for when I heard how ill you were tonight, I was grieved to my very soul. The only thing I was looking forward to tonight was the opportunity to share a conversation with you, dear woman. So when I found that you would not be in attendance, I made my escape to come see to you myself."

"I'm afraid that is most inappropriate, sir."

"Well, I can't very well leave you at home all by yourself, can I? Not in your ailing condition."

"I assure you I am not alone. I am here with my friends and quite safe, thank you, sir." Ice hung from every word out of her mouth. But in fact, her heart was pounding with fear and anger that he would have the audacity to call on her so late and without the presence of her husband.

"Friends? You have friends here with you? Let me meet them, then," Custer blurted, removing his hat and pushing his way past her into the room. Bess took a couple of cautious steps backward.

"Ah, your 'friends,'" Custer laughed. "It's a pleasure to make your acquaintance, I assure you." Sweeping his hat to the floor, he bowed in a low, mocking gesture before Bess.

Tonight, he was dressed like a general. He sported his navy blue velvet jacket, trimmed in bright yellow with two rows of gold buttons down the front and on the cuffs. Gold braid hung from the epaulets on each shoulder. His red scarf hung down the front of his uniform. The pants, stretched tightly around muscular legs, were lighter blue with tan stripes down each side. The broad, flat brim of his navy blue hat touched the floor in this mockingly grand gesture.

"You can go now. Your mistress is quite safe with me," he told Bess like a man accustomed to giving orders.

She looked at Cordelia. A white man had just dismissed her, and in the old days that would have meant she had to leave. But now things were different. She was an employee, not a slave. She made a small income. She was not in servitude. So she looked to Cordelia for direction.

"The general was just leaving, Bess. It's all right for you to stay."

"The general is NOT leaving, Bess. So get out of here this instant. Do you hear me?" he barked, gruffly.

By then, Lucy had entered the hallway and stood peeking around the parlor door.

Cordelia objected strongly, her eyes flashing undisguised contempt. "I beg your pardon, sir. But you are not in a position to come in here and order us around. I take the strictest offense to your being here in the first place. But if you remain, you will behave in a civilized manner. Is that clear?"

Cordelia crossed the room to Lucy. "Go get Robert, dear. Tell him to come quickly," she whispered. Lucy fled out the front door. Bess stood guard as Custer leaned toward Cordelia.

"You know, you don't look ill to me, Mrs. Lawson. Not at all. Quite the contrary, in fact. Especially with the flush coming into your cheeks, you look rather spectacular. Yet your husband said you were not feeling well, you see."

He took two graceful paces toward her and she backed to the wall. "Sir, you have been drinking!"

"Not at all," he laughed. "I never touch liquor. Never have and never will. A promise I made to my wife. If I'm intoxicated, it is only by your beauty."

He stepped to Cordelia and stood with his face inches from hers. Looking fiercely into his blue eyes with as much unadulterated hatred as she could muster, she asked him again to leave.

"My husband will be here at any moment, sir. And I do not think it seemly for you to be here when he arrives."

"Your husband is at the reception being questioned rather intently by the commander and his wife over a brandy, I believe. Seems you may have been heard to say some untoward remarks about today's activities. And here you stand, burning with a fever, poor thing. . ." he crooned to her as he reached out once again to touch her face.

Ducking under his arm, she whirled back at him. "Sir, some illnesses are hidden from the naked eye. And the particular brand of sickness I feel every time I'm in your presence is one of them. And I'm afraid the only cure is complete avoidance. I'll ask you again to leave my house." She pointed to the door.

"Let's see, your husband is a captain, isn't he? And I? I am a general. Yes. Captain. General. You do understand, don't you, my dear? He is under *my* command, you see."

"Whether or not he is under your command is not the question, General," she explained quietly. "The situation is that under no circumstances am *I* under your authority. Do you understand me?"

"Oh, yes, my dear. But I can make things very difficult, Mrs. Lawson. I don't think you'd like to make an enemy of me. Do you understand *me?*"

"What will you do, take his scalp and wave it before the assembly in the fort? Or will you come to scalp me, as well, just as you did Black Kettle's wife?"

With that, he stepped backward in surprise. "Is that it, then? You hate me because of the Indians?" He threw back his head and roared with laughter. "I'll have you know I did not

59

scalp anyone. Those were merely gifts presented to me by one of my more zealous Osage guides." He laughed again, then stepped menacingly toward her.

Again, she quickly backed against the wall.

"Don't touch me! Leave me alone, do you hear?" she cried.

With all seriousness he continued, as he moved closer. "You'd best not worry yourself about the Indians, my dear. My men will take care of them. You'd better get used to it, in fact. A proclamation was issued just today for all the 'friendly' Indians to come in to the fort. Those who refuse to come to the fort will be considered hostile. And therefore, they will be subject to the same sort of . . . shall we say, discipline that was shown Black Kettle's tribe."

"'Discipline,'" she spat at Custer. "You dare to call that butchery 'discipline?' Sir, I find that exceedingly offensive."

"Offensive?" he asked, with raised brows. "Why, doing my duty for my country is an honor. And military service is a noble profession, is it not?" It was more a statement than a question.

Suddenly the words of the book she'd been reading came to mind. She looked him squarely in the eyes as she uttered with a voice so calm and controlled that it belied the panic forming within her, "It is noble when it calls on you to deliver your country, sir, but cowardly, when it merely serves to oppress it or to oppress the people who dwell within."

His face only inches from hers, Custer sliced through the tension between them as he rasped between clenched teeth, "You'd better be careful, Cordelia. It's not popular around here to sympathize overmuch with those savages."

Pushing him perhaps a little more than would be prudent, she quietly replied, "Excuse me, sir. I have never given you permission to use my given name. You will address me as 'Mrs. Lawson.' Is that clear?"

They both eyed each other for a long moment. Then the

general stood back, placed his hat on his head and laughingly said, "It's back to the party I go, *Mrs.* Lawson. If I tarry much longer, I fear I shall be missed. I will look forward to our next meeting, madam. Until then, I'm sure I'll very much enjoy living in such close proximity to so lovely and spirited a . . . 'friend'."

"I assure you, sir, I am no friend of yours." Again that dead level, still, emerald gaze.

"We'll see, my dear. We'll see." With that, he threw open the front door and nimbly descended the steps toward the commander's quarters.

Cordelia slammed the door behind him, then dropped, trembling and breathless, onto the divan as Bess rushed to her side. "Are you all right, Miz Lawson?" Concern was etched on her face, her eyes searching Cordelia's intently. "Can I get you something, ma'am?"

"No, thank you. I'm fine. That was very unpleasant, wasn't it? I'm sorry he treated you so badly. He is no gentleman."

"That's fo' sho'!" Bess's anger blazed from her eyes as Robert and Lucy rushed in through the front door.

"Darling!" he exclaimed, as he swept Cordelia into his arms. "I'm so sorry. What happened? Are you hurt? I can feel you trembling." He looked over at Bess and asked her to bring Cordelia a hot toddy. "She needs a little something to calm her nerves, I think."

Cordelia hid her face against his shoulder, telling herself not to cry. But she allowed the sensation of safety and security to wash over her once more—the kind of security she sensed only when she was in his arms like this.

Bess came back with the drink of warmed whiskey and honey. It was delicious. If she'd been back in Baltimore she'd have put in a bit of lemon juice, as well. Cordelia took another sip and could feel the hot liquid curling warmly in her stomach. Immediately, she felt herself relaxing.

Just then, taps sounded in the distance. Always slow and somber, tonight it took on an especially mournful quality. She took another sip of the toddy.

Robert looked intently into her face. She could sense the questions behind those concerned eyes, but he resisted the impulse to quiz her just now. First, he had to make sure she was all right.

He straightened up and looked around him. "I think it's time we all retired for the evening," he announced.

"Yes, sir," Bess mumbled. She and Lucy scrambled out the back door and into the kitchen, where they could climb the ladder to their sleeping quarters.

"Come, darling. You look tired." Standing, Robert offered his hand. Taking it, Cordelia feebly smiled into the face she loved so much and, heaving a great sigh, said, "You don't have to make that suggestion twice, I assure you. I confess I am exhausted just now."

He helped her up gently and led her into the bedroom. Tonight they didn't make love. But as they lay together, they found solace in each other's arms.

Six

Cordelia woke up with a start to find Robert already up and dressed. He sat on a stool by her side of the bed, drinking a cup of coffee as he looked intently into her face.

"Good morning, my love. Did you sleep well?" he asked.

"Yes, I did, surprisingly enough," she yawned, confused by this attention. "I've overslept this morning, haven't I?" Rubbing her eyes, she pulled herself to a sitting position, leaning back against the heavy oak headboard.

"No. I just woke up early and couldn't go back to sleep. I brought you a cup of coffee." He offered her the cup as she propped two pillows behind her back. She took a sip of the hot coffee. He handed her a biscuit, already buttered and dripping enticingly with honey.

"Bess told me to bring this to you for breakfast."

"Hmm. Breakfast in bed?" she asked with a raise of one eyebrow. "What's the occasion?"

"We were just concerned about you, I suppose. I still can't believe he came here last night," Robert said, shaking his head.

"I can't get over it! And I really can't believe I didn't meet him on the way!"

"He was probably skulking in the shadows like the coward he is," Cordelia offered, amused at the unintentional melodramatic sound of that phrase, and took another sweet, tender bite of the biscuit and honey.

Robert disagreed. "Cordelia, Custer is a lot of things, but one thing he *isn't* is a coward. I've heard stories, and from reliable men, of his bravery in the war—at Bull Run, Gettysburg, Yellow Tavern, Winchester, Fisher's Hill, Five Forks, Sailor's Creek. I've heard it said that he rides into battle as though no bullet or saber could touch him! He is no coward, I assure you."

He cupped her face in his hand as he continued, "Regardless of his heroism on the field of battle, though, there can be no defense for his behavior last evening. I shouldn't have gone to the reception. I should have stayed here with you. I'm so sorry, darling."

Cordelia smiled warmly. "If you shouldn't have gone last night, it should have been for a different reason than to stay home for my protection. Protection shouldn't be needed here at Fort Cobb. You weren't negligent to me, Robert. Please stop worrying."

Lifting her legs from the bed and placing her bare feet on the braided rug beside the bed, she stretched and then leaned over to kiss him. "I love you so much. Thank you for being concerned about me."

"This presents quite a dilemma for me, Cordelia. I don't know exactly how to handle it. I would be justified to call him out, but that seems so . . . uncivilized. Yet, just having a quiet, little chat with him hardly seems a fitting punishment for the offense he's committed against you . . . and me, for that matter!"

"Oh, Robert! Promise me you won't call him out over this! Promise! After all, I wasn't hurt. I was just a little rattled, that's all. And if the truth be known, I think I handled the situation quite well. I don't want you to do anything that will jeopardize our life together. Is that clear? I know your pride may be injured. And we both recognize the impropriety of his visit. But can't we please just let it drop right here and now? I don't want to waste another breath on that man! Please, Robert? Promise me?"

Robert's eyes scanned her face, her hair, her eyes before picking up her two hands in his. Very gently he said, "I'm sorry, darling. This cannot be ignored. At the very least, I shall have to confront him and tell him he is not welcome here again. Ever!"

"He already threatened to make things very difficult for you, Robert. Don't bait him further. I don't want anything to happen to you or to your chances for advancement. Please be careful. I don't trust that man."

"I'm always careful, darling, because I want to be able, for the rest of my life, to come home to you at the end of the day. I don't know what I would do without you in my life."

Abruptly he stood up, straight and tall. "So you'll be all right here at home today?"

"Of course! Besides, Bess and Lucy will be here. And I may not be home much today anyway. I thought I might go to the guardhouse to catch another glimpse of that Indian woman we saw yesterday. I was thinking of making her the subject of my next painting. What do you think?"

"That should be fine, but don't go to the compound alone. Have one of the guards accompany you. Or if you like, I can assign someone to keep you company today."

Turning toward the mirrored dresser in the corner of the

room, she studied herself intently before saying, "Don't you dare! I'll be fine."

Turning back to Robert she urged him, "Now go to work. Do something noble and fine and good. And come back to me safe and sound at the end of the day."

"By God's grace." He kissed her lightly on the cheek and left the room. She stood looking out the window for a long time after he left. The snow was almost gone now. The tall, waving grass across the huge expanse of prairie was a welcome sight. Its constant motion reminded her of the Bible passage that said, about the Holy Spirit, that He is like the wind. Though you can see and hear *evidence* of the wind, you don't see the wind itself and you don't know from where it has come or where it is going.

Thinking about Robert's offer to assign someone to her, she smiled. That was sweet, but unnecessary. Perhaps she should have felt frightened, but she certainly did not. She decided that last night's impropriety would not rob her of one more moment's peace. She set about dressing for the day ahead.

While she was still dressing, Bess brought in a note that had just been delivered. Opening the letter, Cordelia read the beautiful, flowing handwriting,

Mrs. Lawson,

Please forgive my barbaric behavior last evening. There was no possible justification for such common conduct. I assure you there will never be another occasion like that again. I humbly beg your forgiveness, though I know I do not deserve it.

Yours respectfully,
G. A. Custer

. . .

Cordelia read the note again and tucked it into her bag. She must get it to Robert right away, she thought, before he confronted the general. The note was so prettily and humbly worded, she almost believed his sincerity. Perhaps there was more to this man than meets the eye. Perhaps she should open her mind to the possibility that he may not be so bad after all. No, she decided, she just couldn't open her mind that much. But she had to admit it was a nice gesture to have sent so sweet and swift an apology.

She answered with a note of her own.

General Custer,

I accept your apology and freely offer my forgiveness as long as your word is kept.

Mrs. Robert Lawson

Stopping by the kitchen on her way out, she read Custer's note to Bess and Lucy. Since they were present for the offense she thought it only fair to allow them to hear the apology. She gave her own note to Lucy to take to headquarters to place it *only* in the hands of the general. No reason to allow any of those nosy soldiers the pleasure of reading and misinterpreting her note.

Picking up her sketchpad, pencils and her bag, she stepped out into a cold but beautiful, sunny day and carefully picked her way across the soggy parade ground. She would see Robert first and then proceed to the guardhouse for a closer look at that Indian beauty.

~*~

Robert was immediately relieved to read Custer's note. He

decided he would still need to confront him but would also admit that he'd read the apology and would hold him to his word that this would never happen again.

Sitting on the edge of his desk, he leaned toward Cordelia to take her into his arms when Todd Otis lumbered in from outside in his characteristic loose-jointed way. Immediately Robert checked his show of affection toward Cordelia and soberly nodded to Todd.

Todd nodded in response and then greeted Cordelia cautiously with, "Good morning, Mrs. Lawson. Are you still angry with me?"

"Life is too short for hard feelings, Todd. I'm sorry I was rude to you last evening. Please forgive me. I'm often convicted of the error of my ways, and I'm afraid this is not the first time my impulsiveness has given me cause for regret. Of course, you must do what your duty demands. I understand that now."

"Thank you, Mrs. Lawson. But there is nothing to be sorry for in this instance. You were, and are, a marvel to me."

"Please, you may call me Cordelia now, I think," she smiled back at him. She spent an instant imagining Robert with the kind of short goatee that Todd sported, a neatly trimmed frame for his big, wide smile.

"Hey, hey. Enough of this," Robert laughed in mock jealousy. Then turning to his wife again, he asked, "So are you off to the guardhouse now?"

"Guardhouse!" Todd exclaimed, jovially. "Cordelia, what have you done to deserve the guardhouse?"

"Nothing, silly. I'm going to do a little sketching of the Indian captives."

"Yes, Robert tells me you are a fabulous artist. I hope you will do me the honor of painting a portrait of my family as soon as they get here. Maybe just a small one?"

Cordelia laughed again and promised to think about it.

Then with a wave of her gloved hand, she left them both watching after her admiringly.

~*~

As she walked toward the other end of the fort, Cordelia met an exhausted Ela Anthony making her way from the guardhouse to the hospital.

"Oh, Mrs. Lawson. I'm so glad to run into you like this. I was going to send for you. Norman has been working all night and has had no real respite. He's in the guardhouse now attending to the Indians. I have to go check on our wounded at the hospital. But Norman could sure use some help if you have the time."

"Of course, I'll help. I don't know exactly what to do but I'm willing to learn."

"Oh, thank you. As hard as I've tried, I still haven't figured out how to be in two places at once," she chuckled.

"But what about you? You look tired, yourself. When will you have an opportunity to rest?"

"If you'll help Norman for an hour or so, I'll take a nap after I see to the wounded. Perhaps Norman will be finished by then and can get a little rest, as well. You might make that suggestion to him anyway."

"Of course, I will. I'll check on you tomorrow, Mrs. Anthony."

"Thanks, my dear. I appreciate this."

"You're quite welcome. I'll do anything I can to help."

"God bless you. You're an angel!" With that, she continued on her way toward the hospital and Cordelia quickened her steps toward the guardhouse.

Upon her arrival, she informed the guards of her intention to assist the doctor. They allowed her to enter the blockhouse, modified to become the jail or guardhouse. Blinking in the damp darkness of the octagonal stone building, it took her several seconds to adjust to the gloom. Weak beams of light streamed into the room in thin shafts through the rifle slits, called loopholes. This building had been constructed initially to provide a safe place for the soldiers, in case they were under siege by the attacking savages. There were two levels of loopholes all around the building. A wooden platform halfway up the walls was intended to support the upper level of soldiers so that they could fire in all directions around the building.

Gathered into small groups across the hard-packed dirt floor were Indians huddled together for warmth. Cordelia involuntarily pulled her shawl more tightly around her own shivering shoulders. It was warmer outside the building than inside!

Finally, her eyes adjusted sufficiently to make out Doc's form bent over the old Indian man Cordelia had seen the day before. The man, withered with age, shivered uncontrollably.

"Doc, he's so cold. Why isn't there a fireplace in here?"

"Mrs. Lawson! You're a welcome sight, I must say. Did the guards give you much trouble about being here?"

"No, I told them I was here to help you. And I am. What can I do? What about this poor man?"

"Unfortunately, a guardhouse is no place for the sick. No, there is no stove or fireplace in here. When our men spend time in the guardhouse, they bring their own army issue blankets. These people had to leave their village so quickly they weren't able to bring their things with them. And the quartermaster says we have no blankets to spare for the captives. I personally saw at least two dozen blankets in his store, but he refuses to distribute them to these people."

"Have you spoken to the commander about this?"

"Of course not. What good would that do? Would you

mind sitting here and just rubbing his arms and legs? We'll use friction to generate some heat. I need to see to the others."

"Of course, I think I can do that." Cordelia sat next to the old man, wrapped her shawl around his bony shoulders and used her gloved hands to rub his arms and legs, urging his aging circulation to do its job. While she worked with him, she noted his rasping breaths, the bluish tinge of the fingernails of his leathery hands, and his tired, unfocused stare.

Quickly scanning the building, she spotted the attractive Indian woman she'd seen yesterday. She was keenly watching Doc, who knelt beside another patient, as he instructed her on wrapping a deep wound with cotton strips. He had cleaned it thoroughly and sewn the wound together. He trusted the lovely Indian woman to apply the dressing. She nodded and immediately began to dress the wound, following his instructions precisely. Although she understood not one word of English, she learned quickly just from his demonstration.

A little Indian girl sat next to her mother in a corner of the stone building. She had sustained a nasty wound to her upper arm where a bullet had grazed her. Doc applied alcohol to the wound and although it must have stung, the little girl never whimpered. The only sign of pain was that her little hand doubled into a fist and her eyes widened as she sought her mother's face.

The pregnant woman huddled closely with an older woman that Cordelia assumed to be her mother. Though the younger woman was also beautiful, the expression on her round face was simple, in Cordelia's opinion. Yes, she was pretty but seemed spoiled and pouting in contrast to the intelligence Cordelia noted in the eyes of the other maiden. The pregnant woman made no move to help anyone else, but she and her mother watched them with interest.

The three of them—Doc, Cordelia and the young Indian

woman—worked on the wounded Indians until they'd all been examined and treated. Out of 53 captives, only 32 had escaped without injury of some kind. Some suffered gunshot wounds; some had been sliced by sabers. One child sustained a dislocated shoulder, probably from being hastily jerked from the ground. Several had varying stages of frostbite, deep scratches, scrapes and bruises from their desperate attempt to escape the soldiers.

One of the women in the group had a bad cough, which wasn't surprising after spending a freezing night in this cold, damp building. The effort of her coughing was so intense that she held her sides with her arms and grimaced with each wracking spasm.

Doc said she sounded like she had the croup. Out of his bag, he fetched a small vial of medicine. He explained to Cordelia that croup could be cured in one minute. All it took was a little alum and sugar—the sugar added to make the alum more palatable. The Cheyenne woman tried to resist at first, then acquiesced in taking the medicine he offered her. True to his word, the coughing stopped almost instantly. The woman looked up to him gratefully. Tenderly, he patted her shoulder and gave her a brief but kindly smile.

Standing, he pressed his palms firmly into the small of his back, stretching his aching muscles, rolling his head from side to side. He was obviously exhausted.

Cordelia offered, "Doc, I'll stay here for a little while longer to make sure everything's okay. I'll come get you if I need you. I really think you should get some rest."

"Thank you, my dear. But I'll need to go check on our enlisted men. For the most part, they sustained only superficial wounds. But one of them was shot almost through the heart. A single rib deflected the bullet and shattered on impact. It's a very painful wound, but thank the good Lord, I believe he'll recover. I need to watch him pretty close for these first few days. I think they'll all be fine, but I do need to look in on them."

"Mrs. Anthony has already done that. Why don't you go home for a while and get some sleep while you can?"

"Perhaps I will. Perhaps I will. But are you sure you'll be comfortable staying in here alone?"

"There are two guards right outside the door if I need them," Cordelia assured him. Surveying the sad faces of the people around her, she continued, "I don't think anyone will give me any trouble. I think they know I'm a friend. Now go on, Doc. Take care of yourself. What would we do without you?"

"You're an angel," Cordelia heard for the second time that day. "I think I may go lie down for just a little while," his voice trailed off as he buckled his medical bag and trudged heavily out the door and across the grounds to his quarters, looking much older than his thirty-six years.

Meanwhile, Cordelia took a place next to the old man and sat on the cold ground. Taking out her sketchpad, she quickly drew, on sheet after sheet, scenes from inside the jailhouse. There were several groupings of women and children spread across the cold and barren ground. Huddling together for warmth, they attended to each other lovingly.

The beautiful young woman sat on the cold, hard ground with her back against the wall of the building, gently cradling the older woman she'd helped into the guardhouse yesterday. Singing softly, she slowly stroked the woman's hair as she rocked side to side. The older woman, eyes closed, gave no sign of acknowledgement and for a moment, Cordelia was afraid she'd breathed her last, then saw the heaving breaths resume.

The mid-afternoon sun shining in one of the rifle loop-holes cast the beautiful woman's face in such a striking pose of light and shadow that Cordelia fixed her attention on her portrait. Her eyes were large and dark with heavy brows and lashes. The curve of her nose between the high, broad cheekbones gave her an aristocratic look. The full, wide mouth moved to the plaintive tune of her singing. Her black hair hung in two long, thick braids across her shoulders, but some of the hair had escaped their constraints to fall limply beside her face. From time to time, she'd lay her head back and close her eyes, but the soft melody of the song continued soothingly in the frigid gloom.

So intent was Cordelia on her sketch that she didn't notice when the music stopped. But when she next looked her way, the Indian seemed to be sleeping finally—her head resting against the graying one of her companion.

Cordelia checked the old man's breathing again, leaving her shawl with him for warmth. It was not like having his old buffalo robe around him, but in this dark, cold and silent "lodge" he needed all the warmth he could find. Cordelia shivered against the cold and promised herself not to complain about the lack of heat in her own quarters—not after seeing this.

Relieved that the old man's breathing seemed to have improved, she was packing up to leave when the two guards rushed in, noisily rousting the beautiful woman from her spot against the hard, block wall. They stood her up and tied her hands together in front of her, then marched her outside the guardhouse. She looked back at Cordelia with desperate eyes, and then she was gone.

Cordelia hurriedly picked up her bag and supplies and rushed out after her. By that time, she was mounted sidesaddle on a horse, her tied hands tightly gripping the saddle horn. George Custer stood there with his back to her as he signed a sheet of paper the guard held out to him. Three of his hounds milled about his feet, sniffing the air.

At first she hardly recognized him, dressed as he was. But no one but General Custer had those long coils of reddish-blond hair hanging so thickly from beneath the fur hat he wore. He was obviously dressed for hunting, having abandoned his uniform for this outing, choosing instead the buckskins he wore during yesterday's triumphant entry.

When he turned, he was obviously surprised to see Cordelia standing there, staring at him, open-mouthed. He held her with those deep-set Viking eyes of his and the blue seemed to drain very slowly from their irises, leaving them gray. Ghostly. Winter bleak. With death in them. And hell.

Placing his finger to his hat in acknowledgement of her presence, he deftly mounted his horse behind the Indian woman. With a brisk nudge to the horse's sides, they were off at a canter across the wind-blown prairie, following the dry riverbed away from the fort.

Cordelia questioned the stoic guard holding the paper. "Where is he taking her?" she demanded.

"Mrs. Lawson, I'm not at liberty to say."

"Why was she tied like that?"

"Sorry, ma'am."

"You know that my husband is a captain." It was more a statement than a question.

"Yes, ma'am."

"And that he can find this information out for me at a moment's notice?"

"Yes, ma'am. That 'ud be just fine. But I cain't tell you where they's goin' 'cuz I don't rightly know."

"Then may I see that paper?"

"No, ma'am. That 'ud be aginst orders."

"Fine. I'll speak to my husband about this immediately."

"Yes, ma'am."

She turned on her heel and although it was getting late in the day, she hurried to headquarters to see Robert.

~*~

"He did what?" he blasted.

"Robert, you should have seen her face. She was terrified," she told him, shivering.

"I'll look into this immediately. Now you go back home, get some rest and warm up. I'll try to come home with the information you want. Promise me, darling."

"All right. I'll go home. I must confess that I am quite tired." Turning to leave, she remembered, "Oh, and you'll look into getting some blankets for the captives?"

"Yes, dear. I'll see what I can do."

"Thank you, Robert."

She walked home quickly, dropped her bags in the parlor and made straight for the bedroom. Rubbing her cold arms briskly, she bent to place additional logs on the fire. Suddenly the true measure of her fatigue—emotional and physical—enveloped her and drawing a heavy quilt around her, she fell asleep across the bed in seconds.

Seven

She awoke to someone gently shaking her shoulders. Looking up through blurred eyes, she saw Robert standing over her. She held her arms out to him, inviting him with a provocative smile to join her on the bed.

"No, thank you, my love. I dare not. Bess will have supper ready in no time."

"Can't we just be late?" Cordelia asked, in sleepy mischief. Suddenly she remembered what had taken place that afternoon and she sat bolt upright in the middle of the bed. "What were you able to find out, Robert? Has she come back yet? Have you seen her?"

"Quiet, now. Settle down. I'll tell you what I found out but I honestly don't know what to make of it."

Cordelia pulled herself to the edge of the bed and reached out for Robert's hand as he sat next to her.

"Apparently, Custer requisitioned her to serve as an interpreter this afternoon on his quest to locate and round up friendly Indians."

"An interpreter?" she asked, incredulously.

"Yes. General Sheridan has offered safety and protection to all who come in peacefully, but to those who don't, only violence awaits them. They will be hunted down and killed, or relocated to one of the other reservations. So Custer himself went out to spread the word. He needed her to translate."

"But Robert," Cordelia protested. "This woman knows not one word of English! I worked with her this afternoon. Doc had to show her what to do because she couldn't understand verbal instructions. Besides, if she were serving in any capacity of her own volition, she would have been riding her own horse, not sharing one with him—with her hands tied, no less!"

"You're right, of course," he whispered. She saw his jaw working, as it did anytime he was in deep thought. He continued, "Then that makes it even more bizarre."

"I couldn't agree more! So you haven't seen her return then. What about Custer? Have you seen him?"

"No, I left headquarters early so I could speak to the soldier outside the guardhouse. I haven't seen either of them return."

"Oh, Robert. What do you suppose he's done with that poor girl?" Cordelia cried. "I hate to even think what he might be capable of."

"You can't worry about it, Cordelia." He gently patted a stray wisp of hair back in place. "There's nothing you can do about this—except to pray for her safe return. It's nearly dark now. I'll go over to check the guardhouse one more time before turning in for the night."

"Would you, Robert? I do appreciate that. You're such a kind-hearted man. Thank you."

"Don't let it get around," Robert joked. "I'm an officer, you know. My men have to respect me."

"As I'm sure they do!" She sent him off with a smile. When she heard the door close, she clasped her hands to her bosom and looked heavenward. Closing her eyes, she prayed with all fervency for God to be merciful to the lovely Indian girl, whoever, and wherever she may be.

~*~

Half an hour later, Robert returned and seated himself at the dinner table where Bess was in the process of serving steaming bowls of potato soup filled with tender carrots, onions and the rest of the mushrooms from last night. After blessing the food, he tore a chunk of freshly baked bread and dunked it into the soup.

"Mm. This is great, isn't it? Another success, Bess. I'll be big as a barn eating like this every evening."

Bess beamed shyly and scurried back to the kitchen. Cordelia took two spoons of soup before raising her eyes to Robert's face. Still he said nothing.

Unable to hold her tongue another moment she cried, "Well?"

He replied, somewhat reluctantly, "She's not back yet, Cordelia. No one knows what happened to her. I saw a lighted lamp in Todd's quarters, so I think we can assume Custer's back on the fort. But the woman was never returned to the guardhouse. That's all I know."

"What are we going to do about it?"

Robert said nothing.

Pushing away from the table, Cordelia stormed, "Well, I'll tell you what I'm going to do. I'm going to march over there right now and ask him what he's done with that poor girl. That's what I'm going to do!"

Robert caught her arm before she reached the door. "No, darling. You won't do that. There's nothing to be gained from taking that tack with Custer. I'll look into it in the morning."

"You will?" she asked, seeking further reassurance.

"Absolutely. Now come back here and sit down. Let's finish our dinner." He pushed her chair back for her then returned to his.

"Were you able to speak to the commander about the blankets for the Indians?" she asked.

"Oh," he said, remembering as he dabbed his mouth with his napkin, "yes, I spoke to him. He absolutely refuses to give them any army blankets. Even though there are nearly three dozen blankets in the quartermaster's store, he says they are not for the Indians. So I made another proposition to him, to which he agreed."

"And what was that?"

"According to the report that Custer filed, he collected—as plunder, no doubt—around 1100 buffalo robes from the Cheyenne. Commander Hazen will requisition enough of them to keep the Indians warm while in our custody. But he says he can't do it until tomorrow.

"Custer's troops will move out at daybreak tomorrow, along with General Sheridan and one of our companies, commanded by Todd Otis. They're going back to the Washita to try to locate Major Elliot's body and the bodies of his men and to reconnoiter the battle site.

"Robert, you're not going, are you?"

"No, dear. I'm staying here. I'll ride out to Custer's camp with a wagon to collect some buffalo robes for our captives. He won't like it, but he'll already be gone by then and his quartermaster will have no choice but to obey General Hazen's requisition. By the grace of God, perhaps tonight will be the last night they'll be cold."

She looked at him with an adoring expression of admiration that would have melted a flagstone. "Thank you, Robert," she said, simply.

~*~

The next day, she sat very still as she put the finishing touches on her painting of the Indian princess, as she had started calling her. Her easel was set up in the parlor in order to capture the last of the morning light. She was careful to keep the drips to a minimum and made sure she was always working over the burlap mat she used to protect the floor from her paints. After the addition of her signature, she sat back, looking into those haunting, yet soft and beautiful eyes.

"She sure is pretty, Miz Lawson," Bess commented from behind her shoulder.

"Do you think so? As hard as I've worked to capture her, I know I still haven't gotten her quite right. I think she's actually more beautiful than this. But I think it's the best I can do without having her here to sit for me."

"How old you think she is?"

"I don't know. Barely twenty, I would guess. What do you think?"

Bess studied the face, turning her pudgy, pleasing face this way and that, then offered, "I think she's less than that. Younger. Maybe seventeen or eighteen but life's been mighty hard for her and she looks a mite older than what she is. That's my take on it."

"You might be right, Bess," Cordelia muttered softly, still examining her work.

"I brung you in a cup of coffee, fixed just the way you like it."

"Oh, thank you, Bess. You're so sweet to me. What can I do to repay you for your kindness? Is there anything you need?"

Bess looked down sheepishly, embarrassed at this sudden focus of attention and shook her head. "No, ma'am. You don't need to do a thing. I like being here with you and the captain. Ya'll's good people."

Cordelia reached out for Bess's hand, searching for some eye contact and then said, "You and Lucy are good people, too. We sort of grew up together, you and me. You were probably about her age when I first saw you." She gestured toward the painting.

Taking the cloth from her apron pocket, Bess began to dust the furniture in the parlor, talking away as she did, careful to collect the dust, not spread it.

"No, ma'am, I was younger. I was only fifteen when I came to your mama's house. Now Lucy's thirteen years old goin' on twenty! Sometimes, Missy," Bess laughed, "I believe Lucy's doing the raisin' in this family!"

"Well, you've done a great job with her. She's very bright, you know. Her lessons are coming along nicely. I think she may have a real talent for figures."

Bess beamed with pride. "Why, thank you, Miz Lawson. She'll be happy you said that!"

"Oh, she knows. I brag on her all the time."

"I'll be right back, ma'am. I got to go shake this cloth out."

"Thanks, Bess." Rising, she took her coffee cup over to the divan and sat down to enjoy it while she read. Occasionally, she would glance over at the portrait of her Indian princess. Worry moved back into her face like clouds before the sun as she wondered again about the welfare of the young woman who had become so important to her.

Robert had left before lunch for the soldier camp to recover the much-needed buffalo robes for the Indians in the guardhouse. They wouldn't need fifty-three anymore. The old man had died overnight, she'd heard, and of course, who knew if the young woman would be back now. Sadness rushed over her as she remembered.

Suddenly, Bess appeared in the doorway, furtively looking left and right. In a hushed, conspiratorial whisper, she said, "It's Miz Hazen. She's a'comin' this way right now!"

"Oh, no," Cordelia thought. Before she had a chance to respond, Mrs. Hazen burst energetically through the door and tapped at the parlor door facing.

"Hello-oo!" she called, peeking around Bess, who was partially blocking her entrance. Stepping to the side, Bess allowed her to pass. Eleanor Hazen marched in and plopped down in the chair across from Cordelia. She tried to give Cordelia a sweet, maternal smile. It didn't quite work, but she appreciated the effort.

"Mrs. Hazen. What a surprise! Bess has just brought me a cup of coffee. Could I offer you one?"

"Oh, no, thank you," she said, "but I'll have a nice cup of tea, if you don't mind."

"Not at all." Turning toward Bess, she asked if she would bring Mrs. Hazen a cup of hot tea and a plate of shortbreads. Bess nodded and backed out of the parlor into the hallway. Cordelia could hear her shuffling step as she made her way out to the kitchen, obviously in no hurry. Cordelia smiled.

"What brings you here, Mrs. Hazen?" Cordelia asked, over her coffee cup.

"I just wanted to see how you're feeling. That tall, good-looking husband of yours told us the other evening that you weren't feeling well. I'm so sorry you didn't feel well enough to attend the reception. It was quite nice. And General Custer was just glorious. How are you now, dear?"

"I'm fine. Thank you for asking."

Cocking her head to the side, she asked, "And what of this fort life, dear? Are you adapting well?"

"I think so, yes," Cordelia replied, her suspicion mounting. "There may not be all the comforts of home here, but the country is beautiful, the accommodations are satisfactory and, most importantly, I'm with my husband. That means everything to me."

She took another sip and asked, "How long have you and the commander been married, Mrs. Hazen?"

"Oh, a long time, dear. Almost twenty-two years. I was a child bride of fifteen."

Bess brought in a tray of tea and shortbreads and placed it on the small table beside Mrs. Hazen's chair. She served her politely and left the room without a sound.

"Your girl is wonderful, isn't she? Sometimes I wish my Sophie were more like her. But I suppose out here, where it comes to these darkies, we must satisfy ourselves with what . . . ." Her eyes fastened onto the painting by the window. Rising with a little grunt, she walked over to the easel and studied the portrait.

Cordelia stiffened, waiting for her comment, wishing she'd set the painting up in her bedroom instead.

Mrs. Hazen turned and fixed a look of utter admiration on Cordelia. "Did you do this, dear?"

"Yes, ma'am. What do you think of it?"

"It's absolutely beautiful! Funny, I've never thought of an Indian as beautiful before. Is this a real person? Or is she merely a product of your imagination?"

"No. She's one of the captives General Custer brought in after the battle the other day," she explained, careful not to say "massacre," though that would have been her word of choice. "I took notice of her when she walked in. She's lovely, isn't she?"

"Yes, very." Mrs. Hazen was pensive as she took her seat again. Her eyes never left Cordelia's as she took a long sip of the hot tea. Cordelia could almost sense the older woman's mind working as she sat studying her. She felt uncomfortable under Mrs. Hazen's scrutiny.

Cutting into the silence, Cordelia said, "Your husband has allowed Captain Lawson to go to the soldier camp to requisition some buffalo robes for the Indians. They are all but freezing in the guardhouse. There's not a stove or a fireplace in there at all, you know. I certainly appreciate his willingness to have the robes brought in from the camp."

"Yes, sometimes I think he actually liked that old Indian, Black Kettle." By her expression, Cordelia judged she disapproved with that sentiment.

"Yes, I would have loved to have met him."

Mrs. Hazen's brow rose suddenly in shock at such a statement, as if to say, "You would?" But she kept her mouth shut all the same. Instead she said, "Dear, will you grant me a favor?"

"I'll try. What is it?"

Looking over at the portrait again, she leaned forward and gave Cordelia a beseeching gaze. "Paint my portrait. No one has ever done that before and oh, how I'd love to hang one in our quarters. Will you, dear?"

Cordelia almost choked on her coffee. "Well, um." She swallowed, wondering what to say.

She'd always chosen her subjects according to her interest in them and had always managed to shy away from commercial opportunities if the subject at hand didn't fascinate her. She'd once painted a landscape of a plantation house in the south for a dear friend who wanted to have it to remember her homestead. It hadn't been exciting but the land was truly lovely and her friend had been deeply touched by the finished product and had paid her the enormous sum of $25 for it! She'd tried to refuse the money but her friend insisted. That was the only time she'd done anything commercially.

Looking now at Mrs. Hazen's plump face, she couldn't imagine spending the amount of time it would take to duplicate her image on paper. And not only that, but most certainly, she would be expected to make her look younger and slimmer in the process until the finished product hardly resembled her at all. She could think of one pitfall after another.

"Dear?"

"Yes, well, I wish I could, Mrs. Hazen, but I've made it a practice not to paint close acquaintances," placing some emphasis on that term. "I can never really get them right. They end up looking like totally different people and I have just avoided that frustration over the years. But thank you for the compliment. I'm honored you would want me to do this. I hope you understand."

Sitting back in her chair abruptly, she folded her arms and puffed up like a toad. Her pout caused a cascade of chins to appear.

Cordelia fought back a giggle.

Mrs. Hazen blurted, "I certainly do *not* understand! It seems you certainly have the time to do it and I'd be happy to pay you, if that's what you want."

"I'm sorry. Forgive me, but I just don't think I could do you justice. Besides, I don't have any canvas! All I have is paper."

"And you can't paint my portrait on paper?"

"Not the kind of quality you deserve, Mrs. Hazen."

Mrs. Hazen rattled her teacup as she placed it roughly in the saucer and stood up. "Then I'll say good day, Mrs. Lawson."

"Oh, do you have to go so soon?" Cordelia stood to walk her to the door. Before leaving, she turned back to Cordelia and barked, "I do hope you'll reconsider. You did a lovely job of that Indian on paper. I wouldn't mind one like that. Really,

I wouldn't! It would mean a great deal to me . . . and to the commander." With that veiled threat, she turned and marched down the sunny boardwalk toward her quarters.

Cordelia looked heavenward, sighed, and shook her head slowly. "Why do You put me in these situations, Lord?" Then she went back into the house.

~*~

Meanwhile, Robert supervised the loading of the robes onto the back of the wagon. Two men jumped onto the wagon seat, awaiting his command. Instructing them to take the robes immediately to the guardhouse for distribution to the Indians, he decided to ride back to the fort alone.

He walked to his big bay, Chief, and mounted. He was proud of his horse. Chief was one of the finest on the fort.

The War had taken such a toll on the resources of the US Army that the members of the cavalry had to furnish their own mounts. Robert was fortunate to have spotted this one running with a small herd at an outpost near Fort Hays. He'd paid dearly for him, but Robert knew what he wanted.

And Chief was more than he'd hoped for. Unable to repress the urge, he patted the thick fur on Chief's muscular neck and flicked some stray strands of the horse's black mane to the other side.

At his command, the wagon pulled out. Slapping the reins across the backs of their mules, the driver began the trip back to the fort at a surprisingly energetic pace. Watching their progress for a few moments, Robert scanned the hilly country-side before starting back toward the fort, taking a wider trail than his men.

Eight

A quarter-hour later, he crested a mesa and nudged Chief into a canter. He rode across its flat expanse, enjoying the sound of the leather creaking with every stride, and feeling his horse's exceeding power beneath him. He easily fell into the joy and rhythm of the run. The waist high plains grasses swished and slapped against his horse's legs, and against his own boots as horse and rider made their effortless way across the mesa.

Though the wind was brisk, Robert relished the sensation of being out in the open air of the plains. He'd grown fonder of its color, beauty and vast horizons than he'd ever imagined. He savored the moment. In this one small space in time, he blocked out all the worrisome thoughts, fears and horrors, wholeheartedly giving himself over to this wonderfully energizing sensation of euphoria.

Giving Chief his head, he sensed the horse slip into a faster gait, running outright now. He felt the powerful muscles bunch and release under him as Chief lengthened his stride. Hearing the rhythmic snorts of breath, and feeling the subtle sting of the horse's mane as it slapped against his face, Robert enjoyed the purity of utter freedom.

As they closed the distance to the other side of the mesa, Robert slowed Chief to a lope and then to a walk. Urging him down the steep sides, he gave him his head, knowing Chief could maneuver the rocky descent better on his own than under Robert's control.

Halfway down, and to the right, Robert spied an object bathed in red underneath the scrubby brush at the base of the mesa. He pulled Chief to a stop and took his bearings. In the gathering twilight, Robert could still see the fort's flag flying up ahead and knew Fort Cobb lay just beyond the ridge before him. Tempted to keep riding, he was instead compelled to investigate that peculiar patch of red.

Turning Chief toward that direction, he trotted the several yards to the short, thick brush. When he was close enough to make out the form of two buckskin-wrapped legs, soaked in blood, he dismounted in one motion and ran to the figure ahead.

A tattered moccasin remained on one foot; the other shoe was a few yards away, half buried in the prairie grass. He dragged her from underneath the bushes. Though Robert suspected this was Cordelia's Indian woman, he just couldn't be sure.

Her face was a bloody mess, and her half-open eyes were glazed and unseeing. The right side of her cheek was gone, leaving a gaping hole from which her dirt-encrusted tongue lolled. Her hands were blue-white with cold, and her wrists, bruised and swollen, still bore the ropes, though they were no longer tied in front of her. The bend of her right forearm wasn't quite right and displayed a deep blue and red bruise. The fringe of her buckskin dress was partially blood-soaked.

Robert lowered her body onto the cushion of thick prairie grass.

Suddenly he heard a low gurgling sound emanating from her throat and he realized she must still be alive. He felt her chest and was able to detect the tiniest flittering motion. She was breathing! Blood bubbled through the yawning wound of her cheek.

Quickly, he gathered her in his arms and placed her across the saddle of his horse. He climbed behind her, holding her securely with one arm, and nudged Chief's powerfully built sides and they were off at a gallop toward the fort. He didn't know how much longer she would be alive but he knew he had to get her to Doc as soon as possible.

Covering the distance in less than a half-hour, he rode around the fort instead of into it. He wanted to get to the hospital with minimal attention. Pulling Chief to a stop behind the hospital, he left the Indian's all but lifeless form in the saddle, lying limply over Chief's muscular neck.

Robert ran into the hospital, hoping against hope that Doc Anthony was there. He was. He'd been making final rounds before retiring for the evening. When he came back to her, Dr. and Mrs. Anthony in tow, they found thick ropes of blood curling out from the open flap of her mouth.

"Let's get her inside quickly," Doc ordered.

Robert carried her into the side room of the hospital, the one Doc used as an office and an examination room. It was the only private room in the building. The hospital was made up of two open wards with ten beds per ward. There were still several soldiers in one of the rooms. It wouldn't do to have them spot an Indian woman in the same building. Mrs. Anthony closed the door behind them as Robert lay the woman down on the table.

"She lost a lot of blood," Doc said, gruffly. "I don't know if

I can help her, Captain. But I'll try. That's all I can say. Now get out of here before people start getting suspicious. Ela, get me some water, bandages, sutures and a lamp. We've got a lot of work to do."

As Ela quickly began to gather the supplies, Robert backed out of the door into the corridor leading to the wards. Noticing the blood on his uniform, he decided to go out the back way, making his way home around the rear of the buildings.

In Chief's small stable, Robert quickly unsaddled him, took off the bridle, and distractedly polished the gold "US" on the bit with his uniform sleeve. He rubbed Chief down with a damp rag, then tossed an armful of hay into his manger. With an appreciative slap to his horse's rump, Robert latched the stall behind him. From the other stall, Sunburst, the palomino gelding he'd bought for Cordelia, snorted loudly and stamped his foot. Furtively, Robert made his way to the back door of the house.

With the first glimpse of her boss, Bess's hands flew to her face as she shrieked. She had just cleaned off the dining table and was heading back to the kitchen with Lucy in tow, carrying the supper dishes. Robert stood in the hallway just inside the door, still covered in blood. They were near hysterics, naturally assuming it was *his* blood.

"Oh, Cap'n Lawson!" Bess wailed.

"Shh!" Robert held his finger over his lips trying to keep them quiet.

Cordelia, hearing Bess's shriek, quickly scrambled to the hallway to investigate, nearly slamming into Robert, who had made his way almost to the parlor door by then. She braced herself against his chest, then stepped back, staring at her bloody hands.

"Robert!" she cried. "What happened? Where are you hurt? Oh, my darling, my poor darling, let me see."

As she frantically began searching him for wounds, all fear vanished from her face, replaced instead with an expression of intense determination.

"Cordelia, Cordelia! Stop! Wait! Please, Cordelia!" he begged, trying to capture her attention. "Listen to me!" he barked at her, taking her by the shoulders.

Her puzzled eyes looked into his as he continued, "I'm not hurt. I'm fine. This is not my blood. Now calm yourself, darling."

"Robert, are you sure you're not hurt?" She needed reassurance. There was so much blood. Even some of his gold buttons were covered with blood.

"I'm fine. Now, if you really want to lend a hand, you can help me get cleaned up. I'll tell you everything. I promise. But first I want to get out of these clothes. Will you help me?"

"Of course I will." Turning to Bess, she instructed her to heat some water for a bath.

In their bedroom, she watched him strip the bloody neckerchief from his collar, and then she began working on the buttons of his shirt. She pulled his shirttail out of his breeches, then worked the buckle of his pants.

"I don't think I've ever seen you do that so quickly before," he teased.

"Oh, Robert. Really. Now hurry up and get out of those pants."

"Yes, ma'am."

He pulled the pants off. Even his underclothes were splotched with red. Cordelia pulled back the screen that enclosed the tub. Lovingly, she wrapped a quilt around his shivering body as he awaited the hot water. She hurriedly placed two more sticks of wood in the fireplace. Immediately the flames leapt higher.

Hearing Bess's lumbering steps, she opened the door and took the heavy pail of hot water from her.

"We'll need another. Here, let me pour this one in and you can take the bucket back with you."

Robert, seeing how Cordelia struggled with the load, stepped over to her and took the heavy bucket from her, careful to keep himself covered with the quilt. After pouring the steaming water into the tub, he handed the bucket to Cordelia, who in turn passed it out the door to Bess.

"Thank you," Cordelia whispered, then rushed back to Robert, who gingerly stepped into the water. Sitting slowly and leaning back in the tub, he breathed a heavy sigh and closed his eyes. "Oh, this feels so good."

She swept a cloth from one of her dresser drawers, grabbed some soap and bent beside the tub to help him scrub the blood from his neck, chest, arms and belly.

"Okay," she said matter-of-factly as she bathed him gently. "Tell me about it. What happened?"

"Cordelia," he weakly protested, "I can do this myself."

"You just relax and let me do it. I want to hear everything. Please tell me."

He began his story with the collection of the robes from the soldier camp where Custer's troops were bivouacked. Seemingly endless rows of tents formed rugged streets across the plains. The wagons were parked on the diagonal around the tents as a precaution against attack. As massive as the encampment seemed, he explained that only half of the 700 or so men under Custer's command were actually still in camp. The others were with the general and Sheridan on the march to the Washita. Robert described the four wagons loaded with plunder from the village, and assured her that the captives had been supplied with their thick, warm winter robes by now.

He watched her face carefully as he told her the part of the story relating to the discovery of the Indian woman. When he began to describe what he'd seen, Cordelia stopped bathing him and sat back on her heels, listening attentively to the story, sadness and heartache in her eyes.

She had a hundred questions, but she kept her mouth shut and let him talk. She knew he needed to get the whole story talked out and was thankful he trusted in her enough to tell her everything.

A light knock on the door broke the progression of the story. Cordelia took the bucket, closed the door and dragged the water to the tub. With Robert's help, she poured the heated water over his broad chest and resumed bathing him slowly and gently.

He explained how he'd left the woman at the hospital with Doc and Ela and how Doc told him she'd lost a lot of blood and he didn't know if she'd make it. Lastly, he told her how he'd decided to ride behind the buildings of the fort to their house.

"I need to go to her, then. I need to see if I can help."

"Darling, I think she's in the best hands tonight. Why don't you wait until morning? I'll walk you over there myself."

"I'll think about it." Standing, she handed a rough towel to Robert. "Here! I'm going to get you some dinner. Go ahead and put your bedclothes on. You look exhausted. I'll be right back."

After giving a short summary of the story to Bess and Lucy, Cordelia asked them to prepare a thin soup in the morning. She wanted to take it to the Indian woman. She carried Robert's tray to the bedroom. His plate was piled high with beans, fried potatoes and cornbread.

Robert was lying on the bed, almost asleep already.

"No, you don't. Here. Eat this. It'll make you feel better."

"I couldn't possibly eat all this. Aren't you going to join me?"

"I've already eaten," she assured him, though she had hardly touched her food. Dining without Robert, she'd felt queasy and her mind was so active that she had trouble calming herself.

Just as she did now. She didn't know if she could wait until tomorrow morning to see the Indian woman or not. It was likely to be a long, long night. But, still shaken by this frightening incident, she decided to stay here, close to Robert.

After he'd finished his dinner, she removed his tray and helped him into bed. Changing quickly into her nightgown, she blew out the candles, slid under the thick covers to lie close beside him, her head resting on his muscular shoulder. Over and over, she quietly thanked God for bringing him home unharmed. Placing her soft hand over his chest, she eventually fell asleep to the rhythm of his breathing.

~*~

Early the next morning, Cordelia woke up slowly, yawned and, once more, snuggled close to her husband. The fire in the fireplace was almost out. She thought about getting up to put more wood on the fire, but she was just too warm and cozy to risk the cold outside the goose-down comforter that enveloped them. Besides, Robert was so warm and smelled so clean and masculine. She kissed his ear and he stirred slightly.

Then she remembered her Indian princess and wondered if she had survived the night. This was Sunday morning. Things would move more slowly on the fort today. She knew Robert would be up soon, studying his Bible in order to lead the

Sunday morning service held in the hospital. He was no preacher but of the men on the fort, he was the most familiar with the Scriptures. The circuit preacher didn't get around to these parts very often. So Robert evolved into leadership of the little Sunday morning group.

Cordelia usually loved Sunday mornings. She eagerly soaked up the word of God and oh, how she loved to sing those sacred hymns. The words were so rich, the melodies as familiar and welcome as close relations at a family reunion. She and Robert harmonized together beautifully and many were the times she'd had to ask God for forgiveness for the sin of pride when "showing off" during the singing.

But today she was anxious to check on the lovely patient before the services began. She would make it there as soon as she could. At least, that was her intention.

Her mind was so active and alive now that she could no longer hibernate in her cozy, little den. She had to get up and get going.

Careful not to wake Robert, she crawled over the side of the bed, and dressed quickly, but not in her Sunday dress. Instead, she wore one designed for function. It was lightweight without the flouncy skirt her Sunday dress had. She pulled on her warm woolen stockings, and wrapped herself in a heavy wool cloak. Pulling her hair up, she tied it securely with a ribbon and let the rest cascade down her back in long, red ringlets. Placing her everyday bonnet over her head, she started for the front door as quietly as she could go.

Bess, who was setting the table for breakfast, confronted her.

"Where you goin' so early, Miz Lawson?" she wanted to know.

"Shh!" Cordelia placed her finger over her lips to signal for quiet. She looked back toward the bedroom and listened for the sound of movement. Hearing none, she turned back to Bess who flashed an accusing glare at her.

Cordelia whispered, "I'm just going out to the hospital to check on the Indian girl. I simply must find out how she's doing. I told you last night what bad shape she was in! When Robert gets up, please tell him where I've gone. I won't be here for breakfast but tell him I'll meet him at the service."

"What about that soup you wuz goin' to take over there?"

"I'll get it later. I must find out how she's doing first."

She started toward the door, and then turned back. "Oh, and Bess, please have Lucy take in another load of wood. I placed the last piece on the fire just now. Thanks."

Bess silently watched as she went out into the frosty breath of early morning.

~*~

She entered the hospital through the side door, then scurried into the small examination room where Robert had told her she'd find the woman. Though he'd described her injuries, Cordelia was unprepared for what she encountered in that room.

A small wooden chair had been placed beside the table. She knew that Ela most likely had watched over her from that chair. She took her seat and gazed upon the silent figure. The Indian's long, black hair hung loose, clumped together in dried, bloody tangles. Cordelia could tell that someone—Ela, she presumed—had tried to clean it up the best she could. She was lying with her face turned away from Cordelia and her hair partially covered the ashen skin.

Cordelia gently reached over and touched her to reassure herself that the Indian was, indeed, still alive. She heaved a gentle sigh of relief when she felt the warmth of her skin. Then she slowly pulled the hair back from her face.

When she did, the patient stirred, and turned toward Cordelia, who almost fell back into the chair when she saw the dreadful injury to the poor girl's face.

"Oh, dear God!" Cordelia whispered, huskily, stifling a little scream. Then, heart beating wildly and breaths coming in quick bursts, she finally calmed herself and leaned forward to examine the wound.

Doc had stitched her up the best he could, she knew. But there were stitches from the corner of her swollen lips in a curved line upward toward her ear. The slash must have been a good three inches long. Cordelia realized that even if the girl survived, her beauty was forever destroyed.

She surveyed the puffy cheek, already a deep shade of blue from bruising. There was a lump on her forehead, red in the center and blue around the edges. Dried blood had gathered in the corners of her swollen mouth. Her nose had been broken, she thought, because the line she'd been so careful to copy in the portrait was different now. She didn't think it was just because of the swelling. The bone structure had been altered.

There were bruises on her delicate neck. Bruises on both arms. Her right forearm was splinted and wrapped in a white, cotton dressing. She was covered with a sheet and a blanket but Cordelia removed her own heavy cloak and covered her with it as well.

Then she sat back, placed her face in her hands and wept. She didn't know what could have happened to this girl, but whatever it was, she knew it was horrible. She didn't want to think about what pain the poor thing had experienced. Every time she did, the tears flowed harder.

When she at last was able to raise her head again to look at the woman, she saw her eyelids flutter half-open. There was no light in those almond-shaped eyes anymore—just . . . death. Yet, she watched Cordelia and followed the jeweled wash of tears flowing slowly down her cheeks.

With a trembling hand, Cordelia gently stroked the Indian's head. She made soothing, shooshing noises, the kind she'd make if she were comforting a hurting child. The girl continued to watch her with that same far-away, empty stare, with no emotion Cordelia could read, except defeat—total and utter defeat. Yet, she was alive.

Just then, Doc slipped into the room.

"Mrs. Lawson! I didn't expect to see you. How long have you been here?" he whispered.

"Not long," Cordelia sniffed, wiping the tears from her cheeks with both hands. "I had to check on her. Look, she's awake."

Doc bent over his patient and examined the wound on her cheek, turning her face gently by her chin. "That's quite astounding! I didn't know what to expect from her this morning. She's lost an awful lot of blood. I don't know if she'll pull through or not, but I've done all I can do for her."

"Doc, what happened to her?"

"God alone knows, dear," he said with a shake of his head. "I don't think her face was cut, like with a knife. The tear was too ragged for that. It was more like it was blown away, maybe by a gunshot. Several of her upper teeth were blown away as well. Her arm is broken. There are deep bruises on both legs and I believe she may have suffered some broken ribs on the right side. I have her taped up pretty snugly. That's the only thing we can do for now. The rest is up to her . . . and to God, of course."

"Doc, was she . . . violated?" Cordelia asked timidly.

"I take it you mean in a sexual way. No, I don't believe so."

"Well, thank God for that." Grimly, she sat watching the Indian as she fell back into a deep sleep.

"Custer did this, you know."

Doc paused before replying to her, quietly. "Mrs. Lawson, we don't know what happened. You simply cannot leap to such conclusions."

"What 'leap?' He took her out of the compound with her hands tied and came back without her. What else could have happened except that he did this to her?"

"She may have tried to escape. Or she might have fallen. Or her own people might have captured her and done this."

"Oh, you don't believe that any more than I do." Cordelia turned her attention back to the Indian.

Looking thoughtfully at Cordelia, Doc leaned forward and whispered, "May I ask you a question, dear? And feel free to refuse this request, if you need to. I understand I'm asking quite a lot."

"What is it, Doc?"

"I can't very well keep her here. It's only a matter of time before she's discovered. But moving her into the guardhouse would be murder! She wouldn't survive the hour over there. I need someone to take her in, to watch over her until she's strong enough to go back to her people. Do you think . . ."

"Of course, she can come to our house. We can make room for her in the pantry, next to the kitchen. We'll set up a pallet for her and keep her warm and well fed. Why, I think Bess could have her up in no time!"

He chuckled, "Slow down, my dear. What do you think Robert will say? If people found out, it could jeopardize his commission. He has a bright future, Mrs. Lawson. I wouldn't blame him if he opposed this proposition."

"Of course he'll agree to it, Doc! She's a human being, after all. He's not likely to turn her out into the cold in the condition she's in. And you'll come attend her daily, won't you?"

"Yes, of course."

"Then it's settled. We just have to find a way to move her safely, yet discreetly."

"Can we do it now?"

"What do you mean?"

"Well, she doesn't weigh very much. She's tall but very thin, poor thing. I think we could transport her to your quarters by stretcher, just you and me. You could take the foot of the stretcher and I'll take the head. We'll go around the back of the buildings between here and there. The fort won't really come to life for another half-hour or so. What do you think?"

Cordelia stared at him, open-mouthed. "Well, I might need a little preparation time, Doc. I don't know."

"If you take time for preparation, we won't be able to move her until tonight after everyone retires for the evening. And by then, she'll surely be discovered in here. I think we must avail ourselves of this opportunity."

Cordelia nodded, "All right. We'll take her over there right now."

Doc left the room and came back with a stretcher. He rolled her gently onto her left side and slid the stretcher as far as he could underneath her, then rolled her to the right to steady her on it. She moaned softly as her weight shifted to her bruised and broken right side, but she continued to sleep.

"Let's go," Doc said, lifting the head of the stretcher. Cordelia took the handles at the foot of the stretcher and was surprised at how light it was. Doc backed out of the door, made a turn out the side door and they were off, taking it slow and easy around the back of the buildings. Since their hands were occupied, the whirling winds swept dust unimpeded into their eyes and mouths. The hens in the chicken coops cackled loudly at their presence, but they continued on determinedly.

"How are you doing, Cordelia?" Doc asked, spitting out sand.

"I'm all right, Doc. It's not that difficult. What about you? You're the one having to walk backwards," she answered, squinting into the wind.

"I'm fine."

They walked the rest of the way in silence. When they reached the back of the officer's quarters, they placed the stretcher on the ground while Cordelia entered through the kitchen. Doc heard her giving quick commands and then she reappeared.

"Let's go. By the time we get her in there, Bess will have her pallet made."

They climbed up the step into the kitchen where Bess took the foot of the stretcher from Cordelia. "Miz Lawson, you don't need to be doin' that. I'm stronger than you. I'll take it from here. Lucy is making up a bed for her."

"And the captain?"

"Up and gone. Just took a biscuit with him and went on to the Sunday meetin'."

"It's not that late, is it?"

"No, ma'am. He was worried about you and said he might stop by the hospital on the way."

"Oh." Cordelia led the way to the tiny room next to the kitchen. Lucy was putting the finishing touches on a soft pallet on the floor. They transferred the patient to the pallet and covered her with blankets. Lucy stoked the fire in the kitchen fireplace.

"Good thing I brought all this wood up this morning. It was right here where I needed it."

"That's good, Lucy. Thank you so much."

Doc took Cordelia's hand and pressed his lips to it. "You're an angel, Mrs. Lawson. And in case you haven't realized it yet, you might very well be saving this girl's life."

"What do I do now? How do I take care of her?"

"Just keep her warm. Try to get her to take some water or broth. Her mouth is going to hurt badly, so she won't be able to chew anything. So make sure whatever you give her is just a soupy consistency for now."

Reaching into his pocket, he pulled out a vial of medicine. "She's going to be in significant pain, Mrs. Lawson. But she may not let on. Indians have strong constitutions. So watch for other signs like restlessness, a change in her breathing, facial grimacing, lips pressed together tightly or eyes squeezing shut. Just give her a few drops of this every few hours, as she needs it. I can't spare much of it, so use it judiciously."

Nodding, she replied, "I will."

Retreating from the makeshift hospital room, he called back to her, "I'll come by late this afternoon to check on her. You'll be fine until then, won't you?" Not waiting for an answer, he was out the door in no time. Cordelia knew she should go on to the Sunday morning meeting, and that the girl would be fine left in Bess's care. Why, she was already on her knees, wiping the Indian's brow with a cool cloth soaked in clean water. But Cordelia didn't want to leave her just yet. She felt the need to be there if the young woman opened her eyes again.

She asked Lucy to bring in the rocking chair from the kitchen, which she did right away. Taking her seat in the chair, Cordelia thought about Robert and the church meeting, feeling guilty for not being there.

Then she looked at the tortured but sleeping face of the Indian woman and knew her place was here with her for now. Putting herself in the Indian's place, she couldn't imagine the terror of waking from such an ordeal only to find yourself in a place you don't recognize, with people you don't know.

She sat slowly rocking back and forth, thinking about the events God had brought into her life here at the fort. As she meditated upon God's sovereignty, she recalled favorite passages from His word. Her tension slowly drained away as she remembered His faithfulness to His children. There is no safer place in the whole universe than in the palm of God's loving hand.

Looking heavenward out the tiny window of the pantry, Cordelia marveled at the deep blue-green color of the sky. She prayed, "Dear Lord, please be with us as we try to nurse this poor girl back to health. I feel so inadequate, Father. Give her a portion of Your strength and if it be Your will, bring her to wholeness once again. Equip me for this task, and help me reflect Your loving kindness. Amen."

Turning her attention back to the Indian maiden, she studied her intently, confident that her prayer would be answered. Slowly she rocked back and forth in cadence with her own gentle breathing, until her eyelids closed and sleep overtook her, too.

Nine

"You did *what?*" Robert snapped. "I can't believe it!"

"Shh. Robert, do you want the whole building to hear you? Please lower your voice!"

Looking down at Cordelia with pain-filled eyes, he shook his head and more calmly asked, "Have you no respect at all for my position here, Cordelia?"

"Of course I do, Robert. But . . ."

"But nothing." He took several long strides to his chair and plopped down heavily like a fat, old man who'd been on his feet too long. "I fear you've gone too far this time, Cordelia. The very idea! An Indian sleeping practically in the next room! And when she regains her strength, will our throats be cut? Our house burned down?"

Stiffening noticeably at his words, she replied icily, "No, dear. That's what *we* do to *them*, remember?" She spoke with a dead-quiet voice, more shocking than a scream.

Faltering, he eventually continued, "Cordelia, why didn't you talk to me about this first? Why?"

He watched her soulfully, waiting for her answer.

Earnestly, she replied, "Really, Robert, there was just no time! And I didn't think there was any way you would have refused her protection in the state she's in. I mean, after all, you're the one who found her and saved her life by bringing her to the fort. You risked your own position when you did that. So I didn't think . . ."

"That's just the problem. You didn't think!" he spat at her.

"Robert!" He had never spoken to her this way. His words punched her in the gut with surprising pain. She turned toward the window, directing her attention to the flag with its thirty-seven stars and its red and white stripes, whipping out around at the top of the 100-foot pole. On another occasion, she'd want to share its beauty in flight with Robert. But right now she needed to come up with a better explanation for what she'd done. She was puzzling over what to say when Bess came to the parlor door.

"'Scuse me. But Sunday dinner's ready."

"Bess, I'm not very hungry just now," Robert said, still looking at his wife.

"Nor am I," Cordelia agreed, crossing her arms in front of her. But the fallen look on Bess's face touched her bruised heart and she quickly continued, "but everything smells so good, I think I'll give it a try. Thank you." Then, to Robert, she pleaded, "Please, darling, Bess and Lucy have worked hard to prepare Sunday dinner. Won't you try to eat?"

Standing, he groaned, "Oh, I suppose so."

Once they were seated and their plates served, Cordelia folded her hands and waited for his prayer as usual. After a few moments of silence with her head bowed, she looked over at him to find him staring at her.

"Robert?"

Finally, he muttered, "Let's just eat today. We can pray silently this once."

Cordelia gasped in shock. Then, bowing her head, she blessed the food herself and excused Bess and Lucy. She knew where they were headed. It was Lucy's turn to sit with the Indian. Cordelia didn't want her to wake up alone in a strange place. But there was nothing to worry about. She had, so far, continued to sleep.

Meat wasn't always available on the fort unless they killed a chicken or Robert shot some game, so they were having a meal of steaming hot turnip greens with tender turnips on the side, a small portion of boiled potatoes, slices of onion and a steaming pan of buttered cornbread. Since Robert and Cordelia were both raised above the Mason-Dixon line, they were less accustomed to such foods than Bess. To her, this was a real treat.

In silence, they ate what was on their plates. Cordelia was actually surprised at how delicious it was. The slightly astringent flavor of the greens with the buttery goodness of the cornbread was a wonderful blend of tastes. They were offered seconds but neither accepted. In unison, they hurriedly said, "No, thank you, Bess."

Immediately, each looked at the other, then laughed aloud. With the tension broken, Robert stood, walked to Cordelia's end of the table and offered his hand. As she accepted it, he helped her up and led her to their bedroom, where they could be alone. Tenderly, he took her in his arms and held her.

Neither of them spoke. But in their embrace, love seemed to flow from one to another through arms strong with emotion. When he released her, Cordelia breathed softly, "I want you to be proud of me, Robert. I want you to be happy you married me. I never want to be a disappointment to you. Never."

"I am proud of you, darling. And I know it is a result of that tender heart of yours that our . . . 'guest' is here. I know how strong you are. You'd be willing to stand down the whole world to defend her, wouldn't you? Sometimes I wonder if I'm that strong."

Sitting next to her on the bed, he continued, "I'm ashamed of my own attitude, Cordelia. Do I care more for my own career than I do for the life of another human being?" He looked beseechingly into Cordelia's eyes.

"Do you know what the sermon was this morning? It was on the Good Samaritan. I was teaching it because I had been thinking of *myself* as the Good Samaritan. After all, I found her and brought her back, didn't I? But in the Bible, the Samaritan took care of the wounded man without any concern for the cost to himself."

He took her hand. "That's what *you* did, darling. Not me. Like the Good Samaritan, you found her lying bruised and beaten on the road, and without a thought for yourself, you took her in and cared for her, though she is of another race than yourself. That's sacrifice. That's true Christian charity. And I love you for having the heart and the courage to do what you did. I just have to think of some way I can allow this, and still keep my reputation as an officer."

He thought for a moment then concluded, "Reputation is important. But her life is more important. So if I lose it, I lose it. So be it."

Standing, she took his face in her slender hands and beamed through tears of happiness and pride, "Oh, Robert! Thank you!" With that, she planted a light kiss on his cheek and twirled away from him.

Seeing her swaying before him in a dress the misty color of prairie sage, the creamy lace collar next to her soft skin, the green eyes and red hair, something caught in his heart again. Once more, he swore to himself that she was the most beautiful woman he'd ever seen.

"Will you forgive me, Cordelia? Will you forgive my

hateful attitudes toward you *and* toward her?"

Love flooded her heart as quickly as the sudden tears filled her eyes. As he'd done before, Robert stood amazed that those eyes could hold so much, held like great pools of liquid diamonds before escaping the confines of her lower lids to run in sparkling tracks down her cheeks.

"Yes, Robert. I freely forgive, just as I've been freely forgiven time after time."

He leaned over and kissed her welcoming lips.

"Shall we go out to check on our patient, darling?" he asked.

"Well, no," she sniffed, dabbing at her wet cheeks with a handkerchief. "It wouldn't be proper for you to go in there just yet, I'm afraid. She's not clothed right now—just covered. We haven't wanted to move her enough to dress her. Not just yet."

"Very well, then." As an afterthought, he said, "Oh, Cordelia, we may have yet another problem on our hands."

"And what is that?" She eyed him suspiciously.

"Mrs. Hazen."

"Oh! What about her?"

"She is obviously offended that you refused to paint her portrait."

"Oh, she told you about that! You know, I thought that might be trouble." Cordelia busied herself with the pleats of her skirt. "Robert, I just can't do it. It would be like a prison sentence to sit for hours looking at her. How could I possibly find the inspiration to paint her?"

Robert still said nothing.

"Well, surely you don't think I should do it!"

Nothing.

"That's not what you're suggesting, is it? Well, is it, Robert?"

Finally he responded, laughingly. "Actually, I don't see

what the problem is! I know you don't want to do it. I know you don't like her. But I have two things to say to that. First, there are thousands of fine portraits in the world. They had to have been painted by someone! And you can't tell me that every painter found deep inspiration in the faces of his subjects. But they did an admirable job, nonetheless. Couldn't you do the same?

"And secondly, I seem to remember a verse that you've always professed to be special to you. 'Inasmuch as ye have done it unto one of the least of these my brethren, ye have done it unto me.' You may not like Mrs. Hazen. But I know how devoted you are to Christ. So doing this kindness for her would be like . . ."

" . . . doing it for Him," she finished for him, glumly. "You're right, darling. I'll do it."

"Fine! I'll tell her tomorrow at headquarters. Just think of this as a . . . mission of mercy."

Cordelia quietly studied her boot tips.

"It would mean so much to her," Robert offered. Taking her hand, he continued, "Our world is very small now, Cordelia. And it seems a small enough price to pay for peace, does it not?"

"I suppose it would seem that way to you." Cordelia's voice had taken on a defeated tone. "But I'll do it." She tried to offer a smile but the corners of her mouth seemed suddenly stiff and immobile.

Robert didn't notice, for he had already picked up his pipe and book and was moving to his chair for a little relaxation. She searched her drawer for a nightgown. Finding one, she whipped it out of the dresser drawer and held it up to herself. It was a little worn, but still very pretty. Made of white muslin, it had a bodice of lace, trimmed in a ribbon of robin's egg blue.

Then she stole out to the kitchen to peek in on the patient.

Lucy was sitting in the big rocking chair, looking out the window and humming quietly to herself. A pegboard covered the pantry wall behind her, filled with hanging aprons, ladles, and pots and pans, polished and gleaming. A washboard leaned against the back wall.

"Oh, hello, Miz Lawson. She hasn't moved a muscle yet. And listening to her breathing is almost putting *me* to sleep!"

"I know. That very thing happened to me earlier. I'll take over for a while. But first, let's try to get her decently covered, shall we? When she wakens, she'll be horrified to find herself naked under these quilts. I think this nightgown will fit her. She's taller than I, so it will be a little short, of course, but that shouldn't matter, should it?"

Before disturbing her, Cordelia placed three drops of the pain medicine into the Indian's bruised mouth, hoping it would offset the pain she was sure to feel by being moved. She winced slightly but her eyes stayed closed.

"I think she's all right, Lucy. Help me get this poor arm through here."

She and Lucy managed to get the arm through the sleeve and the gown over her head. As they were inching it down her bruised body, Cordelia asked, "Do you know how they got the name 'Indian?'"

Finishing up, Lucy sat back and placing her finger beside her chin, she replied, "Let's see. When Columbus discovered America, he thought he'd found India. So he called them 'Indians.'"

"Very good! That's one theory. But before coming out here, I read up on the subject and one book explained it this way: Columbus discovered America, all right. And the natives he found here were gentle people, very accepting of him. In his journal, he wrote, 'These are people of God.' And in his language, he wrote "In Dios." Later the *s* was dropped and

111

'Indio' eventually became 'Indian,' which originated as 'people of God.' They became known as Indians because of that."

Lucy stared at her thoughtfully. "That's a nicer explanation."

Cordelia smiled. "Yes, I suppose it is!"

Covering the Indian with a quilt, they searched her face again for any sign of waking. They repositioned her on the pallet, adjusting the pillow under her head until she looked comfortable again. The Indian moaned softly but made no other response.

Hearing voices in the hallway, Cordelia opened the door just wide enough to distinguish them. It was Dr. Anthony. Though she could still hear Doc talking to Robert in the hall, Ela's sweet face appeared in the doorway. Her basket was bulging with supplies for the Indian girl; dressings, ointments, and more medicine.

"How is she?"

"Still sleeping. She opened her eyes early this morning while she was still at the hospital, but not since."

Ela's hand fluttered to her throat. "Poor thing."

"I know. It breaks my heart to look at her," Cordelia admitted. Ela nodded as she bent down to examine the wound on the patient's cheek. "This was a brave thing for you to do, my young friend."

"I don't know about bravery. I just know it was the right thing to do."

Ela pulled the covers back to check her arm, making sure the splint wasn't on so tight it might restrict her circulation. But it was fine.

"Bless her heart. She looks so ashen and still, doesn't she?" Stroking her hair, she added, "You did a much better job on her hair than I did, I must say."

"Don't give me any credit for that, Mrs. Anthony. Lucy

and Bess did it. They washed it and brushed it out. It's so thick and straight and gleaming. I wouldn't know anything about that from my own experience with this mop of hair." Cordelia had always battled her natural curls.

"Your hair is lovely, dear. Surely you must know that."

"Thank you," Cordelia murmured, suddenly embarrassed. "I promise I wasn't courting flattery just then."

"I know you, dear. I didn't think you were," Ela smiled.

Dr. Anthony lumbered into the tiny pantry from the kitchen. "How is she?"

Ela answered him, "She's still not responsive, dear. But she appears to be resting comfortably."

"Well, that may be the best we can hope for at this point." He bent to examine her. "The wound looks fine. I don't see any sign of infection yet, which is a miracle in itself. Let me know immediately if you start to see any redness or drainage, Mrs. Lawson. And if she starts running a fever, come for me right away."

Holding his back as he stood, he stretched one side and then the other. "Why don't you allow me to send a cot over for her? It's awfully hard getting up and down every time you check on her. At least it is for an old man like me." He chuckled.

"Won't people wonder about that, Doc? Why we would need a cot?"

"Good point, my dear."

Suddenly Robert spoke up from the kitchen door. "I have an idea. I'll go to work on it right away."

"Why, thank you, darling!" Cordelia said, appreciatively. It pleased her that he wanted to help.

Turning to leave, Doc ushered Ela out the door before him, then said, "I think it's wonderful the way Robert supports this effort, isn't it? He's quite a man, that husband of yours."

113

Cordelia smiled, "Yes, he is," she agreed, not caring to disclose Robert's previous apprehensions about the arrangement.

"I'll call on you tomorrow."

"Thanks, Doc." Cordelia sank gratefully into the rocker and studied her patient, scrutinizing her breathing, and watching for any sign that she might be waking. She wondered for the hundredth time what to call her. Certainly she couldn't keep calling her "Princess."

She closed her eyes for just a moment.

~*~

When she opened them again, it was almost dark in the room. She heard sounds of activity from the kitchen and then Robert's baritone voice and soft laughter as he conversed with Bess and Lucy.

"Hello, darling," he called out to her. "I think I've figured out a satisfactory sleeping arrangement for our guest. We use it sometimes when we camp out on the prairie—when the ground is too wet to lie on, or the bugs too numerous. But I think it should suffice for now."

As he talked, he brought in and positioned two carpenter's horses with the legs sawn off by half. Then he grabbed four boards and placed them side-by-side across the saw-horses, making Cordelia's Indian a bed.

While the maiden continued to sleep, he lifted her from her pallet and held her while the women moved the soft pallet atop the boards of her new bed. Carefully, he lowered her onto the bed and stepped back, appraising his work.

Cordelia and Bess straightened the covers and made sure the Indian was comfortably tucked in.

"Well?" Robert smiled, expectantly.

"Yes, Robert. You did a marvelous job. I would never have thought of it! It's a lovely bed for her. Thank you." Standing on tiptoe, she brushed his lips lightly with her own.

Lucy lit a lantern and placed another log on the fire as Robert departed for his quarters again. She and Bess busied themselves in the kitchen as Cordelia turned back to her patient.

Before lowering herself into the rocker, she thought she detected a slight movement from the bed. Giving the woman a closer inspection, she saw the girl's coal black eyes open slowly. She blinked a few times then cast her somber gaze upon Cordelia. The young woman stared at her steadily, making no sound, showing no emotion, no light—just watching her.

Slowly moving to her side, Cordelia softly stroked her shoulder and cradled her good cheek in the palm of her hand.

"Shh. It's all right, Princess. You're safe here. We'll take care of you," she crooned. Offering her a little smile, she tried to let her know by touch and expression that she was her friend. She hoped she would remember working side by side with her in the guardhouse. Was that just two days ago? It seemed like weeks!

Gliding to the door, still keeping her eyes fixed on her patient, Cordelia called to Lucy. Bess responded, instead. "Yes, ma'am?"

"Please bring a cup of water and a little bowl of soup, will you?"

"Yes, ma'am. I'll be right there."

In no time, Bess was at her side. Together, they helped the Indian girl to a sitting position and propped pillows and folded quilts beneath her head and shoulders. The Indian squeezed her eyes tightly shut for an instant, and perspiration broke out on her head and upper lip, but there was no other response to the movement. As she was lowered carefully upon the pillows,

115

she relaxed into this new position. Warily, she studied every move Bess made. Cordelia wondered if this was the first time she'd seen a Negro woman.

Carefully, Cordelia spooned a little of the thin broth between her parched and swollen lips. A tiny trickle ran down the side of her mouth. Bess gently dabbed her jaw to catch it. But at least some of the hot liquid made it into the Indian's mouth. She held it there for what seemed an eternity, then finally swallowed.

Cordelia and Bess exchanged excited and victorious smiles. Cordelia fed her another tiny spoonful and another. After about five or six spoonfuls, she tried to give her a sip of water. The Indian greedily slurped the water, spilling some of it in her effort to grip the cup with her left hand.

"Take it easy. Easy now," Cordelia pleaded softly, withholding the cup just a little. She seemed to understand and took another couple of sips before collapsing back against the pillows in a heap, breathing heavily, eyes closed.

Cordelia laid the cup aside and sponged the girl's forehead and face gingerly. Almost immediately she was fast asleep again. Cordelia removed the bulky quilts from under her head so she could lie back and rest. The Indian's breathing eased as it resumed its former quiet, steady rhythm.

Cordelia and Bess hugged each other. Funny how such a little thing could bring them both such a feeling of accomplishment!

Without a word, Bess gathered up the bowl and left the cup of water. Flashing another smile in Cordelia's direction, she went back into the kitchen.

This kind of elation was a rare experience for Cordelia. Falling back into her chair and looking out the window into the moonlit sky, she thanked God for this hopeful sign.

Ten

The next afternoon, Bess warmed a bowl of thin soup for their patient. Cordelia carefully carried it into the large pantry on a tray with a spoon, napkin and a cup of cool water.

When she walked into the pantry, she was amazed to see the bed empty, the covers rumpled. Quickly scanning the room, she located the Indian girl standing in the corner, leaning against the shelves for strength. Her fierce eyes cautiously watched Cordelia with a mixture of fear, anger . . . and confusion. Crouched as she was, cradling her broken right arm with her healthy left one, she reminded Cordelia of a wild, wounded animal backed into a corner, baring its teeth.

Slowly, Cordelia stacked the extra quilts under the pillow on the bed, sat on the rocking chair and placed the tray in her lap. Reaching out to the pile of blankets, she patted them and motioned for the woman to come back to bed. She picked up the bowl of soup and stirred it, letting the steaming broth trickle from the spoon back into the bowl, allowing the aroma to permeate the room.

The Indian resisted for a moment. Then, too weak to fight

or flee, she staggered back to the bed and with surprising grace and agility, floated back onto the covers, leaning against the pillows breathlessly.

Cordelia tried to give her a little of the soup, but the young woman turned her head away. Tentatively reaching out, the Indian took the bowl and turned it up to her poor, battered mouth, taking a sip or two before lowering it again.

Cordelia placed the spoon in the Indian's left hand and made the motion of lifting a spoonful of soup to her mouth. The Indian imitated the motion, spilling some in the process, but the majority of the liquid made it to her mouth this time.

Smiling, Cordelia wanted to reward her effort. She reached out to touch her shoulder, but the Indian recoiled from her touch.

"All right, then," she said softly, "I guess we won't be doing a lot of touching, will we?" She nodded and smiled in an attempt to show approval and understanding.

The girl, never taking her eyes from Cordelia, dropped the spoon to the floor with a clang and turned the bowl up again to drink in the warm nourishment. She must have been famished, because she didn't stop until the bowl was empty.

Then, tentatively touching her bruised mouth, she reached for the cup of water, and drank it dry. Cordelia took it from her slowly, still nodding her approval.

The young woman, obviously at the end of her strength, lowered herself onto the softness of her bed. Cordelia covered her with the quilts, allowing her hand to linger over the woman's good arm.

"Sleep now, my friend. There will be plenty of time to get to know each other."

As if she understood, the Indian closed her lovely eyes and snuggled into the comfort of the covers. Cordelia watched her for a long time, reliving this encounter in her mind, and feeling a subtle afterglow of joy.

~*~

The companies from Fort Cobb arrived at the Washita battle site a day later. While Custer and Sheridan explored and searched the area where Major Elliot was last seen, Lieutenant Otis's company was assigned to reconnoiter the site itself.

Todd and his men combed the campground beside the Washita River. Black Kettle had reported 180 lodges in this village. Scouring the site, Todd tried to picture what that must have looked like, here in the rolling countryside of the Antelope Hills. The lodges must have been set up alongside this narrow part of the river, no more than 40 or 50 feet wide, lined with low, sandy banks.

The camp was situated in a depression, with low, steep cliffs on all sides making a winter den of sorts for the people, providing a natural windbreak in the rolling and barren landscape. It was an excellent choice for a campsite. All the primary considerations were present—water, wood, good ground, and protection from the elements.

But, however suitable it was as a campground, it was a horror from a military standpoint. Located in this depression, the Indians were boxed in, making easy opportunities for target practice, which Custer's sharpshooters must have relished. Surveillance would have been simple from this location.

Todd ordered his men to dismount and collect any Indian paraphernalia they could locate, so they walked about, scouring the ground. Though the bodies of several Cheyenne braves lay sprawled across the melting snow, there were relatively few. Todd suspected that most, especially the scalped bodies of

Black Kettle and his wife, had already been gathered by the Arapaho or Kiowa camped downstream.

It was a cold, blustery day where clouds intermittently blocked the sun, leaving a gray pall over the search. He had heard someone say the signs pointed to another winter blast and now he could feel it in the air. They had to work quickly and efficiently.

A pitiful number of scattered items were collected; a few silver armbands, a small pouch of colored beads, two small pouches filled with ropes of dried tobacco, and the singed remains of a beaded doll. Though Custer had assigned them a wagon to collect the Indian articles, a large box would have sufficed for the paltry remnants they gathered. Custer's men had been very efficient, indeed.

Charred remains of buffalo hide lodges and clothing lay strewn across the ground next to the evidences of the small campfires they'd used to warm themselves. The bubbling river next to the camp made the only noise in this clearing within the thicket of short scrubby red cedar trees. Even the birds were silent. The men were unusually quiet, as well.

Suddenly the wind shifted and they were enveloped in the most disgusting stench Todd had ever experienced. The smell was almost tangible! You could taste it in the air! Several of the men coughed and sputtered; some nearly vomited. Others gagged and held their kerchiefs over their noses, shaking their heads and squinting their eyes to the stench.

"What the hell *is* that?" one of them asked, gruffly.

"Something dead," was Lieutenant Otis's reply. He and three others began walking into the wind in the direction of the reeking odor. The others made for the wagon.

The stink of death was sickening. To keep from gagging, Todd held his scarf tightly across his nose and tried to breathe through his mouth. His fellow soldiers were doing no better but they managed to control their urges—at least until they discovered the source of the smell.

As the men topped a small knoll, frightened buzzards left their prey in a wild flurry, flapping their wings and squawking loudly as they scattered to the nearest trees to furtively survey the intrusive activity below. Todd and his men froze when they saw what lay just beyond the ridge.

The Indian ponies had been slaughtered—almost a thousand of them! Their rotting carcasses lay heaped onto the bloodstained ground, one on top of another. This was a field of death. Insects, even in winter, crawled over their lifeless forms and evidence of other scavengers was present as well. Many of the ponies had been shot. Some showed indications of having their throats hacked by the soldiers' dull sabers.

One of Todd's men turned away, heaving into a cluster of big blue-stem brush beneath the closest tree. The two others turned back toward the camp without permission.

Todd didn't mind. At the moment, he was too stunned to care about protocol. "Even their horses," he kept repeating to himself, quietly. "Even their horses! God! What kind of hatred is this?"

His face was white and drawn when he walked back into the camp. His laughing blue eyes were somber now as they studied the men assembled next to the wagon. Looking into their eyes, he saw in them the recognition that something horrible had happened in this place. The men were packed and ready to leave.

Todd ordered them to mount. They eagerly did so. Two climbed aboard the wagon seat, and then looked toward him, awaiting his command. He mounted his horse, who was noticeably unsettled by the smell of rotting flesh. Todd reassured him gently and patted the glistening neck of his sorrel gelding. Then holding his gloved right hand in the air, he gave the signal to ride.

They would join the other companies in the search and burial of their fallen comrades. Flicking the reins across the backs of their mules, the driver of the wagon led the way at a quick walk. They couldn't get away from there quickly enough!

Turning in his saddle, Todd sadly gazed back at the hill that separated him from the carnage on the other side. Nudging his horse forward, he caught up with his men, thankful for the silence in which they rode. It enabled him to think about what he'd just seen, and to lose himself in his tormented thoughts.

~*~

The men returned to Fort Cobb several days later. The day after their return, several significant events occurred. The first was that early in the morning, Indians began arriving by the hundreds. The few survivors from Black Kettle's tribe had obviously assimilated with the tribe of Southern Cheyenne led by Little Robe, who brought his people obediently to the fort along with people from the Arapaho tribe led by Yellow Bear, and the Comanches led by Tosawi. They'd heard about Sheridan's proclamation and warning to those who refused to come in to the fort.

Each tribe raised their villages in a valley less than a mile from the fort. The men came into the fort while the women stayed behind to erect the tipis and build the camp—something they could do in little less than an hour.

On the crowded parade grounds, Cordelia wove in and out of the throng of Indians and soldiers, carefully observing the unfolding events. Therefore, she was present in the crowd when the chiefs were presented to General Philip Sheridan.

Little Robe came forward first, standing before General Sheridan with quiet dignity, a blanket wrapped around his shoulders and thrown over his arm. He told Sheridan his people were starving; Custer had burned their winter supply of meat and slaughtered their ponies so they could no longer hunt buffalo. His people had already eaten their dogs. Now, their bellies soured from the bark soup they'd been reduced to eating. They were here because of the white soldiers' promise to take care of them. General Sheridan listened impassively to his words, spoken through an interpreter, Jeremiah Running Bear.

Then Sheridan said boldly, "You cannot make peace now and commence killing whites again in the spring. If you are not willing to make a complete peace, you can go back and we will fight this thing out."

Puzzled by these words, Little Robe looked left and right at the other leaders gathered there. Finally, shrugging his shoulders, he heaved a great sigh, and said, "It is for you to say what we have to do."

Next to be presented was Chief Yellow Bear, who, having seen the custom of the whites, stuck his hand out to the general without a word. The general reluctantly and briefly took his hand. Wiping it along the side of his pants, he motioned next for the Comanche chief, Tosawi.

The old chief, wearing, instead of a headdress, a flat-brimmed hat with a great yellow star and ratty-looking feather on the front, approached General Sheridan with an innocent grin and an outstretched hand, as he'd seen Yellow Bear do. After another half-hearted handshake by the general, Tosawi pulled himself straight and placed his fist over his heart. He proudly addressed the general in his best, broken English. Cordelia clearly heard him say, "Tosawi, good Indian."

General Sheridan let out a "humph." Cordelia couldn't

quite make out all of his muttered response. Making her way forward through the crowd, she spotted the familiar face of one of the enlisted men. She asked him, "Did you hear what he said?"

"Sure did, ma'am," the soldier laughed. "Said 'the only good Indians I ever saw were dead.'" Cordelia gasped in disbelief.

Tosawi must not have immediately understood the general's words because he still stood on the platform, nodding and smiling. After the interpreter explained what the white chief of the soldiers had said, Tosawi's grin turned to a scowl and he walked back to his people and stood with his arms folded in front of him.

By the end of the day, Sheridan's quote had been perverted to, "The only good Indian is a dead Indian."

~*~

One wonderful circumstance of this momentous day was that along with the Indians, came the interpreter, Jeremiah Running Bear. Though he was a free man, and had the run of the fort, he chose to ally himself with Black Kettle's captives in the guardhouse. Having made an impassioned plea to Commander Hazen for their release, he was told they would be held until the Cheyenne acquiesced to their demands to stop their raids and camp peacefully within the reach of the fort.

General Hazen had heard that Little Robe, suspicious already and now insulted by Sheridan's comments that day, had removed his people back into the hills, away from the fort.

Jeremiah Running Bear, himself a half-breed, promised to speak with Little Robe and to encourage him to come back to the confines of the fort. As he rode out that afternoon, he was stopped by Captain Robert Lawson. They spoke briefly and

Robert gestured toward the officers' quarters. Running Bear nodded and left to search out Little Robe's tribe of Cheyenne.

~*~

To Cordelia, the loveliest event of all was that Todd moved back into his quarters. Both generals, Custer and Sheridan, joined their men in the soldier camp, choosing their tents over the comfort of their rooms away from their men. Cordelia celebrated their decision and joyfully welcomed Todd back into the house.

~*~

That evening, during their dinner of beavertail, which Todd had brought back with him, they shared their stories with one another. Finding beavertail altogether too greasy to enjoy, Cordelia hardly touched her dinner, except for a few fried potatoes. She and Robert listened as Todd told about the battle site. Cordelia felt a twinge of nausea, a combination of the fat meat and the description of the pony slaughter (even though Todd softened it considerably for her benefit).

Then Robert told him about finding the Indian woman. Now it was Todd's turn to listen in amazement as his two friends took turns describing the events surrounding her presence here with them.

"May I meet her?" Todd asked.

Robert and Cordelia exchanged glances before she shrugged her shoulders and replied, "Certainly. But you know this has to be kept just between us."

"I understand that, Cordelia. I assure you I won't breathe a word to anyone about this."

"So you'd like to meet her right now?"

"Yes, of course."

Always the gentleman, Robert pulled Cordelia's chair from the table and took her hand as they led the way to the kitchen. Bess was wiping down the stove with brown paper when they entered—a task she did whenever she cooked something greasy, as she alleged that it cut through the grease and left the stove shining. She and Lucy were surprised to see them in their kitchen, but when she saw Todd's eager eyes looking beyond them to the pantry, she realized why they were there.

"I'll just peek in on her first," Cordelia whispered, glancing into the pantry, then waving them on. "Everything's fine. Come on in."

At the appearance of the two men in uniform, the Indian girl cried out. Surprised by her reaction, Cordelia tried to comfort her, but she pushed Cordelia's arms away and ducked off the bed. With her one good arm and both legs, she crabbed across the floor to the far corner of the room. Standing with great effort, she glared ferociously at the men.

Cordelia stood, breathless, unable to tear her eyes from the woman in the corner. Firelight from the kitchen flickered over her, forcing her face to take on an even more dreadful countenance. She looked like a shadowy fiend with her permanently demented suture-smile. Her hair hung loose around her frail shoulders. She held her right arm across her body and her left fist clenched the gown she wore.

She glared at Robert and Todd, branding them with her eyes. Such hatred emanated from her that Cordelia was glad there were no weapons of any kind in the room. She shuddered to think what this poor, frightened woman could do with a knife. Fortunately, the shelves only held jars of canned goods, and sacks of flour, salt and sugar.

Taking a step toward her, Cordelia felt Todd's strong arm

hold her back. "Please, let me try to talk to her," he said in a whisper.

He moved slowly and with great gentleness, carefully inching ever closer to her. Holding his hands out, and open for her to see, he approached her as if he was approaching a wild horse.

"That's it! Thaaat's it!" he repeated softly, soothingly as he moved toward her.

Her eyes darted around the room seeking a means of escape but, finding none, steeled herself for a fight. As he drew near, she threw herself onto him with a fierce shriek that shattered the quiet like a knife slashing through canvas. Attempting to zigzag around him, she stumbled in her weakened condition, and would have fallen if he hadn't caught her. She struggled for a moment but, with no reserve of strength, collapsed into his arms.

He held her tenderly, rocking her slowly back and forth. It reminded Cordelia of the way this woman had held the older Indian woman in the guardhouse that day. Todd's eyes carefully studied the woman in his arms as Cordelia and Robert straightened her bedding once more. Positioning the pillow, Cordelia smoothed out the covers and pulled them down.

With Todd's help, they cautiously lowered the Indian woman onto the bed. Her eyes fluttered open, once more taking on their look of fear. But she was simply too weak to fight.

Todd gently stroked her good cheek as he looked into her face. Tenderly, he wiped a trickle of blood from the corner of her broken mouth. Cordelia was touched by the degree of pity and gentleness she saw so utterly exposed in his face.

Keeping his eyes on the young woman, he said to them softly, "She's so afraid of us. Bless her heart. There's no telling what she thinks when she sees us, but whatever it is, it scares her to death. Poor thing. I wonder what that man did to her. How could he have hurt this beautiful creature? Look at her poor face. You know, I just can't believe he would do this!"

He continued quickly, "Don't get me wrong. I know Custer certainly has his faults, but I find it unbelievable that he is capable of this kind of brutality."

The Indian woman's body slowly began to relax as she eased back against the pillow. Todd stroked her hair a few times before leaving her to her rest. When he turned toward Cordelia, who was standing in stunned silence next to Robert, she saw the tears standing in his reddened eyes.

"I'd better go," he said, his voice choked with emotion. "But I'd like the opportunity to visit her again, if you'll allow it." Turning back to gaze at her again, he said, "I'd like to show her that not all soldiers are bad. I want to be able to look at her and see something besides fear in those eyes, something perhaps resembling . . . trust."

"You're welcome here anytime. You know that, Todd," Cordelia replied.

"Thanks."

He picked up his hat, placed it on his head and with a glance toward Robert, started out of the room.

"Won't you take coffee with us? or brandy?" Robert called after him.

"No, thank you." There was a pregnant pause as Todd stood in the doorway. "Not tonight." They heard his heavy boot-steps on the porch outside the kitchen. Then he stepped into the house.

Cordelia and Robert exchanged a long glance. As Cordelia bent to the task of tucking the patient in for the night, Robert retired to their quarters without a word. Lieutenant Otis's touching display of kindness had left both of them a little stunned.

Eleven

The next day brought an unwelcome visitor to Cordelia at a most inopportune time. Seated beside the makeshift bed, Cordelia was feeding her Indian some soup, thickened slightly with potatoes mashed to a mush and added to the broth.

The sunlight shining through the high pantry window gave the woman's hair a bluish cast, not unlike the color rising from her bruised and swollen cheek. But her dark eyes had abandoned their dead stare and watched Cordelia cautiously and attentively as she spooned the warm soup into her mouth. Eating didn't seem to hurt her as much today, and much to Cordelia's relief, she was tolerating the soup just fine.

This being the frontier and not their comfortable house in Baltimore, Bess had to use the kitchen also as a laundry room. And today was laundry day. She was boiling a load of dishtowels and dishcloths on the stove and folding clothes she'd just removed from the clothesline outside when she suddenly cocked her head, listening.

"Did you hear that?"

"What, Bess?"

"Sounded like a knock on the front door. I'll go see 'bout it." Wiping her hands on her apron, she exited the kitchen to answer the door.

Cordelia strained to hear what was being said, but to no avail. When Bess entered the kitchen again, she looked worried.

"It's that Miz Hazen again, ma'am. I showed her into the parlor and she's in there snoopin' around, pickin' stuff up and lookin' at everthang. You'd best be getting' in there 'fore she comes pokin' her head in back here!"

"You're right. I'd better go to her immediately. Here, finish up for me?" she asked, pushing the bowl into Bess's willing hands.

"Surely! Me and lil' Princess here been gettin' along mighty good lately," Bess smiled.

Cordelia whispered to her, "Whatever you do, try to keep things quiet in here. The last thing we need is for Mrs. Hazen to find out about her. I'll be back as soon as I can."

Bess smiled at the Indian. "Miz Lawson, you take all the time you need. We'll be just fine in here, won't we, Princess?" The woman's dark eyes never left Bess's round, pleasant face, but there was still no sign of emotion in her expression. Cordelia took momentary pleasure in noting there was no sign of fear there, either.

"Thank you, Bess," Cordelia whispered as she walked briskly to the parlor and her waiting guest.

Mustering a smile, Cordelia entered the parlor and crooned, "My, my. You do have a way of surprising me, Mrs. Hazen. And don't you look nice today?"

Mrs. Hazen stood in her Sunday finest, complete with bonnet and gloves. It was a nauseating shade of lavender, trimmed in white lace. Mrs. Hazen's plump, white face dimpled as she smiled back at Cordelia.

"I couldn't decide what to wear for my portrait, dear. I hope this is suitable!"

"Your portrait?"

"Why, yes. Robert told me you'd had a change of heart and I thought, 'No time like the present to get started.' Is that all right with you?"

"It's not a good time for me right now, Mrs. Hazen. I wish you'd spoken to me first before going to such trouble today." Seeing the downcast look on the older woman's fleshy face and remembering her promise to Robert, she quickly added, "But since you're here we may as well get started. I suppose my chores can wait."

Brightening instantly, Mrs. Hazen's high, affected voice lilted, "Oh, thank you, my dear. Oh, and here, this is for you," she continued, taking an envelope from her bag. "I saw the mail-sergeant ride in a little while ago and I happened to be near the adjutant's office at the time. So I stopped by there to see if my husband had heard from his brother in Dakota. He hadn't, but I happened to see this letter addressed to you. I think it must be from your mother, isn't it?"

Cordelia looked over the envelope back and front. She tried to hide her irritation that Mrs. Hazen would have retrieved it for her. She was dying to read it but decided it would wait until later, when prying eyes and nosy questions could be avoided.

"Yes, it is. Thank you, Mrs. Hazen. You're very kind," she said quietly, careful not to look into the other woman's face, afraid her annoyance would be much too transparent if she did. "I always look forward to hearing from my mother. What about you? Do you have a lot of family?"

"No, dear. I'm an orphan now. And no brothers or sisters either. And our only child died when she was only three years old, bless her sweet soul. I suppose I'm the only person on this post who doesn't care if the mail runs or not. I know I won't get anything. My whole life is right here on this fort." When she smiled, Cordelia could detect genuine pain in Mrs. Hazen's puffy eyes.

Quickly recovering, she added, "But I know the mail is important to everyone else. My main consideration is that I get to digest the newspapers my husband receives. I read them before he does though, because once he gets his hands on them, I don't see him for two days! He gets lost behind the pages of that newspaper!" She chuckled before adding, "Aren't you going to open your letter, dear?"

"No, not just yet. I think I'll save it for tonight when the captain and I can read it together over dinner." She stretched to place it on the side table next to the divan.

Retrieving her sketchpad, she motioned to Mrs. Hazen. "Why don't you sit here in the light?"

Taking a seat opposite her, she assessed her "subject."

"Are you sure you want to wear a bonnet in your portrait?"

"Do you think I shouldn't?" she asked, fidgeting with it uncertainly.

"I think the portrait might be more appealing without it."

"Well, if you think . . ." her voice trailed off as she removed the hat, and sat straighter in her chair. "How's my hair?"

"It's lovely, Mrs. Hazen. Yes, that's better." Cordelia looked at her first one way, then the other, urging her to shift a little more toward the window. When the angle was best, she stopped her. "There. Just hold that pose. This shouldn't take too long."

"I'm fine, dear. Take all the time you need."

Cordelia began with a light outline of her face, neck and upper body. Little by little, she added detail in layers until she was satisfied with the result. She'd been careful to make the needed adjustments to the accuracy of the sketch—the chin was firmer, the skin was smoother, the hair a little fuller and the face a little thinner, but it was recognizably Mrs. Hazen, perhaps as she'd looked ten years ago. The whole sketch had only taken about half an hour.

"There! We're through! Thank you so much for your patience, Mrs. Hazen. I'll bring the portrait to you as soon as I'm finished with it."

"What do you mean, dear? Why, you've barely started!" she protested. "Where's the paint? I don't understand."

"Oh, I have my own way of painting, Mrs. Hazen. Now that I have the sketch, I can paint the portrait anytime. I have a good eye for color. I have no doubt that I can duplicate the shades without your having to sit for long hours while I work."

"But I really don't mind, dear, if it would be of benefit to the portrait."

"No, no, I wouldn't hear of tying up your time like that. I think you'll be satisfied with the painting. And if you're not, you just tell me. I'll understand and I promise my feelings won't be hurt. Now, I hate that you have to run off so soon," she said, standing and ushering a blustering Mrs. Hazen to the door.

"Well, thank you, dear," she finally said.

"Oh, don't forget your bonnet. I'll get it for you," Cordelia said as she stuffed the bonnet into Mrs. Hazen's hands.

"Thank you, Mrs. Hazen. I'll talk to you later."

Closing the door, Cordelia leaned back against it, exhaling heavily. Then she felt it open again.

"Oops! Did you forget something?"

"Yes, I did. Aren't you going to show me my sketch? And just how soon may I expect the painting?"

"I'll try to have it to you by next week. How will that be?"

"Well," she began, as Cordelia closed the door again, shaking her head.

~*~

That evening, they received another unexpected visitor—unexpected, that is, for Cordelia.

It happened as they were finishing dinner. Todd Otis had joined them again. Todd, making it his habit to eat in the officers' mess hall, eagerly accepted these invitations for some of Bess's fine cooking and his friends' enjoyable company.

Throughout dinner, he questioned Cordelia about the Indian. What was her name? How old was she? Had she tried to speak yet? What was the extent of her injuries?

Though Cordelia didn't have the answers to many of his questions, she tried to respond to as many questions as she could before asking, "Todd, why are you so interested in her?"

"I don't know really," he said, thoughtfully. "All I know is that I can't get her out of my thoughts. I've been thinking about her all day, as a matter of fact. Maybe it's the fact that she's so pitiful. I feel sorry for her. Maybe it's because I want to help her get over her fear of white people, though God knows she has reason for fear."

"I hope you don't mind my being indelicate, Todd," Robert began, "but could this attraction to her be a less than honorable one?"

Todd immediately cut his startled eyes toward Cordelia, who was poised, mid-bite, awaiting his answer. Then back to Robert, questioning, he said, "What do you mean, sir?"

"I mean, you've been alone here for a long time. And we both know that young men . . ."

"Captain, please," Todd said quietly, nodding his head in Cordelia's direction, and obviously horrified at this line of questioning, especially in the presence of a lady.

Robert laughed. "It's all right, Todd. Cordelia and I discuss such things freely and openly. I don't think you'll shock her with your answer." He viewed Cordelia warmly, and she smiled under his gaze, making an attempt at being coy and failing miserably. She was hungry for Todd's answer and Robert knew it.

Smiling to himself, Robert continued. "It wouldn't be the first time a white man was charmed by an Indian. I've heard of several examples of white men even *marrying* Indian women!" Shooting Cordelia a quick glance, he said, "Why, I was just talking to the Indian interpreter yesterday and he is the product of such a marriage."

"Is that so?" asked Todd, hotly. "Well, you can forget it. The poor girl may have been beautiful once but she's hardly anything to look at now, with that poor, broken mouth of hers. No, my accusing friend, I am not drawn to her in that way. Not in the least. I am not the kind of man who would fancy himself with a savage."

"A 'savage?' Really, Todd," Cordelia smiled. "You certainly were not treating her as a 'savage' last night. In fact, you were surprisingly tender."

"Don't you people recognize pity when you see it?" His irritation was becoming evident.

"At ease, Lieutenant. We're not here to pass judgment on you. We just want to make sure neither of you will be hurt at some distant juncture."

"Rest assured, that will not happen. I would merely like to befriend her, to earn her trust. My only motive is to help her. My affections and my loyalty belong now and always to my wife, Nicole."

"That's good enough for me," Robert concluded. "Cordelia?"

"Yes, of course. It makes perfect sense." They smiled at each other, and both allowed the awkward subject to drop.

"Shall we retire to the armchairs, Todd? I have some excellent cigars I've been saving for a special occasion."

"Yes, let's," Todd quickly, and with great relief, replied.

"Coffee, gentlemen?" Cordelia offered.

"Thank you, dear."

"I'll take care of it."

As the men settled into their chairs, Cordelia gathered up some dishes and took them into the kitchen.

"Miz Lawson! You shouldn't be doing that!" Lucy was horrified. "I'll get those."

"You may get the rest of them. I was coming in here anyway, so why not bring a few dishes in with me? There's no harm done. I've done it many times before. Is the coffee on?"

"Yes, ma'am, we thought you might be wanting some coffee after dinner tonight, what with Lieutenant Otis here and all."

"Marvelous!" Cordelia started pulling down cups and saucers, preparing the rich coffee for the three of them.

"Miz Cordelia!" Lucy cried, her hands holding her face in horror.

"Really, Lucy! I can do this just fine. I'll do it while you're clearing the table. It only makes sense."

"Mama would shoot me dead if she knew you were doin' this," Lucy whispered.

"Where is she? Upstairs?"

"Yes, ma'am. But she might be comin' back down any minute!"

"Don't worry about it, dear," Cordelia whispered to her, conspiratorially. By that time, she'd poured the coffee, placed the cups on the serving tray and made her way to the kitchen door.

"Lucy, will you get the door for me?" she asked.

"Surely, ma'am," Lucy muttered, opening the door to the hallway and, sighing heavily, watched Cordelia glide toward the parlor. It would be her hide if her mother found out. Shaking her head warily, she followed her to the parlor and started to work clearing the dishes.

As Cordelia finished serving the men, and had just settled herself on the divan to enjoy her coffee, there came a knock on the door. Startled, she gave an imploring look to Robert. "Who could that be?"

Robert gently placed his cup back into the saucer on the reading table beside his big chair. "We'll soon find out, darling."

Her first thought was the memory of the last late caller she'd received—that horrible night when General Custer . . . no, she forced the thought out of her head. She had promised to forgive him for that indiscretion.

She watched the grace with which her husband crossed the room, the ease of a man in perfect form. Once again, she felt that familiar longing for him—longing to touch him, to allow her eyes to linger over the length of his sinuous body. She felt her breathing quicken, but her curiosity cut through her naughty thoughts, as she watched, with apprehension, for who was at the door at this hour.

She heard Robert's welcoming voice, "Come in, come in. I'm so glad you could come." She strained to see who it was but Robert blocked her view. So she was surprised when an Indian walked quietly into the parlor.

He stood roughly five-feet eight or nine. Round shouldered and stocky, Cordelia observed that he was dressed from the waist down in buckskin breeches and moccasins, but wore the shirt and coat of a soldier, except instead of a leather belt like her husband wore, his was a colorful woven sash, with long fringe hanging down below the hem of the coat. Around his short bull-neck, he wore a necklace of colored beads, a large red one in the center with alternating yellow and white ones on either side. His hair was shorter than most Indian men wore their hair, and combed in an American style. But a feather was worked into the strands on one side of his head. Such a blend of American and Indian was unusual, but Cordelia thought it quite captivating, once again admiring the burnished bronze of his skin.

"Allow me to introduce my wife, Mrs. Lawson, and my friend, Lieutenant Otis. May I introduce Jeremiah Running Bear." Mr. Running Bear nodded respectfully to Cordelia and murmured, "Mrs. Lawson," and shook Todd's hand, his eyes lowered, bowing slightly in a submissive posture. "Lieutenant."

"It's nice to meet you, Mr. Running Bear. Are you a friend of my husband?"

"I hope to be, ma'am. But we just met two days ago."

"I see. Could I offer you a cup of coffee?"

"No, ma'am. Thank you."

He and Robert stood awkwardly for a moment, and then Robert gestured toward the chair next to the window. Cordelia was ever so slightly embarrassed as Robert pulled the curtains shut. After all, she thought, we wouldn't want anyone to know we had an Indian in here, now would we?

Once seated, he looked questioningly at Robert, prompting him to say, "You see, darling. I asked Mr. Running Bear . . ."

"Please," he interrupted, "call me Jeremiah."

"Thank you. I asked Jeremiah to come here tonight. He is the interpreter for the Indians. You may have seen him in the ceremony the other day. I thought he could be of some service to us regarding our . . . guest," he said, gesturing toward the kitchen with his head.

"Oh, yes, he certainly might!" Cordelia's eyes brightened as she realized why Robert had asked him to come. She told him as much as she knew of the story, and that they were now trying to nurse the woman to health.

"But we don't even know her name! I've been calling her 'Princess' because she has such a grace and beauty about her."

"Yes, she does," Todd volunteered. "That's a good name for her, Cordelia."

She continued, "There are so many things I want to know about her. Do you think you could speak with her?"

"I would be honored to help in any way I can. And I appreciate the risk you are taking to help her. I didn't know there were any whites who would be willing to do such a thing for one of my people . . . except my father, of course."

"Oh, this is wonderful. Robert, you are such a dear to have thought of this. Thank you!"

Embarrassed, Robert asked, "Would it be more appropriate for us to help her in here? Or would you feel comfortable going to her room?"

"If she has been as badly wounded as you say, I wouldn't want to move her. Perhaps this time I will go speak with her, if she would like to speak. I will not force her if she doesn't want to."

"Oh, that's most reasonable. I certainly understand," Cordelia assured him. "Just allow me to go make sure all is ready for you."

Rising, she raced down the hallway and out the door like a young girl, holding her long, full skirts up as she ran.

After placing more sticks of wood on the fire, pulling the covers up to just under the Indian's slender arms, and brushing the wrinkles away from the quilt, she called to Robert. "I think she's ready."

Her Indian had been asleep and was now following her with drowsy eyes. She jack-knifed into a sitting position when

Jeremiah Running Bear entered the room with a softly spoken greeting.

He recognized her immediately, saying, "I know this girl. She is the daughter of Little Robe, who is now the chief of the southern Cheyenne after Black Kettle! In that way, Mrs. Lawson, she *is* a princess. Her mother and father will be joyful at the news that she lives. We thought she had died at Washita."

"What is her name?" Cordelia wanted to know.

"Her name is Min-nin-ne-wah-hah-ket."

"Oh, my. Will you say it again?"

"Min-nin-ne-wah-hah-ket. When the People name their children, the old ones call them by the things the four winds show them. The one who named her must have been shown a little whirlwind on the day of her birth. That's what her name means—Little Whirlwind."

"Minnywaket?"

"No, ma'am. It's 'Min-nin-ne-wah-hah-ket.'"

"Gracious, I think I might just call her Minnie. Would that be all right, Jeremiah?"

He smiled and looked at the floor, "In this case, I think so, ma'am."

Cordelia excused Bess because there were so many people gathered in the tiny makeshift bedroom, and then she waved Jeremiah toward the rocking chair. He pulled the chair close to the bed, then took his seat next to the woman. Standing behind him, Cordelia leaned into Robert's side as he held her close. Todd was on the other side of the bed, resting his hand gently on Minnie's shoulder until one of her thunderous gazes warned him to stop.

Running Bear, not touching her in any way, spoke softly to her in Cheyenne. Their voices were low and melodious as questions were asked and answers given. Listening to their mysterious dialogue and hearing the crackling of the fire in the background, Cordelia was transported into a magical state of intense respect and appreciation for the scene unfolding before her.

She had thought that French had been a complicated language to learn, but this . . . this strange and extraordinarily exotic language was a wonder to her. It was like candy for her ears and she greedily listened for more.

Minnie's voice was clear, though weak, but she had pushed herself into a sitting position and leaned back against the pillow, bracing herself with her good left arm.

They watched sudden expressions dance across her face as she told her story, though they understood not one word. One moment it was an expression of fear, replaced suddenly by one of intense sorrow, then anger. They appeared, constantly changing, in seemingly random order as her story unfolded.

Running Bear listened intently with his eyes lowered respectfully, occasionally nodding his head.

Finally, her eyes flooded with bright tears that fell in silvery traces down her cheeks, illumined by the soft glow of the fire-light. When they reached her wounded cheek, she winced with pain and covered her face with her hand.

Cordelia gasped in the realization that the salt from her tears was burning her stitched face. She quickly poured some clear water into the basin and, with a clean cloth, wiped her cheek and held the cloth in place.

"Here, I'll do that," Todd volunteered, carefully taking the compress in his own large hand and holding it gingerly over the Indian's bruised cheek.

Ashamed of her pain, she tried to hide her face but Running Bear held his hand up and uttered a phrase that calmed her again. Finally, exhausted, she lay back on the pillow and closed her eyes, still stringing faint words together, pausing longer and longer between the words until she was fast asleep again. Cordelia recognized the gentle rhythm of her breathing.

"She's sleeping. Shall we go back inside?" she suggested.

They all nodded their agreement and made their way to the parlor, leaving Minnie in Bess's care once more.

Cordelia was alive with fascination and curiosity. They hardly had a chance to sit down again before she began plying Jeremiah with questions.

With one gesture of his hand, he silenced her inquiries.

"I'll tell you her story now, as she told it to me."

Twelve

They sat before the warmth of the fire, mesmerized by the woeful events Jeremiah Running Bear relayed to them. Minnin-ne-wah-hah-ket's story started with the massacre itself. She knew the men had stayed up late into the night before—the night Black Kettle and his men had come back from the talk with Commander Hazen at the fort. Sitting in a circle in the Medicine Lodge, where the men held their councils, they talked among themselves until a decision was reached.

Jeremiah continued the saga as he sat next to the hearth. The blazing fire set his black eyes aglow with soft light. His deep, melodic voice was hypnotic as he told her story. The sizzling and popping of the fire filled every poignant pause in the narrative.

After one of those pauses, Jeremiah explained that Black Kettle had decided that this time would not be a repeat of the events of Sand Creek. This time they would not trust the white soldiers. But neither would they fight. They would flee, instead. Medicine Woman, Black Kettle's wife, wanted to leave right then. She had a bad feeling about this, she told him. But he reassured her that the white soldiers would never come out to fight in such conditions. He thought it was too cold, the snow too deep and the storm too fierce for white men to think of battle.

They would move the next day. Some of the men wanted to take up arms against the soldiers, but Black Kettle resolutely clung to the promise he made when he smoked the sacred pipe at Medicine Lodge when the peace treaty was signed. In that treaty, he and the other chiefs had agreed to make peace with the whites, had agreed they would not engage in battle against them. So Black Kettle intended to move his camp of peaceful Cheyenne farther north, where they could still live and hunt in the old ways until the winter had passed.

However, just before dawn the next morning, while the whole tribe was sleeping, Min-nin-ne-wah-hah-ket woke to hear a woman screaming, "The soldiers! The soldiers!" Sitting up, she listened intently for a few more seconds when she heard the crisp crack of a rifle outside. Gathering herself, she threw open the door flap to peek outside. Through the heavy snow, she saw Medicine Woman leading Black Kettle's pony to him. Other braves gathered their pitiful weapons and mounted their ponies. Her father rushed out of their lodge with his shield and club.

She watched as Black Kettle reached his arm down to his wife and pulled her up behind him. They galloped off in the direction of the river.

Terrified, Min-nin-ne-wah-ha-ket ran to her grandmother's side, wrapping her in a blanket. She and her grandmother, Raven Cloud, fled on foot toward the thicket of scrubby trees around their camp, hoping to hide from the soldiers. Her mother lingered behind placing some possessions in a buckskin pouch before making her escape.

Before Min-nin-ne-wah-hah-ket and Raven Cloud could

reach the thicket, they heard strange music and drums that seemed to surround them with sound, though it lasted only a few seconds, but it frightened them even more. At once, she heard the muffled sounds of hoof beats in the deep snow. As she tried to guide the older woman to safety—her assigned duty in case of attack—Min-nin-ne-wah-hah-ket heard the screaming of horses from somewhere behind her.

Looking back at the camp, she saw the heavy blue jackets of the soldiers, and heard their rifles as they blasted everyone in sight. The braves tried to engage the troops long enough to allow the women and children to escape but one after another dropped to the ground in contorted twists and turns.

Suddenly three soldiers on horseback burst forth from the thicket ahead, almost running them over! Min-nin-ne-wah-hah-ket swerved, pushing the older woman out of the way with so much force that it knocked her to the ground. Quickly pulling Raven Cloud to her feet, they fled toward the river. Just as they were about to enter the frigid waters of the Washita, they froze in mid-stride.

There, on the muddy bank on the opposite side of the river, they saw the mud-splattered bodies of Black Kettle and his beloved wife, shot many times and scalped. Their blood mixed with the murky, swirling water and floating ice around them.

Min-nin-ne-wah-hah-ket tried to move her legs, tried to keep going, but the sight of the great Black Kettle butchered in such a disrespectful way made her feel sick and weak. Her reluctant limbs refused to obey her command to run. So she just stood there.

Out of the curtain of falling snow, a soldier rode up behind them and hit the older woman hard on the shoulder with the butt of his rifle, knocking her to the ground once more. When Min-nin-ne-wah-hah-ket bent to assist her, she was kicked in the side with the soldier's heavy boot. She fell next to the old woman and covered her protectively with her arms, hiding her face in the folds of the woman's robe.

The soldier angrily shouted something at them and waved his arms. Unsteadily, they stood and cowered together before him. He herded them to a gathering place with the other captives. Holding each other tightly, they stood, watching the horror around them.

So many of their people, some men but also women and children, lay in distorted shapes across the snow-covered earth. Their blood turned the blue-whiteness of the snow to red. Bright red everywhere! And there were the sprawling bodies of their friends. And over there was Min-nin-ne-wah-hah-ket's brother, Spotted Owl.

To her right lay the crumpled, lifeless body of a little girl called Standing Deer. Wasn't it just yesterday Min-nin-ne-wah-hah-ket had sung to the little girl while braiding her hair? Standing Deer had been so full of life and giggles and happiness. Even in her terror, Min-nin-ne-wah-hah-ket marveled that in one senseless moment, such vibrant life could have been so violently and abruptly snatched from this bloody, disheveled pile of flesh and rawhide—with two black braids lying twisted across the snow.

Hiding her face next to her grandmother's gray head, she fought back the despair that threatened at the corners of her existence. Scouring the camp with her piercing eyes, she searched for her parents, but could find them nowhere.

Her ears were ringing so loudly from the many shots fired that she had trouble hearing, so that as she witnessed women and children around her, screaming and trying to run away, she saw their open mouths without hearing their desperate cries. Most of them never made it to safety. The soldiers overtook them, cutting their throats with their blades or shooting them at close range. She wondered why they hadn't joined the small group of captives she found herself a part of.

Her friend, who had been heavy with child lay across the charred campfire looking with dead eyes into the snowfall, her belly slashed open, covering the lifeless body of her unborn baby boy with frothy blood.

She saw two of the soldiers half-dragging, half-carrying her uncle's 12-year old daughter into a thicket of trees. The scruffy soldiers looked to be laughing but she heard no sound.

As suddenly as the battle began, it was over. The soldiers forced them onto ponies and drove the frightened captives toward the fort like cattle. Abruptly, a sound cut through the ringing in her ears—a sound she couldn't identify at first. With a shudder of recognition, she realized they were shooting the Indian ponies, numbering almost nine hundred! She looked back toward the herd but could see nothing. She could only hear their screams. Those cries would forever be with her, she'd told Running Bear.

Min-nin-ne-wah-hah-ket scanned the camp one last time, seeing their lodges destroyed, their belongings stacked in piles and set ablaze. The stringent smell of burning flesh and hair and gunpowder assaulted her nostrils as the icy wind shifted in their direction. Everywhere she looked, their campground was littered with sprawling bodies. But though the tears wrestled behind her eyes, stinging her throat, she did not cry. Seeing Raven Cloud slipping to the side, she shot her hand out protectively to keep her from falling and to help her straighten herself on the pony. Then she focused on the road ahead.

Running Bear paused in his narrative and turned to Cordelia as he continued. "In the stone lodge, she remembered seeing the Red Hair, which is her name for you, Mrs. Lawson. She said you and your medicine man tried to help the people. She knew you were her friend. She saw your fear for her when

147

Hi-es-tzie came to take her. She wanted to call out to you but she didn't know the words."

"Hi-es-tzie?" Cordelia asked, tentatively.

"It means 'the long hair,' which is what the Cheyenne call your General Custer."

She wanted to tell him that he was certainly not *her* General Custer. Instead, she nodded silently, hand to her throat, and resumed her listening pose, urging him to continue.

"She didn't want to talk to me of this Long Hair. I told her she didn't have to speak of such things if she wanted to keep it within herself. But she said she didn't want it inside her heart, so she told me what happened.

"She doesn't know what he wanted with her, but while they were riding from the fort, his dogs ran over a hill. A little later they happened on the dogs. One was in great pain from porcupine quills in his mouth. Long Hair pulled her down from the horse and cut her hands free. Then he ran to the dog and took his head in his lap. While he examined the wounds, Min-nin-ne-wah-hah-ket climbed on his horse and tried to ride away. But the horse did nothing. The Long Hair laughed at her, and turned his attention back to his wounded dog, plucking the quills from the dog's injured mouth. Min-nin-ne-wah-hah-ket jumped from the horse and ran away. The Long Hair shouted something at her but she kept running. He didn't follow. She thinks he was more concerned about the dog.

"She ran very far, she told me, but finally she had to stop to rest. She rested upon a rock at the top of a mesa. She was very afraid. Her people were killed or captive in the fort. She was free but didn't know where to go to find more Cheyenne. She is ashamed that she hid her face and cried.

"Weak from crying and with sorrow, she failed to notice her surroundings. So while she cried, a soldier came upon her without her seeing him. He grabbed her arm and pulled her from the rock. He spoke softly to her like a friend. But she didn't trust his eyes. He pulled her to a place near some trees and tried to hold her in his arms. She fought against him and turned her face from him. He slapped her across the face and sent her to the ground. She tried to get up but he kicked her in the side, the one the other soldier had kicked in the battle, and she screamed out in pain.

"He threw himself on her and covered her mouth with his hand. When he tried to raise her skirt, she bit his hand as hard as she could. As he cried out, his hold on her weakened so that she rolled away from him and tried to run. But he caught her and threw her to the ground again.

"He said something to her and laughed at her as he sat on her and pinned her arms down with his knees. It was a struggle for her to breathe with him sitting on her chest like that. He slapped her many times. He took out his gun and placed it between her teeth, screaming words at her but this time his face was red and fierce and she knew she was going to die. She tried to die proudly, looking him in the eyes, but at the last second, she turned her head away. She is most ashamed of this.

"The next time she opened her eyes, she thought she was in the spirit. She felt nothing at first. It was still day but the first stars had appeared in the sky. She remembers the freezing cold all around her. Everywhere there was blood. She looked for the soldier but he was not there.

"She tried to stand, but all she could do was crawl. Blood flowed from her open mouth. She tried to close it but she couldn't. The way she told me was that her *face* was open, not that her *mouth* was open."

"Oh, dear God," Cordelia cried, burying her face in her hands.

Running Bear continued, "When she reached the tree, she was able to pull herself up. She wanted to walk back to the camp but she didn't know which way to go. She saw the big flag over the fort and walked that direction. When she reached the edge of the mesa, she tried to climb down the side, but she lost her footing. She's remembers falling but nothing after that.

"The next thing she remembers, she was here, and you and the buffalo woman were watching her. She wanted to run away but she had no strength to run."

"The buffalo woman?" Cordelia asked.

"That is the name she calls the woman with skin the color of the buffalo."

"Oh, she means Bess."

Nodding, he resumed the story, "She knows you are not her enemy. She told me she knows she would be in the spirit now if you had not helped her.

"But the soldiers still frighten her," he said, glancing toward Robert and Todd. "She sees kindness in their eyes but when she looks at them, she also sees the other one. She's afraid he will come back for her. She asked me for a knife so she could kill him if he comes for her again."

"What did you tell her?" Robert asked.

"I told her she was safe here with you. And that when she returns to health, I would make sure she was returned to her people. I hope I spoke the truth to her." He looked from one face to the other.

"You spoke the truth," Todd volunteered. "If I have to take her back myself, I will make sure she returns to her people."

Cordelia and Robert quickly exchanged concerned glances, surprised by Todd's impassioned vow.

Turning back to Running Bear, Cordelia softly explained, "Of course, she may return to her people. I hope she'll allow us to care for her until she's strong enough for travel, but we have no intention of keeping her here as a prisoner, Jeremiah."

"Good. That is what I thought."

"This soldier," Robert asked, with a frown on his face, "did she say what he looked like? Did she tell you anything that might identify him?"

Jeremiah shook his head. "Even if she knew, who would take the word of an Indian over a white soldier?"

"We would," Cordelia exclaimed. "This man should be brought to justice!"

"I agree, my dear," Robert softly explained, "but I'm afraid Jeremiah is right. Unless there is more proof than just her word, they probably would not convict a white man. But I wish I knew who he was. He'd have to answer to me."

"And me," Todd growled. "Whoever he is, may he rot in hell."

Silence lay heavy in the room, where all they heard was the crackling and popping of the fire. What was there to say after hearing this horrible account?

Finally, Cordelia gazed into the kindly face of Jeremiah Running Bear. Her expressive eyes became petal soft, and in the glow of the fire turned the hazy green of distant hills. "Will you come back again?"

"Yes. I would like that. I will go to her people and inform her father that she is alive and safe. They cannot come to her, but I can enter the fort freely.

"Min-nin-ne-wah-hah-ket feels she has dishonored her people by her fear and because she was touched by the soldier and still lives. I told her she was as brave as a warrior and that she should lift her head high.

"Many of my people have suffered. Many have died. They are rubbed out by the whites. It is the way of the world now. We know that. Only a few still hold to the hope of returning to our land, to hunt the buffalo, to live in our lodges with our wives, and to raise our children in the way of the People."

Sadly, he looked into the fire.

Cordelia wanted to tell him that was preposterous, that of course, there would be a time when they could live in peace, that the whites didn't really want to annihilate the Indian people. But, in her heart, she realized his words, however horrible, were likely true.

When he spoke again, his voice seemed to come from far away. Looking sorrowfully into the dancing fingers of the flames, he said softly, "As snow before a summer sun, our people will fade away before the whites until we are no more."

Even in the warmth of the fire, a chill hung in the room, thick and tangible. Cordelia felt a heaviness too great for tears. There were no sounds except those of the fire and the staccato clicks of the grandfather clock.

"I will go now." Jeremiah stood and clasped Robert's arm, then Todd's. He bowed low before Cordelia and thanked her again for what she was doing for Min-nin-ne-wah-hah-ket. As he silently stepped toward the door, Cordelia blurted, "Wait! Please!"

Turning, he eyed her curiously.

"I have something for her parents. Will you take it to them, please?"

"Of course."

Quickly she retreated to her bedroom. While she was away, Jeremiah noted appreciatively the lovely pictures on the wall, a thing most Indians do without. Cordelia could never do without them! She held that pictures on the wall add a pleasant element to any room. He was examining one particular landscape when Cordelia came back carrying the portrait she'd painted of the beautiful Indian princess. Timidly, she offered it to Jeremiah. With great gentleness, he held the portrait at arm's length, scanning the image thoughtfully.

There was an unspoken sadness as he lifted his eyes to

Cordelia. They both realized the beauty captured on this paper was destroyed now.

"Where did you get this?" he asked her, wonderingly.

"She painted it," Robert explained.

"May I see it?" Todd asked.

Jeremiah passed the portrait to Todd.

"It's breathtaking," he finally said, in a hoarse whisper. Reluctantly, he passed it back to Jeremiah, bestowing a look of true admiration on Cordelia.

She blushed under that look.

Jeremiah Running Bear opened the heavy door, paused, then turned back to Cordelia. "Her parents will keep this close to their hearts forever. You have honored them with this gift." Bowing again, he ventured out into the chilled shadows of the night.

Part Two

Thirteen

January 3, 1869

Cordelia strolled toward the trader's store in the uncharacteristic sunshine of the morning. The biting January wind had lessened to a breeze now and if she closed her eyes she could almost imagine springtime.

The character of contentment marked her life now. The past couple of months had taken an emotional toll on her, but they had also caused her to grow up in ways she might not have otherwise. There had been wonderful times of intense happiness—like sharing Christmas with their new Indian friend and introducing her in that sweet way to the baby Jesus, who became the Savior of the world.

She had to smile when she remembered the amateurish Christmas production they'd put on at the fort. Todd had stolen the show with his wit and dramatic prowess. Even George Custer, who took time out from rounding up stray Indians and saving damsels in distress to participate in the comedic antics of the players, made her laugh so hard she had to grip her sides.

Robert surprised her on New Year's Eve with a bottle of French champagne that Griff procured for him for the occasion. Together, her little family had toasted the New Year. The tiny spray of bubbles tickled Minnie's fancy when she took a sip and she'd covered her crooked smile with her hands. Even Lucy was allowed a small amount of champagne, the first alcohol she'd ever tasted. Todd made an eloquent toast and touched Cordelia's heart when tears rushed to his eyes at the mention of his wife's name. Todd—the clown, the comedian, the light-hearted one of the lot of them—was also the most tenderhearted of the bunch, it seemed.

And then there were the quiet times alone with Robert. His tenderness toward her continually enslaved Cordelia's heart, uniting them in a way that eclipsed anything else she'd known.

Minnie made wonderful strides in her recovery. The Lawsons discovered a woman who loved to laugh and tease, one who had easily worked her way into their affections. Half of the little pantry room off the kitchen had been made into her quarters. She still slept on the makeshift bed Robert crafted.

Bess raved about how quickly she caught on to things in the kitchen and Cordelia gained special delight in listening to Lucy teach English after the supper dishes were washed and put away.

Minnie's arm healed quickly. Her forearm remained wrapped, but the bulky splint had long since been removed. Bess had made her two simple dresses. Shoes were bought from the trader's store. Min-nin-ne-wah-hah-ket seemed to gain strength and stamina with each passing day.

Cordelia smiled, remembering the conversation of the

night before when she, Bess, Lucy and Minnie had been in the parlor together. Cordelia was trying again to capture Mrs. Hazen's image on paper (for the sixth time). Bess was sewing and Lucy was reading a picture book to Minnie, explaining the figures on each page. Robert had retired to the bedroom to read. These times after dinner each night when they gathered together, though engaged in their own activities, were the most special and anticipated hours in the twenty-four.

The conversation among the women turned to the subject of men.

"No," Lucy explained to Minnie, "this is the farmer. He works outside in the fields all day. This is his wife. She works in the house."

"All the days, she work in house?"

"Yes, *every day*," she corrected. "That's her job. That's what she does."

"I no like." Minnie shook her head. "In my family, women work outside in sunshine. Men sit in tipi—smoke, talk."

Bess piped up, "Sounds like a lot of the menfolk I used to know! Don't your menfolk do no work?"

"*Any* work, Bess," Cordelia corrected, nodding toward Minnie.

"Men work plenty. They hunt for food. They keep safe whole camp. They work with horse. But they no do woman's work," Minnie explained.

Lucy continued with the lesson. "See? These are the children. Father. Mother. Children."

Minnie looked up to Bess, who was rocking in her chair, then back to Lucy. "Bess – mother? You – children? Where father?"

Bess stopped rocking. Her every motion seemed frozen in time. Lucy's mouth dropped open and Cordelia looked anxiously from one face to the other. Just as she was about to explain to Minnie that they didn't talk about such things, she was surprised to hear Bess speak up.

In her unhurried, deep velvet voice, Bess said, "Minnie, Lucy's father was a very bad man. He never was my man. His name was Jessie. He was big and strong, the 'head nigger in the stable.' The white men listened to what he had to say about horses. He saw hisself as more important than what he really was."

She shook her head, remembering. "He said he loved me, but I knew what he really wanted. I was jest fourteen years old then, Minnie, jest a child myself. An' I didn't want no part of that man. But one night after the whole house was celebratin' gettin' the crops in, he was stinkin' drunk and he found me and he hurt me. I never told no livin' soul. Later, I found out I was goin' to have a baby of my own. Nobody never knew who Lucy's daddy was. I knew if my brother found out, he'd try to kill him. But Jessie was so mean. I was afraid he'd hurt Toby instead. So I never told nobody till now."

Bess looked down at Lucy. "Jessie don't know it, but he give me the best thing I could ever hope for, even though the gettin' was hurtful. He give me you, Baby." Her eyes brimmed with sudden tears.

"What happened to him, Mama?" Lucy breathed.

"I don't know, child, an' I don't want to know! To me, he's dead. I hope he is, too!"

Minnie asked, "You no want no man now?"

"No, Baby. I don't want no man never agin'."

"Maybe someday you'll meet someone you'll love, Bess. I'd hate to think about you going through life all alone." Cordelia was thinking about the closeness she had with Robert.

"I ain't alone, ma'am. I got you and the captain and Lucy and now I got Minnie. An' if I lose ever' last one of you some-day, I'll still have the good Lord. He's with me all the time!"

There were several minutes when nobody spoke. Then Minnie broke the silence with, "I think some man like you, Bess!" She smiled her broken, innocent-devil smile.

"Now what you talkin' 'bout, child?"

"Running Bear! I see how he see you. He all time say how good you cook, how nice - you. He come here too much to see me."

"Now wait jest a minute!" Bess started.

They all laughed, then Cordelia added, "I *have* noticed his attentions, now that you mention it, Minnie. He is awfully complimentary of you, Bess."

"And Mama did wear that pretty blue dress the last time he was here, remember?" Lucy added. This brought on a new round of laughter.

"Lucy! Why, I never!" Bess quickly packed up her sewing and padded out of the room. "I don't have to listen to this kind of stuff, that's fo' sho!"

They all giggled as she left the room.

Cordelia chuckled now to herself, remembering.

Jeremiah Running Bear had become a frequent guest in their home, usually arriving after dark. He was instrumental in getting messages from Minnie to her family and back to her. During his last visit, he'd hinted that it might be time for her to go back to her people. In her heart, Cordelia agreed. But she didn't want to just *send* her back. She wanted to *take* her back!

She didn't dare mention that to Robert. He would be adamantly opposed to her going to the Indian camp. But she was so attracted to these people and to their ways. She heard the drums at night sometimes. There were times when, if the wind was just right, she could smell their cooking.

She listened to some of Minnie's stories and even in her broken English the magic and color of these people intrigued her, capturing her imagination. She wanted to walk among them, to see their faces, to learn their names. And Jeremiah had told her they wanted her to draw them as she had Min-nin-ne-wah-hah-ket. Her portrait was one of the tribe's most prized possessions. She just had to figure out a way to make that happen.

As she walked into the store, Griff looked up from a conversation he was having at one end of the long wooden counter.

"'Mornin,' Mrs. Lawson."

"Good morning. Have you received my package yet?"

"No, ma'am, not yet, but I figure it should be here any day now."

Cordelia's eyes had adjusted to the dark room by now, so she could see the man he'd been talking to. She recognized him as one of the scouts that accompanied Custer on his . . . assignments.

Just as she was about to make a query regarding Custer's whereabouts, the door opened. A young black man walked in, quickly scraping his cap off his head and wringing it in his hands. Though he never actually made eye contact with anyone in the room, Cordelia could tell he was nervous about coming here.

"What do you want?" Griff asked, brusquely.

"Me and my missus, we been travelin' for nigh onto two weeks. We be needin' some supplies and food. We saw the flag and came here to the fort."

"We don't serve no wooly-heads in here, boy," Griff barked, spitting toward, but missing, the spittoon in the corner. "Find your grub somewhere else!"

Cordelia looked outside the grungy window and spied a plump but pretty black woman sitting on the seat of a buck-board wagon. She clutched her dirty cloak tightly around her shoulders and looked side to side—for signs of trouble, Cordelia surmised.

"They ain't no other place to go, sir," insisted the man.

The scout turned around to face the black man and tucked his fringed coat behind the hilt of his knife. This did not go unnoticed by the black man.

Cordelia jumped in by saying, "Where are you going?"

"Probably runnin' from some plantation down south, I'd bet," said the scout, spitting onto the plank floor.

"Oh, no, sir. We be free, now! We're headed west. We have kinfolk out there but we're runnin' out of food and supplies."

"Sorry. We don't have no food or supplies. Now git out of here!" Griff all but yelled at him.

"Wait just a minute, please." Cordelia stared hard at the trader, and then asked the black man, "What do you need?"

He listed several items, including a blanket, coffee, flour, bacon, eggs, and oats for his horses.

"Do you have any money?"

"Yes, ma'am, I have a little."

Facing Griff, she said, more authoritatively than she had a right to, "Then I don't see that there's any problem. You've got the supplies and this gentleman has the money. If he doesn't have enough, I'll make up the difference."

Resentfully, he gathered up the supplies and dropped them with a thud onto the counter. "That'll be $7.50."

"Yes, sir. Thank you, sir," the black man said as he quickly handed over the money. "And thank you, ma'am." He bowed to Cordelia and gathering his supplies, hurriedly left the store.

After he was gone, she whirled to face the roguish trader. "Really, sir. I cannot believe your manner with that man," she stormed. "We just fought a war to abolish slavery in the south. Here is a man who is trying to make a life for himself and his wife. And you treat him without the slightest courtesy. He *is* a man, after all."

"To you, he is. To me, he ain't." He spat toward the spittoon, missing again.

"I think I'm finished with my business here today. Will you send word when my package arrives?"

"Yes, ma'am! Sure will!" he drawled, leaning heavily on the counter.

Cordelia pulled herself to her full height and stormed out of the store in time to see the little buckboard leaving through the front gate, two dark figures arm-in-arm on the seat. Looking back at the store, her eyes flashed undisguised loathing in its direction, before heading back home.

It was such a pretty day that she decided to try to shrug off the frustration she felt at the injustice she just witnessed. By the time she got back to her quarters, she'd decided to go for a ride. Robert didn't mind her riding, but so far had insisted she not ride alone.

"The prairie has its own surprises," she could hear him saying. But today she needed to clear her head. She wanted to ride alone. Besides, Robert was much too busy at this time of day to accompany her. Summoning one of the enlisted men walking nearby, she asked if he would saddle her horse for her. He quickly agreed. The whole fort knew which horse was hers. They'd seen Robert and Cordelia on many rides across the hills. And Sunburst was a remarkably beautiful animal. Robert had scoured the countryside looking for the ideal horse for his wife and found near perfection in Sunburst.

Quickly changing into her riding skirt, Cordelia left word with her busy household staff that she would be out for a ride. No, she wasn't hungry for lunch; no, she wasn't riding with the captain; and no, she didn't know how long she'd be gone.

Minnie, already feeling comfortable enough to express her opinion, shook her head in Cordelia's direction.

"Captain no like."

"I'll be back before dinner, long before he gets home." With that, she headed for the stable behind their quarters.

A small stable stood in the two back corners of the lot behind their house. The two lieutenants' horses shared one stable and the captain's horses were boarded in the other. There was an identical arrangement for the other side of the house. A stockade had been constructed around the back of the house to allow their horses freedom to graze. After all, officers could hardly be expected to keep their mounts in with the general population of horses for the enlisted men!

The huge back lot also housed a chicken coop and a small garden where a winter crop of potatoes, cabbage and greens were planted, fenced off from the horses' ravenous violations. A small cellar and a well were also apportioned to each half of the house (although the water from the well, smelling of rotten eggs, was so sulfurous that it was used mostly for cleaning, not drinking).

She marched to where the enlisted man stood holding Sunburst for her. She climbed onto the little stool they'd made for her in the carpentry shop and pulled herself onto the saddle. Adjusting the reins in her strong, but shapely hands, she thanked the soldier and headed for open prairie.

The main gate of the fort faced to the southwest. The Indians were camped close to a mile toward the east. As much as she'd have loved to ride to their camp, Cordelia decided to head west.

The wind was blowing colder now, but she didn't mind. She loved the brisk feel of it on her face. Besides, her wool jacket and skirt kept her warm enough. They walked or cantered farther from the fort as the afternoon passed. To her left, she watched as a small herd of seven antelope gracefully bounded away from her and disappeared over one of the many mounds of red clay dotting the countryside.

A little farther south, she startled a flock of wild turkeys, who ran with surprising speed, as they escaped down the gulley and over the next hill. Cordelia marveled that their movement seemed more like one unit than the thirty or forty individual birds they were. They looked for all the world like a herd of tiny buffalo as they stampeded away from her.

Up ahead, she spied soft, blue-black tendrils of smoke rising into the sky. Wonderingly, she headed in that direction. As far as she knew, there were no Indian camps out here.

She looked behind her, making sure she could still see the flag flying over the fort. Reassured, she nudged her horse in the direction of the smoke.

As she topped a little ridge, she pulled Sunburst to a halt. There, in the middle of the meadow before her, was an over-turned buckboard wagon, charred and smoldering. One of the huge wheels still turned. Occasional flames leapt from the other side of the wagon. Provisions lay scattered about the wagon, barely visible amid the tall grass. There were no signs of mules. In fact, there were no signs of life!

Cordelia thought about riding back to the fort to report this, but she wanted to get a closer look first. So she rode slowly toward the overturned wagon. She suspected it belonged to the Negro couple she'd seen at the fort, but she didn't want to believe it.

As she drew closer to the wagon, she dropped from the saddle, standing in Sunburst's protective shadow. She scanned the plains in every direction around her. There was a copse of trees to her right but otherwise, nothing but wide, open spaces of prairie stretching before her for miles. It was probably a day's ride to the mesa in the distance.

She felt flushed and slightly afraid as she tiptoed around the wagon, holding her middle with both hands, trying to keep her breathing under control. Her pounding heart seemed to beat so hard she could almost hear it. She swallowed hard as she inched forward.

Cordelia had always viewed courage, both moral and physical, as one of the finest attributes of character. She considered herself a fairly courageous person, on the whole, and tried to call that courage into action for this investigation.

As she rounded the corner next to the seat, a buzzard screeched loudly and amid much flapping of wings he and his companions flew up to the nearby cottonwoods to observe her meddling intrusion.

She took several deep breaths before continuing her exploration. When she viewed the other side of the wagon, she uttered a surprised, stifled scream at what she beheld!

She tried not to look, but couldn't tear her eyes from what lay before her. Sprawled on the ground lay the young black man she'd met earlier. There was no sign of the woman. The man had been stripped and butchered; pierced with arrows in both arms and legs, and his throat lay open like a yawning mouth before her. Each of his thighs had been vertically sliced to the bone. One of his eyes was pecked out, and an arrow impaled his severed genitals to the wagon.

She took in all this carnage in less than thirty seconds and back-stepped as fast as she could, tripping over the tongue of the wagon in the process. Lying there on the red earth, amid the waving buffalo grass, she wept into the crook of her arm, shaking with each wracking sob.

All at once, a shadow fell across her clenched hand. She whirled around to see what it was and saw, standing over her, the leering face of a man she could only describe as "savage." He held a bloody tomahawk in his leathered hand.

Screaming, she tried to rise to her feet and run, but he grabbed her while she was on all fours and pulled her up by her hair. He smelled of blood, grease and unwashed flesh. Though still unfamiliar with *all* the customs and habits of the plains Indians, one fact that Cordelia knew for certain was that most Indian men are obsessively clean, insisting on daily morning plunges in whatever water was available. This man had obviously broken with that tradition. His pungent odor, a stink that could have made a polecat run for cover, assailed her nostrils and she surely would have retched if he hadn't, at that very moment, begun pulling her toward their horses by her hair.

Several other buckskin-clad Indians joined him from out of nowhere! They must have hidden in the trees somehow. The one holding her had a strip of black hair standing straight up all along the middle of his otherwise shaved head. His face was painted red from his cheekbones to his brows, like a mask. One of the other men held the horses, she noticed, and her searching eyes spotted Sunburst among them, his reins tied to the wooden saddle horn of another horse.

The black woman's body was draped across a mule. Cordelia choked back another scream when she noted the blood dripping down the woman's legs and onto the red clay below her. She saw no sign of struggle and guessed that she was unconscious, though still alive.

Two of the Indians came to where she was being held and lifted strands of Cordelia's red hair, laughing and gesturing to each other. The one holding her uttered some guttural command and the other two returned to their horses.

As the one holding her turned to gather the reins in his hand, she twisted out of his grip, leaving a clump of hair behind, and started running toward the wagon. All she could think about was finding some kind of weapon to ward these savages away from her.

She felt a whack to her head, and sensed something wet running down her face . . . then blackness swallowed her up as she fell endlessly forward into darkness.

Fourteen

~~~

She hated being cold. She especially hated waking up cold. For a split second she forgot about her capture, lost in the haziness of thought that accompanied her thudding head. She opened her eyes very slowly, first only a slit to try to locate her captors and figure out where she was. It was dark, but the moon was almost full and the stars were bright. A few heavy, fast-moving clouds raced overhead. Because of the way the flickering light illumined what she could see, she surmised that there was a fire built to her left.

Methodically, she went through a mental inventory of her body to ascertain any injuries, careful not to move too much for fear of attracting unwanted attention. The best she could figure, she was uninjured, and, except for a throbbing headache, was not in any pain.

She was lying on her belly amid the tall, waving grass. The ground beneath her was cold and hard. She could hear, but not see, running water somewhere close. Her wrists were tied behind her and something bound one of her ankles.

Somewhere in the distance she heard the shrill song of

some kind of prairie bird. Curious that he'd be singing in the dark like this, she thought, *I wonder what kind of bird sings at night like that. And why in the world am I thinking of something like that at a time like this?* She cursed her stupidity.

She could hear the men speaking their guttural language from the general direction of the fire. Was it her imagination or was that bacon she smelled cooking? The bacon she'd secured for the young black man that morning. Squeezing her eyes shut, she steeled herself from threatening emotion.

She needed to get a better look at what was going on and detail her surroundings a little better if she was going to find a means of escape. She feigned sleep, but flipped her face slowly toward the small campfire. Opening her eyes only slits again, she was comforted to note that none of the four Indian men looked in her direction, but instead were consuming the half-cooked bacon, slurping it into their mouths with a flick of the wrist, then licking their burned fingers. There were occasional bursts of laughter, but otherwise they spoke in their low, atonal speech. In the distance, she heard the mournful *yip, yip, yip, howl* of a coyote.

Opening her eyes again, she slowly scanned her surroundings. She fought back her fear and forced herself to remain calm. Yes, there seemed to be a creek running through the cracked earth of the prairie. Curly grama and taller mesquite bushes lined its banks. The horses were picketed a short distance from the creek. Then the campfire filled her visual field. She thought she could see the black woman lying face down on the other side of the fire, but she couldn't tell. It might just be a crumpled blanket—a vague darkness amid the tall, dried grass. Whatever it was, the form was deathly still.

As she scanned the territory beyond her feet, she saw a slight rise in the dry, cracked earth. She could see the shadows of scarred trenches in its steep sides, where water and snow had eroded the sun-baked red clay. It was about as far from her as the stable was from her back porch at the fort.

The fort! Robert! He would be out looking for her by now! Oh, how angry he would be that she'd chosen to go out riding alone. She vowed never to disobey him again. That is, if she got another chance.

Oh, Robert, Robert, she sobbed, silently. *I need you, Robert. Please God, let him find me before . . .* She couldn't think of that now. She couldn't give in to the emotion that lay just beneath her otherwise calm surface.

There was a rock or something under her right hip. She hadn't perceived it at first, but now she noticed it digging painfully into her flesh. She tried to shift slightly to her left, so that she could lift herself off the rock. When she did, two of the men looked her way and grunted something to the others.

The one with the red painted face stood studying her for a long time. Her eyes were slits again, trying to feign sleep once more. He must have figured it out because he reached her in three quick, long strides and kicked her over onto her back.

She yelped in pain and surprise!

From her vantage point on the ground, he looked ten feet tall. His spiked hair blew softly in the insistent wind. She couldn't see his face. He was in silhouette with the fire behind him. He stomped the ground, kicking dust and dirt into her face. Kneeling beside her on one knee, he looked back toward the fire and barked commands to the others. They reluctantly covered the fire until only the tiniest flame still burned. Cordelia saw glowing embers amid the dust and ash of the campfire.

Something flopped in the creek. There was no other sound.

Suddenly came the loud crash of thunder in the distance, causing Cordelia to jump in fright and gasp slightly. Huge drops of rain pelted her face—first one and then another as the quick-moving storm approached. The men pulled their belongings under the sparse grove of trees beside her, then the red-painted one grasped her arms and pulled her over to the trees, dropping her face down onto the hard-packed earth.

A clap of lightning zigzagged across the sky followed by another deafening crash of thunder. Again and again. The rain started in earnest. Those first tentative drops gave way to a hard, cold, pelting rain. She shivered and tried to keep her mouth above the rivulets of water streaming down the slope.

The lightning flashed again and a curious sound of thunder followed instantly, then another immediately after! The rain was falling in torrents now, but two thunders? The Indians were looking around, too. She could see the perplexity on their faces.

Another quick flash of lightning and an instantaneous thunder boom—then BOOM! Two of the Indians scrambled to their feet, looking around. One of them turned to her and yelled something, pointing at her. He had painted a stripe of blood red under each eye, and a single dot of red on his shaved temple. She didn't know what he said, but she could tell he was angry and confused.

"Something is wrong!" Cordelia screamed inside her head. She twisted to glimpse the other two Indians, leaning back asleep against the trees. One more lightning flash revealed blood trickling from a hole in each forehead. "They've been shot!" she thought, feeling a powerful surge racing through her veins.

She raised her head, looking all around. The red-painted Indian stepped on her back, crushing her back to the earth, leaving her gasping for air. He drew his tomahawk, and raising it menacingly above her, snarled angrily. Another clap of thunder, but this time without the lightning! And the red-painted Indian dropped onto Cordelia in one fluid motion, landing with his face six inches from hers, his lifeless eyes staring unseeing into hers. His body lay draped across her.

Cordelia gasped and tried to wriggle out from under him.

The other Indian ran for the horses but halfway there, the shot rang out again and the Indian plunged headlong into the grass and moved no more. This time Cordelia clearly heard the gunfire. It wasn't thunder! She couldn't move because of the load atop her, but she continued to struggle against it. Finally she lay breathing heavily in the silence, listening past the rain, through the rain for any other sound. Her eyes searched the darkness for any movement at all. Her heightened senses struggled to comprehend.

After what seemed an eternity, in another flash of lightning, she spied a figure standing on the rise beyond the camp. Carefully, he made his way toward her. Cordelia prayed he was friend, not foe. The last thing she wanted was to trade one evil for another.

Her heart thumped wildly as the man approached. His buckskin coat, trimmed in long fringe from the sleeves and the hem, swayed with every cautious step as he crept ever closer to her. The rain was a soft shower by now. The worst was over. Or was it?

Cordelia felt herself begin to panic as he came steadily toward her. She struggled again to free herself of the load across her, but again ceased after realizing it was impossible, tied as she was.

The brim of his hat covered his face as he bent to pull the Indian off her, but there was the hair—long, reddish-blond curls falling in wet ringlets across his shoulders!

"Custer," she breathed, sinking into the realization. Something like relief flooded her heart.

Agile fingers quickly released her from her bonds and strong arms helped her to a standing position. Struggling for balance, Cordelia rubbed her wrists with relief, as she watched him go about a methodical check of the campsite. He dragged the men next to the creek, stacking them next to each other like the logs of a raft, checking each one for any sign of life. She watched him kneel down on the other side of the campfire, then drag the dark, unmoving form of the woman over to the lifeless row of bodies.

As she made her way tentatively to the man, Cordelia's boot slipped in the mud, almost sending her into a sidewise slide. With surprising strength he grabbed her and pulled her upright, holding her next to him until she could regain her footing. When she raised her eyes to his, she saw her suspicions realized. Indeed, it was George Custer. No blue uniform. No gold braid. Instead, he looked the part of a frontiersman again.

"We'd best get you home, Mrs. Lawson." He walked catlike to the horses, untied them and separated Sunburst from the others. He released them into the night. As Custer walked Sunburst over to her, Cordelia could feel his eyes on her, quickly assessing her condition. Effortlessly, he lifted her onto the saddle and led her like a child over the mound of earth to his own horse, waiting obediently beyond the rise of land. The rain slowed to a trickle as he mounted his horse and headed slowly toward the fort with Cordelia riding close beside him.

"General," she began tentatively, not really trusting her trembling voice.

"Please, call me George."

She swallowed hard. "George. I don't know how to thank you for what you just did. I am so . . ."

He sighed, "Forget it. I'm just glad I was around."

Silence separated them again.

"You're not hurt?" he asked, finally.

"No, I don't think so," she responded, touching the large lump at her hairline. "A few bumps and bruises, that's all."

He studied her for a moment then told her, "You have no idea how lucky you are, madam."

"I don't believe in luck, sir. I believe in grace."

"Yes, and the good Lord's given you more than your share tonight."

"Yes. I'll agree with that," she said before losing herself in thought, imagining with a shudder what *might* have happened apart from that grace.

After riding a few more feet in silence, Cordelia asked, "What tribe did those men belong to? They didn't look like Cheyenne."

"Don't know. These Indians didn't belong to any tribe, really. They were renegades, my dear. Broken off from their own tribes, they formed their own little band. These are the ones who refuse to follow the leadership of their chiefs. They're the worst kind."

Cordelia eyed him suspiciously, giving herself over to the feeling of safety that settled over her now. "How was it that you just *happened* to be here when I needed you most? What were you doing out here?"

"My scout told me about your . . . let's call it 'interference' in the store this morning. Told me he saw you set off by yourself in this direction. Well, ma'am, I just didn't like that, so I set out to watch after you, to make sure you got home safe."

"But I didn't know you were in the fort! I . . ."

"I wasn't," he interrupted. "My men and I are camped about a mile to the south of the fort. Joe knew where to find me."

"That's right. You're at the soldier's camp. I knew that." She felt suddenly embarrassed, thankful he couldn't see the flaming redness suffusing her mud-smeared, tear-streaked cheeks.

"I'd rather be with my men than in the fort."

For some unexplained reason, Cordelia suddenly felt angry and cynical again where George Armstrong Custer was concerned. In a catty assault, she assailed him with the rumor she'd heard the day before.

"Besides, you have other distractions these days, I've heard."

He peered into her face with a puzzled expression. "What are you talking about?"

"I heard you've taken an Indian wife." Cordelia instantly hated herself for bringing up such a distasteful subject. Ashamed that she'd repeated such gossip, she immediately wished she could somehow suck those ugly words back into her mouth, and wondered why his presence brought out the worst in her character—especially after he'd just saved her life!

"I'm sorry. I shouldn't have mentioned that," she said. "It seems I'm quite distraught at the moment. I'm not thinking well."

"Understandable, my dear. Ah, yes, my Indian wife. Actually I do have one," he volunteered.

"What? You mean it's true?" Cordelia pulled Sunburst to a sudden stop and stared, slack-jawed at her rescuer.

"Oh, yes! An old Indian woman gave her daughter to me. I didn't know what was happening at the time, of course. One minute I was listening to her yappin' on about something and the next thing I knew, I had a wife! She's quite becoming, too, I must say," he grinned at her. "Her name's Mo-nah-se-tah."

"But I thought you were already married! Robert said your wife's name was Elizabeth."

"Well, I know that, and you know that, but they don't have to know that, do they?" he teased.

They rode on slowly, in stony silence.

After giving her time to stew over this revelation, he volunteered, "Actually, I don't have an Indian wife anymore. I gave her to my brother, Tom. Have you met him?"

She shook her head.

"Nicest fellow you'd ever want to meet. Always wanted him to find someone who's as special to him as my Libby is to me. But it hasn't happened. Well, at least now he's got someone to help him pass these cold winter nights," he grinned.

"General Custer! Now I don't know *what* to believe. You are a master at the art of deception, I must say! I hope you're enjoying this because I most definitely am not!" she flung at him hotly.

"I'm sorry. I shouldn't tease you at a time like this. I actually did give her to Tom. And this 'wife' of mine just had a baby boy two nights ago."

Cordelia remembered the pregnant captive huddled with her mother in the guardhouse that day. This must be the girl he's talking about, she thought.

"Tom's just looking after them," he continued. "That's all. But who knows? With some time, she really might warm his bed!" He grinned at her mischievously in the moonlight.

"G-g-g-eneral! Really!" Cordelia exclaimed through chattering teeth. The rain had stopped. But the cold wind sweeping over her seemed to have caused Cordelia to take a chill. She shivered violently and her tiny chin quivered with cold.

"Mrs. Lawson, are you quite certain that you're all right? They didn't hurt you?"

"No, thank God. I'm okay. Yes, I'll admit I'm pretty shaken by all of this. And the cold doesn't help matters at all. My clothes are soaked and I'm suddenly very tired and so very cold and . . . and still just a little afraid, I think. While I was held captive, I was able to keep my head about me. But n-n-n-now, after it's all over, I'm t-t-terrified!" Quick tears filled her widening eyes.

"You? Afraid? I never thought I'd see the day!" he chuckled.

"Well, I've never been captured by a mob of angry savages before!" she snapped at him, forgetting her exhaustion and fear for the moment.

"Oh, they're 'savages' now, are they?"

"Well," Cordelia argued, "*those* men were!" She glared at him angrily. She'd done it again. She'd already broken her vow to try to be more civil to him. Swallowing hard, she changed the subject.

"General . . . I mean, G-g-g-george, that was some fine sh-sh-shooting back there."

"Oh, that was nothing. Shooting's not at all difficult, ma'am. It's shooting *people* that's hard. Knowing that in one instant, you're going to end their very lives! Despite what you may believe to the contrary, I don't enjoy being crowded into killing a man just because I have the wherewithal to terminate his hopes and dreams in my hands. That's an awesome ability, Mrs. Lawson. But sometimes we're faced with the choice of killing or being killed. And when you're given that choice, our natural instinct is to protect ourselves, or those we . . . love." This last word was spoken while he looked softly into her upturned face, lit by the moonlight escaping the racing clouds above.

"However, my dear, that doesn't mean it's ever easy," he quickly continued. "Everything stops for the ones whose lives you take—everything except, of course, the judgment, if you're inclined to believe in that kind of thing. That dreaded moment when we'll come face to face with our Maker, and have to give an answer for our sins. Now *that's* a moment that makes *me* tremble with fear, ma'am, because even though the good Lord showed His grace to this wretched sinner, I, for the life of me, can't figure out why."

Surprised by Custer's profession, Cordelia nevertheless said, through teeth clenched and chattering, "George, God shows grace to those He loves, not because of anything good or bad we've done, but because we are cleansed by the blood of Christ. When He gazes upon us, it's *His* righteousness He sees, and not our poor wretchedness."

"Well, that's something for which I shall be forever thankful," Custer confided softly, looking straight ahead.

They rode in silence for the next half-mile. They were in nearly total darkness now, the moon again held captive by the angry clouds above.

From the darkness, Custer broke the silence as Cordelia shivered ever more violently. "You know, Mrs. Lawson," he began, "that husband of yours should procure for you a weapon so you can protect yourself in the event that I'm not here to do it." As the moonlight flooded the scene once more, Custer flashed her a most charming, and disarming, smile. "I bought Libby a little lady's pistol. A double-barreled derringer, 41-caliber, over 'n under. Pretty little thing. But deadly. She knows how to use it, too."

"I don't know, George. I don't know if I could really use it, if I could actually take the life of another."

"Even if he was threatening yours? or your husband's?"

"Yes, even then." Her words trailed off to a whisper, then she added, "Maybe I could. I just hope that God never puts me in that particular situation."

"I'd be glad to talk to the captain about it, ma'am. Seems he'd be glad you'd have something to protect yourself with— protection from those lonesome polecats at the fort when he's away." Again came the boyishly bright and ready smile that changed his whole face into one that was almost handsome!

"No, thank you. I'll m-m-mention it to him m-m-myself."

"You hungry, ma'am? All I've got is a little dried buffalo meat, but it's pretty tasty when you're hungry."

"Thank you . . . George. I'm actually more c-cold than hungry, but I'll try it." Cordelia reached out for the jerky. Her hand was shaking so violently that she almost dropped it. There was an awkward touching of fingertips when she took the piece from his hand and she was surprised at the feel. Pleasant, somehow. Even as she felt the butterflies fluttering in her stomach, a stab of guilt shot through her for this unexpected, and unwanted, reaction.

She shook her head as if to clear it of any similar thoughts relating to the *pleasantness* of his touch. Again, she silently admonished herself. George Custer, seemingly reading her mind, smiled but said nothing.

She nibbled on the dried meat for a moment then offered, "You know, about the time I'd decided there was nothing good in you at all, you have to go and save my life. Now I just don't know *what* to think about you! You have me most confused, sir."

"Mrs. Lawson!" he laughed with mock hurt in his voice.

"No, you may call me Cordelia. I believe you've earned that right."

"Thank you. Frankly, *Cordelia*, I'm surprised at you. You are obviously a dangerously intelligent woman. Yet you are still naïve enough to believe that a person can be totally good or totally evil?" He laughed into the chilly night air—a free, hearty laugh. "All of us are good, Cordelia, and all of us are evil. Some lean a little more to one direction or the other, but both exist within our helpless and ever-wicked hearts. No one is truly good. Don't you remember Romans 3?"

"Yes, of course," she answered with surprise. "I know the verses you mean. 'There is none righteous, no, not one: There is none that understandeth, there is none that seeketh after

God . . . There is none that doeth good, no, not one.' I know those verses, but I must admit my surprise that *you*, of all men, know them. In fact, this night has been full of surprises for me! I had no idea you'd entertained even the idea of salvation. Yet, your knowledge of the scriptures and devotion to the Lord are . . . well, quite astonishing to me!"

"Delia, just what have I done to cause you to have such a low opinion of me? Was it that night I came to you? If it was, you promised me your forgiveness, remember?"

Momentarily shocked to hear the name with which her grandfather addressed her coming from George Custer's lips, she, still shivering, replied, "Yes, I d-d-d-do remember, George! But that's not it. I can't help but also r-r-remember the way M-m-minnie looked the night Robert brought her in."

"Minnie? Who, pray tell, is 'Minnie?'"

Irritated by his casual clipping of her name, and still upset from the night's trauma, she felt like kicking herself for opening this particular topic. For the second time that night, she wished she could suck her careless words back into her mouth. She wondered if she even had the energy to engage in a discussion of such delicacy. She yearned to ride the rest of the way to the fort in silence.

"Never mind," she snapped, staring straight ahead.

"Ho, now! What's this? I must *insist* you tell me about this 'Minnie.' What has she to do with me?" he demanded.

"She's the young Indian woman you ruined, General," she blurted. Suddenly, all the softness had left her voice and again, the hatred seethed as she added, "Surely you haven't forgotten that!"

"Delia, my dear! You slay me! I truly don't know what you're talking about! And besides, is this any way to speak to someone who just saved your delectable little hide? I find your gratitude completely *under*-whelming, I must say!"

"Well, you asked me, General. I was just answering you. What do you have to say for yourself?"

"What happened to 'George?'" he asked, then continued, "I do not recall this event I allegedly participated in. You'll have to illumine me, I'm afraid."

"That day you requisitioned the Indian girl from the guardhouse. One of the Cheyenne captives? Don't tell me you don't remember. I saw you there myself!"

"Of course I remember. But I never laid a hand on her! In fact, I released her! The last time I saw her she was high-tailing it across the prairie as fast as her legs would carry her. I let her go. That's why you're so angry?"

"Yes! I mean, well, no," she answered, confused. "It's what happened after that causes me to be angry. She was savagely attacked, shot and left for dead, sir, and by one of your soldiers!"

"One of *my* soldiers. How do you know it was one of mine?"

She had to think about that. She'd assumed it was one of his men because she didn't believe that anyone stationed at Fort Cobb would be capable of such a thing.

"Well," she hesitated. "I suppose I don't know that. But I can't imagine anyone at Fort Cobb doing anything like that."

His silence condemned her line of thinking more effectively than a rebuttal.

"I'm sorry. You're right. I don't know who attacked her. And apparently, it doesn't matter who did it. I've been told that no one would condemn a white man on the basis of an Indian's testimony. Fair or not, that seems to be the way our justice system works in cases like these. We've decided not to pursue it."

"But you'll hold it against me anyway. And blame me for what happened. Right?"

"Well, it would never have happened if you'd left her alone in the first place." She tried to place severe emphasis on her words, but most of the steam had dissipated from her argument by now. She wished again that she'd never raised the issue.

"Well, I'm sorry for that. I was told she would be a reliable translator. After a while, I realized she didn't have any idea what I was saying to her. I was going to take her back to the fort. Ironically, the woman my scouts had informed me of was Mo-nah-se-tah, my 'bride.' She knows a bit of English."

Cordelia, confused by this revelation, remained unusually quiet. Her head throbbed and the last of her energy ebbed from her shivering body. She thought she'd never been so exhausted in her life.

Custer broke the silence by asking, "How is the woman now? Did she survive?"

"She's improving. And we have taught her about Christ and she's taken Him as her own. Since she was shot in the face, her beauty is gone forever, of course. But she continues to grow stronger—physically and spiritually. No one can destroy the loveliness that comes from *within* her. That beauty continues to blossom."

Custer stopped the horses. "Well, we'll resume our conversation at some later date, my dear. There," he said, pointing toward a light up ahead. "I believe that must be your faithful puppy of a husband. He's out looking for you, no doubt. He'll want to get you to the warmth of a fire as soon as possible, I would imagine."

Cordelia squinted her eyes to try to see her husband.

"That appears to be the place of the buckboard wreckage, isn't it?"

"Yes," he answered. "I believe you're correct."

"But I thought it was much closer to the f-f-fort than this."

"My dear, I'm afraid you were quite foolish to ride out into the wilderness this far. I'm surprised your darling Robert allowed it at all."

"He didn't," she confessed sheepishly. "In fact, he will be frightfully angry with me, I'm afraid. I rode out alone against his wishes. He has told me I am not, under any circumstances, to ride alone. This is all my fault, I hate to say."

"Perhaps I should stay close to protect you from his wrath?"

Cordelia giggled like a little girl, in spite of herself. "Of course not, George! I don't think he is going to beat me or anything!" Then with her face a mask of somberness, she continued, "No, just knowing I've displeased and w-w-worried him will be punishment enough for me. And by disobeying my husband, I have sinned against God, too. That's what grieves me the most. No, I shall never disobey him again."

"Tell that to your husband, Delia. Here he is! Ah, Captain!"

"Cordelia!" Robert raced to her on foot, leaving the others to continue their search of the wreckage. She leaned down for a tender kiss, then explained, "I'm so sorry. I . . ."

"Never mind, darling. Not now. We'll talk about it later. Right now, I'm just so thankful you're alive!"

He placed his hand over her leg, protectively and, with confusion etched on his face, looked up at her "companion."

"General?"

"Captain."

"Robert, I owe my life to him. George just rescued me from the Indians who killed these poor people," she jumped in, gesturing to the overturned wagon. "They were renegades, he says. They captured me earlier and he . . ."

"*George* saved your life?" he interrupted.

"Yes, and in the most amazing fashion, too, I might add. They had me all tied up and . . ."

"Yes," he interrupted a second time. "I want to hear all about it, but my dear, you are soaked to the bone. Let's get you home and into some warm, dry clothes, shall we?"

Robert turned to Custer and offered his hand. Custer took it.

"There are no words to express my gratitude to you, sir. You have not only saved Mrs. Lawson's life, but have returned mine to me, as well."

"It was my honor, Captain. She's quite a woman, this one. You may need to place a tether on her to keep her close from now on, but other than that, she is a most remarkable young woman."

"Yes, a tether and a leather strap to her behind, I think." Robert threatened, only half-jokingly.

"All right, you two. Enough! Can't you see I'm chilled to the bone?"

Leading Sunburst to his own horse, Robert climbed upon Chief and his men followed his lead. Custer, uncharacteristically, dropped back to allow them all to pass and followed them to the fort. As the entourage turned into the gate, Cordelia allowed her gaze to find George Armstrong Custer as he tipped his hat to her and rode off in the direction of the soldier camp.

Fifteen

She was still sleeping when she heard a knock at her door. Groggy, she threw back the heavy comforter and, rubbing her eyes, stumbled to answer it.

"Bess! What is it?"

"Missy, I just heard, and I thought you'd want to know. The soldiers are gettin' ready to go fight them Indians. They're heading out to the Indian camp to wipe 'em off the face of the earth, they said."

Immediately alert, Cordelia gasped, "What?" Her hand flew to her throat. She was afraid to ask the next question, "Why?" but she did.

Bess looked down uncomfortably and fiddled with her apron as she muttered, "'Cuz of what happened to you last night."

"But those Indians weren't from the camp! They were renegades! I told them that last night!" she cried.

"Don't matter, ma'am. They're goin' after all the Indians now. I heard 'em talkin' about it just now when I went to get supplies from the tradin' post! They're all talkin' about it!"

"Where's Robert? Does he know?"

"Yes, ma'am. I reckon he does. I saw him talkin' to some soldiers outside the livery stable. He looked pretty mad, he did!"

"Help me, Bess. I have to stop this right away!" Cordelia whirled into action, stripping off her nightgown and stepping into the first dress she found. She left the house with her hair falling loose around her shoulders—not even taking the time to lace her boots!

It seemed to Cordelia that she was moving through water as she ran the diagonal from the officers' quarters to the headquarters. Every muscle felt sore and bruised. Bursting into Robert's office, she was distressed to find it empty. Quickly, she turned and ran to the livery stable, dodging soldiers and horses, hearing the clank of the metal artillery as they prepared for a march to battle against the unsuspecting—and innocent —Indians.

She met Commander Hazen as he strode toward his headquarters.

"General! Please!" She held to the arm of his rough wool coat and tried to catch her breath. "Please, sir! This is a mistake. You just can't go after the Indians! They didn't do anything! Please don't go! They're innocent! Completely innocent!"

"Mrs. Lawson. We cannot allow this gesture of utter disdain for our women. If we let them get away with it once, they'll do it again and again!" Shaking his head, he firmly declared, "No, we'll have to teach them a lesson they'll not soon forget!"

"But General! You're not listening to me! They are innocent of any wrongdoing! I told you that last night! Those men who attacked me were renegades! If you don't believe me, talk to General Custer. Please! Just talk to him. He'll tell you!"

"General Custer is not in the fort, Mrs. Lawson."

"Then ride out to talk to him. His men are camped less than a mile away! Please talk to him, sir! You can't do this! You can't!"

"I'll do exactly what I see fit to do and will thank you to allow me that privilege, Mrs. Lawson!" the general growled at her. "This is still my fort, madam, and I am still in charge."

"Haven't those poor Indians been through enough, General?"

"Those p. . . Mrs. Lawson!" he barked. "You have gone too far!"

He broke her grasp upon his arm and stamped, fuming, to his office. Just then, she heard the command, "Mount!" The soldiers dutifully mounted their horses, anxious to be going to battle again. Life around the fort had been too slow and tedious for the young men itching for adventure. They took their places in formation, riding two abreast. Cordelia heard the bugle blare out the familiar bars of "Advance" and the officer and first battalion made their way past her toward the gate.

Frantically, she searched for Robert and finally spied him standing on the other side of the stream of soldiers, looking dejected and angry as he watched the soldiers—*his* soldiers— parade by him.

"Robert!" she screamed. Her heart caught in her chest when she saw him lift his eyes to hers. He looked utterly defeated and humiliated.

"What have I done?" she breathed to herself. She had never felt so powerless in her life. Even last night while she was tied and pushed to the ground under the foot of that red-painted savage, she didn't feel this alone and helpless.

She kept repeating, "No!" In disbelief, she followed the long line of horses out the gate. She was aware that Robert was slowly making his way to her, but she couldn't tear her gaze from the straight backs of the men in blue, bound for the Indian camps to destroy the people she had grown to admire.

She thought about throwing herself in front of them but the prairie was too large. They could easily ride around her. She thought about riding ahead to warn the Indians. Sunburst was fast as lightning. But by the time she had him saddled, the soldiers would already be about their gory mission.

Her sight began to fade at the outer edges and her face tingled unexpectedly. Dizziness threatened to envelope her and she staggered several steps before the lone rider caught her eye. He rode to meet the leaders of the cavalry division, Robert's cavalry division. She watched as the officer raised his white-gloved hand in a silent order to halt. Her ears strained to hear what was said, but she could make out none of it.

Leaving the rest of the division, the officer and the lone rider cantered back into the fort. The blond curls bounced across his shoulders with every stride and the swaying buckskin fringe danced as he rode past her without any acknowledgement at all.

"George!" she exhaled, allowing herself a small glimmer of hope for the first time, and followed them into the fort. They dismounted before the commander's office and strode in, the quick tempo of their boots drumming in unison across the wooden boardwalk.

She and Robert met at the horses. They exchanged silent, emotionless looks, then turned their attention to the door of the office and waited. It was then that Cordelia realized she had run out without a wrap of any kind. Until now, the fire of her outrage and desperation had provided warmth enough for this chilled morning.

Condensed breath formed a wreath around the two of them as they waited in hushed agony for the door to open. When it did, Cordelia was the first to move. She leaped onto the boardwalk and clung to the post, searching the faces of the men making their slow exit from the commander's office.

Custer observed Cordelia's screaming emotions lying just under the surface of her control, gazed into her wide, green eyes and slowly made his way to her as the officer climbed onto his horse and took off toward his waiting cavalry. Pulling at each finger of his gloves until his hands were free, he, with great tenderness, lifted her chilly hand to his lips.

"Madam," he whispered huskily. "It's over. They're calling off this absurdity. The commander has decided to investigate the incident further before rendering punishment to the Indians. I will be leading them to the bodies of the men who attacked you. They'll see for themselves that those men were not of these tribes. The ones who troubled you have already paid the price for their crime against you."

He watched her emerald eyes widen in her small, heart-shaped face until he could see nothing else, so drawn was he to their pure, undisguised emotion. Then, behind the sudden down-rushing desolation of her tears, she searched his face with sublime appreciation.

"Oh, George," she sobbed. "How can I ever thank you enough for this? Thank God you came along when you did, or else . . . ." Crystalline tears continued their descent over her reddened cheeks. "Thank you," she whispered as she stood on tiptoe to brush her lips lightly across his cheek in a chaste kiss, a gesture of the depth of her gratitude and emotion.

"Cordelia!" Robert's voice was ice shattering in an empty room, reverberating through her consciousness.

Quickly, she released the general's hand and lowered her eyes to the frosty boards under her feet. She stepped off the boardwalk and drew close to Robert's side, leaning into him for warmth and comfort. He continued to look incredulously at his wife.

"Captain," General Custer barked. "I'd be honored for you to accompany us to investigate the site."

"Yes, I should like to come along, sir. Thank you, sir." Still, his gaze never left Cordelia's blushing face as she continued to carefully examine each thawing blade of grass under her feet.

Addressing her curtly, he said, "Cordelia, I will see you tonight. Go back to the house. I'm sure you'll need to rest today."

"Yes, Robert," she replied, meekly, sneaking a quick peek into his eyes. Looking for a sign that all was well and finding none, she squeezed his hand and turned resolutely toward their living quarters.

Further evidence of Robert's anger toward her was his tone, so harsh she scarcely recognized his voice, as he ordered an enlisted man to saddle Chief and bring him to headquarters.

Stiffly mounting the steps to their front door, Cordelia took one more look their way but they were no longer standing on the boardwalk. She supposed they'd gone into Robert's office to wait for Chief. Meanwhile, the officer had ordered half his men to accompany them on the investigation and the other half to stand down. The latter rode back in disappointment to the huge corral to unsaddle their horses. Thanks to George Armstrong Custer, there would be no battle today.

~*~

Three nights later, Robert sat in his old, familiar chair reading a book he'd started almost a month ago. He picked up his old, familiar pipe, tapped the tobacco into it in the same old, familiar fashion and lit it in four long pulls. The old, familiar aroma of his tobacco filled the room as it wound around his head and traveled upwards.

Everything was old and familiar except the thickness of the

tension between them. Cordelia tried to write a letter to her mother, but rereading the previous two paragraphs, she recognized a sorrowful tone in her letter. She wadded it up and threw it toward the fireplace. It only made it halfway. Out of the corners of her eyes, she peeked at Robert, searching for some reaction to her errant toss, but there was none.

Sighing, she decided to go to bed, though it was still early. Happy voices in the hallway delayed her retreat to the bedroom. She quickly gathered up the wadded letter and tossed it into the flames, watching the edges curl and darken.

Through the clouded glass of the parlor door, Cordelia saw Bess standing with Jeremiah Running Bear at the front door. Bess was smiling, listening to something he was telling her. Coyly she hid her laugh with the back of her hand. Jeremiah reached up and took her hand. For a moment they stood holding hands, and looking more than a little awkward.

Jeremiah had become a frequent visitor now. Cordelia suspected he was postponing Minnie's return to her people in order to offer him the opportunity for these visits. Bess denied any kind of romance between them, of course, but Cordelia knew better.

"Kiss her," Cordelia silently urged him. But he didn't. Instead, he did an abrupt half-bow and rushed out the front door. As Bess turned to walk back toward the kitchen, she found the smiling face of Cordelia Lawson peeking through the smoky glass of the door.

Cordelia giggled and stuck her tongue out at Bess. Bess wagged her finger at her and continued her trek to her own quarters.

Turning with another laugh, Cordelia caught Robert looking at her sternly. Immediately the smile disappeared, replaced by the somber expression she had borne for the past several days.

"Robert, how many times do I have to apologize before you forgive my foolishness?"

No response. Nothing. He just bent to his book and pipe again.

Other times, she had skulked away from him but this time she straightened to her full height, pulled her chin up to a determined angle and walked directly to him, kneeling with her hands on his knees. Taking his book from him, she closed it, careful to mark his page, and placed it on the little side table. Imploringly, she looked into his face.

"Robert."

"What do you want, Cordelia?" His voice was old and tired.

"I just want you to love me."

"I do."

"Then I want you to *show me* you love me. I want things to be back to normal between us."

"You want a lot, my dear."

"You know I can't bear this, Robert. I can't bear to disappoint you. I can't stand it when you push me away from you. I love you. Only you. You teach about forgiveness. Why can't you forgive me?"

"I think I have forgiven you. But I don't seem to be able to engage my heart just now. You say you don't want to disappoint me. Yet I'm disappointed. You say you don't want to make me angry. Yet I'm angry. Angry and humiliated."

"Why humiliated? I guess I just don't understand."

"Cordelia," he barked, exasperated. "Let me see if I can make you understand. I command a cavalry troop. I am a captain in the United States Army. And I can't even control my wife's foolish actions! How do you think that makes me look to my men, or to my superiors? Am I the one who rescues you? Am I the one you turn to? No. General Custer is! How do you think I look to your new friend, *George,* when you stand on tiptoe to kiss him in my very presence, as if I'm not even there?"

"Robert, I have explained that again and again! Please! It was impulsive, I know, but he saved my life *twice!* For I know that if I believed I had caused the loss of even one innocent life, I would have gone mad! I would have had to fill my time with nightly wanderings through the prairie mist, an ethereal being, a lost spirit at war with body and mind. He stopped that battle when no one else could. He saved those lives . . . and by so doing, he saved mine."

She noted him tense when she said that. Quickly she said, "I know you tried to stop it, too, Robert and I'm sure that had something to do with Hazen changing his mind. It's just that . . . well, it's just . . ."

"Do me a huge favor, wife. Don't condescend to me. That, I will not tolerate!" he said with quiet intensity.

"I'm sorry, Robert. Can't you understand that I was just . . . grateful to him? That's all!"

"Cordelia, I was grateful, too," Robert explained softly. "But I didn't kiss him."

She sat back abruptly on her heels, unable to speak. She had to admit he'd made a good point—a very good point. She hadn't thought of that. She began to question whether there was another reason she'd kissed him. She continued to study her hands for a moment longer before offering, "Again, I'll tell you. I'm so sorry. I'm going to bed now, darling. Won't you come with me tonight?"

"No, I don't think so. You go on," he told her, reaching for his book and pipe once more.

Sadly, she rose and trudged into the bedroom. This would be another night she'd cry herself to sleep.

~*~

The next day she awakened to a glorious morning. Cordelia breathed in the fresh air as she curried Sunburst, who busily munched on a fresh installment of oats. His coat gleamed golden in the sunshine.

Though it was still winter, it felt like spring on the prairie today. The wind whipped the tall prairie grass back and forth. Birds flitted and twittered over the landscape. The sky was a brilliant blue, punctuated with clouds so white she had to shield her eyes from their brightness.

She rubbed her hand behind each stroke of the brush. His rich coat felt soft and silky smooth to her touch. As she moved toward his hindquarters, Sunburst turned his head to nuzzle her shoulder, then shoved her away from him.

"Stop that! I'm almost finished," she scolded. She knew that the enlisted men were in charge of grooming the officers' mounts, and usually performed this duty twice daily, but this was something she wanted to do today. She could talk to Sunburst about anything. He proved to be a very good listener.

Clapping the dust from her hands, she lifted her head, hearing the tinkling sound of laughter carried by the breeze. As she poked her head around the stall, she saw Minnie walking toward the house from the garden, carrying a basket of turnip greens, their winter crop. Next to her, walked Todd Otis, tall and graceful. They were lost in conversation—at least Todd was in conversation. Minnie just listened, cackling openly in staccato bursts from time to time. The sound of Todd's deep laughter floated behind them. He took her elbow protectively as she stepped onto the porch in front of the kitchen.

Cordelia watched as he lifted an errant strand of her raven black hair from her face and moved it behind her ear. Once more, worry clouded Cordelia's countenance. Todd was not free to take such liberties with Min-nin-ne-wah-hah-ket. He was, after all, a married man. And she was, after all, an Indian.

She shook her head in disbelief that she'd just formed that thought. She had always believed she was above that sort of thing, that her own mind was somehow exempt from the prejudices that directed other people to make such distinctions. But she had to admit that it bothered her to see how close Minnie and Todd had become. To Cordelia, Todd was like a little brother. She felt protective and proprietary at the same time!

It was time, she decided. Time to take Minnie back to her own people. Yes, she was a joy to have around. She was bright and had picked their language up with surprising ease. She was hardworking, always pleasant and grateful for everything that had been done for her.

Still it was time. Her cheek had healed without complication. Though that reddened scar would mark her forever, she no longer had any problem eating or drinking. She could move her mouth naturally and open it wide for Doc. Her arm had mended, too. Doc still kept it wrapped with stiff cotton dressings, but she was using her hand and arm without any problem. Her pain had all but disappeared and her demeanor demonstrated that she was not mentally deranged as a result of her experience. A lesser woman might have been.

No, on the contrary, she had proven herself to be completely open, hard-working, lovable and capable over the past several weeks. Her honesty and integrity were above reproach.

Cordelia knew she would miss her greatly, as would her staff, but she knew the time had come. She decided to broach the subject with Robert and Todd that evening. It would be difficult. She didn't look forward to bringing up an issue like this one to Robert regarding the Indians. Anything pertaining to the Indians was a delicate subject these days, but not as risky as the mention of one certain flamboyant general's name.

It was Friday. So she knew Todd would be dining with them. He dined with them several evenings every week now. It was such a relief this week to have him at the dinner table. Cordelia was beginning to lose patience with Robert's glum silence, and having Todd's cheerful presence in their home brought much-needed life and vitality back into her existence.

Yes, tonight would be the night. She wanted to propose the possibility of accompanying Minnie when she went back to her people. Jeremiah had already offered to escort her to and from the Indian village. Cordelia knew she'd never venture away from the fort unaccompanied again. Still, this would be a difficult topic to introduce and she feared that her request would cause Robert to explode with new objections. But since he was upset with her anyway, she reasoned she had nothing to lose.

"If he denies me the right to go to the Indian camp with her, I'll accept that without murmur," she told Sunburst, as he chomped away on his oats, unconcerned. "I'll obey his every desire. I'll . . . but what harm is there is going to the village with her? I mean, Jeremiah will be right there next to me! There would be nothing to fear from the Indians. Besides, they have repeatedly asked for me to come to sketch them."

She absently stroked Sunburst's massive neck and asked him, "What would be so terrible about riding into the village during the day and riding back before Robert returns from work? What do you think about that, boy? We could just go during the day to sketch some village scenes, and get to know some of them. I mean, I would need to check on Minnie from time to time, wouldn't I?"

Sunburst chomped away. The twitching of his ears was the only sign that he was listening to the sound of her voice. "Yes, I could do that. Robert may not even need to know . . ."

She stopped herself immediately. "Of course he needs to know! I mustn't hide *anything* from him. His trust in me has suffered enough without my adding to his pain."

She tossed the brush into the tool bin and brushed the dust off her hands once more. "But Sunburst, what if he says no? What do I do then? I'll accept it. That's what I'll do. I'll be good and submissive. I'll do the right thing. I'll make him proud of me again. But . . ." she cocked her head to the side and heaved a great sigh. "Oh, who knows *what* I'll do. Who *ever* knows what I'll do?"

With that, she slapped her horse on the rump and headed back to the house.

Sixteen

At precisely 5:42 that evening, as they sat around the dining room table, they all heard the sounds of a wagon pull into the fort. It was almost dark, much too late for traffic, so Robert went quietly to the window to investigate.

"My word," he said. "It's a stagecoach! At this hour!"

Todd's fork fell out of his usually nimble fingers. "A coach?" he asked. "Is anyone getting off?"

Robert squinted his eyes, and moved his head side-to-side, trying to get a better look through the thick glass. "I don't think so. The driver seems to be asking directions or something. One of our guards is pointing over this way. No! Wait! Someone *is* getting off."

Todd and Cordelia locked eyes as Robert exclaimed, "Good heavens! It's a woman! Now who . . .?" He turned his eyes upon his friend.

"Todd, I think you'd better come take a look."

Todd, frozen in his chair, could only shift his hopeful eyes to Robert's face. "Come here, man. Come see if it's her!"

Suddenly Todd moved with such speed that he almost

knocked his chair over backwards. He flew to the window and watched as the guard took the bags the driver handed down to him. The woman, dressed in a dark traveling gown, picked up a bundle from inside the coach and putting that bundle to her shoulder, turned to their direction and carefully picked her way across the grounds toward them.

"Nicole," he croaked, tears springing to his bright blue eyes. Turning to his friends, he laughed, "It's Nicole! She's here! She's really here!"

In the next second, he had exited the room, leapt down the steps to the parade ground and stood enveloping this poor woman in those big arms, kissing her lips, her cheeks, burying his own wet face into the crook of her silky neck. Then, standing back, he took the bundle from her and examined it carefully.

Robert and Cordelia watched from the window. The growing darkness could not cover the radiance in the smile he flashed at them. Then he ushered his wife and baby into their presence.

Cordelia, who had long awaited her coming, felt suddenly shy and awkward, and wondered what to say, what to do with this new arrival to the fort. She was unprepared for the emotion that pricked her own eyes and stung her throat in anticipation of this meeting.

When Nicole walked in the door, Cordelia rushed to her side, crushing her in a huge embrace. She was so fragile, so pale, so thin. Cordelia held her gently in her arms, afraid she'd break her if she held her any more tightly. The all-black traveling garb accentuated her thinness, her pallor. But even so, she was utterly lovely, like a beautiful little bird too weak to fly.

"Please come in, come in. You must be exhausted." As she ushered Nicole to the divan, she called out for Bess.

Before they could sit down, Todd next to Nicole, holding

his daughter in his arms as if he'd been doing this all his life, Bess was there.

"Bess, meet Mrs. Otis. She's just arrived on the coach. Make sure the lieutenant's quarters are ready for her, will you? She'll need to lie down soon. And have Lucy bring us some tea or coffee or something." Cordelia could barely contain her excitement.

"My pleasure, Miz Lawson," Bess replied. Then to Nicole, she said, "So nice to finally get to meet you, Miz Otis."

"Thank you, Bess," came Nicole's exhausted reply.

Cordelia observed the two lovebirds maternally as they sat side-by-side in awkward silence, obviously aware of her attention. She didn't want to stare, but she couldn't seem to take her eyes off them.

Not knowing exactly how to break the awkward silence, Cordelia asked, "May I see the baby?"

Todd, as if waking up suddenly, said, "Yes, of course," and handed her the treasure in his arms.

Gingerly receiving the baby, Cordelia stared into the bright blue eyes of Nora Alice Otis. "Oh, Todd, Nicole, she's such a beauty! And she has Todd's big, blue eyes! How lovely!"

They didn't seem to hear. Todd's lovesick eyes traced every contour of his beloved's face as she soulfully returned his gaze. With the same surprising tenderness Cordelia had witnessed once before, Todd reached up to touch Nicole's cheek, lightly caressing her delicate jaw, then holding her chin in his trembling fingers.

"My love," he whispered. She smiled at him with such complete happiness that light seemed to fill her eyes.

Cordelia realized, in a heartbeat, that she'd had nothing to fear from poor, scarred Minnie. This exquisite woman held Todd's heart totally and completely, and nothing she'd ever witnessed compared to this tender moment in time.

Bess entered the parlor. "Lieutenant, your quarters is ready."

"Shall we?" he asked Nicole, shyly.

"Yes, please."

Turning her attention to Cordelia and the baby, Nicole breathed, so quietly she could barely hear her, "I'm sorry to leave so soon. But I am dreadfully tired. Perhaps we can visit tomorrow?"

"Oh, yes, absolutely," Cordelia blurted, feeling big-boned and awkward compared to this delicate creature before her.

"Thank you," she whispered. Todd held her as she stood. "Thank you, Cordelia," he told her as he bent to take the baby in his arms. "I'll show my wife to our quarters."

Cordelia noted the caress in the words, "my wife," and nodded in acknowledgement. "Please let us know if there's anything you need, Todd. Anything! You have five of us over here longing to help in any way we can."

"Thank you," Nicole responded, sweetly. "That's good to know." Then the Otis family disappeared behind the door to their new home.

Robert, Bess and Cordelia stood watching after them for a full minute before any of them moved. Then Cordelia unexpectedly collapsed onto the divan, burying her face in her hands, weeping as if she'd lost her best friend.

And in a way, she had. Seeing the love so obvious in Todd and Nicole only accentuated the estrangement between herself and Robert. Robert moved toward her momentarily, as if he were going to comfort her, then retreated to the bedroom, leaving his wife in tears and Bess collecting the dishes from the table, shaking her head.

~*~

The next day, while Cordelia was in the kitchen visiting with Bess, Lucy and Minnie, they all ceased from their labors preparing dinner when they heard a baby crying. Each looked at the other and smiled.

Bess spoke up first. "There's just something special about having a baby around."

The baby didn't cry for long. And the kitchen staff resumed their preparations. The new "family" across the hall was coming over for dinner this evening. It would be their first real chance to get to know Nicole. She had been so exhausted and so happy to see Todd the night before that little was accomplished in making her acquaintance, as far as Cordelia was concerned.

Cordelia enjoyed meeting new people—especially one so eagerly anticipated as Nicole. Todd had told her that his wife was uncommonly beautiful, but he couldn't have described to what degree that was true.

She was of moderate height—fully as tall as Cordelia—but willowy thin and pale, the poor thing. When she walked, she seemed to glide across the room making no sound except the subtle swish of her dress along the floor. Every gesture was poised and graceful, as was every turn of her head on that exquisitely sculptured throat of white porcelain. Her hair, soft and dark—though not nearly as dark as Minnie's—was braided and coiled at the nape of her neck. Even after days of travel, every hair was in place when she arrived.

Her full lips were of the palest pink color and the corners actually turned up a little when she smiled. Her hazel eyes appeared huge in such a thin face, but were framed by thick, dark lashes and perfect arching brows.

There was something angelic about Nicole, Cordelia thought. No, not angelic really, but certainly something ethereal, not of this world. That was it. Ethereal!

While she stood there, peeling potatoes, Cordelia made up her mind to honor Todd's request to paint their family portrait. In fact, it would be a pleasure.

"I can't wait to see that baby," Lucy was saying.

"She's a pretty, little thing," Bess offered.

"Do you think Mrs. Otis will let me hold her?"

Cordelia chuckled, "Lucy, I'll bet you'll get plenty of that in the days and weeks to come. There are plenty of times a woman needs to have someone reliable to sit with her child. And I can certainly vouch for your reliability."

She gave the potato an extra couple of strokes with her knife, then added, mischievously, "Of course, you'll have to fight *me* for her."

"Miz Lawson, when are you and the Captain gonna get us a baby to love on?" Bess asked innocently.

At the moment, Cordelia could think of no reply to that. The question seemed to paralyze her, in fact. Then she said a trifle too cheerfully, "Oh, I don't know. We haven't really talked about it. It would be hard to have a baby out here in the middle of nowhere."

"My people have them, no problem," Minnie volunteered. "Plenty of them."

They all laughed.

"Well, you have a point there, Minnie," Cordelia agreed, still chuckling.

"Lucy, check those rolls and see if they're risin'," Bess instructed. Then she explained, "These are Lucy's first yeast rolls. She did 'em all by herself, she did," then cackled a little as she watched her daughter's face.

"Yes ma'am, they're rising. Look Minnie!"

"Um," said Minnie, disinterestedly.

"Why are you so glum today, girl?" Bess wanted to know.

"What means 'glum?'"

"Quiet, and sad-like."

"I no sad-like," she protested, but her face said otherwise. Cordelia watched her closely for a few moments.

"Are you certain about that, Princess?" she asked.

"Yes, ma'am." Almost as an afterthought, she looked up at Cordelia and asked, "Ma'am, do I have to meet that lady?"

"Why, yes, Minnie! It is the polite thing to do! We are going to be living very close to her. It's only fair that she meet the ones she's likely to be spending most of her time with! Why do you ask?"

"I go outside to make water," she said, hurriedly getting up from her stool, where she had been shucking the last of the winter corn.

"Oh, no you don't." Cordelia blocked her exit and put her hands on Minnie's strong shoulders. "What's wrong?"

"Nothing."

"Look at me, Minnie. Tell me what's bothering you."

"Lieutentant Otis won't make talk to me now, will he? He won't be my friend now. She here now. I like Lieutentant Otis. He is my friend."

"Oh, Minnie," Cordelia said, hugging her close. "He's still your friend. You knew he was married, didn't you?"

"Yes, ma'am," she said, pulling back and looking at the floor. "And I know white man don't want no Cheyenne wife. But he told me I was his friend."

"Well, friends are too hard to come by to cast them aside so easily. You and the lieutenant have had some good talks and have gotten to know each other very well. I don't think that will change. Although, I doubt if he'll have as much time for *any* of us anymore, now that his family is here with him. Sweet Minnie, can't you be happy for him? You should have seen his face last night."

"Jes' like a little puppy-dog he was!" Bess cackled. "I never saw that look on his face before!" Cutting her eyes toward Cordelia, she added, "But I seen that look on the Captain's face lots o' times!"

"Humph." Cordelia rolled her eyes ceiling-ward and said, "You haven't seen that look on his face lately, I'll bet."

"Hmm. No, ma'am, I haven't," she agreed. "But I bet I'll see it agin' real soon."

"I wonder." Cordelia spoke so softly Bess could hardly hear her.

~*~

That night, before dinner, Todd and family came shyly into the parlor. Todd cradled baby Nora on one side and held Nicole's hand on the other.

"Both my girls. I still can't believe it," he grinned, looking from one to the other.

"I'm so delighted for you, Todd. Mrs. Otis, I've heard so much about you. I just know we'll be good friends."

"Todd's letters are full of you, too, Mrs. Lawson. I'd be honored to be your friend. You're a strong and courageous woman. I admire that already."

"Why, thank you," Cordelia replied, surprised. "Please, come sit by me until dinner is served."

The two women retreated to the divan as Todd crossed to his customary chair across from Robert's. Robert's chair was empty. He hadn't come in yet from some projects he had to evaluate, Cordelia had explained earlier.

As the young women chatted easily, Todd looked from one to the other. He couldn't help but compare. They were exact opposites of each other. Nicole's skin was pale, her hair dark and straight. Cordelia was all peaches and cream with that little dusting of freckles over her nose and she had that crop of curling red hair piled atop her head. Where Nicole was frail and delicate, Cordelia was strong and hearty. Being around her, you could sense her energy and vitality, whereas, Nicole seemed to struggle to raise a thin arm, so fragile he feared she would break. They were daylight and dark, night and day. Yet, both were beautiful, inside and out.

Just then the parlor doors opened and Bess, Lucy . . . and Minnie brought in the food. Bess and Lucy stood facing the divan after they had carefully arranged the meal on the table. Minnie stood back against the wall with her head down.

"Oh, good! Mrs. Otis, now you'll get to meet these very special people." Cordelia rushed to Bess's side, taking her hand in both of her own. "You've already met Bess. She runs the place around here."

"Oh, Miz Lawson, I don't neither," said Bess, bashfully.

Cordelia continued, "This is Lucy, Bess's daughter. Lucy is my prize pupil—then again, she's my *only* pupil," Cordelia laughed, "and she is a great help to all of us." She kissed Lucy's cheek and moved to Min-nin-ne-wah-hah-ket.

Taking her by the shoulders, she moved Minnie closer to Bess and Lucy. "And this is our newest addition. We call her Minnie." Turning back to her friend, she said, "You tell her your real name."

Minnie still looked at the floor but softly uttered, "Min-nin-ne-wah-hah-ket. It mean 'little whirlwind.'"

Nicole stood and effortlessly transported herself (and once again Cordelia marveled at her new friend's elegance) to Minnie's side. She took her hand and held it to her own white cheek.

Startled, Minnie raised her eyes to find tears streaming down Nicole's cheeks.

"Miz Otis! Why . . . do you cry?" she asked.

"My husband wrote to me about you. He's kept me

informed about your recovery and now that I see your beauty, my heart breaks to think about your pain. Are you healed then?"

"Yes, ma'am. Almost healed. No pain, now."

"I'm so glad," Nicole said. It was obvious that Nicole cared a great deal for this once-beautiful Indian girl. Cordelia found Nicole's tender emotion very moving.

Turning to the other two women, Nicole regally touched each of them on the shoulder and said, "I'm so happy to meet you both. You have been very helpful to my husband while he's been here alone. I hope I'll be able to take some of that burden from you now that I'm finally here where I belong." She glanced at her husband and smiled.

Bess spoke first, "He ain't no burden, ma'am. You got a good man there."

"He keeps us all laughing around here, Mrs. Otis," Lucy grinned.

"Thank you. Yes, he's a very special man." She floated to the divan and sat smiling in his direction, signaling the completion of the introductions.

Just then, the door opened and Robert entered the room like the gentleman he was. He bowed low before Nicole and kissed her hand. "Mrs. Otis, once again I am happy to make your acquaintance." As he motioned for them to take their seats at the dining table, he continued, "It's about time you got here to take this long, tall fellow off our hands. He can be quite a nuisance, you know."

"Thank you, friend," Todd said laughingly. Then to Nicole, "Wait until you taste this food."

Lucy moved quickly to Nicole's side and asked, "May I take care of little Nora for you during the meal, ma'am?"

"Well . . . yes, I think that would be wonderful, Lucy.

Thank you. I've just fed her so I think she'll go off to sleep very quickly."

Lucy took the baby in her arms and beamed at everyone.

Robert blessed the food and thanked God for bringing Nicole back to her husband safe and sound. Then he nodded to the staff and they left for the kitchen, each chattering on about the baby.

"I guess you know that little girl will be spoiled rotten before too long. It's been a long time since we've had a baby around," Cordelia smiled. "In fact, she's the first!" Looking at Robert, she continued, "Who knows? Maybe we'll enjoy her so much we'll have one of our own before long!" She was only half-way kidding. Robert made no comment.

Todd broke the tension by saying, "Come on! Let's dig in!" and then bowls were passed, meat was served and drinks were poured. There was never a quiet moment as they talked and laughed throughout the meal. They had a lovely dinner and coffee afterwards.

Todd and Nicole expressed their appreciation for the meal and the hospitality. As Cordelia and Robert waved them home across the hallway, Lucy came out of their door.

"Little Nora is asleep now. She's a good baby, ma'am."

"Thank you, Lucy," Nicole replied, and then glided into her quarters for the night.

Meanwhile, Robert turned away from Cordelia's upturned lips and walked into the bedroom like a tired, old man. Her smile faded as she stood looking after him.

Slowly she closed the parlor door, blew out the lights and made her careful way into the bedroom, which had lately become several degrees colder!

~*~

Their little Sunday morning meeting was almost unbearable for a number of those gathered in the hospital. The hospital ward in which they met was a large open room lined with out-sized bunks that could hold two patients when needed. A small table equipped with a lantern and basin separated each bunk. The stove rested upon a brick platform situated in the center of the room. The stove-pipe rose straight up from the stove, made a right-angled turn and traveled to the back of the room and out the wall. To either side of the stove was a large table with chairs. A chessboard was set up on one of the tables. Books and bones, or dominoes, were stacked on the other.

Today the chairs formed three lines for their little "congregation." Much squirming and exchanging of glances was noted by all but the one doing the preaching . . . as well as Cordelia.

Robert had chosen his text carefully, Ephesians 5:22-24, "Wives, submit yourselves unto your own husbands, as unto the Lord. For the husband is the head of the wife, even as Christ is the head of the church; and he is the saviour of the body. Therefore as the church is subject unto Christ, so let the wives be to their own husbands in everything."

It was painfully apparent to all gathered that his lecture was for one pair of ears only. Cordelia's! Even George Custer, who sat in the back of the room (actually half-lying on one of the hospital beds) kept cutting his eyes in her direction.

But Cordelia sat with straight back, head held high, hands in her lap, holding her Bible, and listened attentively to her tedious husband. She looked neither left nor right, and other than to survey the words on the page, never took her eyes from Robert's face.

After the meeting, Doc Anthony closed in prayer and asked God's forgiveness on all those gathered therein. At the final "Amen," people began to chatter as they gathered their bags and Bibles and headed to the Anthonys' quarters for Sunday dinner.

Robert closed his Bible, gathered his notes and tucked them under his arm. As he walked resolutely toward the Anthonys', Doc caught up with him and said, "Interesting lesson, son. I've never actually witnessed the word of God used as a club before. It seems you may have forgotten the next verse, 'Husbands, love your wives, even as Christ also loved the church and gave himself for it.' Excuse me. I have to catch up with my dear wife." Then he jogged the few yards over to Ela. Robert stopped in his tracks as he watched his friend move away from him, wondering what in the world he had been talking about!

General and Mrs. Hazen moved to Robert's side. "Good sermon today, Captain," the general told him, nodding in his wife's direction. "A good reminder for *all* the wives." Mrs. Hazen laughed good-naturedly and took her husband's arm.

"Captain, we certainly enjoy the portrait your Cordelia presented to us last week, don't we, dear? It was worth the long wait, I assure you. I finally found a place for it in our quarters. It looks marvelous there, doesn't it, dear?"

"Yes, she's humbly placed it directly over the fireplace mantle in the parlor," her husband teased.

While they were talking, Cordelia and Nicole ambled by, deep in conversation. Nicole had chosen to wear as a head covering, in lieu of the bonnets worn by most of the women, a soft scarf of black Spanish lace. Todd lagged behind to walk with Robert, waiting patiently for his turn to speak to his friend.

"Come on, dear. We mustn't monopolize the captain's attentions!" Mrs. Hazen said, without a word to Lieutenant Otis. With that, the Hazens walked away.

Turning his attention to Todd, Robert resumed his walk

toward the Anthonys' quarters. "Look, Robert," Todd began, "this may be none of my concern, but as your friend I feel compelled to tell you that you are making an ass of yourself. I don't know exactly what Cordelia did to make you so angry but *nothing* she could have done could justify your behavior over the past week—and this so-called sermon today.

"You know what my wife just told me?" he asked. "She said that all that I wrote about the people on this fort was accurate, except for what I wrote about you. She couldn't understand why I'd told her that watching you and Cordelia reminded me of us. She said she hoped we would never be like the two of you!

"I had to tell her that you were not yourself lately, that she hadn't seen the side of you that I called my friend. Now I don't know what is going on in that stubborn head of yours, Robert, but whatever it is, you have to address this thing between you two and resolve it at once!"

Robert stared at Todd for a moment, then said, "You're exactly right, my friend."

"You think so?" Todd asked, hopefully. This had been easier than he'd imagined!

"Oh, absolutely. This *is* none of your concern." And with that, he changed his direction and strode, alone, toward his own quarters.

Todd looked after him in open-mouthed surprise. Then, shaking his head, he ran after his wife and Cordelia.

George Custer, carefully and uncharacteristically bringing up the rear, leaned back against the block wall of the hospital, tugging at the corner of his heavy moustache and watched the procession toward the Anthonys'. He especially enjoyed watching Cordelia stroll languorously next to her new friend, who was too frail to keep up with Cordelia's usual fast-paced strides.

"Nicole is pretty, yes," he thought, "but my taste goes towards those with more . . . what is it Cordelia has? Fire? Spirit? Yes, but that's not it exactly. No. Perhaps it's energy and passion. That's what it is! Pure passion. For life. For her beliefs, and yes, probably even for that childish husband of hers. She reminds me so much of my Libby that being with her makes me feel quite at home! I just wonder . . ."

He allowed that absurd thought to trail out of his mind as he turned his collar up to the chilly wind and mounted his horse, Dandy. He'd had enough of "civilized society" for one day. He suddenly felt the need for the company of his dogs.

He always had dogs with him—sometimes two or three and sometimes forty! One thing was certain; he preferred their company to any of these people—except perhaps one.

Seventeen

"Robert, where were you? We kept thinking you'd be there for Sunday dinner, but you never showed up! Are you feeling all right, darling?" The concern in her voice was genuine, he decided, feeling the first twinge of shame creep into his conscious thought.

"I just wanted to be alone today. Bess made me a ham sandwich and I tried to read a little. But I must have fallen asleep. What time is it?"

"Almost 2:30. The others are still at the Anthonys' quarters. But I just couldn't enjoy myself over there without you. I was afraid you weren't feeling well."

"I suppose they're all over there talking about my sermon. What did you think of it, Cordelia?"

"No, no one said a word about it, Robert. Not to me, anyway. What did I think of it?" Her eyes turned upwards and her thin index finger rested next to her mouth in a thoughtful pose. "Hmm. Well, you did an excellent job expositing the text, Robert. It was very accurate, as far as I could tell. And I'm sure we all need to be reminded of that text from time to time.

"But I've studied Ephesians many times so I was pretty familiar with it. Others may not be. It was likely very relevant to those more unfamiliar, like Nicole, for instance. Now that she's reunited with her husband it will be important for her to understand the wife's role of submission to her husband, not that I've noticed any *un*submissiveness in her. But I, myself, have no problem with the concept, especially with a husband as fine as you are, my love."

Her words fanned his shame into flame as he leaned forward in his chair, grasping his head in his hands. He burst into tears before her.

"Robert! My word! What's wrong with you?" She caressed his shoulders as they shook with his heavy sobs.

"Please . . . just leave me alone, Cordelia. I can't . . . talk to you just now," he managed to get out.

Feeling his rejection again, she returned to the safety of her bedroom, lying on their soft bed, and listened, in agony, to his sobs.

She woke some time later when he knelt beside her. "Cordelia," he whispered. "Cordelia, wake up!"

Seeing the way she looked right then, warmed by the fire-light, he almost decided against waking her. His hand tentatively touched the wild-tangled mass of tawny fire-spun hair on the pillow, and seeing her lithe-limbed, sweet curving, something deep inside gripped his heart hard.

Slowly, her heavily-lidded eyes fluttered open and settled that infinitely wise gaze on him. She stretched in a most fetching way, then murmured softly, "I must have fallen asleep. I'm sorry." She made a motion to get up, but he pushed her gently back to the bed, finding his place next to her.

"No, my love. I'm the one who's sorry—in more ways than one, I fear. I have been a sorry husband to you, Cordelia. And I'm sorry for the way I've treated you. In fact, the thought of my actions toward you is intolerable to me! I am afraid it will take some time to undo the damage I've caused, both to us and to the others who witnessed my brutality toward you."

"Robert, you haven't been brutal."

"Yes, I have! Doc told me this morning that I used the scriptures as a club. He was right. May God forgive my soul! I don't deserve your forgiveness—or His—yet I'm asking you for just that. Will you forgive me, Cordelia? I've been a fool and a child about all of this. I let my pride get the best of me. I shall spend the rest of my life making it up to you, if you'll only let me."

She saw such pain in those deep, brown eyes that she could scarcely bear the sight. "Yes, Robert. Yes, I forgive you. We have both been foolish, my love. But we can start afresh. That's the lovely thing about love. There's an unlimited supply of it!"

Her smile was radiant as he bent his head to her bosom and cried again. She held him, stroking his head, offering what comfort she could to a heart bruised by the recognition of his own sinfulness.

She caught his face between her two slim, surprisingly strong hands. Bending to him, she softly, sweetly, clung her mouth to his, her lips trembling against his with such anguished tenderness that their warmth breached the very last of his defenses.

He told her one more thing before he lost himself completely in the comfort of her arms. He whispered, "I've missed you."

"And I, you," she smiled back in return. "Welcome home!"

And such was the reconciliation of Robert and Cordelia Lawson. They never left their bedroom the rest of the day, except for the occasional hurried trip to the privy and back. And Bess made sure that absolutely nothing or no one disturbed them.

Part Three

Eighteen

~~~

February 2, 1869

Cordelia slowly rode alongside Min-nin-ne-wah-hah-ket on their way to the Cheyenne camp. Jeremiah Running Bear rode behind them, eyes darting to and fro, conscious of his obligation to get them there safely. The prairie grass energetically waved them along their short journey.

Indian Territory was lushly blanketed with thick native grasses; big and little blue-stem, Indian grass, sawgrass, and witch grass. The reason the large herds of buffalo loved this country was because of the abundant and highly nutritious grasses here. Their roots reached deep into the earth, protecting it from threatening erosion brought about by the torrential rains and ever-swirling winds. These roots also acted like a massive sponge holding precious water during times of drought.

The buffalo, to a lesser degree, and the occasional wildfires, to a greater degree, kept the grasses under control. Other vegetation across the expansive plains was mesquite, sage, cactus and thorny shrubs. The stunted trees, which all grew leaning in the direction of the persistent wind, were red cedar, blackjack oak, cottonwood, hackberry, chinery oak, and an occasional willow. These grew mostly in the ravines, gullies and creek bottoms. If they happened to take root elsewhere, they rarely survived the harsh growing conditions.

Gazing upon her surroundings with an artist's eye, Cordelia marveled at the textures and hues of this beautiful grassland. Besides, studying the countryside took her mind off the difficult task at hand. They continued to ride in silence.

Cordelia and Minnie shared two mixed emotions, making this the longest mile they could remember. Cordelia was excited and exuberant about the imminent opportunity she had to visit the Indian encampment at last, to see first-hand how the Cheyenne live. However, looking at Minnie's proud profile, her heart was seized with sorrow, knowing that awaiting her in much too short a time was a tearful goodbye. Then she would turn back toward the fort without her friend.

Min-nin-ne-wah-hah-ket, on the other hand, was filled with excitement and exhilaration to be able, at last, to rejoin what family and friends she had left in her own village, steeped in her own traditions. Once more, she would enjoy the company of her mother and father. However, she was also filled with foreboding as she contemplated her reception back into the tribe—she had lived with the whites for over two months. And there was the matter of her assault by that filthy soldier. She shuddered at the thought. Absently her hand drifted to the scar on her right cheek.

Cheyenne women were the most chaste and modest of all the tribes. How would the other women in the tribe view her? And what about the men? She remembered the oath her father had made with Black Kettle and his son, Gray Horses Coming.

She was to have become his bride by now. Would he still want her, scarred and ruined as she was? Was he even alive? Did he survive the massacre? She didn't know. She had dared not ask Running Bear, afraid of what his response would be.

And then there was the other thing—the thing she didn't care to admit even to herself. She had grown accustomed to her life with the whites. She had come to love Cordelia, Todd, Dr. and Mrs. Anthony, and even the captain, a little. Bess and Lucy had become like her own family. And they were of the black skin, far worse in the eyes of "the People" (as she referred to her tribe) than being white. She had gotten used to being warm and dry, to being well fed and protected. The work wasn't nearly as hard and the company was always pleasant. She would miss these things. She would miss speaking in the white tongue and wearing the comfortable clothing Bess had made for her.

Her eyes filled with tears as she remembered the tight hug Bess had given her when she left the fort. Lucy had kissed her poor, scarred cheek and told her to come back to see them whenever she could. Minnie steeled herself against her rising emotion as she presented each with a gift. Since she didn't have access to the leather she normally used, she gave them each a hand-painted bag made of leftover muslin as a way of thanking them for all they'd done for her. The bags were lovely examples of the precision work of the Cheyenne, with colorful markings and figures on it. Bess and Lucy were truly touched by the expression of her friendship and appreciation.

Minnie glanced at Cordelia's pert profile and her heart seized with sorrow as she imagined the difficult goodbye awaiting them when her friend turned back to the fort without her. Still, she successfully fought back the threatening tears. Instead, she fixed her gaze on the distant signs of life in the village ahead—the sinewy plumes of gray-white smoke writhing over the tipis, and the smoky tips of the lodge poles now coming into view.

Both women felt their heart rates quicken as they spotted them. They looked at each other with eyes close to panic. They were almost there!

Running Bear finally broke the silence by saying, "Your parents will be watching for your return. They are overjoyed at your coming, Min-nin-ne-wah-hah-ket."

She merely nodded. Words would not come. Even Cordelia's usual chatter failed her at that moment.

Suddenly, a cry rang out as the Indian people ran out to greet the little entourage. Cordelia was surprised to see the open expressions of joy on their faces, having thought these a stoic and stern people, with Minnie's light-heartedness as the exception.

Quickly, Minnie was surrounded, and her horse was led to a spot just outside the village where an older couple waited patiently. Minnie dismounted hastily and ran to them, clinging to her mother and finally letting the sobs come forth.

It was a painfully sweet scene for Cordelia to witness, especially when Minnie's mother lifted her face and audibly gasped when she viewed her scar for the first time. Minnie tried to hide her face with her hand, but her father caught her wrist and lowered it to her side, speaking to her in a quick, bass rumble, holding his head high. With his finger under her delicate chin, he lifted her head high as well.

Cordelia may not have understood the language, but the gesture was clear. Min-nin-ne-wah-hah-ket was not to be treated as a beaten victim, but as a proud survivor. She was to wear her scar with honor. Cordelia choked back the sudden onrush of emotion as she felt the quick sting of tears.

Minnie's mother took a necklace from her own throat and placed it over Minnie's head. Minnie looked at it with obvious pleasure and turned to show Cordelia, who planted a grand smile on her face in acknowledgement of Minnie's reception back into her world.

It was then that the Indians seemed to take any notice of her at all. The children stood back shyly, watching her from the safety of the women's skirts. Cordelia recognized most of them from the guardhouse. She smiled. Some smiled back. Others withdrew behind their human shields.

The crowd grew silent, watching Cordelia. Jeremiah Running Bear spoke to them, explaining Cordelia's presence, she assumed. There was some nodding of heads and then Minnie's parents approached her. As they neared, Cordelia dismounted and took a step toward them, careful not to look them in the eyes, as Running Bear had told her that was a sign of disrespect in their culture.

The chief said something in his low rumble. His wife nodded her head at his words.

Jeremiah translated, "They say they are glad for all you have done for the daughter of their hearts. They want to know if you are the one who gave them the image of their daughter. I told them you were."

"Tell them," came Cordelia's clear, confident voice, "that it has been my pleasure to know their daughter and that she has been a blessing to us all."

"There is no Cheyenne word for 'blessing,' but I'll do what I can to pass along the thought." He turned back to the Indians and spoke to them warmly.

Little Robe, Minnie's father, nodded and motioned for her to join them in their tipi. Quickly, Cordelia grabbed her drawing pad and pencils from her pack and left Sunburst in the care of an adolescent male who stepped up to receive the reins.

"Thank you," she said, with a smile. He made no response, except to take the reins.

Walking beside Minnie as they followed the happy parents with Jeremiah bringing up the rear, Cordelia noticed how much healthier the people looked now than they had in the cold, damp guardhouse. It was a known, if not fully understood, fact that those who spent their days in the fresh air and sunshine were of superior health to those, especially of the white culture, who spent their time cooped up without the healthful benefits of the sun—even this winter sun.

The tipis were arranged in an orderly fashion. In front of each tipi was a campfire and scattered throughout the village were racks from which strips of meat hung. The racks were simply constructed by shoving two sticks with forked ends into the ground and placing another stick onto the forks, suspending it in the air. Over the horizontal stick, they hung the strips of meat. In their old habitat, these strips would have been of buffalo meat. Now, they were strips of elk, deer, or rabbit—whatever they were fortunate enough to find and kill, after first showing respect by asking its permission and thanking it for giving its life to feed their families, Jeremiah had told her.

Coming to the central tipi, they stooped to enter. Cordelia was immediately surprised by the roominess of its interior and comforted by its warmth and the smell of the fire in the center. Lighted torches were situated around the room. Still, it took a couple of seconds for her eyes to accommodate to the dimness.

Little Robe took his seat at the back of the lodge. Cordelia, looking questioningly at Jeremiah, sat at the chief's right side, trying to remember the protocol she'd learned earlier. She was not to ever walk between the fire and the chief. She was not ever to walk on the left side of the room.

She sat very still, trying to observe all things at once—the sights and smells and sounds of this setting. No one spoke for a long time.

Then the chief, made so by the death of Black Kettle, motioned for her to begin. Cordelia looked toward Jeremiah, who explained that the chief was ready for her to draw him.

Eagerly she set up her drawing pad to just the right angle on her lap. In near ecstasy, she took advantage of his permission to stare at him boldly, then turned her head to her drawing.

He sat very straight, cross-legged with his wrists resting lightly upon his knees. He looked straight ahead into the fire, so the shadows played across his leathered features. He wore a bonnet with beaded trailers made of eagle feathers, ermine, horsehair, and what looked to be eagle's claws. His shirt and trousers were the same fringed buckskin worn by all the people. Only his moccasin boots were beaded. Behind him, leaning against the wall of the tipi at an angle, stood a long war lance with some kind of protective charm. She tried to include that in the background of the portrait. The charm was small and round, like a ring wound with rawhide. Spidery workings were spun inside the circle and in the center was a bead holding a tassel of something like tiny feathers or fur.

She worked silently, repeatedly looking from his rugged face to her drawing pad. Out of respect, no one spoke. No one interrupted her. No one moved; they just watched her hand fly across the page.

At last, she smiled and held the pad out to Little Robe. He took it in his weathered hands and cocked his head this way and that, examining his image on the page. Finally, he placed the pad in front of him and nodded. Gesturing toward his wife, she quickly gave Cordelia a silver armband, intricately etched and set with turquoise stones. Little Robe made a quick, horizontal movement of his hand and closed his eyes. The interview was obviously over.

Jeremiah said, "That is a gift to you, Mrs. Lawson, in

return for his image. He is very pleased. But now it is time for us to go."

"Oh, not yet, Jeremiah," she started to protest, but with one look at Jeremiah's face, she obeyed. Standing, she bowed to Little Robe, smiled at his wife and stepped out of the golden warmth of the tipi into the cold brightness of this early February day.

Minnie, who had removed the page with her father's image and retrieved the rest of Cordelia's pad, joined them outside, passing it to her.

"My father is very happy. He want you to come again to draw my mother and the rest of his tribe."

"All of them?" Cordelia laughed. "Tell him I'll be happy to come back again." Taking in a long pull of fresh air, she continued, "Oh, Minnie, what a wonderful world you live in. You're happy to be back then?"

"Yes, but . . ." Minnie looked down. Now was the time. "I want to thank you, Mrs. Lawson, for what you did for me. You save my life. I know this is truth! You let me live with you family and I am sad to leave them. You told me about precious Jesus and His Father, the Great Spirit. You are my friend. You will come back quick?"

"Yes, I will, dear," noting that she made a correlation between God and the Great Spirit, though Cordelia had never used those words. "And, as I told your parents, it has been my pleasure to know you. You are my friend, too. I shall miss you very much." Blinking back tears, Cordelia embraced her and whispered, "You will always be welcome in my home."

Minnie nodded to her, and then to Jeremiah, and ducked back into her tipi. Cordelia knew her opportunity to view the village was over, that it was time for her to leave. She and Jeremiah walked silently past the campfires and the racks with strips of drying meat to the outskirts of the village where their horses were brought to them by the children, braver this time, as they smiled and waved at their departure.

She waved back and turned resolutely toward the fort. Jeremiah accompanied her As they rode he indicated he was looking forward to taking his evening meal with Bess and Lucy in the kitchen. Smiling he added he had left Bess working on a peach pie and that his mouth was already watering in anticipation.

~*~

That was the first of many days for Cordelia and "her" Indians. The Cheyenne proved to be a people of great dignity and honor.

Even in areas whites believed *dis*honorable—like stealing horses. They were experts! The Cheyenne didn't view it as thievery, but as a learned skill, a craft they'd perfected. Even the young boys were taught to determine quality breeds of horses. They were among the best riders of all the tribes and had the best herds of horses. Other tribes came to the Cheyenne to trade for them. Thus, even though their herd of over eight hundred horses was slain at the Washita massacre, their present herd numbered around seventy-five.

Cordelia didn't ask where they'd gotten them. That was one of the things she felt it best to ignore. She noticed they kept the horse Minnie had ridden to the camp. During the next three weeks, she sat for many days within the village, drawing the scenes that unfolded around her—the laughing children running and playing, the women cooking outside their tipis, the men smoking their pipes and talking, talking and smoking, seated in a circle in the chief's lodge or in front of the lodges on the fair days.

She was amazed at how creative they were. One buffalo was

able to provide so much. They used every bit of the animal. They tanned hides for lodges and to wrap their small canoes to make them more watertight. They used them for making drums, shields, and kettles, as well as creating soft clothing from them. Thick buffalo pelts became their sleeping robes and coats to keep them warm. With the horns they carved out ladles, spoons, and cups. Bones were carved into saws, needles, and spear tips. Hooves were boiled down to make glue. Muscle sinew was made into bow strings. Hair was braided into ropes, or reins for their ponies. Shoulder blades were used to make axes and hoes. With the rib bones, they made sledge runners. Blood was used to mix paint. Even the tails had a use as fly swatters and brooms.

She illustrated their clothing, their utensils, their tack, and their weapons. She wanted to know all about them. She agreed with Jeremiah's prediction that their ways would soon die out, so she was engaged in documenting their lives with a pictorial diary, of sorts.

Many of them proudly hung their portraits from the lodge poles of their tipis. Some allowed her to keep their images. She became nearly obsessed with these frequent pilgrimages to the Indian village, with Jeremiah's accompaniment, that is.

It wasn't like she was becoming a part of the tribe. It was more like she was becoming accepted by the tribe. They allowed her to go where she wanted, to draw what she wanted, to speak to whomever she pleased. She relied on Jeremiah or Minnie to translate for her because, try as she might, she could not seem to wrap her tongue around their language. She found it more and more remarkable that Minnie had picked up the English language as easily as she had.

One morning, after a ride from the fort, Cordelia dismounted and was overtaken by a wave of nausea. It soon passed, but she felt odd. Pasting a smile on her face, she removed her supplies and moved into the circle of lodges. Seating herself on her favorite "chair," an overturned tree trunk, she swallowed hard and placed the back of her hand on her damp forehead. Two of the older women exchanged glances, then smiled at Cordelia, who didn't quite catch the joke.

"Minnie!" she called. In a few seconds, Minnie, who had been fetched by one of the children, appeared next to Cordelia, greeting her with, "Hello, my friend."

"Oh, Minnie," Cordelia breathed. "I'm afraid I'm not feeling well today. I don't know what's wrong."

"Maybe it is baby," Minnie offered.

"Baby! What baby?"

"The one here." Minnie said this matter-of-factly, placing her hand over Cordelia's mid-section.

Cordelia sat in stunned silence. The two older women covered their mostly-toothless grins with their hands. One spoke to the other and they giggled like schoolgirls.

"What did they say?"

Minnie laughed with them, then translated, "They say you only one who don't know about baby. They say they know many days ago."

"That's absurd, Minnie! I think I would know such a thing if it were true."

"You sick in the morning? Yes. You miss your moon? I think yes. You here get bigger (placing her hand upon her chest)?"

Cordelia's hands flew protectively to her breasts. "Well . . ."

"You go to privy many time?"

Cordelia didn't need to agree. It was obvious. Minnie continued, "The women see because you skin is change. New color they see in face, Mrs. Lawson." Minnie sat, quietly smiling at her friend as she let it all sink in. From across the camp, an Indian flute's lilting melody filled the silence.

Finally, Cordelia allowed herself the tiniest smile as she thought about the baby she was now certain she was carrying. "A baby, Minnie. A baby!" She hugged her knees to her chest and rocked back and forth, laughing. "I can't believe it! I can't wait to tell Robert! I think I'll go back right now and tell him!"

Standing quickly, she grasped her mid-section and reeled awkwardly and would have fallen if not for Minnie's sturdy arms to steady her.

"Oh, I'm so dizzy. Will it be like this the whole time?"

"No. Only at first. You need to get up slow."

"I see that, Minnie." She sat down again, grateful to be among friends on this glorious winter day. She scanned the village for sight of Jeremiah, then, spotting him in the distance, she waved her arm at him. Seeing her, he trotted over to them.

"Yes?"

"Jeremiah, I think I shall be going back to the fort a little early today. Could you get our horses please?"

"But we just got here. Is something wrong, Mrs. Lawson?"

"No. Everything is just wonderful," she smiled back at him. Shrugging his shoulders, he went after the horses.

Nineteen

Dinner that night was an intimate affair. Bess had roasted a turkey for them, complete with cornbread stuffing, giblet gravy, melt-in-your mouth yeast rolls and candied sweet potatoes swimming in butter and cinnamon. Thanksgiving in February!

Jeremiah had killed two wild turkeys. So while Robert and Cordelia enjoyed their repast, he was able to reap the benefit of his hunting skills as he, Bess and Lucy shared the other turkey at their meal together at the thick kitchen table.

Delicious as all this was, Cordelia picked at her food, waiting for the appropriate time to break her news. Robert was talkative tonight, rambling on and on about an assignment he'd been given to escort the stage carrying representatives from Washington safely to Camp Supply. They were coming here to satisfy their curiosity about the Indians and to see for themselves what the "Wild West" was all about.

Fort Cobb was part of their tour. From here, they would travel to Camp Supply to the northwest. Robert and his men would be responsible for guarding the coach until it reached that destination.

Cordelia tried to listen attentively, but she was completely uninterested in the affairs of two Washington representatives and any reason they had to come out here. But it was all Robert seemed to talk about. On another occasion, perhaps she, too, would find it all very interesting but not tonight.

Finally, somewhere between his second and third roll, Robert paused long enough for Cordelia to jump into the conversation, pretending that she thought he was finished with his story.

"You know, my visit to the village today was very short."

"It was? Why?"

"I . . . um . . . wasn't feeling well."

"Oh? What was wrong? Feeling queasy again?"

Cordelia smiled at him and nodded.

"Yes?" he laughed. "And this makes you so serenely pleased?"

She nodded again. "Robert! I think we're going to have a baby!"

Robert dropped his fork onto his plate and pushed himself back in his chair. He stared at her for what seemed an eternity to Cordelia.

"Well, are you pleased, Robert?" she asked, timidly.

Sighing deeply, he quickly replied, "Well, yes, of course, but I'm a little stunned by this news. Cordelia, how can you be sure?"

"Actually, the Indian women diagnosed my condition. They pointed out some facts that I'd frankly overlooked. And I think they're right."

"Have you spoken to Doc about this?"

"Not yet. I thought I'd go see him tomorrow."

Robert stood uncertainly and strode to Cordelia's side.

Standing, she wrapped her arms around his trim waist and placed her head lovingly on his chest as he cradled her in his arms. "Darling, I am very happy," he told her, his voice husky with emotion.

"I am, too," she whispered. Breaking the embrace, she stood at arm's length holding his hands as she continued, "But let's not spread this news around just yet. I'd like for Doc to confirm my suspicions first."

"Oh, of course. I won't say a word. The less people know of our private affairs the better, as far as I'm concerned." He walked thoughtfully back to his seat.

Cordelia didn't like that look on his face. She could almost see the wheels turning behind his sudden frown.

When he spoke again, he said, "Darling, this necessitates some changes. Surely you realize that."

"Changes?" Cordelia asked, suddenly on alert.

"Why, yes," he replied, suddenly all business. "For one thing, you shouldn't be on horseback anymore, in your condition. You'll have to curtail your visits to the Indians, I'm afraid. In fact, it may be necessary for you to travel back to Baltimore. You'll receive better care there, among our family and friends, during your confinement."

"Confinement!" Cordelia was beside herself. "Me? Confined?" Chuckling, she continued, "Really, Robert. Be serious! I will *not* need a period of 'confinement,' I assure you! I can have this baby just fine without that!"

"Cordelia. Isn't that what is done when one is . . . you know, in the family way?"

"For some, perhaps, but not for me. I have nothing to be ashamed of. I don't need to be sent home like an unmanageable child. I'm going to have your baby. That is a beautiful thing. Robert, my life is with you, out here on the prairie, with my friends. I don't want to go back without you! And I just *can't* stop visiting the Cheyenne! There's so much more I want to capture about them, so much more I need to learn!"

"Cordelia, you will have to consider the welfare of this child. That must take precedence over your other desires. A woman in your condition must take it easy. If you must, you may resume your activities after the child is born. Do you know when that will be yet?"

Dumbfounded, Cordelia shook her head, not trusting her voice at that moment.

Leaning forward, he looked around surreptitiously and whispered, "What about . . . you know. Will we need to wait until the baby is born before we . . . you know?"

"Robert, really!" she gasped. "You don't expect me to lie next to you in that bed for months without touching you, without wanting you! My word, Robert. This is not at all the reaction I thought I would get to such blessed news. Already you have me fairly bedridden until childbirth! When did you become such an expert on babies, Captain Lawson? Why not just let *me* worry about my condition? You know I won't do anything to jeopardize the health of this child."

"Yes, of course. I was just . . . oh, let's just wait until we find out if this is really true before we continue this discussion further."

"Yes, let's." She held him with eyes turned to emerald ice.

They both resumed their meal. Cordelia noticed Robert's eyes on her. She could feel the color rise to her face.

"What?" she asked.

"You really *are* radiant, darling. I've always heard that was true. Now I see it for myself," he smiled. "I can't believe we're having a baby!"

She couldn't help herself. A broad smile covered her face, despite her agitation with her husband. In fact, all that was forgotten in a moment.

They were still seated at the table smiling at each other when Bess and Lucy came in to clear the dishes.

~*~

"Don't you need to examine me or something?" Cordelia asked.

"I just did!" Doc laughed. "I don't have to physically examine you, if that's what you mean. No, just obtaining the answers to my questions is enough of an exam to tell you that you are probably right about your suspicions. You're showing some of the signs. There will be more to come."

"How far along do you think I am? When will the baby come?"

"Hard to know for sure, but if your dates are correct, I would say around September."

"A September baby!" Cordelia smiled. "You know, Robert's birthday is in September, too!"

Doc placed a hand on her shoulder and said, "My dear, I am very happy for you and Robert. This is truly a blessed event."

"Doc, I have to ask you some things. Robert wants to 'confine' me to our quarters, I think, possibly even to our bed, if he has his way about it," Cordelia pouted, dramatically. "I won't have to do that, will I? That really won't be necessary, will it? And he wants me to stop riding out to the village. And he even mentioned that he might send me back to Baltimore until the baby is born! What do you think of all that?"

"You understand that this is not exactly my area of expertise. I can count on . . . one finger the number of births I've attended. I would think that for some women, these precautions would be absolutely necessary. But you, my dear, are one of the healthiest and most robust women I have ever known and I think we'd have to hog-tie you to keep you 'confined' for the rest of your time.

"So in my opinion, which is really my best guess, you comprehend, I would say that it wouldn't hurt for you to limit your physical activities without eliminating them completely. Perhaps, he's right about your riding horseback every day. But may I offer a compromise?"

"Please!"

"Why don't you just use one of the buckboards when you and Jeremiah go to the Indian camp? I would think that would be easier on you."

"I suppose I could do that," she admitted.

"And about Baltimore, I would suggest you and Robert resolve this between the two of you. I, personally, would feel more secure knowing you were getting expert medical care in Baltimore. You certainly can't get that from me, you know. I've already confessed my limitations in that respect."

Cordelia pondered this news for a moment before offering, "But the Indians know all about childbirth! They have their babies without the aid of any doctor! Perhaps they could deliver the baby when the time comes."

"Oh, Mrs. Lawson! Really! Only you would contemplate such a thing. Yes, I suppose they could provide that service for you. But I certainly would feel more comfortable if you had a doctor at your side when your time comes."

Cordelia scanned the dusty volumes of books on the shelves.

"Well, if I need a doctor by my side, then I want you. So you'd better start reading up on childbirth." She smiled impishly in his direction.

Chuckling, he said, "You're such a delight. For you, I'll read. I'll read every book I can get my hands on, but that's not the same as having an experienced physician. Think about it.

You may decide it's in your best interest, as well as the baby's, to go back to Baltimore, or maybe even to Topeka! I'm sure they have a doctor there who would be more experienced in this area."

"All right. I'll think about it. But I may talk to the Cheyenne, as well."

"You really enjoy them, don't you?"

"Oh, yes! I really do. Doc, people talk about how savage they are, how uncivilized. But I see just the opposite. I see a civilization that, in some ways, is more ordered and reasonable than *ours*! They live in tune with nature, with the land, with the sky and with each other. The chief's word is law, but he doesn't make his decisions until all the men express their opinions. He hears all sides of an issue, then rules on it. And the people accept it without question! And a more peaceful people, I've never seen. They are loving and clean and funny— all the things that you *wouldn't* expect from a bunch of 'hostile savages.'"

"I hope they know what a treasure you are, Mrs. Lawson."

"Oh, I think they appreciate me, Doc. Their acceptance means a great deal to me. And I think I've made some very good friends in the weeks I've gotten to know them."

"What about Minnie? How is she adapting to life back with her people?"

Cordelia looked down at her hands before answering. "Minnie is doing fine. She lives with her mother and father. But I think she is very sad. She was betrothed to Black Kettle's son. After she returned to her people, he took one look at her face and turned his back on her. They glimpse each other from opposite ends of the village, but he has not spoken to her. She has made it known to others that she releases him from his promise, but I think she's very unhappy about it. She doesn't think anyone will ever love her because of her face. She feels she has nothing to offer. And you know that's not true. Why, she'd be a sweet and faithful wife, a wonderful mother, and I think you can still see her beauty, don't you, Doc?"

"Yes, but these issues must be overseen by her own people, my dear. There's nothing you can do about it."

"I know."

"Oh, curse George Custer for ruining that girl."

"Doc! Really! I told you he didn't do it."

"Yes, I know, but none of it would have happened if he'd left her alone in the first place. Folks can bow and scrape at his feet all day long, as far as I'm concerned, but I have no use for the man. He's a ruthless, arrogant, power-hungry scoundrel, if you ask me."

"Doc," she reminded him softly, "you know, that 'scoundrel' also saved my life and the lives of all the Indians around the fort. There's more to General Custer than meets the eye."

"Well, I never thought I'd hear *you* defend him! Frankly, I'm surprised!"

"Oh, I don't defend everything he's done, or not done, for that matter. But people love to talk about him, good or bad. It seems he's always the topic of conversation. Some think he's a hero and others, like you, my friend, think him a scoundrel. But one and all have to admit that George Custer is something special, something different. I've never met anyone like him. He has his faults, of course, and they're huge! I think he knows that. But he has been a perfect gentleman to me, and has honored his word to stay away from Minnie. He wanted to come over to apologize to her, but she never wants to see him again. I told him so. Hopefully, she'll never have to."

"Yes, I certainly agree. But I'm not as trusting as you are. I don't doubt that he wanted to come over, but to apologize? Not likely. That doesn't sound like the General Custer I've heard about. I think it more likely that he wanted to come to see you, my dear."

"Me?"

"Don't look so surprised. I'm sure you've noticed the way he looks at you, the way he hangs on your every word."

"I've noticed no such thing. In fact, he's completely devoted to his wife, Libby, and talks about her all the time."

"Hmm. I wonder."

"Doc!" Cordelia teased. "I've never seen this cynical side of you before. What would someone like General George Armstrong Custer want with a big, fat, married lady like me?"

Doc laughed. "Well, I couldn't imagine—such a plain, gawky creature you are! What could I have been thinking?" He patted her shoulder, affectionately.

Hopping down from the exam table, Cordelia picked up her bag and shawl. "I've taken up far too much of your time, my friend. Thank you."

"My pleasure, Mrs. Lawson. May I tell Ela about this blessed event?"

"Yes, of course!"

He opened the door to his office for her, but she turned just before he closed it. "Oh, Doc!"

"What is it, my dear?"

"One more thing." She could feel the color rushing to her cheeks again, but, with eyes lowered, she asked, "What about . . . . marital relations during this time? Surely we don't have to stop . . . you know, until the baby is born."

"No, I don't think so. But in the last months, you may want to . . . curtail such activities."

"Thank you, Doc. That's another thing Robert hinted at denying me!"

Once the door was closed, she heard his laughter inside.

Tapping on his window, she wagged her finger at him in mock annoyance. He waved her away, still grinning.

~*~

Minnie gave Cordelia another piece of rabbit, saying, "You need more meat now, ma'am. You eat this."

"No, no," she protested. "I've had plenty. Thank you."

"You eat!"

Cordelia straightened herself a little, as if to make room for another bite or two. Sitting on the fallen tree trunk that was "her spot" in the village, she took another delicate bite of the succulent meat, much to Minnie's satisfaction.

She and Robert had reached an agreement. She and Jeremiah would come to the village in one of the fort's little buckboards. The giant spring under the seat would support her better and be easier on her, Doc had said. The second point of compromise was in the frequency of her trips. Instead of coming two or three times per week as she'd been doing for the last several weeks, she agreed to come to the village only once per week.

They'd also decided that there was no need for her to return to Baltimore this early in her pregnancy. However, Cordelia agreed to go back by her sixth month, though she didn't especially see the need. But that would buy her some time here with the Cheyenne before she had to go.

The issue of their marital relations was settled once and for all last night. The memory of it caused the sensation of myriad fluttering butterflies in her stomach and she felt a quick warmth rush to her cheeks.

Goodness, I'd better not dwell on that right now! she thought, forcing herself to concentrate on the scene before her.

The weather cooperated with her today. With the soothing

warmth of the campfire nearby, it was quite pleasant. Some of the children were playing a game with a stick and a ball filled with dried grass and covered with skins. Their laughter filled the clear, clean air and made Cordelia smile.

The older boys were practicing their skills as hunters—throwing their spears, or tomahawks or shooting their bows. Ammunition was too scarce for them to practice with the rifles their people owned. But all the boys in the tribe were taught to be hunters from early on.

They were also taught the more subtle skills of the hunter; how to be still and silent, how to fast during the day, how to move long distances without complaint, how to track animals and learn their habits. Most of all, they learned the value of patience.

Two women fussed over the deer stew simmering in the kettle over the fire. This current dispute seemed to be about how much of a certain green herb to put in the pot. The older won the argument and tossed in another pinch, just to make the point.

Minnie had told her that her people usually had two meals per day. They ate whatever meat the men provided—deer, antelope, rabbit, squirrel, fish or buffalo, as well as their daily meal of boiled beans. The bread they made consisted of a mixture of corn and beans. Cordelia had watched them mix the corn meal with mashed, cooked beans. They formed the dough into loaves, which they wrapped in corn husks. In that form, they baked the bread. Even now Cordelia noted several husks laid end to end around the edges of the fire.

The men kept their distance and occupied their time with wood-working, tending the horses, making arrows (careful to wing them with turkey feathers), or their favorite pastime—smoking their pipe while sitting and talking . . . or *not* talking as was more often the case.

All eyes suddenly turned toward the sound of horses entering the camp. The men stood to face the oncoming visitors—fierce men with scowls on their faces. Cordelia counted eight men, in all. She recognized one of them, the one who had lagged behind to study her at the fort that first day! She'd wondered why she'd never seen him in the Cheyenne camp, and assumed he had been killed at Washita. Though she didn't fully understand why, her heart rejoiced that he was still alive and well. He rode with the others to the front of the Medicine Lodge, where they held their meetings, or councils, as they called them.

The children openly watched their movements as they dismounted. Little Robe and the other men of the tribe followed them into the Medicine Lodge. The familiar Indian caught a glimpse of Cordelia as he was about to enter the tipi. He immediately halted and stared into her eyes briefly before disappearing into the lodge.

Cordelia looked with a puzzled expression to the women for some clarification, but they just resumed their tasks at the big, black pot. Another woman examined the deer hide that was drying on a large rock to the side of the fire, flapping the hide from one side to the other, then back. Minnie, who had wandered off a few minutes ago, was nowhere in sight.

However, Jeremiah was moving quickly towards Cordelia, stopping when he saw her looking his way. Motioning for her to come, he waited for her in front of the Medicine Lodge.

Immediately, she grabbed her pad and pencils and scurried to meet him. "What is it?"

"Come, we must go," came his hurried reply.

Cordelia tugged on his arm. "Who are those men, Jeremiah? What are they doing here?" she wanted to know.

"Friends. Arapaho and Kiowa. They are here for a council with Little Robe. They bring news from their village to the south. These council meetings can be quite lengthy and most solemn. We should go now."

"Do you think they would mind if I sit in on the council, Jeremiah? I'd love to try to capture the scene."

"No, Mrs. Lawson. First they will smoke and make the small talk with each other until it is night. Only then will they share the news they bring. This is our custom. You won't be here when the council begins."

Wheels were turning in her mind. "Perhaps I could stay here tonight and witness this council. You could ride back to the fort and leave word with Bess and Lucy about where I'll be. Tell them I could come back home tomorrow at first light."

"I don't know, ma'am. The captain will not like this, I think."

"Please, Jeremiah." Cordelia looked up into his face with eyes wide with wonder and excitement.

Sighing, he agreed to discuss the matter with Little Robe. "You wait here," he told her.

"Fine! I will!"

He disappeared behind the door flap of the Medicine Lodge. She waited a long time—so long that she began to shift her weight from one foot to the other, moving with a little hopping motion that made it look like she was dancing one of their own steps. Finally she moved back to her place on the tree trunk but kept her eyes fixed on the door of the lodge.

About the time she'd decided to go in there and see just what was going on, Jeremiah stepped out again, looking for her, hands on his hips in annoyance.

"You said you would wait here."

"I know. But you were in there for at least an hour! In my delicate condition . . ." she protested coyly, teasing him almost into a smile.

"Little Robe agreed for you to be in the council meeting

tonight but you cannot speak. You must stay in the background. You must draw no attention to yourself. Do you understand these things?"

"Yes, of course. And I agree." Though Cordelia didn't realize it, Little Robe viewed having his own illustrator as a sign of prestige, and one he was counting on to impress the other chiefs, even if the illustrator was a woman. The drawings of himself and his family were proudly displayed on the walls of his own tipi.

Jeremiah snorted, then set off for the horse pen. He would use one of the Indian ponies for this mission. It would be much faster than the buckboard.

Watching him ride around the windbreak toward the fort, she felt a twinge of guilt anticipating Robert's reaction to this news. But she hoped he knew she would be safe here with her friends. And it was, after all, just one night, a once in a lifetime experience.

She realized she'd better find Minnie and make sure there was room for her in the tipi tonight and that permission would be granted for her to stay. "Probably should have checked with her *first*," she reprimanded herself.

Twenty

Just at dusk, Jeremiah returned to the village, entered the Medicine Lodge and immediately came back out for Cordelia. He motioned for her to come now.

Once again, she grabbed her supplies, grateful and excited that the time had come. She was getting chilled now that the sun had set and the warmth in the tipi would soothe her, she knew. But more importantly, she was thrilled with the opportunity to witness the council meeting.

Entering the lodge, several heads momentarily turned her way, and then, as if white women *always* attended these council meetings, casually turned back to their host. The air was filled with the pungent aroma of the heavy tobacco they smoked.

The scene was utterly lovely, she thought as her hands flew over the page—drawing them, and trying to capture the atmosphere of this somber moment.

Outside the lodge, some of the Cheyenne played drums and others shook rattle-type instruments to the beat. The mournful melody of a lone flute lilted through the winter cold. It played a song that began slowly and gradually gathered speed. Cordelia seemed to feel the beat of the drums inside her heart.

Little Robe, as always, sat in the back of the lodge. The men sat cross-legged in a circle around the fire-lit room, leaving space for Cordelia and Jeremiah to sit with their backs against the taut skins of the medicine lodge. Even so, she felt the warmth of the fire begin to creep into her bones again.

The men's angular features cast amazing shadows all around them, while the fire's red-golden flames licked the inside of the darkened lodge with shades of red and yellow, like sunlight on the red earth they sat upon. Articles of war hung from the sides of the lodge; shields, lances, bows, parfleches and arrows. Several guns leaned against the wall next to the door.

These items were in stark contrast to the homey items hanging in their family tipis, things like combs made from bone, brushes made from bone and porcupine quills, cups and plates stacked on small wooden shelves hanging from the lodge poles. The pallets on which the family slept were rolled and placed against the edges of the room. There were pallets in here, too. They made a firm cushion for Cordelia's aching lower back.

One of the visitors began to speak. He didn't stand, as a white man would have done. And the other men didn't look at him. In fact, they seemed bored and apathetic. Cordelia found it nearly impossible to read their expressions. They sat as if made from stone. Jeremiah explained in a whisper that it was considered disrespectful to watch the speaker.

This satisfied her curiosity and she began to listen to the man's speech as she drew. Of course, she couldn't understand a word so she leaned over toward Jeremiah, who quietly translated. Cordelia was bright enough to realize that he wasn't telling her *everything* that was being said. He was obviously editing and condensing as he went.

She knew this because the speaker would say something like ten or twelve slow and careful sentences punctuated at intervals with deep grunts to which Jeremiah would say something like, "He thanks Little Robe for his willingness to hear him."

But Cordelia didn't argue. This was an amazing experience and she wanted to soak it all in. She leaned to her right until she could see the face of the familiar one. He looked at the ground, listening intently to the speaker.

"Who is that one, Jeremiah?" she whispered.

"Which one?"

"The one there, looking down at the ground."

Jeremiah nodded when he saw him. "He's an Arapaho chief. His name is Yellow Bear."

"Oh. Do you . . ." she continued.

"Shhh. Mrs. Lawson, please."

"Oh, sorry," she whispered.

Jeremiah listened for a few seconds before translating to her. "It seems there has been talk," Jeremiah whispered to her, "that the people will be forced to move to the south. They have heard that the hunting is poor there. The people will be dependent on government rations."

Someone else took over the speech, as Cordelia listened carefully. This *was* important, if it was true.

"He says he will not depend on the White Father in Washington," Jeremiah whispered. "The rations that have been promised through this winter have still not arrived to the fort. It will only be worse there, he says."

Yellow Bear added, in a velvety smooth baritone voice, "Yes, but Commander Hazen allows us to hunt for our food. Some other commander may not allow this. Our people will starve if we cannot hunt."

Grunts all around, with much nodding of heads.

"Our numbers are few since the battle at Washita. We cannot fight the white men. Their numbers are many and their strength is mighty."

Another spoke up, "The whites seem to have an endless supply of men. The more we kill, the more they send," Jeremiah translated.

Little Robe spoke for the first time. "We cannot fight the whites. Our chiefs have signed the treaty at Medicine Lodge. It is our word of honor that holds us from this fight. There may again be war but it will not be by the misconduct of our people. We are held by the chain of friendship, made when friendship was worth the price. If they kill us for our lands, in a state of innocence we will sleep with our departed people."

He looked from face to face until he fixed his gaze on one young man in particular. "Our great chief Black Kettle refused to take up arms against the whites. He refused to allow even our young men to break the promises made in the treaty."

"Yes," another man added, nodding his graying head in agreement. "I remember when three of our young men rebelled against Black Kettle's word and attacked a house of logs where a white family made their home. Our braves were only there to take their livestock, but when the white man came out with a rifle, they shot him dead. When Black Kettle heard of this, he banished the boys from the camp, forcing them to flee to another tribe for protection."

"He speaks the truth," said another, "for one of those boys was the son of my brother. They still live as if he has died."

Again, the nods from all in attendance.

The attractive young man began to speak. "My father was a wise chief, always on the side of the people. But if he had taken arms against the white soldiers, he might be with us still. Why should we honor this treaty when the whites have broken it many times?"

"Is that Gray Horses Coming?" Cordelia asked Jeremiah in a hushed whisper.

He merely nodded as the conversation continued.

Cordelia noted this information. This was the young man Minnie loved, and had been promised to. He was the one who shunned her now. She immediately labeled him an immature fool to have turned away from one as gifted and loving as Min-nin-ne-wah-hah-ket.

Little Robe responded, "The whites have no honor. We cannot do as they do. We die to protect our word, our honor. Black Kettle died for honor."

The room was silent except for the grunts of the nodding men around the campfire.

"How soon will we be forced to the south?" Little Robe wanted to know. This time all heads shook side to side, accompanied by some unenthusiastic shrugs.

Cordelia had long since ceased her drawing, so mesmerized was she by the content of this council and the wisdom of the men gathered here.

"I have been to the land to the south many times on my searches for horses," one said. "It is a barren place with no fort. Where are they going to take us?"

Another answered, "They have built a fort there, I've heard. It is much larger than this fort with many more soldiers. I fear for our people if we are forced to go there. We have few horses since the battle. Our old, our weak, our women and children are feeble from this hard winter. The road to the south will be the burial ground for many. Even our few ponies eat the bark of trees, such is their hunger and weakness."

Cordelia, though not understanding their words, listened as intently as if she could. Jeremiah's soft translation in the background became as a voice in her own head, so that she felt she understood the words of their worried conversation as they were being spoken.

She was surprised when suddenly, she heard Jeremiah refer to "Red Hair Woman," which was the Indian name Minnie had given her. Several half-turned in her direction. Little Robe looked toward her. Jeremiah stopped whispering. All was completely silent except for the crackle of the fire in the center of the lodge.

Little Robe said something, apparently, to *her*. Confused, she looked to Jeremiah for a translation. Leaning toward her, he said, "The chief wants to know if you have heard of plans to move us to the south to this new fort."

Thoughts flew through her mind like bats out of a cave at dusk. What she was left with was . . . nothing! She knew nothing of this! All she could do was shake her head, "No."

Finally she found her voice and said, "No, I know nothing of this!" Jeremiah translated into Cheyenne, which the Arapaho understood as well, being their sister-tribe.

Again, there was no speech for several minutes as the men drew smoke from the pipe and blew it into the heights above.

Following the smoke's delicate ascent, Cordelia noticed how bright the stars were through the hole at the top of the lodge, left for ventilation for the campfire. The silence crushed her senses as she waited for their next words.

Finally, Little Robe spoke, saying, "Red Hair Woman knows nothing of this. Perhaps the news Scorched Lightning has brought us will not happen. Let us wait to hear more before we make our plans. Each of us will think on this problem. We will meet again to decide what is to be done. I have spoken."

Without further discussion, the men rose from their seats and made their soundless exits, leaving the empty room behind them, except for Cordelia and Jeremiah. Suddenly realizing she had been holding her breath, Cordelia breathed deeply, letting it out slowly.

Neither of them spoke as Jeremiah rose and left her alone to her thoughts and her drawing pads. Soon she followed him into the cold night air. Quickly locating Minnie, Cordelia joined her for a bowl of stew, while sitting around the campfire. When she sat close to the fire, the blaze burned her face and arms, leaving her back chilled to the bone. When she moved to her fallen tree trunk she felt chilled all over. She couldn't seem to stay warm. She was glad when the women began to move into their lodges.

She and Minnie entered the tipi of her parents. Cordelia sat cross-legged on the ground, freshly swept clean, with her dress carefully covering her legs. Not knowing how to help, she watched as the women made their preparations for the coming night.

She had planned to bathe tonight in her little tub at home as she did two or three times a week. Out here in the frontier it was hard to do it with any greater frequency—a daily sponge bath, yes, but a tub bath every day was out of the question. Still, some only bathed on Saturday nights!

And others—especially "mountain men," Robert had informed her—did not believe in a water bath at all. They practiced what they called a dry rub. They were completely convinced that if they stripped down to mother naked, as they called it, and immersed themselves in water they would surely die, unaccustomed as they were to such ablutions. Robert had jokingly alluded to the fact that when engaged in conversation with a mountain man it was of primary concern to stand upwind or a person would surely faint dead away from the stink.

The Indians, however, were extremely clean individuals, especially the men. The Cherokee and Cheyenne considered water one of the three holy gifts of the great Spirit (the other two being sun and fire). No matter how cold or scarce the water, they would dip themselves and bathe every morning. The women did this less often but their mild scent was not unpleasant. So there would be no bathing tonight for Cordelia. She didn't mind. Her head was swirling with words and pictures and ideas and questions. All she wanted was a place where she could sort them all out in her mind.

She tried not to think about Robert. Jeremiah said he'd left word with Bess, but they both knew what Robert's feeling would be when he heard the news. Yet another impetuous, ill-advised decision his impulsive wife made without any concern for his position. Thinking of Robert brought dread to her heart. She knew she'd have to face his ire soon enough.

When Little Robe and his wife settled onto their bedding, Minnie motioned Cordelia next to her. Once situated on the pallet, Cordelia marveled at the warmth provided by the heavy buffalo robe covering them.

Out the ventilation opening at the top of the tipi, she watched the stars for a few moments, trying to sort out her confused thoughts regarding the night's events. The Indian flute played on in the distance.

Were the Indians to be moved to yet another reservation? Would the journey really be such a hardship that women and children could die? Why hadn't Robert told her anything about this? She remembered thinking, *I'll never get to sleep tonight.* That was the last she remembered, for slumber fell upon her quickly and soundly.

It was still dark when Minnie woke her the next morning. Minnie held her hand over Cordelia's mouth, placing a finger over her own to indicate silence. Cordelia nodded.

Minnie motioned for her to follow. Wordlessly, Cordelia stood and tiptoed out of the tipi into the first light of morning.

"Come. I show you something," Minnie whispered.

Cordelia rubbed her sleepy eyes but nodded her agreement, throwing a blanket about her shoulders. Together they crept to the creek bank, then followed it up to an area widened by the industrious maneuverings of a family of flat-tail beaver. With their dam, they had created a small pond in the otherwise dry countryside. There, at the water's edge, Minnie and Cordelia crouched and waited but for what, Cordelia didn't know.

A heavy fog covered the surface. The chilled world was completely silent around them. Soon, Cordelia noticed the first ray of sunlight sneaking past the horizon, through the trees lining the opposite bank. Then a magical event began to unfold over the water.

The fog began to move and sway, to break apart and swirl slowly around in myriad undulating figures over the still surface of the water. Each wispy rotation lifted slowly from the water's face, spinning faster and more tightly with the coming of the sun. Cordelia watched in stunned silence as the wispy tendrils whirled and turned ever upward in their slow, fairy-like motion, like throngs of dancing spirits wafting their way to the heavens, trailing their feathery fingers behind them. As abruptly as the misty dance had begun, it dissipated into the brightness of the morning sky.

Neither spoke a word, but when Cordelia turned her delighted face to that of her friend, she found the confident smile of understanding there. This was a sight Cordelia Lawson would never forget.

~*~

"And furthermore," Robert continued, as he paced back and forth before her, "I cannot believe you would place me in this position. No, I never said you couldn't stay the whole night with them. That's true. That's because the thought of such a thing *never* entered my mind. How could I ever have imagined that my wife would entertain the notion to spend the night wrapped in a buffalo skin on the dirt floor of an Indian tipi—and with child, at that?"

Cordelia had lost interest in his exasperation ten minutes ago, yet she continued to listen to the droning of his voice, her eyes lowered to her toe tips, her hands folded primly in her lap.

"Well?" he was saying, "What have you to say for yourself?"

"Nothing, Robert."

"Nothing?" he asked incredulously.

Dramatically she pretended to think about it, then shrugged, shaking her head slightly and lifted her eyes to his. "No. Nothing. I am, of course, sorry to have made you so angry. But given the circumstances, I'm not sorry I stayed. It was, quite frankly, an experience I'll never forget."

That stopped him in his tracks.

Tugging at his jacket hem, and clearing his throat, he nodded a couple of times, then finally said, "Well." Not knowing where to go from here, he decided to end the lecture and go on to his office. This time, he left without her kiss and her blessing. Instead he just trudged out the door.

Bess immediately stuck her head in the parlor door. "Are you all right, Miz Lawson?"

"Yes, of course, Bess."

"You want some more coffee?"

"Please. Mine seems to have grown cold."

"Mm, mm, mm," she said, shaking her head. "The captain sure is fumin' mad, ain't he, ma'am?"

"He certainly is, Bess. No, I don't suppose I'll be doing this again anytime soon." She shot a mischievous glance sideways at Bess.

Bess was quick to wag her finger at Cordelia and respond,

"Well, I don't blame him a bit. I'd be plenty mad at you, too. I still can't believe you'd do such a thing. When Jeremiah brought us that message, I *knew* the captain wouldn't like it. I didn't even want to tell him! I almost sent Lucy to tell him. But I couldn't put that poor child through that. No, ma'am. I had to tell him myself."

"What did he say?" Cordelia asked.

"Nothing, ma'am. You know how he works that jaw when he's good and mad? Well, tha's what he done. Just steady working that jaw."

"Well, truth be told, I don't enjoy distressing my husband, Bess. You know how I feel about him. I'd die for the man! Really I would! But being there last night was really important to me. It really was! I wouldn't have caused Robert the slightest concern if it could have been helped. But sometimes, when a person is offered an opportunity like that, she has to take it— regardless of the consequences!"

"Yes, ma'am. If you say so. But if'n it was me, I'd do no such a thing."

"Well, you're an angel, Bess. A pure angel from heaven."

"You know *that* ain't true, ma'am," came her throaty reply as she, having filled Cordelia's cup, made her way back to the kitchen still chuckling, leaving Cordelia to her steaming cup of coffee and her memories of last night's developments.

She hadn't dared to tell Robert the content of the meeting —not with him in this state of mind. She'd talk to him about it tonight at dinner.

~*~

Lieutenant and Mrs. Otis joined them for dinner that night by previous agreement. Otherwise, Cordelia was convinced her husband wouldn't have allowed it.

But much to his credit, he'd seemed to soften over the course of the day, and was almost himself tonight. Todd also seemed to be in bright spirits. The reason became clear as the dinner progressed.

After a bit of forced laughter, Todd began the conversation. "So, Robert, have you told Cordelia about what is to transpire?"

"Ah, no, I haven't had the opportunity yet," Robert continued, a bit too brightly, as if previously rehearsed.

Cordelia looked from one to the other suspiciously, but said nothing.

Nicole took the bait. "What is it? What is this big mystery?"

"We had a meeting today with General Hazen. It seems he has received orders from General Sheridan. You remember General Sheridan, don't you, Cordelia?" Robert asked, trying to buy time.

"Why yes, dear, I do," came her patronizing reply.

"Well, he sent the commander some orders today regarding the Indian problem."

"The Indian problem? I didn't realize there was a 'problem,'" Cordelia purred politely, waiting with less-than-perfect patience for him to reach the point of the conversation.

He looked to Todd for assistance. Todd, having placed almost a half a potato in his mouth, offered none.

So Robert continued, "It seems the decision has been passed down from Washington—from the President, himself —to relocate the Indians to a more agreeable living situation."

Cordelia put her fork down delicately, and then sat demurely with her hands in her lap, the very image of propriety. But beneath this calm exterior, everyone at the table, except perhaps for Nicole, knew the kind of rage that was brewing inside. Her mind whirred with the memory of last night's concerns about just such a "relocation." And she had said she knew nothing of it.

And here it was! She felt she had betrayed the council of men; she had led them astray, even if it had been completely unintentional.

But she couldn't think about that now. She had to listen attentively to every word being said.

"This has, after all, only been a temporary arrangement since their village was destroyed. We knew the day would come when they would have to be relocated, didn't we?"

Receiving no reaction from Cordelia, he turned to Todd. "Didn't we?"

"Oh, yes. Absolutely. It was always a temporary solution to the problem." He nodded in agreement, not daring to look at Cordelia, who, so far, had remained quiet.

Cordelia drew in a deep breath, letting it escape slowly. In a wee, small voice, very gently, she asked, "And just where is this better living situation?"

Robert, finishing off his coffee, explained, "We have orders to divide the village. The Cheyenne and Arapaho are to be moved to Camp Washita, to the south. The other tribes will be sent to the north to join Red Cloud's reservation."

"Don't you think the Indians should have some say about where they are to live? What they are to do?"

"No, Cordelia. I'm afraid the time for that is over. They are charges of the government now. The Bureau of Indian Affairs was formed to act in the government's interest where such things are concerned. It is their opinion that they will need to be relocated. It will be more cost effective to take care of them down there where they are set up for that."

"More 'cost effective,'" Cordelia repeated, quietly.

"Yes, dear. You know the easterners are steadily complaining about the exorbitant costs of the military, now that the war is over. We hear tales about how they're urging the politicians to whittle our numbers significantly. At the same time, those out here on the frontier are howling for more protection from the Indians. By removing the Indians to a place more equipped to handle them, and utilizing the troops there, it will keep the government from having to add soldiers to this fort. So you see, it's actually for our benefit as well as theirs," he concluded, hopefully studying her face, "a perfect solution."

Cordelia nodded, "I see," she said, quietly. "When will this 'relocation' take place? How will they be transported?"

Believing it was safe now to join the conversation, and surprised by Cordelia's seeming acquiescence, Todd replied, "We are to begin making the arrangements now. When Robert returns from his escort, we are to ride out. So that would mean we'd leave at the end of next week. Right, Robert?"

Robert nodded in agreement.

Todd continued, enthusiastically, "I've been assigned to ride north with Major Humphries from Fort Larned."

"And I," said Robert, with a slight edge to his voice now, "will be riding south to Camp Washita . . . with General Custer!"

Fighting the impulse to raise an eyebrow, Cordelia quickly asked, "Is the general back from chasing Indians then?"

"No," Todd replied, "but he should be back by then, we think."

"And how far away is Camp Washita?" Cordelia asked. "I've never heard of it. I didn't think there was another fort to our south until you reached Texas."

This time Robert answered. "Yes, there are several forts in Texas. But this one is only about thirty or forty miles from us. Actually, General Custer had a hand in the design of the fort. It used to be a designated supply fort. But it was abandoned long ago. Custer and the commander of that fort, General Grierson, have overseen the rebuilding of the fort and it is ready for occupation now."

"General Grierson," Todd explained, "has the detail of soldiers called 'buffalo soldiers.' Have you heard of them, Cordelia?"

"No, I don't think so. Why are they called 'buffalo soldiers'?"

"The 10th cavalry is composed of Negro soldiers. The Indians called them 'buffalo soldiers' because of their skin color and the texture of their hair; short, dense and curly, like that of the buffalo. These men distinguished themselves in the war, that's for sure. They fought bravely and earned the respect of all."

"Interesting. But what of the Indians? Where will they live?" Cordelia demanded.

Robert answered, "They'll be assigned land outside the fort, a large reservation. I'm sure they will like it much better than this place."

"Well, I think not! You're wrong about *that*, darling."

Here it comes, thought Robert, startled by the strength of her assertion. He'd been wondering when the dam would burst. He shot a worried glance at Todd.

"In the first place," she continued, "they have already been warned about this move. They even know it is to be to a fort to the south. Scouts have returned from there, bringing disparaging reports about the unsuitability of the land. They will be removed farther away from their hunting grounds. The land is less conducive to crop production. Here they are allowed to hunt. That's the only way they have survived this winter because, they tell me, General Custer seems to have burned or confiscated their entire winter supply of meat and they still have not received the rations our leaders promised them. Is that true, Robert?"

"Well, yes. It has been one of our prime concerns, Cordelia. We have been in continual contact with Washington, making request after request for these rations and supplies. They say they are on their way, but still we have received nothing. In fact, that is one of the issues we are to discuss with the Washington delegates when they arrive the day after tomorrow."

She nodded. "They are concerned that the new commander will refuse to allow their hunting. Rumor has it that at the new fort their weapons may be taken away completely. Without their weapons they won't be able to feed themselves. So they'll be left to starve to death, I suppose."

"Now Cordelia, really . . ." Robert began.

"Of course, that might fit into the Army's Indian policy of extermination." Her calm demeanor was disquieting to both men. "These people are obviously destined to vanish from the very face of the earth. How did Jeremiah put it? Oh, yes, 'as snow before a summer sun.' Sums it up beautifully, doesn't it?"

Nicole sat completely silent, her mouth open in shock at the turn their conversation had taken.

"Cordelia, I believe you're making too much of this," Todd offered.

"I don't. And the Indians wouldn't think so, either. The hunting issue is of primary importance to them, I assure you," she replied hotly.

Robert spoke up, "And just how are you in possession of these facts, Cordelia? It seems unlikely they would have disclosed them to you, a white woman, after all."

"Yet that's just what they did. They trust me, Robert."

He and Todd sat in stone silence, thoughts churning.

Finally Robert asked, "Who were these people who

brought the information to Little Robe? They were Cheyenne scouts?"

Hearing the chief's name brought her up short. Suddenly she realized she'd betrayed a confidence to have said so much. She should have kept these things to herself. Why couldn't she keep her mouth shut? Her cheeks quickly flushed as she decided to say no more.

"Well, who were they?"

"I don't think I care to say, Robert." She desperately needed to make a retreat somehow. Standing, she began collecting the dishes, "Excuse me. I need to get these dishes to the kitchen."

Nicole stood to help as well.

"No, no. Take your seat, Nicole. I'll get this."

"Cordelia, what has gotten into you?" Robert wanted to know. "You know Bess will get the dishes."

"Now, Robert, it doesn't hurt me at all to help them out every now and then. So if you'll excuse me . . ."

With that, she took off down the hallway toward the kitchen. At the end of the hallway, she tried to figure out a way to negotiate the doorknob but with her hands so full, all she could do was lightly kick a knock at the door and hope it would be answered soon.

Sure enough, Lucy, coming from the Otis's quarters where she'd gotten Baby Nora to sleep ran to open the door, aghast that Mrs. Lawson was standing there with an armload of dishes from the table. Lucy opened the kitchen door for her as well and gave her mother a defensive glance, as if to say, "It's not *my* fault!"

"Don't worry," she said, instead. "I'll gather the rest of the dishes, Mama."

"Thank you. Take the coffee pot in there with you, Lucy." Bess instructed, with her hands on her hips.

"Yes, ma'am."

"Now," she said to Cordelia, "just what do you think you're doing, Missy?"

"Don't scold me, Bess. I had to get out of there and this was the only way I could think of to do it."

"Well, are you goin' back in there? Or have you decided to start bunking in with us now?" Bess teased.

"Bess! Really!"

"No, really! You have to go back in there sometime, you know."

"Yes, I know that but I just need a place to think for a minute," she said, looking around for the rocking chair. Locating it next to the hearth, she sat down and, gripping both arm rests, began to rock feverishly.

"I'm gonna' go help Lucy. Don't wear the rockers off that thing, now."

Cordelia managed a smile, grateful that she'd have a moment to herself.

Anguish filled her heart as she realized the position she was in. She had information she felt duty-bound to get back to the Indians. She had to! She couldn't stand the idea that she'd said she hadn't heard anything about this move and then, the very next day, she'd discovered it was true, after all. Then they would expect her to tell them when and how. Would that be a betrayal of her husband's confidence if she told them? She agreed that they needed to know these things. In fact, they had a *right* to know these things. But would she be placing Robert in jeopardy by being the one to tell them?

And what of Robert? Now he'd want to know information from her that she felt duty-bound to keep in confidence. The Cheyenne trusted her enough to allow her to sit in on a council. She had no business divulging anything she'd heard there.

Cradling her head in her hands, she felt guilty and ashamed

that she'd said anything at all. But didn't her husband have a right to know that the Indians were already in possession of these facts? Now, surely Robert must feel duty-bound to deliver this information to General Hazen and, ohhhh. It was just too much for her to consider.

How did she ever get herself into such a position? And what was she going to do about it? How could she love and honor her husband and be worthy of his trust and then tell the Indians the details of this despised plan? The faces of her Cheyenne friends flashed through her mind—the memory of the sound of the children's laughter, the women's shy and half-hidden smiles, the men's concerned and somber expressions in the firelight the night before. She shook her head as if to clear it of these precious images. How could she consider herself worthy of such trust if she told Robert what she was told in confidence?

Suddenly she realized that Baltimore was looking better all the time. She bent her head in prayer as she whispered under her breath, "Father, You have promised that You are always near, that You will never leave us or forsake us. I need You now, Father. Please give me the right words to say. Help me to know the right course to take. Give me a portion of Your wisdom so that whatever I do honors and glorifies You in the process. Help me to be true to my husband *and* to my friends. These things I ask in Your blessed Son's name. Amen."

Rising from her chair, she placed four apple turnovers on small plates and arranged them on a tray. Slowly, she walked out the kitchen door, walked the few steps outdoors until she reached the door to the hallway, clumsily opened the door, balancing the tray in her right hand, then down the hallway to the parlor doors.

Taking a deep breath and plastering a smile on her face, she entered the room. The three of them had been served coffee and Cordelia served the turnovers, purposely avoiding Bess's eyes (since the turnovers weren't made for tonight).

As Cordelia placed her own on her lap, Bess leaned forward for the tray. "Here, ma'am. Let me take that for you." Cordelia gave her a sheepish little smile and passed the tray to Bess.

"Thank you, Bess."

"Now, Cordelia," Robert started.

"You know," Cordelia said, interrupting him, "I've scarcely heard Baby Nora tonight. She's such a good baby, isn't she?"

"Yes, she is," Nicole agreed. "And I'm so thankful for that. I just don't know what I'd do if she weren't. It seems it's all I can do to care for her now."

"Don't worry, Sweetie," came Todd's soothing bass voice. "You'll feel stronger once you've had the opportunity to breathe some of this fresh prairie air, won't she, Cordelia?"

"Oh, absolutely. It has done wonders for my stamina," Cordelia offered. "And nothing is better for the health than fresh air and sunshine."

Robert launched into his "Now Cordelia" phrase again, his voice stern and fatherly, but Cordelia sat up suddenly and sniffed the air.

"Do you smell that?" she asked. "Well, speaking of breathing in fresh air, I just thought I smelled a hint of smoke! Robert, could you check the other fireplace, please?"

His stare silenced her for the time being. "I don't smell anything, Cordelia. Todd, get prepared for that question. Women out here are always smelling smoke, and at the most inopportune times, too. Like in the middle of the night. Or in the middle of a conversation, for instance," he adding, still glowering at Cordelia. "Has Nicole started that, yet?"

"Why, as a matter of fact, she did ask me that just last night!"

Nicole smiled, her wide hazel eyes moving from one

friendly face to the next, and then settling upon her husband. *See how she loves him?* Cordelia thought to herself. *Do I still look at Robert that way?*

She sat there studying him, a quizzical little half smile on her face. His eyes were downcast as he maneuvered the last bite of turnover onto his fork, unaware of her eyes.

Cordelia's smile broadened with the renewed realization that there was no danger of losing the love she had for this man. They didn't agree on everything, that was true. There had been cross words between them lately. That was also true. But their commitment to each other was as strong and solid as those heavy iron chains Cordelia had seen on the ships in Baltimore harbor. Their link was unlikely to ever break and Cordelia found that a comforting reflection.

Turning her attention back to Nicole, she asked, laughingly, "What's it like to live with your husband again? Is he pretty hard to get along with?"

"Oh, no!" she exclaimed. Nicole reached for Todd's hand. "He wakes me every morning singing to me," she said, timidly. "Did you know that?"

"No! Singing? What does he sing?" Cordelia loved Todd even more now.

"He sings, 'Beautiful Dreamer' every morning. He used to do that back home. I didn't realize how much I'd missed it."

Todd explained, "Well, it's just so fitting for her. 'Beautiful dreamer, wake unto me.'" He squeezed Nicole's hand.

"Well, I think that's just the sweetest thing I've ever heard," sobbed Cordelia, and suddenly the tears spilling over her cheeks were absolutely genuine.

Robert dropped the subject of the Indians for the rest of the evening.

Twenty-One

That night, as they lay in their beds, the winter's last snowstorm whipped and whirled and thrashed and howled around them. They awakened to six or seven inches of fresh, white snow, which enclosed the entire fort in an eerie quiet until the bugle sounded reveille.

It didn't dampen Cordelia's resolve, though. She had to figure something out to settle this quagmire of conflict in which she found herself.

One thing that usually helped her think was currying Sunburst, so right after breakfast, she bundled up and made her way through the snow to the tiny stable in the back.

The pungent smell of hay and oats comforted her spirits as she entered his stall. Great plumes of warm breath from his velvet nostrils greeted her as he snorted and stamped his foot in the hay. Taking the curry brush from the tin pail hanging on his stall, she began to brush him, speaking to him in her soft, quiet voice.

"I just don't know," she continued. "What do you think I

should do? Well, what *can* I do?" Brush, brush, brush. "I mean, one way I betray Robert and you know I can't do that! The other way, I betray my friends and I can't do that either!"

Turning the pail upside down, she sat upon it and rested her head on her dirty hands, and still clinging to the heavy brush, she listened to his rhythmic chomping as he buried his nose in oats. It was in this position that General Custer found her.

"A very pretty picture, I must say," he laughed, resting his arms on the top of the stable door.

"General! I mean, George. How did . . ."

"A very hostile Bess told me where you were. I pretended to walk away but I doubled back here to see you. That's all right, I hope?"

"Well, you're here. I suppose it'll have to be all right. When did you get back? I thought you were off chasing Indians or whatever it is you do out there."

"Yes, it's so nice to see you, too, Cordelia," he laughed. "I got back last evening. It was a most successful campaign, too, I might add. In exactly three weeks, we executed a march of hundreds of miles through the barren wilderness. We never fought a battle and still managed to subdue the hostiles. AND," he added, with a lilt of grandeur, "we rescued the two white women held captive by the Cheyenne. All without incident. Oh, it was pretty grueling, I'll admit and there were times when things were pretty . . . intense. But I'd call that a successful venture, wouldn't you?"

"Yes, very impressive, General. Congratulations. This will put quite a few feathers in your cap, won't it?"

"Yes, I would think it might."

Stroking Sunburst's gleaming rump, he continued, "May I?"

Cordelia handed him the brush and he took over where she'd left off. "I never truly know how to take your comments, my dear. Do you still despise me so?"

"No, George. I don't despise you. I rather enjoy your company, I confess."

"Good! Now I couldn't help but hear you speaking to someone as I approached. I assume it was to this beauty you were speaking."

"Yes. He's a very good listener, you know. And he never judges me," she added.

"You mean, like your husband does."

"No, I did *not* mean that. I can talk to Robert about anything."

"Then why aren't you talking to him about . . . *this*, whatever it is?"

"Because it concerns him, I suppose. Oh, I don't know." Then remembering who was asking the questions, she responded hotly, "Oh, why do you always do this? It's none of your concern, you know. Robert and I will resolve this—not that we have anything much to resolve, mind you . . . Oh, George Armstrong Custer! Why do you have to be so . . . so . . . irritating?"

He laughed heartily. "I believe I've heard that somewhere before."

"I'll bet you have! What are you doing here anyway?"

"I had some news I thought you should know and I didn't know if your 'darling' Robert had told you, yet."

"Well, what is it?"

"The Indians have been reassigned. The captain and I will be taking them down to Camp Washita. It's a good fort. The land is hospitable. I should think they would like it very much. We're moving the Cheyenne and Arapaho tribes," he explained. "Some of the Kiowa and Comanche are coming, too. The others will be sent north."

"Yes, I know. Robert *did* tell me," she said, pointedly. She almost volunteered the information that the Indians would *not* like to move down there, but then she'd be caught in three ways instead of two. So she said nothing, for a change.

"There is an issue I'd like to discuss with you," he went on.

"What is that?"

"Your Minnie. Since she is with the tribe again and I'll be riding alongside them, it's inevitable that she will see me. But this is my assignment and I'll not refuse it because of her. I just want your suggestion on how to best handle this . . . situation. I gave you my word that I'd stay out of her sight. But in this situation, I fear you must release me from that particular promise."

"Well," she lectured hotly, "the best way to handle it would be if there was no situation at all!"

He bowed low to her, dramatically.

"But since there is the situation, you're quite right. And it must be addressed."

From her perch atop the bucket, her tiny face puckered as she thought, her dusty fingers tapping alongside her temple as she did.

"I'll talk to her. I'll warn her that you will be riding with them, and explain that you realize you're a despicable human being, but that you mean her no harm and have pledged your life to her safety. Yes, that's what I'll tell her!"

"A 'despicable human being!' Well, I like that! And after all we've been through together, you and me."

"Yes, especially because of that," retorted Cordelia impishly.

"Besides," George replied, in a hushed tone, "I know you don't believe that. If I gauge the signs correctly, I would assert that you're actually quite fond of me."

"Then perhaps you're not gauging the signs correctly. I hope you don't mistake me for one of the swooning young girls who throw themselves at your feet, General."

"Actually, no. There's no mistaking you for that. In many ways, you remind me of my Libby. She's also full of pluck and vigor. You two are quite the exception to the rule, Cordelia. If you ever got together I'm sure you'd be great friends . . . of course, I'd never allow you to get that close. It wouldn't be prudent, I'm afraid. I don't want the two of you comparing notes about me."

"What makes you think two exceptions to the rule like us would want to spend our time together talking about you? I'm sure we could find more interesting topics."

"See? You've done it again. Insult after insult!"

Laughing, she admitted, "I'm sorry, George. For some reason, you always seem to bring out the wicked side of my personality."

"Would that were true, my dear. Would that were true."

"Anyway, if we could get back on the subject, General, I'll assure Minnie that you will do all you can to ensure her safety. And you'd better do that, too. Please, George, keep her safe. Keep all of them safe, as a personal favor to me. I have become very fond of those people. I couldn't stand the thought of them being hurt. I don't want this relocation to happen, mind you. But I know that it must. So I just ask that you keep them safe."

"I understand and give you my word that I will do my best to move them without incident."

"Just make sure you do. You know, your reputation as an Indian fighter is far from honorable."

"That, my dear, depends upon whom you ask."

"Possibly." She took the brush from him and with great deliberation, placed it back in the pail and hung it up on its nail.

"I'd better go back in. It's too cold to stay out here any longer. Remember your promise to keep them safe. I'll talk to Minnie."

"Thank you, Cordelia."

She had taken two steps toward her quarters when she stopped and turned to him.

"And George . . . please look out for Robert. I know you two aren't exactly friends, but I ask you to lay that aside. Can you do that?"

"Of course."

"Thank you."

He tipped his hat, watching her until she disappeared behind the hallway door.

~*~

As she came in from outdoors, Lucy met her in the hallway.

"Mrs. Otis is not feeling well today. Could you look in on her?"

"Certainly!" Cordelia told her. "Just let me wash up first."

After making sure her hands were clean, she crept to Nicole's door. Knocking quietly, she heard a feeble, "Come in!" from inside. She found Nicole lying on the bed with a cool compress over her forehead.

"Oh, Mrs. Lawson!" She tried to get up, but Cordelia gently pressed her back onto the bed.

"No, you don't have to get up for me. I'll just sit right here next to the bed and we can talk. What's wrong, Nicole? Is there anything I can do for you?"

"No, thank you. Really, I should be better soon. Usually when I take a little nap, I wake up somewhat refreshed and many times I feel better." With a little forced chuckle, she continued, "I seem to have one of my headaches again."

"Really? I'm so sorry. Perhaps Doc will have something that can help you. Shall I fetch him for you?"

"Oh, no! Please don't. I'm sure I'll be fine in a little while."

"Nicole, forgive me if I disturb you by saying this, but perhaps you should find some way to get some fresh air. You're always cooped up inside. Why, that would make anybody sick! I know you may not be able to exercise in a strenuous way, but you could bundle up and sit out on the porch for a few minutes every day. I tell you, the fresh air and sunshine can do wonders, even when it's cold. I never have headaches and I'm quite sure it's because I enjoy the outdoors so much."

She watched as a feeble smile spread across her new friend's face. "Yes. I quite agree. Perhaps that's all I need. And eventually, I may even be able to walk briskly around the fort. You and I could enjoy a footrace or two around the quadrangle."

Cordelia patted her shoulder affectionately. "I'm sorry. You've been ill. Perhaps I shouldn't have said anything at all."

"No, that's fine. I appreciate your concern, really I do. And if I'm not better soon, I promise I'll see Dr. Anthony. Next time you see me, who knows? I just might be sitting out on the porch waiting for you. I know I have to do something. My mother used to say, 'a wife with a headache cannot be companionable!'"

Cordelia giggled. "I haven't heard that one, but I suppose there's some truth to it."

"I never want to cause Todd to suffer because of my infirmities. So I shall have to work hard to make sure there's *no* truth to it in this household."

Nicole held her fragile white hand out to Cordelia. "Thank you for your visit, Mrs. Lawson. I'm feeling better already. I think I'll just take that little nap while I have the chance. Lucy is here in case Nora wakes before I do. I'm sure after a nap I'll feel restored."

Afraid to give her hand the slightest squeeze for fear of breaking one of the fragile bones, Cordelia smiled reassuringly. "I hope so, my friend. I certainly do. I'll see you in a little while."

"Yes," she whispered. "In a little while."

Cordelia slipped out of the room as soundlessly as Nicole slipped into her nap.

~*~

Sitting before the hearth, she could watch the flames dancing in the fireplace or she could turn her head slightly to see the snow-covered parade ground outside her parlor window. It pleased her to be able to fix her gaze on such opposites; flame and snow, hot and cold, orange-red and blue-white.

Momentarily worried about the Indians' welfare in this cold, she recalled the cozy warmth of the tipi and the buffalo hides, and she knew they would be fine. She'd plan a trip to the village as soon as she could. She needed to speak to Minnie about George. She'd need to speak to Little Robe about . . . what?

Then it came to her. Why should she speak to Little Robe at all? If Robert wants information about Little Robe and the Indians' concerns, and if Little Robe wants word about the goings-on at the fort, let them talk to each other! Jeremiah would be glad to translate for them!

That was it!

As she sat upright in her chair, her face reflected the warmth from without and within as she realized God had answered her prayer! She knew what to do!

She would speak to Robert right away and explain that if

he wants to know what the Indians know, he can speak to them himself! And that way he can tell them what they want to know, as well, and only as he sees fit! A perfect solution. This was a solution that absolved her of any responsibility at all, except to set up this unlikely meeting.

~*~

For the second time that morning, she bundled up and walked-ran through the snow to Robert's tiny office. He was bent over his desk, writing. When he looked up, he smiled welcomingly.

"Darling! This is a surprise. You look lovely. I think being in the family way agrees with you."

"I *know* it does! But Robert, I must talk to you about something. Is it private enough here for a sensitive discussion?"

"Well, yes. What is it, Cordelia?" He walked around his desk and sat on the edge, motioning her to a chair.

Once again, she noticed how strikingly handsome he was and found herself staring into those soft, brown eyes for the thousandth time perhaps? Or maybe ten thousand?

"Robert, I know you were disappointed last night when I wasn't disposed to answering your questions regarding the Indians. But I hope you appreciate the awkwardness of my position. However, I just came up with the perfect solution—no, not me, but I believe this is the plan God gave me in answer to prayer."

"Slow down, my dear. We have time to talk. I don't leave until tomorrow."

"Tomorrow!"

"On the escort duty."

"Oh, really? I didn't think the delegates were even expected until tomorrow."

"They're already here. I saw them this morning talking to Generals Hazen and Custer."

"Oh, I didn't hear the coach. But I guess I wouldn't in this snow, would I?"

She didn't want to think about Robert's duty assignment because it would take him away from her for several days. She didn't look forward to the agonizing goodbye they'd say tomorrow morning. She had gotten used to having him home each evening. Bidding him goodbye was more like death each time and grew harder and harder with each separation. Thank goodness, he wasn't sent out as often now as he was in warmer weather.

But, in this case, even when he returned from this assignment, he'd be leaving almost immediately for Camp Washita. That might add another two weeks to his absence. She didn't know if she could stand it.

Besides, she was afraid this might interfere with her perfect plan.

"Cordelia?" Robert inquired, interrupting her train of thought.

"Give me a minute, please, darling. I'm thinking." Well, that settled it. This meeting would have to take place today. There was no way around it. The two of them would have to go to the village today or tonight—snow or no snow—to talk to Little Robe. It wasn't a good day for travel but if Robert was leaving tomorrow, it had to be done.

"All right. This is the plan. You must come with me today to the village to speak to Little Robe. I refuse to be placed in such an awkward position between the two of you. Don't you see, this way you and he could discuss matters alone. He'll listen to you, Robert! He's wise and makes no decision without deep contemplation and discussion with the other men. And this way, you'll have your answers, too. The best part is that I will be left out of it entirely! I need to talk to Minnie about something anyway. Please, Robert. Let's go right now if you can."

"Slow down, slow down!" He moved back to his chair and studied the pen in his fingers for several minutes—minutes that seemed like hours to a waiting Cordelia, seated as she was on the edge of her chair. She was growing cross just watching him. Why in the world was he having such a hard time with this decision? It was perfect! Couldn't he see that?

Finally, he leaned forward. Decision made, she knew. "I'll go. I'll talk to him, but without you. I don't think it prudent for you to travel in this weather. It's near freezing out there. And with the baby . . ."

"Robert, I have to go. I'll bundle up on the drive there and the tipi is warmer than our quarters so I'll be fine, I tell you! I must speak to Minnie and I also need to speak to Little Robe to explain your presence there. Whether you admit it or not, Robert Lawson, you need my assistance in this."

No response. None. He just stared at her for several tense moments. "Fine. As much as I hate to admit it, you do make an excellent point. I'll get the buckboard and pick you up behind our quarters in an hour. Will you be ready?"

She beamed with pleasure. "Yes, I'll be ready."

With that, she bounded 'round his desk and kissed him. But when she began to draw away from him, he pulled her onto his lap and returned her kiss with such tenderness turning to passion that she almost changed her mind about the expediency of their mission. Maybe they could go in two hours, instead of one.

Startled by her readiness to postpone their trip, she pulled away from him once more.

"Good heavens, Robert," she whispered. They stood,

holding each other in a leisurely embrace. He was holding her like that, with her head resting dreamily against his chest, when General Hazen and the two dignitaries from Washington burst into the room, bringing with them a gust of frigid air.

"Oh, excuse me, Captain," he sputtered.

Robert and Cordelia sprang apart and Cordelia gathered her wraps and her bag and sang a sweet, "Thank you, dear. I'll see you later." Then, "Excuse me, General. I have no intention of disturbing your work. I just find it increasingly difficult to stay away from this handsome husband of mine."

She sent her most flirtatious smile in the general's direction, and he returned her smile, shyly. "Gentlemen," he said, "meet Mrs. Lawson."

The first gentleman nodded his head curtly. The second took her hand and kissed it. "My pleasure, Mrs. Lawson. May I say that of all the beauty the West has to offer, you are the most beautiful sight these poor eyes have seen in a long time."

"Why, what a charming thing to say! Thank you, sir," she crooned, graciously.

"Captain, where did you find this one? I want one just like her!"

"You and how many others! I spend the majority of my time these days just chasing all the lonesome polecats away from my wife. I hope I don't have to add *you* to the list, Senator!" he laughed.

"Robert! You don't mean to tell me that you're going to become one of those jealous husbands, do you?" Cordelia scolded him, jokingly.

"Absolutely, and a wife-beater, too, if necessary!"

"Robert!" came her shocked response, accompanied by laughter from the men. Then with one more peevish grin at her husband, she was off to prepare for the trip ahead.

"Please, sit down," Robert offered cordially, but all three men were perched near the window, craning their necks to watch Cordelia as she carefully picked her way across the parade grounds.

A tiny smile crept over Robert's face as he waited.

Twenty-Two

On the way to the Indian encampment, Cordelia held Robert's arm and rested her head against his muscular shoulder, a slight smile on her face. She knew she'd felt this much contentment at some time before but she couldn't quite remember when.

He held the reins in his gloved hands and expertly drove the little buckboard over the hilly terrain toward the campground. His eyes were ever on the lookout for anything out of place, anything suspicious, anything that could possibly bring harm to the precious cargo beside him. In the quickly gathering dusk it was increasingly difficult to differentiate the shadowy shapes and contours that lay before them.

By the time the village came into view, he knew the Indians already knew of his approach. Cordelia, without the slightest fear or trepidation, sat quietly beside him and snuggled deeper under the quilt that covered her.

"Cold?" he asked.

"Not really. You're warm enough to keep me comfortable, darling."

She saw his steely-eyed squint as he scanned the Indian village ahead.

"Swing around to that side over there," she instructed, pointing to the place Jeremiah usually stopped the wagon. She knew Little Bear would be there to take care of the mules.

"Are you worried about this, Robert?" she asked, sensing his apprehension.

"I have never had any sort of council with the Indians, Cordelia. When I've been present for discussions, it's always been as a spectator. I hope you know that I would not be doing this if I didn't trust you so completely."

"I know, my love. Thank you for your confidence. Everything will be fine. I know that. Don't you agree that this is the perfect solution?"

His eyes swept over her upturned face and, once more, he felt that clenching in his gut he sometimes experienced when he looked at her. "Yes, I suppose so," he said, pulling the horses to a standstill.

Instead of immediately flocking around the wagon as they usually did, the children hung back, watching carefully. They didn't quite know what to make of this white-soldier-man who arrived with their beloved Red Hair Woman.

But Jeremiah, hurriedly called to the scene, no doubt, greeted them warmly, shaking Robert's hand in the way of the white men. Cordelia nodded to Jeremiah's abbreviated bow to her and told him why they were here.

"We just didn't have time to make prior arrangements, Jeremiah. Robert is leaving tomorrow on an assignment and won't have another opportunity to speak to him. Do you think Little Robe will see him?"

"Yes. I believe so. But it would be better for Scorched Lightning and Yellow Bear and their men to be here, too."

"I know that," Robert said, "but it just couldn't be

helped. I'd appreciate anything you can do to aid our cause, Jeremiah. We just want a friendly and honest dialogue with Little Robe."

"Come," he said, turning toward the chief's tipi. Cordelia offered her husband a reassuring smile as they climbed the little embankment to the lodges above. They paused outside Little Robe's tipi as Jeremiah went in. They heard muffled voices, then silence.

Finally, Little Robe stepped outside his tipi followed by Jeremiah. His eyes crinkled in recognition when he saw Cordelia standing next to this tall white soldier.

Jeremiah made the introductions. Robert stuck his hand out to Little Robe, who recognized this gesture and took his hand awkwardly.

"Did you tell him that Robert is my husband?" Cordelia wanted to know.

"Yes, Mrs. Lawson," Jeremiah whispered.

"Did you tell him that he is here at my suggestion?"

"Yes, Mrs. Lawson."

"Well, then." Cordelia nodded her approval and shifted her weight from one chilled foot to the other.

Little Robe addressed Robert and opened his tent flap so Robert could enter. With a backwards glance to Cordelia, he bent into the tipi and the three men disappeared from her sight.

Swinging her arms restlessly, she looked about her, wondering what she would do this whole time and wondering why she didn't insist on being in the meeting. She couldn't stand not knowing what was being said. She wondered if she'd remembered all the protocol when she'd briefed her husband on the way here.

Spying Minnie and Little Robe's wife, Running Deer, she made her way toward them. "We can wait in Raven Cloud's tipi," Minnie told her as she approached. "It is warm there. When the men finish their talk, we will know."

So Cordelia, with one last long look toward the chief's lodge, ducked under the flap into the warmth of the room.

~*~

"When will we be forced to march to this new fort?" Little Robe wanted to know. Jeremiah translated.

"It will not be for another week. Preparations have to be made. Provisions have to be secured. There are many people and the way will be hard, I fear," Robert answered, honestly.

Little Robe nodded.

"We have worry for our women and children. Our ponies are few. And the winter has taken much of our strength, I think," he said, slowly.

Robert was careful to keep his eyes to the ground instead of looking at Jeremiah as he translated the chief's words. He didn't want the chief to feel as though he were addressing Jeremiah instead of Little Robe. The chief passed the pipe back to Robert, who took another small pull on it. He, like the Indians, did not inhale. He handed the pipe to Jeremiah.

"Perhaps we could transport them in wagons," he suggested.

The chief nodded.

"The commander there at the new fort. How is he? Is he a good man, like Commander Hazen? Will he allow us to hunt and to ride in this new land?"

"That I do not know," Robert stated solemnly. "His name is Grierson. I know that he is a brave man. In the white man's war, he fought many battles. But I do not know how he feels about your people. I will have to ask General Custer. He knows him well."

At Custer's name, Little Robe's brows raised and he leaned back assessing Robert anew. This even before Jeremiah had a chance to finish the translation.

"If he is a friend of the Long Hair," Little Robe interrupted, "he is likely a man of no honor."

"Not necessarily," Robert told him. "You believe that my wife has honor?"

"Yes," came his reply.

"She is his friend." After a second's pause, Robert continued, "I am his friend."

That had been harder to say than he'd expected. He wondered to himself if it were even true. He despised this feeling of jealousy that washed over him every time he thought of Cordelia's association with that man. The subject of George Custer had become a sore spot for Robert. He was tired of being outdone by that pompous showman—for that's what he was—all show! But he chased those thoughts from his mind and redirected his thinking toward the conversation at hand.

The chief said nothing at first. He puffed again on the pipe sending the smoke curling toward the ceiling. Finally he said, "This, I did not know. I will have to think on it."

This time it was Robert who remained silent, waiting for the chief's next question.

The pipe passed between them three times before he finally asked, "You will guarantee our protection on the journey to the new fort?"

"Yes. General Custer and I will be leading two cavalry companies who will take you to Camp Washita. We will keep you safe."

The chief nodded once more.

Eventually, Robert asked a question. "I know you do not want to go to the new fort. But will you give me your word that you will lead your people there peacefully, without taking up arms to resist these orders?"

It was Jeremiah's turn to be surprised. He paused before asking the chief this question. Little Robe turned to him, waiting for the translation. Robert turned to him and with a nod in Little Robe's direction said, "Ask him!" After a moment, Jeremiah asked the question.

The chief thought about his answer carefully before giving one. "As far as it depends on the Cheyenne, we will go peacefully. I cannot speak for my brothers of the Arapaho and Kiowa. I have spoken." With a sidewise slash of his hand, he crossed his arms over his massive chest. The interview was over.

Robert held out his hand again. After some deliberation, the chief took his hand firmly and nodded his affirmation.

Looking to Jeremiah for direction and following his lead, Robert stood and exited the lodge without another word. The buckboard was brought up and they looked around for Cordelia. Jeremiah ordered one of the young braves to inquire at the tipi of Raven Cloud.

Soon, Cordelia's mass of red curls appeared from behind the tipi flap, a flash of radiant color in the winter whiteness around them. Her eyes asked a hundred questions as she approached the men, but her smile never faltered as she climbed aboard the wagon with Robert's assistance, pleased by the sense of his obvious strength. It reminded her of . . . yes, of the pure physicality of General George Custer.

No one saw the smile falter at that thought. It was too dark by then and the moonlight lingered behind them as they made their way to the fort. Lost in their own thoughts, it wasn't until they were back in the safety and comfort of their own dining room, eating the roast beef sandwich Bess had prepared for them, that Cordelia began plying him with questions. After he had satisfied her curiosity regarding the meeting, they decided to turn in early.

Lying under the covers, shivering slightly, she stared into the red-orange flames in the fireplace, satisfied that she'd made the right decisions about the meeting tonight, about the friendship she'd established with the Indians and especially about her choice in husbands.

She snuggled closer to him. He distractedly patted her shoulder and turning his back to her, fell asleep, leaving her to her own thoughts once more. Tomorrow he'd be leaving for almost a week. She held him a little tighter at the very thought of watching him go.

Part Four

Twenty-Three

March 20, 1869

The next morning, at the sound of the 4:30 bugle call, they hurriedly rose and dressed. After a quick breakfast, they said their goodbyes at home. Robert didn't especially like public demonstrations of affection so it was more appropriate this way.

Inexplicably, Cordelia didn't cry this time, though she felt her heart breaking inside her chest. When he took her into his arms, she smiled in his embrace and told him to come back to her safe and sound.

With his usual, "By God's grace, I shall," he kissed her, not with passion, but with the utmost tenderness, leaving her swaying slightly on tip-toe.

She stood at the door as he tromped toward the stable to saddle Chief for the long journey ahead. The snow had frozen overnight and the reverberating sound of the crunch, crunch of snow accompanied each booted step in the quiet of first light.

Shivering, she closed the heavy door and made her way to the parlor window. From there she watched his tall figure in the saddle as he came around their quarters and rode toward the waiting stagecoach, his heavy cape spread across Chief's rump. He'd chosen six men to accompany him on this assignment. Together they would escort the coach safely to Camp Supply.

She saw the raising of his hand, and heard the muffled sound of his command to advance. He never looked back—just rode straight and tall away from her into the snow-covered countryside. She watched until the silent whiteness of the prairie enveloped him completely.

Watching him go, Cordelia felt terribly alone. Her hand gravitated to her still-flat belly. It was then she remembered that she wouldn't be truly alone again for a very long time.

~*~

Three days later, Cordelia sat on the steps before their quarters, enjoying the surprise nature had bestowed on them. The last of the snow had melted yesterday and today the sun shone brightly, teasing them with the nearness of the warmth of spring.

"How's Nicole?" she asked Doc, as he made his exit from the Otis's quarters.

She'd never seen such sadness in his eyes. He shook his head and descended the steps without another word. Cordelia caught up to him, took his arm and strolled with him along the boardwalk.

"Doc! What does that mean? You know you can't get by me with just a shake of your head!"

"Mrs. Lawson, please. There is such a thing as privacy, you know. Perhaps Mrs. Otis doesn't choose to have you know her intimate affairs. Have you considered that?"

"Well, no, frankly I haven't!"

"Well, consider it! I can tell you nothing."

"But I'm worried about her! I'm no doctor but even I can see how weak and pale she is. I hear her coughing at all hours. I see those dark circles under those incredible eyes of hers. I know she's sick, Doc. I'm not being nosy. I really want to help her."

Softening a little, he placed his hand on his arm over hers. "I know you do, my dear. I have yet to meet a person more loving or caring than you are. But I must leave this matter up to Lieutenant and Mrs. Otis. I *will* tell you this. It's probably not a good idea for you to spend too much time with her right now, not with the baby coming and all."

"So you think I shouldn't get close to her? You mean she's apt to give me whatever she has?"

"Oh, I *think* that's unlikely. But I'm not sure, Mrs. Lawson. Just to be on the safe side, I'd advise against it."

"But Doc! She needs me, doesn't she? That's what friends are for!"

"I know you well enough to know you'll do whatever you want to do. I'm just giving you my advice. Take it or leave it."

"Okay, Doc. I'll consider what you've said."

"That's all I ask, my dear."

Squinting into the sunlight, he took in a deep breath of fresh air. "It's a glorious day today. Some days it's enough just to be alive, isn't it it?"

Without waiting for a reply he was off in the direction of the infirmary again. Todd waited for her at the top of the stairs.

"Todd! I didn't see you there," Cordelia said, surprised.

"I know. I heard what Doc told you—that you don't need to be around Nicole. I want you to know that I understand and I agree. Your baby's health must be your first concern right now."

Cordelia, enjoying the feel of springtime outside, sat on the top step, pulling Todd down beside her. "Tell me about her. How is she, Todd?"

"Not well," he told her. His usually laughing eyes were somber now. "She admitted to Doc just now that the doctors back home advised her not to make this trip. They warned her that it would prove too wearing on her. But she said she just had to get here. She waited too many months trying to get better. When she finally realized she wouldn't get any better, she came anyway."

"Oh, Todd. She loves you so."

Todd's eyes filled with quick tears and his mouth distorted as he fought back tears.

"I wish I'd known she was so sick," he croaked, pounding his fist into the palm of his other hand. "I could have asked for leave to go to her! But she never said a word. Her letters always promised she'd be coming soon, but never said why it was taking so long. I should have figured that something was wrong. I even thought about it, but I supposed it was because of the baby! Nicole's always been . . . well, delicate," he explained.

Brushing a tear away, he continued, "Cordelia, I don't know what I'd do if something happened to Nicole, if, you know, she didn't get better. I'd be utterly devastated!"

Cordelia placed her arm around his waist. "Shh. Let's not talk about that, Todd. Not just yet. There are still many prayers to be said before we get to that point. May I go in to see her?"

"But Cordelia! The doctor just said . . ."

"The doctor just made a suggestion, to which I said I would consider it. I have considered it and now I'd like to see Nicole if that's all right with you."

"Of course, but . . ."

"Todd, may I see her alone?"

He watched the activities on the parade ground for a moment before nodding his head. "I've work to do. Lucy and Bess said they'd watch Nicole and the baby this afternoon." His blue eyes reflected the deep color of the sky. But, like the sky, she saw clouds there, too.

"That's fine, Todd. Go on now. We'll take care of her."

He squeezed her hand, stood tall, took a deep breath while tugging at his coat and headed off toward headquarters.

Cordelia walked as softly as she could to their room, knocked ever-so-lightly and tiptoed inside.

Bess was bathing Nicole's forehead with a damp cloth.

"Here, I'll do that for a while, Bess. Baby Nora seems to be sleeping now, too. Why don't you get a little rest? I'll sit with them for a spell."

"All right, ma'am. You call if you need us. We'll be listening for you."

Cordelia nodded.

At the quiet closing of the door, Nicole opened her soulful eyes. "Ah, Mrs. Lawson."

"What did I tell you about that 'Mrs. Lawson?' It's 'Cordelia!'"

"I'm sorry," she breathed. "I forgot. All right then, Cordelia." She made a monumental effort to smile, but all she could manage was a slight curve to those pale lips. Her heavy eyelids closed once more. Then she started that terrible coughing again.

Cordelia helped her sit up a little until the coughing subsided, then propped her up with some pillows and gave her a sip of water. While stroking her damp hair, she noticed a thin trickle of blood coming from the corner of Nicole's colorless lips. She dabbed at it with the cloth, careful to hide the bright red splotch from Nicole.

"Oh, Nicole, why did you brave this journey to come all the way out here when you were so sick?"

"I think . . . you know why . . . Cordelia," she whispered, raggedly gasping between every few words, eyes still closed. "I've seen . . . in your eyes . . . how much you love . . . your husband." Opening her dark eyes and staring intently into Cordelia's, she continued, "I had to come . . . because I love mine, too."

Searching the room until her eyes lighted on her baby, she continued, "Besides, I had a . . . very important introduction . . . to make." Nicole's feeble smile broke Cordelia's heart as tears stung her eyes.

"Maybe you shouldn't talk, Nicole. Perhaps you should just rest."

"No . . . I need to talk. Please!" She took a deep breath, followed by another couple of minutes of coughing. When she finally lay back against the pillows, exhausted, she said, "I had to make sure . . . Nora would be well-cared for. I had to meet the people . . . she'd grow up with."

Cordelia sat in sorrowful silence as she let her friend speak.

"How long . . . has Robert . . . been gone now?"

"Three days. He should be back tomorrow, I think."

There was a long pause. "You . . . miss him, don't you?"

"Very much."

Another pause.

"Cordelia, I have no right to ask this of you. But Todd . . . won't know the first thing . . . about raising a little girl. You and Todd . . . are very close. Help him? Teach her . . . how to be a lady?"

"Nicole, please!"

"Will you?"

With a heavy sigh, Cordelia said, "I'm an unlikely choice to teach a little girl about being a lady! I hate fiddling around with hair and dresses. I'd rather ride horses or go on picnics than plan tea parties. However, if something happens to you, of course I'll do whatever I can to help Todd with Nora. But you mustn't think this way, Nicole. You have to set your mind on getting better!"

She made yet another attempt at a crooked little smile, then shook her head. "I won't get better, Cordelia. Dr. Anthony just admitted as much to me. I knew that . . . before I came here. But . . . you know I had to come."

"Yes, I know," Cordelia responded quietly.

"Thank you for everything you've done, Mrs. Lawson."

Cordelia was going to reprimand her about the "Mrs. Lawson" again but before she could protest, she noticed that Nicole had dropped, once more, into her deep sleep, her tiny jaw dropping open slightly. Her breathing came in raspy, but regular, intervals.

Cordelia leaned back into the rocking chair. Watching her as she slept, Cordelia wondered how many more days she could manage to keep pulling air into those poor, afflicted lungs.

She closed her eyes and prayed fervently for Nicole. It was the desire of her heart that God would heal her. But she prayed for more than that. She prayed that God would give them to grace to accept whatever His will was in regard to Nicole, for she understood that everything—death as well as life itself—depends on God's perfect and divine will.

If He chose to heal her, then they would all rejoice! And if He chose to take her to Himself, though it would leave great sadness in their hearts, she knew there was no better place for Nicole to be than in the very presence of the living God!

"Lord," she concluded in prayer, "faith is not always easy. And sometimes hope is hard to find. But thank you for the joy of knowing that You are a God of comfort, a God of utter faithfulness and reliability. You promised never to leave us or forsake us. Though our own hearts are often faithless, Your goodness and faithfulness to Your children never wavers. We place our trust in You. Amen."

After her prayer, her thoughts turned to Robert, wishing he were here to hold her, to comfort her through this trying time. But even as she formed the thought, Baby Nora stirred in her cradle and whimpered red-faced, kicking her little legs and waving her tiny clenched fists.

Quickly, Cordelia picked her up and held her close. Nora nestled herself against Cordelia and watched her with those blue, blue eyes, so like her father's. Cordelia couldn't help but smile.

Twenty-Four

Robert didn't come home the next day, or the next. Cordelia strolled along the boardwalk with Baby Nora, delighting in another spring-like day, while keeping her eyes on the distant horizon. The soldiers were enjoying the day, too. They were playing that new game called baseball in the field behind the trader's complex and warehouse.

Cordelia watched them for a while, trying to learn the rules of the game and laughing at their antics. Bill Griffenstein was pitching to one of the enlisted men. The man, whom Cordelia had seen many times before but couldn't recall his name, hit the ball high to left field where Todd was standing. Todd's hands came up as he backed, backed, backed into the field until he stepped in a gopher hole and fell directly on his backside. The ball landed inches from his still outstretched hand.

Cordelia laughed again. When she looked down at the baby, Nora laughed back at her, her whole face alight with glee. "Did you see your daddy? Isn't he funny?"

Brushing himself off, Todd looked her way and pointed his

finger at her. She turned away from him so he couldn't see her laughing.

Big David Schatz, another first generation German American, walked to the plate. He hit the first pitch. The second baseman grabbed the ball, flinging it at the runner, hitting him on the shoulder. Out! Schatz laughingly ambled back to his teammates. Now it was Todd's team's turn to bat. She saw him run in from left field.

Strolling back along the boardwalk, she took a seat on her top step. Her gaze drifted again and again to the main entrance of the fort, watching for any sign of Robert's return. Seeing none, she sighed and directed her attention to the delightful bundle in her arms. Lucy came out to sit with them, holding her arms out for Nora. Cordelia passed her over to Lucy.

"Nicole?" she asked.

"Sleeping."

"It's gotten to where she seems to be sleeping almost all the time now."

"Yes, ma'am," Lucy agreed. "But when she's asleep she doesn't do all that terrible coughing. Not as much, anyway."

"Yes, at least she's resting."

Stroking the downy softness of Nora's dark curls, Cordelia continued, "Oh, Lucy, I wish Nicole could be out here today to enjoy this sunshine. And I wish she could have heard Nora laughing at her daddy a minute ago."

"She laughed?" Lucy was thrilled!

"Oh, yes, have you ever heard her?"

"No, ma'am."

"Well, here, let's see if she . . . ." Cordelia tickled her neck and Nora laughed again, a cute little laugh so infectious that Lucy and Cordelia were forced to join in.

"She's so pretty, isn't she?" Lucy asked.

"Absolutely!" Cordelia had to agree.

"Mrs. Lawson, do you want a girl or a boy?"

"Oh, I don't think I care either way. I shall love him or her with all my heart. You know that."

"Yes, ma'am. Mama and I want it to be a little girl with red curls and green eyes just like yours."

"Oh, my! I don't know if I want a little version of me running around here. No telling what she'd get into!" She laughed again.

"What's going on here?" Todd boomed to them with mock sternness.

"Did you win?" Cordelia asked, blocking the sun with her hand as she looked up at him.

"No. We didn't. Thank you for asking."

She grinned mischievously. "That's so hard to believe, Todd. You seemed to be doing so well!"

"Thank you, Mrs. Lawson," he said, pointedly. "Now may I see my little girl?"

Lucy handed her up to him.

"Todd, have you heard anything yet about Robert?"

"Not a word." He looked out over the prairie towards the horizon. "I'm sure they'll be back before long." Looking into the softness of his daughter's face, he suggested, "Let's go in to see your mama."

Cordelia and Lucy parted so he could pass between them.

"I should go in and help Mama with the linens. She should be about ready to hang them out by now. That's the only part I like." With an impish grin, she got up and started in.

"Coming?" she asked.

Cordelia searched the barren landscape again. "No, I don't think so. Not right now. I want to wait out here a little longer. Everything is ready for his arrival, isn't it?"

"Yes, ma'am."

"I'll see you later, then."

"Yes, ma'am."

She didn't know exactly how long she stayed out on the steps. But when the sun began its descent, the cooler temperatures moved in on the little fort. She watched the soldiers solemnly lower the huge flag. Briskly rubbing her arms with her hands, Cordelia decided it was time to go in. With one long, last look at the darkening horizon, she made her way in to check on Nicole.

~*~

An hour later, about the time she finished her sandwich, she heard the sound of horses' hooves pounding the dusty earth. Throwing a shawl around her shoulders, she ran out onto the parade ground, anxious to greet her husband.

Something was wrong. She didn't know what, but she could tell something was amiss. Why did they ride in with such haste? Why were they congregated before the General and Mrs. Hazen's quarters? Where was her long, tall husband? Where was Chief? She examined each silhouette before realizing that Robert was not among them.

The commander held a lantern while one of the men gave him an excited, clipped report that Cordelia couldn't quite make out. She decided to investigate. As she approached, there was a sudden hushed silence as all eyes shifted to the dirt beneath their boots.

Quietly, she stood beside the commander, looking from one grimy face to the next. She didn't need to ask the question. It hung heavy in the frosty air around them.

Commander Hazen began, "Mrs. Lawson. We have some unfortunate news. Would you like to come in and sit down? I think you'd be more comfortable inside."

Following like a zombie, Cordelia allowed herself to be led

into the foyer of his quarters. He ushered her into the parlor and she lowered herself gingerly onto the edge of one of Mrs. Hazen's treasured 17th century side chairs.

The commander lit another lantern and pulled a chair up so he could face her. Cordelia remained outwardly calm as she awaited the news. But inside her head, she was shrieking, *No! No! No! No!*

She clutched her middle as the commander began to talk. Cordelia tried desperately to hear his every word, concentrating as hard as she could, but things seemed garbled to her and disjointed. Her focus seemed scattered—splattered like paint on a drop cloth.

She squinted her eyes, concentrating on his, and listened with all her might as he recounted the soldiers' story. "Indians . . . attacked on their way home . . . never recognized which tribe . . . he stayed behind . . . single-handedly holding them back so his men could escape. . . . They rode away, expected him to bring up the rear . . . he didn't . . . circled back . . . nowhere in sight . . . searched . . . nothing . . . nothing . . . . nothing," his voice seemed to trail off at the end.

"I'm sorry, my dear. They are quite sure he wasn't there when they went back. They searched most of the day before riding back here without him. They think the Indians have him. They found no . . . well, no body, my dear."

"You don't think he's . . ." She swallowed hard, not able to even say it.

"I'm not sure, Mrs. Lawson. Sometimes Indians hold men captive. They don't always kill them. They may even use him as a bargaining tool. We just don't know, at this point." He left out the less desirable possibilities, not wanting to add to her despair.

Mrs. Hazen, who had joined them at some point during

the narration, placed her chubby arm around Cordelia's shoulders.

"There, there, child."

"No! He's all right! I know he is. I'd . . . I'd *feel* it or something if he weren't!" Cordelia explained to them, hopefully. The commander and Mrs. Hazen exchanged a quick *poor thing* glance before turning back to her.

Steeling herself against the rising tide of emotion, she glared at the commander. "So what are you going to do about this? What's the first step in getting him back?"

He looked down at the floor before answering. When he finally looked into her face again, he said, "We'll organize a search party, of course. We'll send men out to explore every square foot of the terrain where they last saw him. We'll do our best to find him. But Mrs. Lawson, you may need to face the fact that he may not be coming home again."

"No, I refuse to face that fact until it's abundantly clear to me that he won't! Will you be leaving at first light?"

"It will take a little time to organize the search but we'll leave as soon as we can."

"Thank you. And you won't move the Indians until we find him?"

He shook his head.

"I should like to accompany the search party," she asserted firmly. "I can ride as well as any man, and . . ."

"I'm sorry, but I must insist you stay here, Mrs. Lawson. That wilderness is no place for a woman. I'm afraid you'll just have to trust us, my dear."

Cordelia stood very straight as she walked out into the cold night air. She tried to remember her grandmother's rule. What was it? Yes, yes, she could hear her saying it now.

"Don't stoop! Throw up your chin, girl! The whole secret

of standing and walking erect consists in keeping the chin well away from the chest!"

So Cordelia held her tiny chin up and walked away with much more confidence than she actually felt at the moment. Todd came up the steps as she was coming down. She held him with the cool green penetration of her gaze. Falling in step beside her, he held her shoulder as they walked slowly and wordlessly back to their end of the complex.

Like an omen of sorrow came the mournful sound of taps, played right on time—8:45 pm. But tonight the sound pierced her soul as never before.

At her parlor door, she paused, offering Todd a pitifully sad smile and patting his arm to express her gratitude. The truth was that she didn't think she could speak. She was afraid that if she opened her mouth, nothing would come out except the shrieks she heard over and over in her head.

The next morning, Todd knocked lightly on the parlor door. Cordelia answered. At least, her body managed to move from the divan to the door; her hand managed to turn the knob; and her eyes managed to find Todd's face. But she felt disconnected from all that, separated in a way she couldn't precisely define.

"Todd?"

He stood before her, dressed in his uniform, holding his hat in his hands.

"Cordelia, I am going to find Robert. We leave in 15 minutes." Looking over his shoulder at the closed door leading to his quarters, he asked, "Will you watch them while I'm gone? I hate to ask but . . ."

"Of course. But Todd, you don't have to go, do you? The others can search for him. Your place is here with Nicole right now."

After a long sigh, he said, "I can't stand to think about leaving her. I keep thinking, 'what if this is the last time I see her?' But when I think of Robert out there alone, I can't stand to sit here idly while others go to search for him. He's my best friend. How can I sit back and trust anyone else to put out the kind of effort I know I would?"

She had no answers. She'd been thinking the same thing. But she knew they'd never allow her to accompany them. So she'd sit and wait. For what, she didn't know.

"You see? I have to go."

She reached her hand out, placing it on his arm. "Thank you," was all she could muster.

He nodded.

"Between all of us here, Nicole will be cared for, Todd. We'll do all we can for her. And Nora is such a good baby. She's really no trouble at all. Try not to worry. And Todd?"

"Yes, Cordelia?"

"Find him."

~*~

She sat in the chair, mechanically rocking Nora but her mind was miles away. It glided across the prairie like an eagle, searching out the nooks and crannies of the red clay mounds that lay scattered over the entire grasslands, imagining every scenario in which Robert could be found safe and sound. The others she somehow avoided.

Though the cool air wafted through the slightly-opened window, Nicole was covered with beads of perspiration. Her skin had lost its luster and was nearly as translucent as her lips. Cordelia had placed a cool, damp compress on her forehead, but her skin felt warm and clammy.

Nicole's breathing had changed during the day. Instead of

the regular ragged breaths she'd been taking, now she was almost panting. Dark circles surrounded her half-open eyes.

Cordelia didn't think Nicole was really conscious even though she occasionally moved an arm or whispered some unintelligible word. Her lips were swollen and cracked. Cordelia suspected she needed water. But liquids choked her every time they were dribbled into her mouth.

The baby jumped as Nicole coughed again. But she didn't cry. She just settled back into her nap. Nicole's eyes opened slightly and she actually fixed them on something over the bed.

Cordelia heard her say, with some surprise, "You!"

"Yes, dear?"

"What are *you* doing here?" she managed to whisper.

"I'm just here taking care of the baby and looking after you, Nicole. Todd will be back soon."

"You mean *now*?" she asked. Goosebumps crawled up both arms as Cordelia realized Nicole wasn't speaking to her.

Cordelia looked around. *What is she looking at? Who is she talking to?* she asked herself.

"Yes. Soooooon . . ." Nicole breathed, then drifted back to sleep.

About that time, there was a light knock on the door.

"Come in," Cordelia called.

General Custer walked quietly into the room.

"General!" came Cordelia's hushed cry.

"How is she?"

"I don't think it will be long," she whispered to him. "What in the world are you doing here?"

"I'm sorry. But I just heard about Robert. I'm so sorry, Delia. I wanted you to know that I'm taking some of my men, my dogs and two of my best scouts. We'll catch up to them easily enough, I think. Perhaps we can be of service."

Eyeing the baby, he held his arms out and asked, "May I?"

Momentarily confused, Cordelia held Nora out to him. He took her like he'd been handling babies all his life. She vacated the rocker so he could sit there with the baby. While he was cooing and grinning at Baby Nora, Cordelia dipped the compress in cool water and sponged Nicole's face, throat and arms again before reapplying it to her forehead.

Turning to Custer, she placed her hands on her hips and asked, "Now where did you learn to do that, pray tell?"

"I love babies. Always have. Libby and I haven't been . . . well, *fortunate* enough to have one of our own yet but I haven't stopped trying." He winked and flashed a devilish grin at Cordelia.

She didn't want to admit it, especially now, but she didn't like the way that thought made her feel. It was none of her concern, she told herself. George Armstrong Custer was no prize. That's for sure. But watching him with Nora made her a bit *less* sure of that, somehow. She felt the urge to touch one of the pale curls that strayed across his shoulder and instantly experienced a pang of guilt so real it made her wince.

He stood, handing her the baby, and picked up his hat again. "I'll be on my way. Don't worry. If anyone can find the captain, I can."

"Thank you, George. You always come to my rescue, don't you?"

With a grin, he tipped his hat and left as quietly as he had entered.

~*~

Custer wasn't the last of those willing to volunteer their efforts to locate her missing husband. In the mid-afternoon, a party of her friends, the Cheyenne, rode into the fort led by Jeremiah Running Bear.

308

After obtaining permission from General Hazen to join the search, he and the others rode over to Cordelia, who stood watching them from her steps.

"We're going after your husband, Mrs. Lawson. When the People heard of your sorrow, many braves stood to join the hunt for Captain Lawson. Little Robe had to tell all but these that they must stay in the camp. These are the ones he has chosen for the search."

With a hand on his horse's rump, he turned to look at the party of men. "These are the best trackers and hunters from among our people. We will find him for you, Red Hair Woman."

With eyes flooded with tears, Cordelia memorized each treasured face. "Thank you," she whispered, not trusting her voice. Bess came out of the house and stood beside her as they watched the men ride out of the fort.

"You see how folks love you, Missy? They know when they meet up with a real lady what has a heart of gold. Even that ornery skunk's willing to risk his hide to help out. I seen him here this morning."

"You mean General Custer? You *saw* him here, Bess." Cordelia smiled at her friend and hugged her tightly.

That night she sat with Nicole and watched the embers glow red-hot in the fireplace. Thinking of her friends' selflessness, she allowed herself some feelings of encouragement. "The best Cheyenne trackers, the best scouts, a Civil War hero and his hunting dogs and Robert's best friend. My, what a combination he has searching for him."

"But Lord, You know where he is. And wherever that is, I know he's in the palm of Your hand. I beg You to hold him safe for me and for our baby. Please let them find him. Please bring him home to me. Please, Lord. I don't know what I'd do without him."

She suddenly remembered her earlier prayer regarding Nicole. Funny. When she prayed about this poor, sweet child, she was completely resigned to the fulfillment of God's will—whatever it was! But now that she was praying for her husband, she fervently begged for his safe return.

She knew she must make an attempt to conform her thoughts to those expressed earlier. She had to recognize that even if God took Robert home to be with Him, it had to be for her own good, as well as his. After all, He promised in His word, "And we know that all things work together for good to them that love God, to them who are the called according to His purpose." It was one of her favorite verses. So it was from a tender and devoted heart that she was then able to pray, "Thy will be done, Father. Thy will be done."

Twenty-Five

They had been gone two days. The longer they were gone, the more discouraged Cordelia became. If not for her responsibilities regarding Nicole, she feared she would have planted herself on her divan and not moved. Weakness overtook her. Every movement exacted its toll on her energy. Many times, she shook her head at the plates of food Bess brought her.

Breakfast seemed the only meal she could eat, before melancholy swept over her again. She was always most hopeful in the mornings, expecting to see the riders come back with Robert in their midst. But as the day wore on and no riders appeared, she had to battle the despair that, so far, hovered just out of reach.

On the morning of the third day, Cordelia sent Baby Nora back to the kitchen with Lucy so she could focus what energy she had on Nicole. She hadn't thought it possible that Nicole could survive the night, but she did. Her breathing was shallow and irregular now. She hadn't moved or spoken since before Todd left.

A peculiar repugnant smell lingered about Nicole now,

even though Bess had bathed her only an hour ago. The odor seemed to seep out through her pores, poor thing. She seemed to be resting comfortably, though. And she was clean. As there seemed to be nothing more she could do for her friend, Cordelia sat back in the rocker and softly sang hymns to her.

She hoped Nicole could hear the words and find comfort in them. Cordelia found comfort in them, as well. It was in the middle of "A Mighty Fortress" that she heard the horses. She froze, scarcely breathing.

She could hear that one rider rode directly to their quarters as the others headed for the stables. Cordelia's heart pounded as she heard his boots, taking two steps at a time to get into the room. Could it be Robert? or was it Todd?

The door swung open and there stood Lieutenant Otis, a bit rumpled and dirty from the long ride. He anxiously searched his wife's ashen face.

"Todd, you made it back! Thank God! She's waiting for you, I think."

Kneeling beside the bed, he tenderly pressed Nicole's delicate hand to his lips. Tears streamed down his dust-caked cheeks as he sought some sign of life in her face. Pallid as the pillowcase under her head, Nicole made the motions of breathing; her chest and shoulders heaving with the struggle, her mouth opening and closing, but there was no movement of air.

"Nicole!" he cried. "I love you. Thank you for being my wife. Thank you for loving me, my darling."

Cordelia stood to the side with tears flowing, covering her trembling mouth with the back of her hand, still holding the wet cloth.

Nicole's eyes opened slightly, and she winced as if she were going to sneeze, but once her face relaxed again, there were no more breaths. No more movement.

"Go with God, my love. Go with God." He fell across her

chest, holding her and sobbing, repeating her name over and over. Watching the tender scene before her, Cordelia thought her own heart would burst. She moved toward Todd, placing her arm across his quaking shoulders.

Turning to Cordelia, Todd fell into her arms and together they sobbed for the loss of two lives so dear to each of them—their dearly departed, Nicole Otis and Robert Lawson.

Bess found them in this posture. "Oh, Lord God!" she cried. "Is she gone?"

"Yes, Bess," Cordelia cried, holding a hand out for Bess, who took it eagerly. "She's gone."

They cried and held each other as they lingered near Nicole. Sniffling, Cordelia whispered for Bess to bring Nora in to Todd. Bess, dabbing her wet eyes with the hem of her apron, left to do just that.

By the time she returned, Todd was sitting on the foot of the bed with his back to Nicole. His sorrow was apparent. His slumping shoulders and hanging head told the whole story. When Bess held Nora out to him, he looked at her, but made no move to take her.

Just when Cordelia thought he was going to do nothing toward his daughter, he lifted his arms to her. Giggling with delight, she playfully patted his face with her chubby, little hands.

Cordelia saw a smile steal across his drawn countenance. He chuckled at Nora's glee. Then peeked sheepishly at Cordelia.

"It's going to be all right, isn't it, Cordelia?"

"Yes."

"You know, we should be as joyful as this child. Her mother is with Jesus now. She's not confined to a bed or to a body so weak she can't move. Why, she's free now, isn't she? She can soar like a dove through the heavens!" Through tears and laughter, he said, "Her battle is over. But we'll never forget her, will we, little girl?"

To her father's delight, Nora cooed and shrieked with joy, as she kicked her little legs and waved her arms. He drew her to his chest and held her until she made noises signaling she wasn't happy there. Just before she started to fuss, he lowered her again so he could watch her. She seemed to enjoy the sight of him, and her broad, toothless grin elicited another wide smile from her father.

They left Nicole in Bess's care as she was made ready for the wake and together they stepped into the Lawson's parlor as they waited. It was only then that Cordelia timidly asked Todd about her husband.

"Todd, can you tell me about Robert? Did you find anything?"

"Oh, Cordelia! I'm so sorry! I should have told you right away!"

"No, you did exactly what you should have done, Todd."

Shaking his head, he said, "I don't understand it. It's like he just vanished. One of the Cheyenne trackers found a faint trail of blood. We followed it to a rock shelf where it looked like someone must have fallen because there was a large pool of dried blood. Cordelia, General Custer said no man could have survived losing that much blood. If it was Robert, I think it's time we face the fact that he must have died. I'm so sorry."

"But there was no sign of a body?"

Shaking his head, he replied, "I'm sorry, no. I don't know what could have happened to him but there was no trace of him anywhere. We found the bodies of some of the Indians. From the men's descriptions and the bodies we found, we believe these may have been from a tribe called 'Choctaw,' out of Arkansas. No one knows why they attacked or what they hoped to gain by it. We found shell casings, hoof prints, one of their rifles, three bodies—all Indians. The whole area is rocky and barren. We believe a wagon may have driven across the scene. We saw some signs of wheels. But they seemed to lead nowhere. They headed toward a rock outcropping, but we couldn't find where they went from there. Even the Indians were stumped! There was absolutely no sign of Robert. None of his belongings. Nothing! We have no explanation for you, I'm afraid. We called off the search last night."

"Do you think he's dead, Todd?" Cordelia managed to ask.

"If the Indians were using him for bargaining, they'd have sent word by now. We checked at Camp Supply. They've heard nothing. And, Cordelia, if he were alive and able to send word, he would have notified you by now. Especially after seeing that pool of blood, I have to say I don't think he survived. I'm so sorry."

"Well . . . until I hear otherwise, I'll go on believing he'll come back to me," she stated resolutely.

He held her hand. "You know," he said, softly, "losing Nicole is devastating to me. But at least I know she's gone. I'm so sorry we couldn't help you find the answers you're looking for."

"I know. It's all right, Todd."

~*~

It didn't take long for word of Nicole's death to spread to the whole fort. The men filed respectfully through the tiny room the Otis family had called home, where Nicole had been placed in a plain wooden casket. Candles and lanterns provided the muted light that illumined her now-lovely face.

Todd shook each man's hand and received his condolences. The women on the fort began bringing food. The dining table in Cordelia's parlor was filling up with whatever they had to bring. There were slices of turkey, a chuck roast, potatoes, carrots, onions, mashed potatoes, fried chicken, corn, a peach pie and a plate of fried apple pies. There was even a jug of milk to wash it all down with. This was enough food for thirty people! Cordelia didn't know what they were going to do with it all.

Scanning the table and the people all dressed in uniform or in black, seeing the sad faces walking through her apartment, she felt some confusion about just who was being consoled. Were they concerned about Todd? Or was this concern for her? Many had expressed their sorrow about her husband. She wanted to paint a sign that pointed to Todd and said, "This is the grieving widower," and another pointing to herself that said, "I am not a widow!"

Still, she knew they meant well. After the well-wishers had departed, Bess and Lucy tried to find ways to preserve the food that had been brought. Even Todd's ravenous appetite seemed crushed by the weight of sorrow.

Bess prepared a plate of food for each of them and brought supper to them.

"No, thank you, Bess. None for me. Todd?"

"No, thank you. I couldn't eat."

Bess noisily placed the plates on the table along with the forks, spoons and knives. She set the butter dish next to Todd's place, right by the hot biscuits she'd just taken out of the oven.

"Well, that's jest too bad. 'Cause you're both goin' to get yo'selves over here and eat somethin'. I happen to know neither one of you has eaten a bite today. So both of you come over here right now and eat!"

She stood there with her hands on her hips glaring at the two of them. They looked at each other and laughed at Bess's boldness.

Todd stood and held his hand out for Cordelia, who took

it reluctantly. They shuffled obediently to the table, taking their usual seats. For a moment, another wave of sadness washed over them as they noticed the empty seats across from them.

It was hard to take that first bite but, especially for Todd, that's all it took. He realized suddenly just how ravenous he was. Cordelia was surprised by the return of her own appetite as well.

"Bess, what do you do to get these biscuits to melt in your mouth like this? I've never tasted any quite so good!" Todd stuffed another bite into his mouth, grateful to talk about anything but his grief.

"Thank you, Lieutenant. All's I do different from most folks is I add a little carbonate of ammonia. Makes 'em real light and flakey, don't it?" Bess replied.

"She's quite the scientist, I'm afraid," Cordelia told him with a twinkle in her eye. "She's shown me twenty times how just a pinch of carbonate of ammonia placed on the tip of a knife and heated will almost immediately convert into gas and pass off into the air. It's quite impressive."

"I don't know about all that," Bess admitted, "but I know it works every time!"

Todd's chewing ceased instantly, "Then is it safe to eat?" His eyes shifted from one face to the other in mock concern.

Bess and Cordelia both laughed. "Well, I should hope so," came Cordelia's retort. "If not, you certainly wouldn't be in the land of the living with all the biscuits you've eaten around here!"

He chuckled. "You're right about that. All I know is that you make a mean biscuit, Bess."

"Thank you, sir. Now I got to git! Ya'll need anything else?"

"No, Bess," Cordelia said. "We'll be fine. Thank you."

Bess shuffled away and left them to the rest of their meal.

The conversation had taken their minds off their heartache for a few moments. Now they both turned their thinking to the circumstances at hand. There was much to think about. Many decisions had to be made.

After they finished their meal and had their coffee, Todd walked across the hall to his quarters. Mrs. Hazen was sitting with Nicole, taking the first shift. Lucy was due by midnight to take the next.

Todd stood beside his wife's casket and stroked her chilly cheek with the back of his finger. Baby Nora lay sleeping in her crib, noisily sucking on two of her chubby little fingers. The candlelight played across the sleeping child's face. Todd couldn't resist touching her downy head. An unexpected rush of tears blind-scalded his eyes, and flooded the bony contours of his cheeks.

Suddenly weak and exhausted, he realized he had no place to sleep! With the vigil taking place in his quarters, it would be improper for him to sleep in the same room with ladies present. So he picked up his hat and headed for the empty room next door. Tomorrow would be a day he'd never forget. Tomorrow he'd bury his wife.

~*~

A cold drizzle awaited the funeral procession the next morning. Residents of the fort began to gather outside the officers' quarters, awaiting Lieutenant Otis's appearance.

The soldiers were dressed in their best uniforms, the women in their best dresses and wraps. Cordelia didn't usually like to wear hats, but today she was thankful for the wide brim that kept the cold rain from her face. She hoped this would be the last cold front of the winter.

Also assembled and blowing warm breaths of air through

their instruments was the military band, offered for the occasion by General Custer, who stood in full uniform with the Hazens. As an overcoat, he wore a navy blue cape with gold buttons and ornamental gold braid. His red scarf was loosely tied around his throat and tucked into his jacket. Anxiously, he watched Cordelia as she and Lucy descended the steps to join the waiting group of mourners outside. Bess decided to stay home with Nora, not wanting to take the baby out in such weather.

Six men entered the Otis quarters to collect the casket. They gently and somberly loaded it into the waiting wagon and hurried to formation on either side.

Cordelia took her place behind them as she awaited Todd's arrival. Lucy squeezed Cordelia's hand as she started for the back of the crowd, where her kind were expected to follow. But Cordelia drew her back.

"Stay with me, Lucy," she insisted. "You're my comfort, you know."

"Yes, ma'am." Lucy shifted from one foot to the other uncomfortably, but remained close to Cordelia.

Behind her, the Hazens, the Anthonys, General Custer and his officers, and the enlisted men of Fort Cobb began to loosely form into ranks. Cordelia spied Minnie and Jeremiah at the rear of the assembly.

Other than the occasional toots and stray drummings from the band, all were silent. The occasional sharp pattering of sleet broke the quiet pall.

Every upturned face fixed their eyes on the top of the stairs, still waiting for Lieutenant Otis to take his place behind the coffin. Just as Cordelia started up the stairs to check on him, Dr. Anthony brushed by her, restraining her with his arm. An unspoken glance said, "I'll go."

She returned to her place, pulling her heavy shawl around

herself tightly. She longed for Robert's warm, strong arms to hold her against this bone-shattering cold. Visions of Robert, lying out on the barren prairie, looking skyward with lifeless eyes rushed to mind, but she quickly cast that thought from her consciousness. To reassure herself, she smiled confidently at Lucy and drew her closer.

Just then General Custer left General Hazen's side and made his way to Cordelia. Without asking, he took his place beside her.

She could feel, rather than hear, the gasps behind her at such impropriety. Her husband was, in all probability, recently deceased. There had been no time for mourning. Why, he hadn't even been found yet or given a Christian burial! How dare she keep company with another man this soon—especially with a married man, such as the general!

Shocked as she was at his appearance by her side, she admitted that she took comfort in his presence. She whispered something in his ear and the general walked to the waiting band, speaking behind his gloved hand to the director of the group, who nodded enthusiastically then hurriedly huddled with his men.

George rejoined Cordelia in the waiting throng. It was strange, she thought, that she could be alone with Todd for as long as she wanted and never think in terms of his maleness. Todd, for all intents and purposes, was her little brother. But she had to admit that General Custer was another matter. He stood a full foot from her, but she was acutely aware of his presence, and aware of his . . . masculinity. Despising herself for even the recognition of this fact, she turned her head from him, trying to blot him from her thinking. How dare she think of any man besides her beloved Robert? Next to Robert, all men were inconsequential, she reminded herself.

There was one woman in the crowd who didn't worry

about Custer at all. Mrs. Hazen. She knew Cordelia despised the general! She'd heard her say so, hadn't she? She hadn't even come to that delightful reception given in his honor! She watched carefully for Cordelia's reaction. Would she slap him? Would she say something clever that would cut him to the very bone? But, much to her disappointment, Cordelia did neither. Instead, she seemed to accept this gesture graciously.

Finally, the two men, Dr. Anthony and Lieutenant Otis, appeared at the top of the steps. Cordelia instantly noted Todd's red-rimmed eyes and pallid coloring. Yet, he held himself proudly erect as he made his way down the steps and into his place in front of Cordelia's little group.

He looked so forlorn there, swaying all alone, that Cordelia broke tradition to step to his side. He didn't seem to notice her presence until she reached for his hand.

Momentarily startled, he then squeezed her hand so hard she thought it might break. Cordelia looked up into his sorrowful eyes, usually so full of mischief and merriment, but now so full of pain it was almost unbearable.

General Custer crossed to her other side. Lucy walked behind and between Todd and Cordelia. In a moment, the band began to play "Rock of Ages" as they began the procession to the little graveyard outside the fort. Only four people were buried there so far—all soldiers.

When they came to the gravesite, the soldiers pulled the casket from the wagon, and using long leather straps, they lowered it into the earth. Doc Anthony strode to the head of the open grave with his Bible and read from Psalm 116.

"I love the LORD, because He hath heard my voice and my supplications. Because He hath inclined His ear unto men, therefore will I call upon Him as long as I live. The sorrows of death compassed me, and the pains of hell gat hold upon me; I found trouble and sorrow. Then called I upon the name of the

LORD; O LORD, I beseech Thee, deliver my soul. Gracious is the LORD, and righteous; yea, our God is merciful. The LORD preserveth the simple; I was brought low, and He helped me. Return unto thy rest, O my soul; for the LORD hath dealt bountifully with thee. . . . I will walk before the LORD in the land of the living. I believed, therefore, have I spoken: I was greatly afflicted: . . . What shall I render unto the LORD for all His benefits toward me? I will take the cup of salvation, and call upon the name of the LORD. . . . Precious in the sight of the LORD is the death of His saints. . . . Praise ye the LORD."

Then he continued, "We are gathered here today to pay our respects to Mrs. Nicole Renee Rimbaud Otis. She was born July 25th in the year of our Lord, 1848, and died March 26, 1869. She was the beloved wife of United States Army 1st Lieutenant Michael Todd Otis and dear mother of Nora Alice Otis. Mrs. Otis came to know the Lord six years ago and has served Him in thought, word and deed ever since. We didn't know her well, but we honor her with our prayers and our presence in behalf of her husband, whom we love and respect.

"I've spoken with Lieutenant Otis and have been assured of his love and devotion for Almighty God. Though he is grieved, he rejoices in his knowledge that his beloved Nicole is standing today in the presence of our Lord.

"Lieutenant Otis, accept our deepest condolences for your loss. May the God of all comfort strengthen you and sustain you in your time of mourning. And may your memories of Nicole comfort you for your entire lifetime."

Todd nodded his thanks. He took a step toward the grave, bent to pick up a handful of dirt to throw on the casket, finding only clumps of damp, red earth instead. But he dropped the clumps onto the casket.

At that signal, the band struck up "Beautiful Dreamer" as

those gathered began their careful return to their quarters through the slippery grass and red clay. Todd's head jerked upwards and his frantic eyes rested on his friend, Cordelia. They were the only ones who understood the relevance of the song.

Her intention in suggesting the song was to comfort Todd. But now, seeing his anguish, she regretted her impulsive judgment, for the melody seemed to break both their hearts even more. They held each other in a sorrowful embrace until the tune had finished.

Todd stood at the foot of the grave for a long time. Cordelia motioned for Lucy to head back. She and the general braced Todd and helped him home. He went through the motions of walking, back straight, eyes forward, but Cordelia couldn't bear to look into his eyes.

As they started up the steps, they heard the whump, whump, whump of the shovels digging into the wet ground then dropping the clay onto the casket below. With a long last look toward the little cemetery, Todd allowed himself to be led into the officers' quarters and into the Lawson's parlor.

General Custer placed another log onto the fire as Cordelia guided Todd to his favorite chair opposite Robert's. Cordelia delicately sat on the edge of the divan as she removed her wet hat. Custer immediately took it from her, shook it off and placed it gently on the floor next to the hearth to dry. He, then, crossed to Robert's chair and sat down.

Stiffening, Cordelia shot him a glance that said, "Oh, no, you don't!" Todd looked up, too, though not a word was spoken. The general quickly rose and asked, "My dear, where shall I sit? next to you, perhaps?"

"George, I appreciate everything you've done today. Really, I do. But Todd and I have some things to discuss. Would you mind, terribly?"

"No," he said, disappointment evident in his tone, "not at all! I certainly understand. I'll say good day, then." Tipping his hat, he started out of the room just as Bess arrived with a tray carrying three tumblers of hot, buttered rum.

"I brung these to help get you all warmed up agin'. You ain't leavin', are you, General?"

"Yes, I am. Give mine to the lieutenant. I think he may need two!" With a curt bow, and a toss of his curly head, he replaced his hat and marched out into the mix of rain and spitting sleet. After a few minutes, Cordelia heard a horse gallop off into the distance.

She took her drink from the tray and sipped it delicately. Todd took his and said, "Thank you, Bess. Why don't you have the third one?"

"Oh, no, sir. This other one is for you, the general said. I have one for us in the kitchen. I didn't figure Miz Lawson would care."

"No, of course not."

Todd drained his first one, then reached for the second, taking it more slowly.

Bess stood a little uncertainly for a moment, twisting her apron in her plump hands, then said, "Lieutenant, I jest want you to know how terrible sorry I am about your poor wife." Bess wiped her eyes with the hem of her apron as she blubbered, "She was a sweet little thing. She really was. And you don't worry 'bout nothing. Me and Lucy's gonna make sure you got everything you and that baby needs."

"Thank you, Bess. That means a lot to me."

"Oh, and Lieutenant?"

"Yes?"

"Minnie's here. She's back in the kitchen with me and Jeremiah and Lucy. She wanted me to tell you some things but I says to her, 'you go in an' tell him yourself!' Can you see her, sir?"

"All right. Send her in. Is that all right with you, Cordelia?" She nodded.

"Thank you, sir. She'll be in here in no time, I'd imagine. You want another one of them toddies, ma'am?"

"Yes, please. It has a way of warming a person up from the inside out, doesn't it?" She felt the warmth curling soothingly in her stomach.

Todd nodded. "Heavenly!"

"I'll have Minnie bring in two more, then."

"Thank you, Bess." It didn't take long for Cordelia to drift off into her own sorrowful thoughts. She and Todd were certainly a pair. Neither of them needed to speak. The depth of their sorrow united them in a somber alliance.

In a few minutes, a timid Min-nin-ne-wah-hah-ket walked into the room, carefully balancing the tray, sticking the tip of her tongue between her scarred, ever-smiling lips. Todd quickly stood to take the tray from her.

He served Cordelia her drink, then set his on the table beside his chair. Still standing, he faced Minnie and watched as she stood humbly before him. A tear fell down her ravaged cheek as she looked at the floor, searching for the words she wanted to say to him.

With his finger, he brushed a tear from her cheek. "What is it, Minnie? Are you all right?"

"Me? Yes. You? I think no."

"I'm very sad now. That's true. But I'll be all right, Minnie. Don't worry about me."

"I'm sorry for you lose you wife. She nice to me. She pretty."

"Thank you, Minnie."

"I want to come here now. I stay with Bess and Lucy and

help you with baby, with cooking, with cleaning. You need help now."

"Thank you, but I can't ask you to do that. On my wages, I have no money to pay you. Besides, it might not look right for you to be here with me. You are a maiden, after all."

"That no matter. Bess and Lucy have no husband. And they take care of you. And I no want money. Just want to help."

"What about your people, Minnie? They're about to move far away. You'll want to go with them, won't you?"

"No, Lieutentant. I want to stay here on fort. I like it here."

Todd turned to Cordelia, with his eyes pleading for her to help him. She merely returned his gaze with innocent eyes, seen just over the rim of her upturned cup.

"Minnie," he explained, taking her hand, "what I'm trying to say is that I have nothing to offer you. It just wouldn't be fair to you."

"I want nothing. Just to help you and Baby Nora."

"Let me discuss this very generous offer with Mrs. Lawson. I'll have an answer for you before you leave this evening."

"I no leave. I stay. I come to help you now."

"All right. For now, you stay if that meets with Mrs. Lawson's approval."

Minnie looked around Todd's broad shoulders for an answer from Cordelia. Seeing the hopeful, excited expression on her poor face, Cordelia could do nothing but nod.

"Oh, thank you!" With that, she half-ran/half-walked out of the parlor and back to the kitchen.

Settling back into his chair, he sighed and picked up his cup again.

"Well, I must say you were of absolutely no help!"

Grinning, Cordelia shrugged her shoulders.

Todd took a long drink from the cup, spilling a renegade droplet down his short, black beard.

"Oh, I'm sorry," he laughed, wiping his chin with his hand.

"It's good to see that smile again, Todd. I've missed it."

Staring at her for a moment, he replied, "It's nice to see yours again, too."

She didn't realize until then that she, too, was smiling. "I guess we haven't had much to smile about lately, have we?"

"No. And we still don't!" The words may have been dismal, but they smiled anyway.

Twenty-Six

"People will talk. You *know* that!" Todd told Cordelia as he saddled his horse.

"Oh, people will always talk about something. I know *that*! You can't live your life to please other people, Todd."

"I know that. But she can't keep hiding on this fort. Before long, she'll be seen. Already she's talking about taking the baby for a walk in that little carriage Aaron made for us. Where else is there to stroll except outside? Once the men find out she's here, she'll be in danger. I can't stay around all the time to protect her."

"I know. That concerns me, too. But they've treated Bess and Lucy with respect. Perhaps they'll treat Minnie with equal respect."

"Respect!" he spat. "The other day I heard someone say something about you and me! Dumbest thing I ever heard."

"What did you say?"

"I let my fist do the talking! That's what I did. Then I told him he needed to have his mouth washed out with lye soap, but that wouldn't do his filthy mind any good!"

"You certainly handled that well, didn't you?" Cordelia teased.

Leading his horse out of the stall, Todd stepped around Cordelia to mount. "Well, I just couldn't help it. He made me mad. I can handle what they say about me, but I don't want anyone maligning you. You're like a sister to me, you know."

"I know," Cordelia responded. "And I appreciate your defending me, but Todd, that kind of reaction may only serve to convince people that the accusation's true! Don't let it bother you. Let people think what they want. We know what's true. And God knows what's true. That's all that really matters."

"I suppose so. But what about Robert? He deserves better than that, doesn't he?"

"You'll get no argument from me. Will you be back for dinner tonight?"

"Certainly. This is just a scouting detail. I think Hazen's getting ready to move the Indians soon."

"But he promised he wouldn't do that until Robert was back!"

Saying nothing, he looked into the distance. "Yeah. Well, we'll talk about it this evening."

She nodded and watched him ride out the gate, latching it again once he was gone.

Todd and me! How ridiculous! That would be like being with my brother, if I had a brother! she thought, shaking her head on her way back into the house.

~*~

It proved to be a tough day for Cordelia. She ached for Robert—physically ached for him! She sat on the divan with her art pad on her lap, her charcoal pencil in her hand. But her

329

eyes were fixed on the distorted parade grounds outside the thick pane of glass. She wasn't necessarily looking *at* anything. She was not, in fact, seeing—just staring into that bright, sunny day.

Three wads of paper lay at her feet, each with a set of soft eyes missing the mark so badly she had to toss them aside. *Soft, brown eyes,* she thought. She could close her eyes and visualize them before her, the way he could embrace her with those eyes, could see the square line of his jaw, the full lower lip smiling seductively. His thick brown hair was a little too long, by now. She would need to trim it for him when he got back. And he'd probably let his beard grow. She thought she might like him in a beard.

Such were the thoughts she allowed to swim across her mind. They carried no emotion. Her gut remained intact while thinking them. It was those other thoughts that crept unwillingly to the forefront from time to time that caused her stomach to clench and unclench, to tie her insides into knots. The sensation was too intense for mere words.

Her face showed no emotion, only a stony sadness. Her limbs hung limply, her shoulders followed the same drooping angle as her mouth. So depleted was her energy that even holding her head erect or lifting her eyelids proved almost too much for her at times. She toyed with the idea of taking to her bed.

Yes, that's what she'd do. She'd take to her bed—an ethereal creature, weak and fragile. Certainly she'd waste away, waiting day and night for his return. And if he didn't return, she'd shrivel up and die. Someone, probably Bess, she speculated, would come in to check on her only to find out she'd expired during the long, lonely night.

Carefully, she posed herself in a recumbent position on the divan, pretending death. She became very still as she imagined the lovely painlessness of death. Her breathing slowed. People would file by and remark about her youth, her beauty and her intense love for her husband.

For some odd reason, this line of thinking seemed to soothe her. In her heart, she knew she'd never do any such thing. She had a little baby inside her that she had to consider. Still, for this moment in time, she took comfort from her dramatic imaginings.

~*~

Several times during the day, Bess or Lucy would seek her out to ask her some trivial question or another. She'd answer, apathetically, then go inward to her thoughts again.

Earlier, Minnie had brought Nora in for a visit. Cordelia stirred enough to tickle her little chin with her long, slender finger and make the little clicking noises Nora seemed to enjoy. It made her laugh anyway.

"You know, Minnie, there is no sound on the earth sweeter or more delightful than the laugh of a happy, joyous little baby. And nothing dissipates sadness quicker than a good, hearty laugh. We do not laugh enough, do we?"

Minnie puzzled these strange sounding words in her head, trying to make sense of them.

"Oh, I don't mean," Cordelia continued, "that we need to laugh boisterously all the time, but the gladness of our hearts needs to naturally bubble up once in a while and overflow in a glad, mirthful laugh."

She took the baby and twirled around and around, enjoying the innocent laughter this elicited from Nora. And curiously, the sound of her own accompanying laughter made her so sorrowful that she burst into sudden tears again.

Minnie, confused by her strange behavior, collected the

baby and, holding her protectively, retreated to the safety of the kitchen, away from this crazy white woman, Cordelia suspected.

That must have been hours ago. The sunshine was fading and Bess had come in to set the table for dinner, cutting her eyes toward Cordelia, not knowing what to say.

Dinner! Ugh, Cordelia thought. She wondered how she could eat anything. Yet, she knew she needed all her strength for when Robert came home. No telling what shape he'd be in and she had to be up for the task.

So she'd eat, she decided. And Todd, wasn't it about time for him to come home? She didn't remember hearing the sound of his boots against the wooden floor yet.

She spied the art pad in her lap. It irritated her that she couldn't seem to capture her husband's eyes, by far her favorite of his features. She could see them as clearly as if he were standing before her, but when she tried to duplicate them on paper, she couldn't! Why was she having such trouble with this? She'd done many portraits over the years. Eyes were her specialty.

She stacked the pad and pencil on the end of the divan, bent to pick up the "rejects" and stood with a grunt.

Oh, my! she thought. *I sound like a granny!*

Tossing the paper in the fireplace, she walked to the window, stretching her back as she moved. "Not much going on out there," she noticed. They were taking the huge flag down, a process she never tired of seeing. They stood at attention, saluted the flag, lowered it ceremoniously, then folded it uniformly, all hands working together toward the task at hand. Finally, the flag was presented by one soldier to another, who formally saluted before receiving it. Now they marched back toward the quartermaster's store, where the enormous flag was kept overnight.

That's how she managed to see General Custer cross their path, returning their salute, as he strode effortlessly toward her quarters.

"Oh, bother!" she exclaimed, aloud, jumping back from the window. "He saw me watching him! I know he did!" She quickly arranged herself on the divan and picked up a copy of the first book she could reach, opening it to the middle and pretended to read with great concentration as she heard the front door open, then a tap at her door.

"Come in!" she sang out.

He opened the door and peeked around it. "May I see you for a moment, Delia?"

"Of course, George. Please come in. You may leave the door open."

General Custer came over to her and kissed her hand politely before sitting across from her, carefully avoiding "Robert's chair."

"Would you care to stay for dinner?" she asked.

Seeing two places already set, he inquired, "Just the two of us, my dear?"

"No, George. Lieutenant Otis will be dining here tonight as well."

"Yes, I should like to stay if I might."

"Fine, I'll ask Bess to set another place."

As she neared the door, she turned back to General Custer.

"General, I need to ask you something. I've been thinking about this quite a bit. I should like to have the opportunity to view the site where Robert was last seen. Do you think that would be possible?"

"Possible, but improbable, my dear. It would hardly be fitting for a young woman to travel to those parts in the company of so many men." He studied one of his fingernails before continuing, "Besides, that's rugged country up there.

It would be hard for a woman in your oh-so-delicate condition."

"How did you know about that? You know, I'm getting so sick of hearing about the limitations of my 'delicate condition!' But yes, I suppose you're right," the sorrow in her voice tortured his ears. "Todd said almost the same thing when I asked him to take me there."

When she looked up at him, her eyes were crystalline emer-alds—the tears held there, catching the light then running like quicksilver down her cheeks.

"Oh, George, what am I going to do?" Then, in a great and terrible way, she began to sob. She buried her face in her hands and dropped onto the divan.

In one fluid motion, he was by her side, holding her as she sobbed into his shoulder. He gently rocked her side to side as he enjoyed the feel of her in his arms. He placed his cheek against her head, closed his eyes and breathed in her fragrance as she cried.

It was in this position that Todd found them when he walked into the dining room with his daughter in his arms. He politely cleared his throat and the two immediately retreated to separate ends of the divan.

George Custer, with a sly grin across his face, looked calm and comfortable, especially next to a genuinely distraught Cordelia Lawson. "Oh, Todd," she said, rising from the couch and placing her arms around him and Nora.

"The general has just informed me that he will not take me to the site where Robert was. I guess I'm just feeling a little helpless now . . . and hopeless, too, at the moment. I want him back so bad."

"I'm truly sorry, Cordelia," he whispered. Then in a louder, edgier tone, turning his eyes to the general, he said, "You have no idea how much I long for his return, as well."

"Thank you, Todd. Oh, the general will be dining with us tonight. I'll just go and let Bess know." Blowing her nose as delicately as possible, she drifted out of the room and down the hall toward the kitchen.

Sighing and tugging gently on his moustache, the general leaned back and crossed his legs, assuming far too comfortable a position for Todd's liking. It was funny how Cordelia was the one who detested this man in the beginning and ended up liking him. He, on the other hand, held him in high regard at first. It was only after seeing him several times in action that he began to find himself disliking him for his arrogance and egotism. The world was a stage for George Armstrong Custer, he thought.

Todd mustered as much masculine energy as he could, under the circumstances—holding a baby girl in his arms—and confronted the general. "I hope," he began, "you do not have any untoward intentions toward Mrs. Lawson, sir. She is as dear to me as my own sister, and I wouldn't want her to be hurt any more than she already is. I hope you understand my meaning."

Rising to meet him eye-to-eye, the general unflinchingly smiled and assured him, "I understand perfectly. And I'll let your insolence pass this time, because of your grief, Lieutenant. But I'd be careful if I were you. A young, beautiful woman like Cordelia and a grief-stricken young man like yourself. That could be a dangerous combination, Lieutenant, if you don't mind my saying."

"And if I do?" he asked, consciously swelling to his full height.

"Then I'd withdraw my warning," Custer replied, lackadaisically. He strode to Robert's end of the dining table and seated himself there as easily as if he'd sat there every evening for years!

This also grated on Todd's sense of protectiveness. Even with this sweet, pink baby girl in his arms, he could feel the heat of anger ebbing into his face. Just as he was about to explode in rage, Bess entered the room with another place setting in her sturdy hands.

"'Scuse me, sir," she muttered, as she detoured around Todd's solid stance. Tending to the task at hand, she quickly set the plate and ivory-handled silverware before the general, then placed the glass in its proper place at the tip of his knife.

"Here, let me take that baby, sir. It's almost time for her to eat, too. We got her milk heatin' in the kitchen right now."

He wordlessly passed his daughter to Bess. Cordelia carried a pitcher of cool water and filled the glasses.

Todd, expecting a look of warning from her when she spied the general in Robert's place, was disappointed when she accepted the arrangement without even the slightest raising of one exquisite eyebrow.

Todd quickly held her chair for her, as she took her seat at the table, then crossed to his customary place. Still scowling, he was further incensed when she asked the general to bless the food, which he did with great eloquence and ease.

Flicking his napkin to his lap, he turned his attention to the food before him: roasted wild goose (compliments of Jeremiah), fried potatoes, green beans, and steaming hot rolls.

"My dear, this looks incredibly inviting. I must remember to tell Bess." Custer beamed at her.

"Yes, please do," she urged him. "She doesn't get nearly the praise she should for all the wonderful meals she and Lucy turn out from that little kitchen. You must join us more often, General."

"I'd be delighted," he purred, sneaking a peak at Todd's darkening expression. General Custer had a wonderfully free and becoming smile and his bright, blue eyes twinkled mischievously.

The conversation over dinner was sparse but polite. None of them were in a particularly festive or talkative mood, but the evening was pleasant, nonetheless.

Lucy brought in a plate of fried apple pies for dessert.

"Oh, none for me, thank you, Lucy." Cordelia dabbed at the corners of her mouth with her napkin.

But Todd and the general each had one. As Todd finished his, he saw Custer reaching for another, so he also reached for a second. Glaring at the general, Todd poked bite after bite into his mouth as Cordelia chatted easily with them.

As Lucy served the coffee, the conversation took a significant shift away from "pleasant."

Custer ushered her to her seat on the divan before seating himself in Todd's chair across from her. This forced Todd into either taking Robert's chair or sitting next to Cordelia on the divan, which could be considered forward. He sat beside her.

"I suppose the lieutenant has apprised you of Commander Hazen's decision about the removal of the Indians."

Cordelia nodded. "He mentioned it as a possibility, yes."

"Ah, more than a possibility, I'm afraid. In two days, we'll start the evacuation."

Todd jumped in, "Yes, Cordelia. That's what I was going to speak to you about tonight. Remember this morning? I told you we'd discuss it tonight."

"But the commander promised to wait for Robert," came Cordelia's objection.

Custer tried to explain the situation further. "I'm afraid he can't wait any longer. Word from Camp Washita is that they are ready and waiting. And Washington has been patient long enough, Hazen told me. The bureaucracy wants the Indians moved so they shall be moved. The Indians are becoming restless, we've heard, so we must be on our way."

"I was with them just two days ago. They are not becoming restless," Cordelia argued.

"The Cheyenne, perhaps, but can you speak with the same authority about the Arapaho? or the Kiowa? or the Apache, for that matter?"

"Well, no, but . . ."

"It's going to be necessary to move them now. Hazen's already exceeded his orders by waiting this long."

"I see." Cordelia closed her eyes momentarily, before continuing, "I suppose he'll replace Robert then."

"As a matter of fact, I've heard that Lieutenant Otis is accompanying me now."

Opening her eyes wide, she looked incredulously at Todd. "Is this true?"

"Yes, Cordelia, but . . ."

"And that's not all I've heard, as a matter of fact," continued the general. "There is a need for a new captain to take Robert's office and Lieutenant Otis appears to be the man for the job."

Cordelia's eyes never left Todd's face, but she remained silent.

"I wanted to tell you, Cordelia," Todd uttered, "but I just didn't know how to begin. I suppose I have the general to thank for this brutal methodology." He glowered at the general, sitting comfortably in his chair.

"I've always believed in taking a direct approach to any situation," Custer explained, confidently.

"You're to take Robert's place." Cordelia said it quietly, and without emotion. "You're to take Robert's place," she repeated as if trying to absorb the idea.

"I've been approached about it, yes. But the promotion isn't certain, yet."

Sitting very still, very silent, very composed, Cordelia managed to capture the attention of both men by the act of simply doing nothing. Todd tried hard to read her eyes, to see something reflected in her face that would indicate what was going on in that clever mind of hers. The general admired the delicate curve of her neck as she turned to look at Todd. His eyes strayed from her neck to her shoulders, her breasts, her waist, and the slight expansion of her hips. Biting his lower lip, he could only imagine the pleasures that lay newly dormant in her warm and pleasing form. Meanwhile, Todd was in an uncomfortable agony under her gaze.

Oblivious to this, she sat waiting. For what, she didn't know. She just sensed that she shouldn't speak.

After a long break in the conversation, Cordelia took a sip of her coffee, breathed a long sigh and shook her head. "I cannot fathom this turn of events, I must confess. There are so many implications to this promotion."

Standing, she continued to speak while pacing the floor, talking out the thoughts that were rapidly cascading inside her head. "In fact, if you are to be the new captain, then this will be your quarters. Not mine. Not Robert's."

Suddenly she whirled around so quickly that her skirts twirled around her lithe legs in a most fetching way, the general thought. "In fact, without Robert here, I have no quarters! I have no place here! Without Robert, I have no . . . home," she breathed, her hands on her chest. She looked from one face to the other.

"Where will I go? What will I do?" She was thinking aloud at this point.

Todd abruptly cut into her rushing thoughts. "Now wait a moment, Cordelia. If you think for one moment you'll be evicted from these quarters, you're wrong. The commander would never do that to you."

"And why not? I came here to be with my husband, a captain in the US Army. And now, it seems there is no captain. So I have no business here any longer. The commander would not be unkind in doing this. He would merely be doing what is fair and practical!" She resumed her pacing, "But where will I go? And what about Bess and Lucy?"

Whirling toward them again, "Oh, my goodness! I will have no funds coming in either! Without Robert, I'll be . . ." she gasped before continuing, "destitute! And the baby! What about my baby?"

"Delia, really, my dear. You must get a rein on yourself. I know you have more pluck than this!" George stood to guide her back to the divan. Todd bristled when he heard Custer's familiar shortening of her name. She allowed herself to be led back without any resistance.

"Your family back east has money, don't they? Perhaps they can send you an allowance. Or you could always go back to Baltimore. You have a house there, don't you? Your family would welcome you and the baby back with open arms, I'm sure. That is the logical option, I would think."

"Yes. That's one option."

Now it was Todd's turn to join into the conversation. "What other option do you have? There are hardly any towns out this far. Where else would you live?"

Cordelia suddenly seized on an idea, and her whole face brightened. "I could go live with the Cheyenne! I know they would welcome me! I could make this journey with them, recording every detail, and illustrating every facet of their lives. Then, when this horrid journey has been accomplished, I shall publish my work for all to read. I could live on the money I'd make from such a book. What do you think?"

She looked excitedly from one to the other, awaiting their response. She didn't have to wait long.

"Cordelia!" blasted Todd's cry of outrage. "You cannot be serious! To visit them is bad enough, but to live among them . . . well, it just wouldn't be proper, not to mention the fact that it would just be too dangerous. You'd expose yourself and your child to all sorts of peril. There'd be hunger and the exhaustion of a forced march over rugged terrain. There'd be the risk of ambush from other tribes. Why the Cheyenne themselves might turn on you and take your life for breaking some tribal law or another!" Obviously opposed to the idea, he grabbed at any objection he could find.

"And what about you, George? What do you think of the idea?"

"If you were not with child, my dear, I would see nothing wrong with it at all. Yes, I agree with Lieutenant Otis that there would be increased danger for you. That's fine if you are willing to accept the risks involved, for yourself, that is. But should you jeopardize the child? I don't know about that.

"Besides," he continued, "you need to fully understand that these are primitive people, my dear. You'd lose your present level of comfort. You'd lose your present level of safety. The living conditions would be appalling for a white woman, especially one of your sophistication and upbringing. Surely you realize that."

Before she could respond, he added, "Besides I happen to know that it's quite difficult for a woman to find a publisher willing to support her work. On the other hand, the interest of those back east is feverish when it comes to Indians and the Wild West. I, myself, am working with Messrs Harper & Brothers. I am preparing a memoir of my experiences from West Point to Appomattox. I could write to them on your behalf, ask them about the possibilities. It just might work.

"However, as I was saying, you'd have every right to accept these hazards for yourself, being an intelligent and spirited woman, Delia. I don't know that you have the right to subject your child to these elements. I'm afraid I will have to agree with the lieutenant that it just wouldn't be safe."

Todd said, "Why don't you either stay here or go back home, Cordelia? If and when we learn anything else about Robert, we will send for you immediately. Go home and wait for word."

Cordelia held her head in her hands. "Oh, I just don't know. There are so many things running through my mind right now that it's hard to concentrate on *any* of them!"

George stood, placed his hat on his golden head. "You need to get some rest, my dear. A good night's sleep will do wonders for your thinking."

Todd stood as well, kicking himself for not being first to suggest this to her.

"There is no rush, my dear," the general continued in his well-modulated voice. "No one is putting you out into the wilderness any time soon. You have plenty of time to think these things through."

"Not really," she reminded him. "If the Indians are to be removed in two days, then I shall have much to do to prepare for such a trip. Why, I'd need to talk to Bess and Lucy, and pack, and oh! I have to speak to Little Robe about these things, first of all. I need to make a trip to the village tomorrow to consult with him."

She gazed suddenly at Todd. "Oh, Todd! I promised Nicole that I would be here to help you with Nora. But I don't see that it will be possible for me to stay on the fort. Do you agree?"

"Cordelia, you are leaping to conclusions where there are

none! Take your time to sort through these things. I don't have to remind you how much you have at stake."

"No. I'm fully aware of that."

"Besides, Commander Hazen will likely allow you to live here until these quarters are needed. I'm more than content with my own room. It's comfortable enough for my needs."

"Yes, especially when you spend so much of your time in these quarters anyway," the general replied quietly.

Todd glared back at him.

"I'll say goodnight now, Cordelia," Todd said, bending to kiss her cheek. "Please try not to worry. I'm sure everything will work out."

"Of course, it will," the general assured her. "There is no safer place to be than in the palm of God's hand."

Todd kicked himself again for not coming up with this spiritual reminder first! "I'll talk to you tomorrow, Cordelia," Todd managed, angrily leaving the room. Nobody seemed to notice.

As for Cordelia, she stood in open-mouthed amazement. "Why, George, that's what I say all the time! How did you know?"

"I didn't. But I firmly believe that all things remain under the sovereign control of Almighty God. He already knows what He'll have you do, Cordelia. You just have to stumble into His will! That's all. He'll give you the grace to choose the way He has already chosen for you. So Todd's right. Don't worry about a thing."

"I'll try not to. Thank you, George, for caring."

"Oh, my dear," he said, turning to her and taking her hands in his. "If only I were free to . . . well, to care for you in the way I'd like. We'd make one fantastic couple, Cordelia. I believe our life together would be utterly amazing."

"George, please don't talk like that. We're both married and have no right to consider such things. I value your friendship. But there can never be more than that. Surely you realize that."

"Oh, yes. I realize it. But that doesn't mean an ornery cuss like myself can't dream a little from time to time. No, this is a matter against which I usually guard myself, even from the innermost thresholds of my mind." He moved a step closer, lifting her hand to his searing lips. "I know full well that to dwell upon such things is an open invitation to madness."

She gazed into his face, hovering inches now above her own.

"Good night, George. I'll see you soon."

"Good night." Before she could stop him, he bent forward and planted a tender kiss on her forehead. "God be with you, my dear, dear Delia." And with that, he vanished into the night.

Twenty-Seven

The next day dawned gloriously. Though the ever-constant wind still combed its frosty fingers over the scrubby plains, the sun shone brightly, teasing mere humans with the elusive promise of spring.

Cordelia's mind had been churning all night, denying her all but an hour or two of fitful sleep. Excited by the prospect of such a thrilling adventure, she decided to throw caution to the wind and make this journey with the Cheyenne to Camp Washita.

Though she had itemized the dangers on a piece of paper, she'd quickly dismissed them. She knew she was taking quite a risk, but she figured if she had to live her life without Robert, she was willing to take that risk.

The only question that still gave her problems was the issue of the child. Did she have the right to jeopardize the baby's well-being by making this trip? She'd often teased that she had the "spiritual gift of rationalization," but that "giftedness" now told her that there was no safer place to be than with these wise people, who had carried children and given birth for generations and generations. They would take care of her and her baby. She trusted their abilities.

On another sheet of paper, lying on the floor next to her bed, was a list of things she'd need to do to make this trip a reality. She had written:

- *permission from Little Robe*
- *talk to Bess and Lucy*
- *enlist Minnie's cooperation*
- *discuss plans with Hazen*
- *pack*
- *leave a letter for Robert with Todd*

She knew the first thing she had to do was to make sure that Little Robe would allow her to travel with the tribe. She would be useless, she knew, but she believed his sense of mercy would override his practicality in the matter.

That was the task for today. Making all the preparations needed for this spontaneous decision would keep her busy, she knew, but she'd just have to make time to do them. Besides, it kept her from thinking about Robert. No, she mustn't allow herself to dwell on him. What was it that Custer had told her last night? Ah, yes, "to dwell on such things is an open invitation to madness," or something to that effect. Quite right. The man had a talent for the effective turn of phrase, she admitted.

Putting the final touches on her unruly hair, she made her way to the kitchen. Even before she entered, she smelled the rich and comfortably familiar aroma of coffee brewing and bread baking.

When she opened the door to the kitchen she was surprised to find Jeremiah and Bess wrapped in a tender embrace, their lips pressed together in a kiss. She suspected the fresh air from outside, rather than the sound of her entry, permeated their consciousness, as they turned towards the door to investigate.

"Oh, Miz Lawson!" came Bess's horrified cry. "I'm sorry. Me and Jeremiah, we were . . . ah . . ."

"Mrs. Lawson," Jeremiah joined in, trying to explain their behavior, "it's all my fault, really. She was in here working and I interrupted her."

Both looked like they'd been caught red-handed in some sort of sinister crime. The looks on their faces made Cordelia's peals of laughter fill every corner of the room. It was the first time she'd laughed like that since . . .

"Oh, I'm sorry," Cordelia breathed, wiping the tears of merriment from her eyes with her slender index finger and flicking the wetness away from her. "Oh, my goodness! You two looked like you've robbed a bank or something!"

She took a seat in the rocking chair, a smile still playing around the corners of her mouth, and studied the two of them standing awkwardly in the center of the kitchen. Bess looked at the floor. Jeremiah placed his arm protectively around her shoulders.

"Bess, my sweet friend, please don't be embarrassed. Did you think I'd forgotten that you're a real, live woman with real, live feelings? And Jeremiah, did you think I hadn't noticed how often you could be found here in this kitchen? I must say I'm not really as surprised by this as I am just tickled by your reaction!" With that, she bent over with laughter again.

Now Jeremiah's expression turned to one of irritation. "I'm sorry," Cordelia mouthed, unable to speak quite yet. After taking a deep breath, she was finally able to recover.

"Actually, Jeremiah," she continued, trying to return to business, "I was hoping to find you here today. I need to see Little Robe and wondered if you could drive me."

"Well, yes. I can do that, ma'am. When did you want to go?"

"Now? There are several things I must do today but that one takes precedence. How soon can you be ready to go?"

Jeremiah ventured a quick glance at a still-silent Bess and said, "I need time to hitch up the mules, that's all. I can be ready within a half-hour. Will that be soon enough?"

"Perfect. Thank you, Jeremiah."

He gave Bess's chubby hand a squeeze before making his exit from the kitchen.

Bess watched after him, then turned her gaze to Cordelia. "So you're not mad at me?"

"Certainly not. On the contrary, I'm quite pleased for you. Jeremiah is a good man, Bess—kind-hearted and wise. What are his intentions toward you? Have you talked about that?"

"Yes, ma'am. Jeremiah, he says he loves me. Well, you know how scared I am about such as that. I thought I was through with menfolk for good! An' I never thought I'd ever be with a Injun, even though Jeremiah is just half Injun. But he's so good. An' he really does seem to love me. I tried a coupl'a times to chase him off, but he jes' wouldn't go. So I sort of got used to him bein' around."

Bess traced her finger along a crack in the oak table, and shyly continued. "Miz Lawson, we was gonna talk to you about this together, but since you asked, I need to tell you something, I think."

"Surely, Bess. Come sit with me," she said, patting the chair across from her.

Bess, wiping her hands on her apron, obediently followed Cordelia's request. Cordelia appraised her friend in a new way as she took her seat.

Bess was eight or nine years older than she. Though she was on the plump side, she was still an attractive woman. Her features were too large to be considered truly beautiful—her eyes too round, her lips too thick, her nose too flattened for that. But her skin was the color of a creamy toffee, smooth as silk. Her hair—Cordelia had never seen it when it wasn't braided—was thick and black as midnight. She was a strong and sturdy woman, but her figure still had that hourglass shape, but without the need of a corset or any other contrivance. Her loyalty was beyond question and her heart was soft and tender as the new petals of a flower. Cordelia loved Bess as her friend and appreciated the service she'd provided over the years.

"What is it, Bess? We have a little time before Jeremiah gets back."

"Well, Miz Lawson, we want to get married."

"Bess! That's lovely!"

"Yep," she smiled, proudly. "Only thing is that we don't know how to do that out here. Jeremiah, he tells me that most of the Injuns look down on us colored folks. They think the white man is lower than they are. An' they think we're lower than the whites! So he says they ain't no way he'd want us to try to live with 'em."

They both rocked wordlessly for a moment as they thought about the implications of this.

"He says we could build a little house out on the prairie, but he don't really want to do that on account of he wouldn't want to leave me out there all alone and Jeremiah, he has to travel a lot when he's interpretin', and huntin' and all. It just wouldn't be safe."

She gazed beseechingly at Cordelia as she continued, "We was kind of hopin' you wouldn't mind too awfully much if he lived here with me. Upstairs. He wouldn't be any trouble, Miz Lawson, and he's a pretty handy fella to have around! What do you think?"

Cordelia thought about it for a moment, then nodded her head. "I think that would be just fine, Bess. But what about Lucy? Surely you wouldn't want Lucy up there with you all the time? There are times when lovers should be alone," Cordelia whispered to her.

Bess lowered her eyes again shyly and said, "We already thought o' that. But Lucy, she's willing to bunk down here in the pantry, where Minnie is right now. Only thing is that I don't know what we're gonna do with Minnie!"

"I think I can help you with that one. In fact, I wanted to talk to you, too. It seems that Lieutenant Otis may soon be promoted to captain. As such, these quarters will be his. I'm sure he'd want you to stay on and take care of him just as you've cared for me over the years."

"But Miz Lawson! Where you gonna be?" Alarm rang out in her voice. "If you go back home, then we're goin' with you!"

"Well, that's just the thing I want to discuss with Little Robe. I'm considering going south with the Cheyenne when they're herded like cattle to Camp Washita." She didn't seem to be able to keep the resentment out of her voice.

"Miz Lawson, that just wouldn't be proper, would it? No decent white woman would actually live with Injuns, would she? What about the captain? If he comes home and you're not here ..."

"I've thought about that, Bess. I still believe he will come home to me. I cannot accept that he's really . . . you know . . . dead. I think I'd *feel* it somehow, if that were true. But I can't stay on here at the fort if my husband is no longer here. I can understand that, can't you? So my choices are to go east again or to go south with the Cheyenne. Do you have any idea how few white people have had that experience, Bess?"

She could feel the underlying excitement as she explained. "I could write about it and illustrate the Indian's way of life.

Perhaps I can find a publisher who will find it as exciting as I do! The general is going to write to his publisher about it on my behalf. I'm sure there are many, many people back east who would be interested in something like that. Don't you think so?"

"Yes, ma'am, but what about the young 'un? You gonna carry that baby through all that?"

"I don't see any reason not to. I'll be in the best of hands and I'm sure they'll know what to do when the time comes to have him."

"Him? You aimin' to have a boy, then?"

"I don't really know, Bess. But especially now, I think I'm leaning in that direction. He could carry on the Lawson family name, you know. I've thought about naming him after Robert."

"That's real nice, Missy. But it sure pains me to think about you having that baby without me bein' around. I was sure lookin' forward to that little child."

"I know. And if Robert comes marching in here today, then I'll be happy to stay here forever. But chances are . . ." her voice broke a little as she continued, "that won't happen, Bess. So we have to be willing to change our plans. Life goes on, does it not? Though sometimes I wonder how." For several seconds a far-away look crept into her eyes as Bess waited for her to continue.

"Anyway," she said, stirring from her reverie, "if Little Robe gives me permission to travel with the tribe, I'll ask Minnie to accompany me on the journey, to serve as my interpreter. I'm trying to learn their language but it's not coming to me easily. I'll need her, I think."

"You know that child is purely head over heels for Lieutenant Otis."

"I know, but Lieutenant Otis is head over heels for his late wife. And as much as he likes Minnie, I don't think he could ever entertain the idea of marrying an Indian woman—or *any* woman, for that matter. Not now. Maybe not ever. It seems to me that the best thing for all involved would be for Minnie to go back to her people. And Lucy will be here to take care of Baby Nora."

"That's right. You've thought about ever'thing, haven't you?"

"I hope so. But first, I need to make sure Little Robe is in agreement with all this. If he refuses, then I suppose I'll be packing for travel back east. It's just that Baltimore's so far away. And when Robert comes home, I'll be relatively near him at Camp Washita."

"I see. Here comes Jeremiah now," she said, picking up the sound of his familiar footsteps on the porch.

"Bess," Cordelia said, gently, noticing the expectation that filled Bess's eyes, "I'm really happy for you and Jeremiah. When is this blessed event going to take place?"

"I don't rightly know, ma'am. I don't know who'll marry us, yet. Jeremiah says we might be able to find a white man to do it. But he don't think no Indian will."

"Well, we'll work on that," Cordelia whispered as Jeremiah opened the door.

"Wagon's ready, ma'am."

"Thank you, Jeremiah. I'm coming!" She winked at Bess and followed him out the door.

~*~

"So she's already told you about our plans?"

The wagon bumped and lurched over the rugged red earth. Cordelia, careful to hold on to the side with one hand and her hat with the other, replied, "She did. Jeremiah, I wonder if you realize what a huge step this is for Bess. I've known her for a long time and in that time I've never known her to get involved with a man. She has told me she gave up on men years ago. I assume she told you about Lucy's father, and I use that term very loosely."

"Yes, ma'am."

"She was devastated by the experience. It took her years to forget the pain—emotional as well as physical. I wouldn't want anything to happen to hurt her that badly ever again. I know it's not really my place, but I want to make sure your intentions toward her are honorable."

"I assure you they are."

"With the two of you being separate races, life may be more difficult, I think. Are you prepared for that?"

"I think so. I have tried to think this through carefully. I don't want to hurt her either, Mrs. Lawson. She is the kindest soul I've ever met. Her only aim is to please others without much thought for herself. I don't have much in the way of possessions, land or money but I have enough love to last a lifetime. She'll never be rich, Mrs. Lawson, but I hope to make her happier than she's ever been in her life."

Cordelia scrutinized his face as he said this, deciding that he was as sincere as a human being could be. She decided to stop worrying about Bess.

"One thing puzzles me, though. You are half-Indian, Jeremiah. You have lived with them enough to understand how it feels to be looked down upon, to be abused and oppressed because of your color. With this in mind, how, then, can the Indians look down upon anyone else? How can they intentionally oppress any other race of people? How do they justify that?"

"You're asking the wrong person, Mrs. Lawson. I have been sickened by what I've seen at the hands of the whites. There are things I will never speak of—not even to Bess. But I have also seen what my people have done to others, and that sickens me, as well. I have no answer for these questions.

"I can only state the fact that the Indians believe that they are the People. The whites are intruders into our country. They have destroyed our herds, wiped out our land with the railroad tracks to the west. They are slowly dusting us from the earth from which we've come. We can do nothing against such strength and numbers. But my people also see the Negroes as beasts of burden. East of the Mississippi, Indians owned thousands of slaves. Did you know this?"

Cordelia shook her head.

"Never has anyone been as good at field work as the Negro race, they say. And many Indians, Cherokee especially, owned slaves to work their farms and tend their horses. It is an idea passed from generation to generation. First they enslaved the Indians from Mexico. Then when the Negroes began to come into the land, they bought them as slaves for their superiority in the field."

"But you have none of this bias toward Bess? Why is that?"

"I am the product of a white man and an Indian woman. I was raised to respect both races. Even though I have seen the horrors of hatred, I was raised believing all to be equal.

"I did not set out to love Bess, Mrs. Lawson. At first it was just her cooking that I loved. But the more time I spent with her, talking to her, walking in the moonlight, working with her in the kitchen, the more I came to love her for who she is, not what race she is.

"I had a wife once. She was a Cheyenne girl. Very pretty. But she was killed at Sand Creek while drawing water. The soldiers rode in at dawn. She was the first to fall to their swords, I think. I had no chance to hold her, to give her a proper burial. We were on the run for days. I had a choice, Mrs. Lawson. I could go through my whole life hating all whites and seeking revenge forever. Or I could go on without letting this poison take root in my heart. That is what I decided to do. I never expected to marry again. But now I want to be a good husband and maybe even a father someday."

Cordelia's brow arched in surprise. "Really? Have you ever mentioned that to Bess? about being a father, I mean?"

"No, not yet. But it doesn't matter. I will be happy with her either way."

"You're a good man, Jeremiah. I'm glad this has happened between you and Bess. You both deserve some happiness, I think." This she said with a tone so sorrowful that Jeremiah turned to look at her.

"Are you all right, ma'am?"

She sniffed a couple of times, and then said, "I'm fine, Jeremiah. I've known happiness greater than any I could have imagined. I've loved more deeply than I thought I was capable of. I just miss him. That's all." She looked away, looked to the grove of trees ahead where the Indians had made their village.

Cordelia was embarrassed that she'd taken so little interest in Bess's life. She never thought of the possibility of Bess and Jeremiah strolling in the moonlight, sharing chaste kisses or having long talks about their dreams and expectations of life. She had been too caught up in her own affairs, she guessed.

She thought about the first time she'd ever seen Robert Lawson. It happened at her cousin's wedding. It had been a grand affair with people coming from miles around. At thirteen years old, Cordelia believed she was nearly grown up herself. She witnessed her cousin, Pearl and her new husband kissing in the hallway while everyone else was dancing and she longed to have someone to kiss. She'd closed her eyes to imagine it when Pearl's little brother, John David almost knocked her down running from his friend.

The friend stopped in his tracks and politely asked Cordelia if she'd been hurt. She shook her head "no" and stared into a pair of the softest brown eyes she'd ever seen. John David circled back around calling to his friend.

"Robert! Come on!"

"Your name is Robert?" Cordelia ventured.

"Yes. We just moved to Baltimore. My parents and John David's are friends. He invited us here for the wedding. What's your name?"

"Cordelia."

"Cordelia," he repeated. "I'll remember that."

When he smiled at her, she leaned forward and planted a kiss right on his mouth, then ran off among the whirling dancers, remembering the momentary feel of his lips.

Cordelia smiled now with the memory. That little kiss wasn't exactly what she'd longed for at the time, but it was all she had the courage to muster. And it was enough to keep her imagination going for the next several years until she and Robert Lawson were betrothed. She'd decided that day at Pearl's wedding that she would marry that boy someday. And she had.

Jeremiah sensed that she was straining to maintain her composure. So they made the rest of the trip in silence.

Twenty-Eight

As Cordelia expected, Little Robe welcomed her into his tribe. Wanting to thank him for his permission, Cordelia drew out a long piece of yellowed fabric folded into a narrow strip. She'd carefully packed it for her journey west, never imagining its significance for the situation in which she now found herself. Placing the linen bundle on the buffalo hide floor before them, she unfolded it once and again until there was revealed upon the softness of the fabric, one long peacock feather—the gift her grandfather had presented her so long ago, still amazingly intact and lovely.

Little Robe looked at it as if he had never seen anything so beautiful before. She lifted the linen up and held it out to Little Robe, gesturing for him to take the feather.

Gingerly, he grasped the quill of the feather and slowly pulled it from the protection of the linen, holding it high in the air. The sun coming through the opening in the top of the tipi sent shafts of light across the feather, brilliantly displaying its vibrant, iridescent colors. He slowly and carefully twirled the feather around and around studying its every contour, every hue. His black eyes filled with approval and gratitude for such a magnificent gift.

Never one for profuse dialogue, he merely nodded and grunted something to his wife, pointing his finger to the right. His wife, Running Deer, smiled at Cordelia and led her out of the tipi, leaving Jeremiah alone with the chief. Running Deer called to a young warrior, Two Dogs. He jogged to her obediently. She said something to him quickly and he bent into the tipi of the chief.

In a moment, he came out of the lodge with a frown on his face. Jeremiah followed. Without emotion, Two Dogs looked Cordelia over as if he were studying a horse to buy, then sliced his hand through the air in a horizontal fashion in front of him.

"Sold!" Cordelia could imagine someone saying.

"What is it?" she asked Jeremiah.

"In the Cheyenne tribe, each tipi is under the protection of a warrior. Two Dogs is a good hunter, a good horse thief. He has a wife who is heavy with child. You will live with them. He will provide for you and you will assist his wife."

"What about Minnie?"

"If Minnie agrees to come with you, she will stay with you under his protection."

"So the chief just told him he has two more mouths to feed. Is that why he seems less than happy?"

"He is not unhappy. He has three women in his tipi now—three women who will take care of him. In exchange for the services you will provide, he will provide food and defense for you." Jeremiah smiled crookedly. "Don't worry about his bad expression, Mrs. Lawson. He is proud to have you in his lodge. This will make him an important man in the village."

They watched Two Dogs angrily stride away to join the other men who were sitting outside their tipi, smoking and

---

talking. No doubt, he would have much to say to them. The men didn't seem busy but the women in the tribe scurried around, gathering and packing their meager possessions and scant winter stores of food in preparation for the trip. The tipis would be last to be broken down, packed and pulled along on the journey.

"What about his wife?" Cordelia asked.

"His wife is good. Kind. You will have no problems. Draw one of your pictures and show her how handsome she is. She will like you."

"I hope so." Cordelia sighed. Then, with new determination on her face, she said, "Let's go back home, Jeremiah. Now I must speak to Minnie. Oh, there's much I have to do before tomorrow."

~*~

"But what about Lieutentant Otis? Will not he need me?" Min-nin-ne-wah-hah-ket searched Cordelia's face earnestly.

"Minnie, Lieutenant Otis cares for you as his friend. And who wouldn't? You are very kind and gentle. Your heart is good. But Lieutenant Otis will have Bess and Jeremiah here to care for him, and he'll have Lucy to watch after Baby Nora."

Minnie's downcast expression tugged at Cordelia's heart as she continued to explain, "I'm afraid it is I who need you now, Minnie. I simply cannot travel with your people without someone to translate for me. I won't force you to accompany me, Minnie. But I'm asking that you will."

With that, she leaned back against her chair and waited for an answer. The answer came quickly enough.

Minnie raised her head. Cordelia could already see the resolve on her poor, broken face. The eyes were iron. Strong.

"I will go with you. I will return to my people. It is great thing to do help to you. My heart is glad to have you for my friend. But it is sad, too, little bit. Lucy and Bess, Jeremiah, Baby Nora, the lieutentant . . . and the captain," she whispered that last part. "These I will be sad to leave."

"I know," Cordelia whispered as well, her eyes going somber as she spoke, as she remembered. "I shall miss them, too, Minnie."

Quickly recognizing her friend's pain, Minnie regretted her mention of the captain.

Cordelia straightened in her chair with businesslike resolve and, with a hint of a smile said, "We will leave tomorrow. There's much I have to do before we go."

"I help you?"

"No, I don't think so. The things to be done, I must do myself. But thank you," she said, placing her hand on Minnie's shoulder in an almost regal gesture.

As Minnie hustled out of the parlor, Cordelia rose and slowly walked to Robert's big desk. On her way, she spied his shaving mug and razor and his brush on the dressing table. She picked it up as if it were made of porcelain, stroking it lovingly with her finger. Suddenly her eyes were a scald of tears, filling and spilling down her cheeks. Funny how such little things affected her like this.

When she anticipated something would be hard, she had time to brace herself against it and thereby keep her composure. It was these little, unexpected things that caught her off-guard and unhinged her emotions—emotions she desperately tried to ignore.

Hardly able to see the shaving mug through her tears, she now wondered what to do with it. She had no need to pack it. But she couldn't leave it either. If only he would come home right now. She didn't want to have to think about what to do with any of Robert's things.

She lovingly traced every curve and turn of the hand-carved wood desk before opening it. Then, slowly, she sat down to begin the task she dreaded most—writing this letter to Robert. For the next half-hour, she worked on the letter. It began, *My darling Robert, my heart.*

For several minutes that's all she could write, for she was seized again with weeping, picturing his face, his eyes caressing hers, his lips, opened slightly . . .

"*Oohhhh.* I am undone!" she cried. "How can I write this letter? How?" She closed her eyes and worked the words out in her head. Bending diligently to the task, she continued,

I have every confidence that you will one day read these sorrowful words and already my heart is glad to think that, if you are reading them, our reunion must indeed be imminent!

Faced with the prospect of returning east without you, or traveling with the Cheyenne to Camp Washita to await you, I have decided on the latter. I shall only be two days' hard ride from you, I'm told, and there I, and your child, will be waiting.

I know not when we will see each other again, my dearest love, so I shall leave that in the hands of our faithful Lord. I pray He will protect you, as I know He is even now. Come to me quickly, Robert. My empty arms yearn to hold you again.

Eternally yours,
Cordelia.

Rereading the letter made her cry. She realized how utterly sentimental it was. But if this situation did not call for sentiment, she couldn't imagine one that would!

Sealing the letter and applying Robert's own seal, she tucked it into her bag. She placed a scarf over her head, throwing the ends over her shoulders and out she went to deliver the letter and to say her good-byes.

Her first stop, in the gathering dusk, was to Doc and Ela. To her dismay, Doc was still at the hospital. She had hoped to see them together instead of bidding them separate good-byes.

As she sat facing her friend, she sighed deeply.

"I've come to say good-bye, Mrs. Anthony," she started, coming right to the point.

"Good-bye? My dear, wherever are you going?" The alarm was evident in Ela's voice.

"This may sound foolish to you, but I'm traveling with the Cheyenne to Camp Washita tomorrow. Lieutenant Otis is soon to become *Captain* Otis. You know what that means. General Hazen is replacing Robert! He has called off the search for him and is assuming him to be . . . well, deceased. I'm afraid I shan't be allowed to stay here in my quarters under those circumstances, though he hasn't mentioned anything to me about leaving yet."

"I'd heard about Lieutenant Otis. He's distraught about the whole subject, Cordelia. He didn't want to advance in this manner."

"I know that. But I'm happy for him. He deserves this position and it makes good sense, really. I don't fault the general's judgment in the least, I assure you."

Standing, Ela paced around her tiny parlor. "But Mrs. Lawson, the baby! Wouldn't it be wiser for you to go back home to your own folks? Wouldn't the baby have a better chance there among . . . well, more civilized people?"

"Ela Anthony!" Cordelia was aghast at the term *civilized.*

Hurriedly, Ela continued, "Now don't look at me that way. You must admit that, though I'm an advocate for the welfare of the Indians, I'm also a practical woman. I know the Cheyenne have their own civilized ways, but you must admit that back home, things will be *more* civilized!"

"Yes, I suppose you're right. But the main reason I'm going to Camp Washita is to await Robert there. I can't stand the thought of being separated by so great a distance as I'd be back in Baltimore. And the baby will be fine. The women will know what to do. After all, they've been doing this for generations, you know."

That elicited a little smile from Ela. "Yes, I'm sure you're right." Worry was etched on her face, but she decided not to spend their last few minutes in argument.

With that, Cordelia rose to leave. Very quietly, Ela began to cry, her tears chasing one another in steady progression down her cheeks. Cordelia gave her friend a long hug.

"Good-bye, Mrs. Anthony. Thank you for your friendship and your kindness to me. I shall miss you more than you know."

"Yes, and I, you, dear," she sniffed. "Please take care of yourself and that little one," she pleaded, patting Cordelia's only slightly rounded abdomen.

"You know I will." Cordelia flashed a brave smile her way. "I'll stop by the hospital to see Doc on my way back from seeing the general."

"Please do. He'd be heartbroken if you left without seeing him."

"I wouldn't think of doing such a thing!"

Ela clasped her hands. "Good-bye. You are always welcome here."

"I know that. I'm sure we shall see each other again some-day," Cordelia said, much more confidently than she actually felt at that moment.

With that, she headed to the commander's quarters, certain he would not still be in his office. The first stars were appearing in the sky now and the men were lighting the lanterns that hung at intervals along the boardwalks.

Looking up at the grand doorway that led to the general's quarters, Cordelia resolutely mounted the wooden stairs. The general opened the door.

"General," she said pleasantly as she marched into his residence before he'd had a chance to respond.

"Mrs. Lawson! What brings you here?"

"I must speak to you, General."

"But, but . . . can't this wait until tomorrow?"

"I'm afraid not, sir." Cordelia made herself at home in the parlor. General Hazen followed her uncertainly and sat across from her, waiting for her to begin.

He didn't need to wait long.

"I agree with your decision to promote Lieutenant Otis to captain. He is quite deserving of this confidence, General, as he is a man of honor and integrity. His duty to his country is uppermost in his heart, I'm sure. If you are waiting on my account to proceed with this promotion, then I urge you to wait no longer. I have made arrangements to travel with the Cheyenne to Camp Washita tomorrow. I will be vacating the captain's quarters at that time and there is no reason why Lieutenant Otis and his daughter can't move in immediately. My housekeeper, Bess, will be staying behind to serve him as she has faithfully served me all these years. Her daughter, Lucy will remain to serve as nanny to Baby Nora."

"I see. But what brought this on, Mrs. Lawson? I've said nothing to you about vacating the premises."

"You've called off your search for my husband, I believe."

"Well . . . yes, I had to. Mrs. Lawson, I don't believe your husband survived the Indian attack!"

"So, you believe that he is deceased, is that correct, General?"

"That would be a reasonable assumption, madam, since if there were still breath in his body, I believe he would find his way home to you."

This sudden tenderness surprised Cordelia and, for a moment, knocked her off-balance.

"Yes, General," she whispered, "that would be a reasonable assumption. But one I'm afraid I cannot afford. They say that hope springs eternal. That's true in my case, General. Until I see clear evidence that points otherwise, I shall go on believing in his survival. I shall go on believing that one day he will find himself free to come back to me."

"Quite admirable, my dear," the general admitted, softly.

"So, on your assumption that my husband has died, the captain's quarters should go to your new captain, Todd Otis."

"Yes, I agree, but I feel no haste in putting you out of hearth and home. You may take whatever amount of time you need. In fact, I have no quarrel if you'd like to move your quarters to one of the lieutenant's rooms, if you want to stay on the fort indefinitely. But frankly, I assumed you would most likely go back east. I happen to know that a coach is expected here tomorrow afternoon and will leave the next morning for a journey back to Topeka where you could board a train and travel home by rail."

"No, thank you, General. I have given it much thought and have decided to align myself with the Cheyenne for this journey. I will accompany them to Camp Washita and live among them on their new reservation where I will await my husband's return. I have been given a rare opportunity and I intend to take it."

Cordelia, who had never thought of the general as kindly, now found herself gazing into a pair of the saddest, kindest eyes she'd ever seen.

"Thank you, sir." Standing, she adjusted her scarf and

moved slowly toward the door. "Please give my regards to your wife."

"Yes, I will, but I must correct you on one point, Mrs. Lawson. The trip south has been postponed until the day after tomorrow. The men would never forgive me if I sent them off on the day Miss Lauria is to arrive."

"Miss Lauria?"

The general smiled. "Lauria Post, a most . . . remarkable woman, I've heard. She's an actress from back east."

"Oh," Cordelia gasped. "I think I *have* heard of her. She's coming here? Why?"

"Just a stop-over. She is actually heading to Fort Larned. She's doing a show there, I believe. But she wanted to stop by here first."

"Whatever for?" Cordelia asked.

"I think she's got her eye on a certain general—and I don't mean me."

"You mean George Custer?" Cordelia was incredulous.

"The very one."

"How does she know General Custer?" Cordelia wanted to know.

"Rumors, Mrs. Lawson. All rumors. But I've heard she set her cap on our young general years ago and has never stopped searching him out. I think she's catching up with him tomorrow. It should be a rousing good show," he laughed, leaning toward her in a conspiratorial gesture.

Cordelia noted that unlike George Custer, whose smile changed his homely face into one almost handsome, General Hazen's smile totally transformed his kindly face into that of a rogue.

"You're right. It will be very interesting indeed." Her voice was ice.

"However, her visit will be a short one. She'll leave on the stage the next day. They shall take a route from here to Camp Supply and then head north to Fort Larned. She'll get off there, but the stage will go on to Topeka if you should change your mind."

"Thanks, but I won't change my mind. However, this will give me an extra day to prepare for my journey. I'll send word of the delay to the Cheyenne this evening through Jeremiah. Oh, Commander, I almost forgot. It seems that Jeremiah and Bess have decided to marry. I have granted him permission to live in the loft over the kitchen with Bess, but I need to clear that with you, I think."

A deep scowl covered his face as he pondered this information. "I had heard he was a frequent visitor to the fort, but a resident of the fort is something entirely different."

"I shouldn't see why. He is always respectful and courteous and has proven to be a great help to us these past months."

"Yes. Well, I suppose it would be all right. Perhaps I should write to General Sheridan for his opinion."

"Why, General Hazen! I've always thought you had full authority over this fort! Don't tell me you have to consult General Sheridan to make a little ol' decision like this!"

She smiled sweetly as she waited several more seconds while he studied her. He suspected she might be manipulating him with this argument but wasn't absolutely confident of that fact.

"Oh, very well then. Tell him he is welcome to remain here as long as he adheres to the regulations of this fort."

"Thank you, sir. I certainly will. Oh, and another thing. Could you send for a chaplain to perform the ceremony?"

Another pause. Finally he plastered a most insincere smile on his face and clicked his heels, saying, "Certainly, my dear. Will there be anything else?"

"No, that's all. Thank you, General."

With that, she proceeded down the steps in the direction of the hospital. However, seeing no sign of light through the windows, she decided to go on home. Bess would have dinner ready by now, and she needed to discuss her plans with Todd over dinner. She'd see Doc tomorrow.

Twenty-Nine

After dinner, Cordelia walked Todd to the parlor door. They'd had much to discuss. Dinner had stretched almost two hours, reminding her of the European custom. Todd was resigned now to Cordelia's plans to travel south with them.

He took note of her excitement when she spoke of her adventure. He also noted that the only time he didn't see the abject sorrow on her lovely face was when she discussed the Indians. *So let her go,* he thought, *if that will bring some happiness back to the green jewels of her eyes.*

She'd also shared the news about Miss Lauria. To that, Todd just laughed. Yes, of course he'd heard the rumors that she was stopping here at Fort Cobb, but he doubted it was true. Cordelia reassured him that it was.

It bothered him that Cordelia seemed so concerned about Custer's possible relationship with Miss Lauria. But then, the twinge of protectiveness and jealousy he felt every time Custer was in Cordelia's presence also gave him cause for concern. After all, none of this was any of his affair, he told himself. But as the closest thing to a brother to her, he felt responsible, nonetheless, for Cordelia's protection, especially from the likes of General Custer. He hoped that once Cordelia was safely out of Custer's grip, she would lose all interest in the topic of George Armstrong Custer.

Cordelia's words intruded now into these thoughts as he heard her say, ". . . so I want you to take this letter, Todd. Give it to him when you see him. Will you?"

"Yes, of course," he agreed, relieved to see Robert's name on the envelope. "I'll never stop hoping for his safe return, Cordelia."

"Then do more than hope, my friend. Pray!"

"I will. And I *do!*" he assured her. "Thanks again for helping me out on the problem with Minnie. I'm most grateful to you."

"Todd! Haven't you been listening? I really do need her. This is as much for me as it is for you. Good night. I'll see you tomorrow."

She stood on tiptoe as she leaned into him, surprising him with a sisterly kiss on the cheek. Even so, he could feel the blood rising to his cheeks as he all but shuffled his feet with embarrassment.

"Good night," he managed, as Cordelia closed the parlor door.

As soon as she'd closed the door, Cordelia's mind had immediately shifted its focus from Todd to the trip ahead, itemizing in her organized way all she still had to do.

~*~

Early the next morning, Cordelia dressed and made her way to the kitchen. Seated at the old oak dining table, she poured a sufficient quantity of heavy cream into the strong, hot coffee before her. She wanted to spend as much time as she could with Bess and Lucy before she had to say good-bye.

"You hardly touched your breakfast, Missy," Bess told her. "What is that you're workin' on over there?"

"My list of things to do before I leave tomorrow. I'm through with everything except to say goodbye to Doc and finish packing. I'm not taking a lot. I'm leaving almost everything here for Todd. I have a favor to ask you, Bess."

"What's that? You know I'd do anything for you."

"Yes, but this will be difficult, I think. I can't bring myself to pack up all of Robert's things. So I was wondering if you could do it. Don't get rid of them or anything, just pack them away for me."

Bess studied Cordelia's face for a moment before she walked to her and took her in her arms.

For a moment, Cordelia thought she might lose control again and burst into tears. But she gave Bess a little squeeze and turned back to her breakfast.

"Are them eggs too hard for you?"

"No, they're perfect, Bess, as always," she sniffed. "All right. I'll eat, though they're a little cold by now."

"You want I should fry you up some more?"

"Heavens, no! I'm fine," she assured her as she took another bite of egg with a tiny nibble of her biscuit. Plopping the last bite of bacon into her mouth, she said, "There. I'm finished now, Bess. Really, I'm not that hungry. I just want to enjoy my coffee and visit with you."

Bess reluctantly removed her plate and Cordelia grasped her wrist as she did. Looking down at her smiling, impish face, Bess suddenly had to choke back the tears that had threatened for days now. She patted Cordelia's hand and quickly turned away from her.

"There is one more thing I wish I could to do before I leave."

"What's that, Missy?"

"I wish I could see you two get married. I spoke to Commander Hazen about it. He's sending for a chaplain."

"Thank you, ma'am."

About then, Lucy walked into the kitchen with the baby. "Mrs. Lawson, you have a guest. I showed him into the parlor. I heard him knocking on the door. Thought he never would stop, so I let him in."

"Who is it, Lucy?"

"The general, ma'am."

"Hazen?" came Cordelia's surprised response.

"No, ma'am. Custer."

"Well, why ever did he come here so early in the morning?" Cordelia wondered aloud as she stood, straightening her skirt as she did. "I'll see him, Lucy. Bess, will you bring us both some coffee?"

"Yes, ma'am," she answered, flashing Lucy a look that Cordelia totally missed.

"I do have a thing or two to discuss with the general," Cordelia said as she hurried out the kitchen door.

Making her entrance into the parlor, Cordelia held her head high as she greeted the general.

"General! What a pleasant surprise! To what do I owe this honor?" she asked, playfully.

"Good morning, Cordelia. I've just heard that our journey to the south will be postponed until tomorrow. I've sent a rider to inform the Indians. We shall leave tomorrow at first light."

"Thank you. I've already sent Jeremiah to inform the Indians. So they already know."

"But how did *you* know?"

"The commander told me last night."

Looking down at his hat in his long slender fingers, he asked, "What else did he tell you?"

"Please sit down, George. For heaven's sakes, you look more nervous than a long-tailed cat in a room full of rockers!"

Smiling, he took Cordelia's elbow as she sat on the divan, taking his seat across from her. Bess brought in the coffee service on their only silver tray. Then she expertly served them before leaving with a backwards glance at Cordelia, who answered with a warning glance of her own.

"Now, George, why are you so upset this morning?"

"I'm not upset, my dear. What makes you think that?"

To his credit, Cordelia noticed how quickly he had composed himself and fallen back into his confident, easy manner. She waited until he had raised the cup of steaming coffee to his lips before asking him, "So what is this I hear about you and Lauria Post?"

He almost dropped his cup, spilling a bit of the hot liquid on the fringe of his buckskin jacket. Quickly grabbing the cloth napkin from the table beside him, he dabbed at it.

Buying some time, Cordelia thought, watching his every move. Trying to come up with an answer.

"Laurie who?" he asked, innocently.

Cordelia thought to herself, *look how easily he lies, how well he does it.* Aloud, she said, "Why, if I didn't know better, I'd actually believe that act, George. But I hear you and Miss Post know each other rather well."

"Cordelia! Please! You can't believe those preposterous rumors! I didn't take you for the kind of woman who would put much weight on nasty, unsubstantiated gossip. Remember, there are two sides to every story."

"So, you deny any knowledge of the woman, then?"

"I know her. That much is true. I met her long before I had

met my dear wife, Libby. But even then, I was a little more . . .
well, selective than *that*, my dear, I assure you."

Enjoying the rare sight of the great General Custer
squirming like this, she continued, "I hear she may have more
than a casual interest in you, George."

"Perhaps. But, my dear, I do have standards, you know."

"Do you?" she teased. "I'd forgotten!"

"You're enjoying this much too much, Delia. Perhaps I
should take my leave!"

"What!. And miss the show? Her stage is due here this afternoon, as I'm confident you already know. Surely you'll be here
to meet it."

"I hadn't planned on it."

"Oh, but General!" she laughed. He was right. She *did*
enjoy toying with him.

"This is just nonsense, and I shall leave if you do not
change the subject at once! If you will remember, I am a
married man!" His piercing blue eyes studied her from under
his heavy brow.

"All right. I'll show you mercy this once."

"Thank you," he said, nervously stroking his bushy moustache. He proceeded to tug at the ends, then changed the exercise by twisting them to needle-like points that he seemed to be
coaxing upward. So lost in thought was he that he seemed
scarcely aware of these uneasy fingerings.

Finally, he continued authoritatively. "Now, on to the
subject of this journey, I have assigned one of my men to drive
your buckboard to the fort. I'd do it myself if I didn't have
other duties to attend, you understand. I want you to stay in
the buckboard at all times while we're moving. No riding. No
walking. It will be a hard trip, Cordelia. I'll not mislead you
about that. And I take my responsibility for you very
seriously."

"Thank you, George. I know that. And I'll do whatever you say. I'll be the best little traveler you've ever seen."

"Yes, I'm sure of that," he said, sarcastically. "I'll have to watch you like a hawk, but you *will* obey orders. Is that clear?"

Placing her coffee cup on the table next to her, she saluted with a curt, "Yes, sir, General."

"Go ahead and make jokes, Delia, but once we start the move, it will be imperative that you behave and follow my instructions. The way will be fraught with risks and danger. I cannot spend all my time worrying about you. Do you understand?"

"Yes! I told you I'd behave and I will!" she protested.

"Did that husband of yours ever obtain that little firearm I spoke to you about?"

"No, he didn't. In fact, I confess I never addressed it with him. I don't want a gun, George."

"Well, you need one. Here, I brought this for you. You probably couldn't hit the broad side of a barn with it, but if you were close enough, it might offer you some protection."

He handed her a Colt M-1860 44-caliber Army revolver.

"No, I don't want it!" she protested.

"Take it," he ordered. "I don't care if you never touch it again. But I want you to have it available if you need it. I've loaded it already, so be careful with it."

"But George," she began.

"But nothing, Cordelia!" He looked at her sternly. "You take it or you won't be traveling with me. Do you understand?"

"Yes, thank you, General."

She took the weapon gingerly, surprised by its weight.

"I'll take it, but I won't use it."

"Whatever you say. I just want you to have it."

"All right. I have it now. And I'm going to pack it for the

trip. Feel better now?" she teased, as she set it on the table beside them with a clunk.

"Yes, I do." Taking his last sip of coffee, he stood and made a little bow to her as he walked to the parlor door. Following, she almost ran into him when he turned suddenly and caught her in his arms.

"George!"

"Oh, please forgive me. I thought you were falling."

She saw the mischief in his face, the twinkle in his eyes, the smile playing around one corner of his mustached upper lip.

"Thank you, George. I'll bet you did."

"Be ready to leave at the sound of reveille in the morning. I'll have the driver pick you up then."

"All right, George. Have a pleasurable evening now!" she called after him with a laugh as he descended the steps. He stopped to look back at her with a wag of his finger. Then he walked on without another word.

~*~

Around four o'clock that afternoon, she heard the stage pull up to headquarters. She'd already decided she wasn't interested enough in its passenger to bother with it, yet all afternoon she'd been listening for its arrival.

Now, she looked out her window, but the passenger was getting out on the other side and she couldn't see a thing. She looked for George among the young men gathered to meet Lauria's stagecoach. She realized she felt more than a disinterested amount of relief that he was not in attendance.

Cordelia made her way to the steps in front of their quarters and sat down to watch the activities. Once the stage pulled off in the direction of the livery stable, she saw the short, not-too-plump figure of a woman in a blue dress with an enormous feathered hat. General Hazen greeted her, apparently, and a scowling Mrs. Hazen stood next to him, clutching his arm like a mother desperately holding her child back from the edge of a steep precipice!

As Lauria approached the boardwalk, there was still some standing water in a puddle extending from the boardwalk. One young soldier picked her up by the waist and took a little kiss from her before passing her to another, who took his little kiss and passed her to the next man, who kissed her cheek before placing her safely on the boardwalk.

From her perch on the steps, Cordelia could see the wide smile on her pale face, imagining her silky voice telling them how sweet they all were. "Humph!" Cordelia rolled her eyes at the scene. Then she saw two soldiers lugging a trunk in her direction.

"Why in the world are they bringing it this way?" she wondered, suddenly sitting bolt upright on the steps. "They're coming over here!"

Standing, she watched the soldiers carry the trunk up the steps and into the front door of the empty room adjoining Todd's quarters. Standing at the door, she stared in disbelief as Lauria made her way up the steps.

"Hello," she smiled at Cordelia. And Cordelia, who had already decided she wasn't going to like this girl at all, felt her heart soften, as she looked into the pale, plain face and responded, "Hello."

Lauria didn't look anything like she'd imagined. She was not painted up like a woman of ill repute. She was far from beautiful. In fact, her thin blonde hair was pulled back into a twist, her face was dusted with a pale face powder, and her thin rosy lips stretched into an open, friendly smile.

Catching herself staring, Cordelia blurted, "I suppose

you'll be staying across the hall from me tonight. I'm Cordelia Lawson. My husband is Captain Robert Lawson."

"Lauria Post. Nice to meet you, Mrs. Lawson. I hope you don't mind me staying here tonight?"

"No, of course not."

"That's mighty kind of you, ma'am. Most decent women don't much like me bein' around." Hearing her common speech, her quiet voice and seeing what Cordelia interpreted as shame etched into her face, she impulsively leaned forward, gave her a little hug and said, "Welcome to Fort Cobb, Miss Post. Please let me know if you need anything."

"Thank you, ma'am. I appreciate that. It's been a long trip and I'd like to get changed. I promised the boys I'd give them a little song later on. Maybe I can get some rest before then."

"Are you hungry?"

"I sure am! Is there anywhere to eat around here?"

"Well, you could dine with the men in their mess hall, but they only have coffee and left-over bread. Or you could take your meal with the officers in the officers' mess, which is very little better. Or you could dine with me here," she suggested, surprising both of them!

"Thanks, but I'd appreciate it if you could just point me in the direction of the officers' mess if you think they wouldn't mind." This time when she smiled, she saw the leering expression of a woman used to being in the company of men.

"Yes, of course. It's just over there, behind the quartermaster's store," she said, pointing the way. "Actually, they'll be serving dinner in less than an hour, I think."

"Good. I can get a little nap in before then. Thanks." With that, she sauntered off in the direction of the open door. "Oh, and where might I find General Custer? Do you know? Does he take his meals at the officers' mess?"

Cordelia fought to hide her shock at the mention of his

name. "I don't think so. He's most likely with his men outside the camp."

"Thanks." She disappeared behind the door.

Cordelia had to admit to herself that she was more than slightly annoyed at this woman's rejection of her gracious offer of dinner, and at her mention of General Custer's name. She decided that she'd warn Todd to make sure the latch on his door was securely fastened tonight. She didn't trust this one.

~*~

Cordelia lit another lantern in the kitchen as Jeremiah pulled a stool up to the table. Cordelia planned to take her dinner with them tonight. Minnie, wearing one of the simple dresses Bess had made her, transferred mounds of mashed potatoes into a bowl and lavished it with several dollops of sweet, creamy butter. Lucy rocked Nora to sleep by the fire. She said she'd eat later. Bess took the biscuits out of the oven and set them aside to cool while she took the chicken out of the heavy, iron skillet.

Cordelia enjoyed watching all this activity. She'd miss it terribly. But what she enjoyed most was observing Jeremiah as his gaze followed Bess around the room like a lovesick puppy! She smiled at the thought. Even more gratifying was the way Bess kept glancing in his direction, wrestling with the smile on her own face.

The domestic bliss of the moment was interrupted suddenly by a persistent rapping on the door. Jeremiah stood up, scraping the stool across the brick floor, and strode protectively to the door.

On a blast of cool air came the nervous utterance of a stammering General Custer. "I'm s-so sorry t-to interrupt, but is Mrs. Lawson in there? Could I speak to her?"

Blocking the door with his arm, Jeremiah looked at her questioningly.

Cordelia hurried to the door. "It's all right, Jeremiah. Thank you. What is it, General? You look as if you've seen a ghost!" Then, seized by blind hope, she blurted, "Is it Robert? Is he back?" Her eyes held his in a frenzied grip.

"Robert? No, my dear. I've heard nothing of Robert. But I was wondering if I might intrude on you this evening for dinner. Am I too late?" he asked, trying to see into the kitchen.

Cordelia burst into laughter. "I know why you're here! You're hiding! Big war hero and Indian fighter!"

Custer looked at her angrily, "I am not hiding. And I won't stay another moment talking to you through a doorway! I'm sorry if I interrupted your evening, Mrs. Lawson."

As he turned to make a hasty retreat out the back way, Cordelia grabbed his sleeve. "No," she laughed, "I'm sorry. Poor George. Of course you're welcome to stay for dinner."

Bess spoke up, asking if Cordelia would like her to set up dinner in the parlor. The look on Bess's face told Cordelia that's what she'd personally prefer. "Yes, fine, Bess. We'll be in the parlor, then."

Taking Custer's arm, she strolled down the hallway with him and into the parlor. He held Cordelia's chair for her, then took his own place in Robert's chair, as usual. By then, Bess and Jeremiah had arrived with the table setting and the platter of food.

Without being asked, the general blessed the food. Then, pleasantly, he said, "Thank you, Bess, Jeremiah. It looks and smells absolutely delicious. All the more because it will be the last meal like this we'll have for a long time. You realize that, don't you, Cordelia?"

"I do." Bess and Jeremiah cast a last worried look in her direction and retreated to the kitchen.

George took two biscuits, a heaping spoonful of potatoes, one of the boiled, buttered onions and two pieces of chicken, over which he generously ladled the white gravy. Cordelia watched this plate-loading procedure with amusement.

"I wonder if I need to gather up food for the trip. Should I?" she asked.

"It wouldn't be a bad idea. I think you'll find hard tack and dried meat palatable for only a very short time."

"I'll ask Bess to make some sandwiches. That should be easy enough to transport."

"Oh, this is delicious," George mumbled, appreciatively. "Is Bess coming with us?"

"No, George."

"Pity," he said, between bites.

"I thought I'd told you the arrangements. Bess and Jeremiah are to be married, and will stay here with Lucy to tend the house for Todd when he returns from this horrid assignment. Lucy will be Nora's nanny. I'm confident she'll make a good one. That girl is so bright. I do hope she continues with her reading and studies on her own. She needn't be a nanny forever, you know. In these modern times, she may aspire to many other professions."

"Or none at all," Custer volunteered. "It would be quite an accomplishment for her to fill Bess's shoes one day. That Bess is an amazing servant, is she not? Reminds me in many ways of our own Eliza. No one bakes a better peach cobbler than Eliza!"

"George, I'll thank you not to refer to Bess as my servant. I *employ* her as a cook and housekeeper, that's true. But she is much more than that. She's my friend and my . . . well, like a *sister* in many ways."

"Cordelia, please. That's all very fine sounding, I assure you, and perhaps somebody else would believe that hook, line and sinker. But as for me, I know that you and I will never be able to see their race as fit for anything other than servitude. Oh, and soldiering. The buffalo soldiers, for example, who are now a part of Camp Washita, are really quite excellent marksmen, very courageous in battle and they obey orders to the letter. But they will never attain a position of leadership. They are unable to think analytically, Cordelia. They can only follow instructions, and that only if given in the simplest terms."

Cordelia's fork crashed to the plate as she glared at him. "George Armstrong Custer, I don't care who you are. I will not allow such speech in my home and tonight, this is still my home."

"See? Your tolerance extends to your *employees* but not to your guests? Am I not allowed my own sentiments, my dear? I cannot believe you're the type of person who would allow only shared opinions to be voiced. Why, then we'd all be just alike, wouldn't we? And what a boring place this poor earth would be if that were the case."

Cordelia's glance faltered just a little. Then, thinking of a different tack, she picked up her fork and took a delicate little bite of potatoes. In her softest, sweetest voice she replied, "You're right, George. If I am truly a tolerant person, I must be tolerant of all people. If I allow the Indians their culture and the Negroes theirs, then I must allow the heathen swine who hold to your opinions theirs as well."

George's hearty laughter filled the dimly lit parlor. "Well done, Delia, my dear! Well done!" he laughed, applauding in mock appreciation. "I have never been more prettily insulted, I must confess."

That big, booming laughter proved to be his undoing tonight because almost immediately, they heard a knock on the door. It opened before Cordelia could rise from the table to answer it. And there stood Lauria Post, hands on her hips, in a faded rose-colored dress that dipped low in the front and bustled out in the back. She wore a simple rose-colored feather in her baby-fine hair.

"Why, George Custer! I'd know that laugh anywhere!" She sauntered, uninvited, into the room with bouncy, deliberate steps as she continued, "Where have you been keepin' yourself, Georgie? I've been lookin' for you all over the place!"

"Hello, Lauria," he snarled.

"'Lauria!' Why so formal? Whatever happened to 'Laurie, me darlin'?' A person could get the impression you were tryin' to avoid me or something." She flashed her wide-mouthed grin at him while looking up through her pale feathery lashes.

"I am," he stated somberly. "Now, if you'll be so kind," he said softly, rising from his chair and taking her elbow, guiding her back to the door, "we are engaged in our supper and you, Lauria Post, are *not* invited."

"What's the matter, Georgie? Have you forgotten how much we . . . like each other?" she asked lasciviously, looking him up and down.

"I was unmarried and a fool, at the time. Both of those conditions have been remedied now, so I'll thank you to leave us in peace. Go back to whatever you were doing before you barged in here." With a little shove, Lauria found herself back out in the hallway, but not for long.

"Just you wait a minute," she argued, pushing herself back into the room, angrily. Cordelia merely sat and watched the show, eyes wide and mouth opened slightly. "I've been looking for you ever since you left that night. Honey, I've missed you somethin' awful. I have! There won't never be anyone else like you. Let's go somewhere where we can talk in private, Georgie. There's so much I want to tell you."

"I am not interested, Lauria. Really, I'm not."

"Well, listen to you, Georgie. When did you start putting

on airs? You're suddenly a gentleman to the manor born, aren't you? No, more than that! You're a prince right outta the story books, I think, like all us poor silly females dream about."

Looking shrewdly toward Cordelia, Lauria nodded her head in her direction and said, "So you're married now, Georgie?"

"Yes," he said, taking Cordelia's arm and helping her to her feet. Holding her protectively next to him, he continued, "Darling, this is an old acquaintance of mine, from way before I knew you. And Lauria, this is my wife, Mrs. Custer."

Cordelia's left eyebrow arched in surprise.

"Oh, this is your wife, then, is it?" Lauria seemed to play along. Then, with fury in her voice she argued, "I'm afraid Mrs. Lawson and I have already been introduced, *General*. Nice try."

Placing her hands on her hips, she began to walk around Cordelia, ogling her speculatively. "But come to think of it, where is *Captain* Lawson? This is a cozy little arrangement you got for yourself, isn't it, Georgie? Send the husband away on some phony assignment somewhere and have the little lady all to yourself."

"Watch it, Lauria, before I forget that I'm a 'gentleman to the manor born,'" he warned.

"I gotta hand it to you, Honey," she said to Cordelia, "you got it pretty good here, don't you? I should have taken you up on your offer. It's plain to see that all the fun is over here tonight! Yeah, Georgie here is quite a prize, isn't he? Oh, he's a mite too skinny for some, but he's all man, ain't he, Honey?"

George's hand grasped Lauria's shoulder and whirled her around to face him so rapidly that Cordelia scarcely knew what was happening! Holding her by the shoulders tightly, he shook her violently. Cordelia followed the descent of the dusty rose feather as it fluttered to the floor.

"Go have your fun somewhere else. You've just insulted a great lady, Lauria. You're not good enough to even stand in her presence. So get out of here before I forget that I'm a gentleman."

She stood there, tears welling up in her eyes, which had suddenly gone all simple and childlike. Pouting, she rubbed her arms and shoulders and wailed, "Why'd you go and do that, George? I was just tryin' to have a little fun!"

"I'm warning you, Lauria," he snarled, raising his hand as if to strike her.

"Nooo!" she cried, as she ran from the room. "You'll be sorry, George Custer! Just you wait!"

"I'm already sorry. Sorry I ever met you!" he called after her as her door slammed shut. He knew that if he wanted, he could go in there right now, make everything right with some pretty words and a kiss or two, but the way he saw it, he already had a few too many women in his life. Why play with fire?

"I'm sorry, my dear. Usually I'm a man who honors womankind, but in this case . . ." he began as he turned back to Cordelia. He stopped abruptly when he saw her face. There was a most unusual expression there—one he'd never seen before.

He saw her shrink back against the dining table, and her eyes seemed to reach searchingly into the very recesses of his mind. He forced himself to empty any but the most chaste thoughts from his head.

That is, he tried to. But seeing her standing there, swaying a little, the color rising to her cheeks, her nostrils slightly flaring, her mouth, held tender and sweet, her lips open just enough, just enough . . .

He swept her into his arms, pressing his lips to her throat, taking in the smell of her hair, her skin. Her hands came up to push him away, yet lingered as she held him. For a brief moment, a scant instant in time, he felt her eager lips on his, parting, softening ever so slightly.

Though she told herself to draw back from him, her rebellious lips continued to cling to his, moving in that tactile, sensual language that every lover instinctively knows, wordlessly informing him, helplessly, hopelessly of all her terrible longings, all her aching needs. His hand slid down the curve of her spine, pressing her into the searing firmness of his body.

"George!" she cried. "George, please. Stop." Then, more insistently she cried, "George, stop it this instant!" He pressed himself into her, crushing her with his embrace, buoyed by her struggle against him. Suddenly, she stopped fighting, became still in his arms and the death in her voice stopped him cold when she quietly said, "Let me go, George."

"Delia, my love," he croaked, planting one last kiss on her flaming cheek. Slowly, he released her, stood away from her with his head hung low like a dog skulking under his master's cry of displeasure.

"Oh, Delia, I'm so sorry. Please forgive me. I couldn't help myself. This will never happen again, I assure you," he insisted breathlessly.

"Yes, you're right, General," came her soft reply, struggling to control her own breathing. "This will not happen again. I'll make sure of that."

"You're angry with me, aren't you? And I don't blame you a bit. I'm a wretched, wretched man. Say you'll forgive me. Please."

Cordelia stepped close to him and took his rugged hand in her soft one. Looking up into his face through the blind scald of tears, she said, "I forgive you, George. How can I blame you for what just happened? Who will hold me to account for my part in it? You shouldn't have kissed me. We both know that. But for a moment, I wanted it, too. I shall never forgive myself for that. In the meantime, my husband may lie somewhere cold and wounded, unable to come back to me. I shall loathe myself forever for my actions tonight. First light comes soon, General. I'll be ready to travel by then. But for now, you'd better go."

Without another word, he took his hat in his hand and set out for the parlor door, stepping around Todd, who stood in the doorway.

~*~

Cordelia stepped delicately to the divan. "Come in, Todd. Pour us both a brandy, will you?"

Todd entered the room slowly, retrieved Robert's brandy from his desk and poured them a drink. Handing her the glass, he noticed she avoided his eyes. He took his seat across from her, crossed his legs and leaned back against the plush chair, spinning the brandy in his glass slowly.

"How long were you standing there?"

"Long enough. From your statement of your own condemnation I can ascertain the rest, I think."

She rolled her eyes, "I doubt that."

"You want to tell me about it then?"

"No. I'm too ashamed."

"Because of Robert?"

"Yes, because of Robert."

Todd leaned forward, taking her hand in his. "Cordelia, you're like a sister to me. You know that. And as your brother, I'm telling you that you have to face the fact that Robert may not be coming back. Don't condemn yourself for this breach in faithfulness. It is entirely possibly that you are a widow and free to follow your heart wherever it leads you."

"No, Todd," she said, tasting the salty quick-silver of her tears, "I'll never be free of him. I'll go to my grave loving

Robert Lawson, which makes my behavior tonight even more depraved."

"What happened, Cordelia?"

"He kissed me, Todd." She searched his face but it remained impassive. "He kissed me and for a moment, I didn't want him to stop. I'm as cheap as that little tart down the hall!"

"Cordelia, really!" he said, resuming his cross-legged posture and sipping his brandy.

"Todd, she is perhaps more honest than I. She follows her lecherous heart wherever it leads her, and tonight it led her to our friend, the general. I, on the other hand, hide my lechery behind decorum. She may be adrift in an ocean of worldliness, but I should be better than that, Todd. I belong to God. I am supposed to practice self-control!"

"You say you belong to God. And I know you do! But what does He say about sin? He says that when we sin, we are to repent and He is faithful to forgive us. That's all He requires. Your repentance. His forgiveness. It's as simple as that. You feel bad about your reaction to *Custer's* impropriety, yes, *his*. He's a married man, an officer and supposedly, a gentleman. He had no right to touch you. He's the villain here."

"No, Todd. Even if I am a widow, which I believe I am not, it was still sin on my part to kiss him. He is, as you said, a married man."

"Even so, God will honor your heart-felt repentance with forgiveness. Should it be harder for you to forgive your own indiscretion than for a holy God?"

"Thank you, Todd." Cordelia took another sip of her brandy. "You're right. If He can forgive me, and He tells us He will, then I must try to forgive myself. The past belongs to the past. I must look to the future and I vow this indiscretion will never happen again."

"With General Custer? I hope not. Like you said, he's a married man. But even if he were not, he's just not good enough for you, Cordelia. He's all flash and glitter! One day, it is my prayer that God will bring someone into your life who will appreciate you and love you with a love that rivals Robert's own devotion to you."

Cordelia shook her head vigorously. "No, Todd. That will never happen."

Wisely, Todd let the prediction pass unchallenged. They sat together before the fireplace and comfortably shared their silence for the next three-quarters of an hour. Todd decided it was time to turn in. They both had a big day ahead of them.

Thirty

Like a zombie, Cordelia shuffled from one lantern to the next, snuffing each in its turn. The last lantern, she carried into her bedroom. Pulling the curtains to, she moved listlessly through the motions of undressing but her arms felt weighted as she turned each button on her dress, and then watched it float to the floor around her bare ankles. Leaving it there, she changed into her warm nightgown and sat before the mirror, looking at her image dispassionately. Removing the pins from her hair, she brushed it until it hung curling and loose around her shoulders. With a heavy sigh, she slipped between the crisp covers of her bed, conscious that it would be the last one she'd sleep in for a long time.

Reaching for the lantern on the bedside table, she turned the light down low, noticing the shadows playing across the opposite wall. There, in her bed, she lay silent and unfeeling . . . and more alone than she'd ever felt in her life.

Where was Robert? She said it aloud, "Robert." The sound of his name seemed strangely unfamiliar. She'd always felt his presence near her, but tonight he seemed so very far away. Yes, this was the last night she'd sleep in this big, comfortably lumpy bed, the bed she shared with her beloved. She turned to her side so she could follow the contours of the pillow next to her.

In the dim lantern-light, she tried to remember exactly how he looked lying next to her, to remember the times they'd gazed at each other in the dream-lit night. To her disappointment, she found the image fuzzy around the edges. Willing herself to recreate, in her mind, a clearer vision of his face, his eyes, the hollow of his throat, the strong chest and chiseled abdomen, she found she was unable to bring the vague form into clarity. She squeezed her eyes shut, admonishing herself for her faithlessness; opening them, she tried again to formulate the image.

It was no use. She could see him in her mind's eye for a mere second before the image began to distort. His soft, caressing brown eyes became piercing, observant and devilishly blue. His neatly trimmed moustache became longer, bushier, curling slightly at the corners.

Cordelia covered her eyes with her hands to block the vision as she flipped onto her back, watching the play of light on the ceiling. "Robert." She said it again, hoping to bring him to life in her mind.

"Is he still alive?" she allowed herself to ask for the first time. "If he is, why hasn't he come back to me? Where is he? Does he feel my presence with him? Are thoughts of me his companions now? Please, God, take care of him. Please bring him back to me."

She took a deep breath, trying to relax into the feathery comfort of her bed. But sleep wouldn't come. Not tonight. Instead, she remembered in flashes of clarity, not her husband's gentle hand upon her face, but the feel of another man's lips upon hers—sweet, soft moving, searing her with unspoken passion, longing. Feeling the firmness of his body pressing hotly against her own, Cordelia's lips had parted to allow the tentative exploration of her mouth, his warmth permeating into her being.

She bolted upright in the bed. "Stop it!" she cried into the night. "I will *not* think about this anymore!" She threw the heavy down comforter off her and walked to the window to open the curtains. Tonight she wanted to see the stars, the moon. She wanted to sense that she and her beloved, though separated by distance, could search the face of that same big, glowing moon together.

There was no way for her to have known that there *was* another gazing up at that same glowing orb—someone standing outside his tent, remembering her softness, and the heat of her skin upon his own, and her strong but delicate fingers entangling the soft curls of his hair.

Lying in her bed once again, Cordelia felt hot tears trace their way from the corners of her lovely eyes and pool in her ears, making the sounds of the night go muffled. But even through her tears, she felt oddly disconnected from her emotions, an unfeeling shell, just lying there thinking its thoughts and breathing its soft, even breaths into the night.

~*~

With the sky's first illumination, Cordelia shoved her pads, paints and brushes into her carpetbag, ready for travel. She placed her hat at an angle and tied the attached scarf clumsily under her chin. Tugging at her gloves, she picked up her bags and wrestled them into the parlor.

Just then, she heard the rattle of wheels outside. While she gathered last-minute items from her quarters, she heard Bess answer the door. She ushered a smiling, young soldier into the parlor.

"You may go ahead and load these bags into the wagon, please. And I'll want this easel packed, too."

"An' I have a basket for you," Bess added. She shuffled down the hall and out the door and returned with a big basket packed with items wrapped in red and white checked cloths.

"I packed this up for you, Missy," Bess said, wiping a tear from her eye with the hem of her apron. "Just so you don't have to travel hungry. I packed the sandwiches you asked for, but there's some of your favorite things in there, too!"

"Oh, Bess," Cordelia replied, holding her in her arms as they sobbed into each other's shoulder. "Thank you."

The young soldier, who told Cordelia to call him "Bug" (short for Doodlebug, he said) went about his task briskly and happily. Like the other members of the 7th cavalry, he was as anxious as a schoolboy to be on the move again.

"Mrs. Lawson, we're all ready now," he grinned energetically.

"I'll be right there . . . Bug," she forced herself to say.

Noting Bess and Lucy's wet eyes, Cordelia struggled to maintain her composure. "How can I travel with a man I have to call 'Bug?'" she laughed, easing the tension just a little.

"I just want to tell you both how much I've appreciated," she began, "everything you have done for Robert and me." Her voice broke, as she tried to go on. "You know how much you both mean to me. And I want you to know that we'll see each other again someday. I intend to go east eventually and I'll send for you when I do. You may have lives here then that you won't want to leave, so I want you to know you will be under no obligation to move east when I do. But you'll be welcome. You know that."

She looked from one face to the other. Lucy was trying hard not to cry, but Cordelia heard a sniffle from her direction. Lucy pushed Bess aside and placed her thin, young arms around Cordelia's shoulders. "Good-bye, ma'am. Thank you for all you've done for me, for teaching me and everything. I won't forget you, not ever!"

"You'd better not," she sniffed. "Take care of each other. And Bess, you take care of that man of yours. Remember me on your wedding day. I'm sorry I can't wait for the preacher to get here. But General Hazen assures me that one has been requested and is adding this stop to his circuit."

"I'll write to you, Mrs. Lawson," Lucy assured her.

"Good! Just send your letters to Camp Washita. I'll pick them up there. I'll look forward to hearing from you. Now, where's Minnie? Isn't she coming?"

"She said good-bye to us a little while ago," Bess explained. "She said she'd meet you out back."

"All right, then. So I guess this is good-bye."

She waved and followed Bug to the buckboard. He helped her up and, with the agility of the young, quickly climbed up beside her with a partially toothless grin.

Doc had told her once that many of the men suffered with missing teeth while stationed on the Great Plains. Besides the lack of oral hygiene, scurvy was the chief cause of this. The soldiers rarely ate the fruits and green vegetables that could prevent the disease. He'd tried unsuccessfully to mandate the growing of a garden for the sake of the enlisted men on the fort. It was not of vital importance, he was told. They didn't have the manpower to delve into agriculture out here. As a result, many succumbed to the disease.

Cordelia remembered, with a little shiver, Doc's words as he told her that he had seen men reach into their mouths and extract a perfectly healthy tooth with nothing but their own fingers. That's one of the devastating effects of scurvy, he'd said. The men who would listen to his advice had to rely on wild green plants like lamb's quarters, wild garlic and wild onion.

That was something George Custer would never have to worry about, that's for sure, Cordelia thought. Not only was he privileged enough to eat a balanced diet most of the time, but he was fastidious about hygiene. He even carried a toothbrush in his shirt pocket at all times so he could immediately brush his gleaming white teeth after a meal. She shook her head at the memory.

Turning her attention back to young Doodlebug, she told him, "You'll need to drive around back to pick up my horse and supplies; we'll have an extra passenger, to boot!"

"Yes, ma'am."

With a shout of "Hyah!" to the mules, Bug turned them around and looped back to the small stable where he jumped down from the wagon. He breathed an appreciative whistle when he laid eyes on Sunburst.

"What a beauty!" he exclaimed. "I never saw him up close before!"

"Thank you. He was a gift from my husband. He picked him out for me himself."

"Come on, boy," he said to Sunburst. "Let's go." He led him out of the stall by his halter and tied him securely to the back of the buckboard, next to his own horse, "Freckles."

Minnie slowly made her way to the wagon.

Bug looked at her a long time, and then glanced up at Cordelia. "This is our other passenger?" he asked.

"It is," Cordelia said, authoritatively.

"Well, let me load this here saddle up first and then I'll make a spot for her to sit in the back. There's not much room up front, you know."

Minnie said nothing, just stood there drilling holes through Bug with hostile eyes, while unintentionally leering with her permanently demented smile. Her hair hung in two thick braids, tied with rawhide strips. But she wore an American-style dress and apron that Bess had taught her to make, adding her own touches with beads and fringe.

Bug tried to help her up into the wagon, but Minnie shied from his touch and jumped into the wagon unassisted, glaring at him all the while. Shrugging his shoulders, Bug checked the knots securing the horses, then hopped onto the seat beside Cordelia and slapped the reins lightly across the backs of the mules.

"We're off!" he cried, gleefully.

Cordelia looked back at the officer's quarters, then at the fort itself and wondered if she'd ever see it again. Filled with excitement, satisfaction and even a tinge of dread, she set her eyes on the horizon, following the scattered procession of soldiers gathering outside the Indian camp—broken down now—for the forced march south.

Once away from the fort, her gaze fell to the vast expanse of prairie. The wide, empty prairie lay in all directions around her, the tall grasses moving like the boundless waves of the sea. She asked herself, *Am I sailing on the ocean or traversing the Great Plains?* Above the sound of distant voices and the rattle and thud of the wagons, she heard the birds' echoing cries of protest.

She knew George had to be about, but she didn't see any sign of him yet. By the time they reached the village, a line of travelers, Indians as well as soldiers, could be seen extending into the distance ahead of them. Some of the Indians rode horseback, but most walked. The men walked first, unencumbered, Cordelia noticed, while the women followed with the burdens and perhaps even a baby on their backs. Most walked in single file, without a sound.

Others attached themselves to the line behind them. The

wagon train carrying supplies stretched toward the rear, followed by a few head of cattle and the soldiers and rear guard that protected the more vulnerable end of the train. The cattle were brought along to provide beef for the journey. Bug explained that during a forced march such as this, they usually killed one every other day.

Meanwhile, he whistled happily beside Cordelia, which brought some relief to her troubled heart. The last thing she wanted to do was spend almost a week of travel across the washboard expanse of prairie carrying on a senseless conversation with this gawky youngster beside her.

She smiled at the thought that, as George had told her, he had hand-picked her escort. What a sensational choice he'd made! *Not taking any chances, are you, Georgie?* she thought, picking up Lauria's term of affection for the wayward general.

Several times, she turned to look at Minnie, to try to engage her in some way, but Minnie was sitting at the back of the wagon with her legs dangling off the back. She'd wrapped a blanket around her shoulders for warmth and never once tried to return Cordelia's gaze. Wisely, Cordelia realized they both wanted nothing but peace and quiet and time to nurse their breaking hearts. She was content to leave it so.

Three hours into the journey, after being jostled and tossed left, right, up, forward and back by the topography of the plains, Cordelia felt like her own teeth must certainly be loose by now. She'd already bitten her tongue three times. She'd never had to think about tongue-safety before and she smiled at the fact that she was actually expending mental energy trying to find the perfect placement for her tongue to keep from biting it in two!

Her back ached, and her legs were black and blue, she suspected. The seat that had felt surprisingly comfortable on short trips from the fort to the village, now felt like jagged stone to her behind. She longed to stop so she could stretch her legs and walk about, but she had already decided she was not going to be a delicate flower on this trip. She'd prove to all who'd advised her otherwise that she had as much "pluck," as George called it, as anyone else on this trip.

Still, she wondered whether she could handle the extreme discomfort of days of this kind of travel. It wasn't yet noon on the first day and George had estimated a full four or five days to reach Camp Washita. On horse-back, it would only be two or three days, but with so many women and children walking, less than ten miles a day could be expected.

It was a task of monumental proportions. The nine supply wagons carried food, blankets, barrels of water, medicines, guns, shovels and ever-present whiskey. The procession of travelers was over a mile long. There were less than two hundred Cheyenne but the Arapaho numbered over four hundred, she was told.

Repositioning herself repeatedly, she was about to ask "the merry whistler" as she was calling him now, to desist at once, please, when she glimpsed the figure of General George Armstrong Custer himself! And what a sight he was. He was truly in his element now.

Whether she wanted to admit it or not, the way George Custer rode a horse was purely a thing of beauty—so at one was he with his steed. As if reading her mind, Bug spoke up.

"In my whole life, I ain't never seen nobody who could sit a horse like the General, ma'am. Sometimes when they's aridin' along real fast, it's kindly hard to tell where the horse stops and the man starts," he grinned at her.

"Yes, I see what you mean," Cordelia admitted.

With his hunting dogs running with tails wagging beside him, Custer rode down the ranks of the procession dressed in his own self-designed uniform; his large flat-brimmed hat, red kerchief wrapped around his throat, and buckskin jacket with its long fringe moving rhythmically with Dandy's every stride. The brass buckle on Dandy's bridle, with the "US" insignia, gleamed golden in the sunlight. Custer sported a holster in which rested his Remington 44-caliber Army revolvers. He'd belted a saber dramatically around the waist of his Union-issue navy blue pants with gold lace sewn down both sides. Leather boots and leather gloves completed the picture-book ensemble. Impressively, he sat in the black leather saddle, completely comfortable and at ease. His golden curls flowed behind him, catching the glint of the sun. His fierce blue eyes seemed to observe everything at once. Raising his gloved hand toward Cordelia, he flashed a dazzling smile, as Dandy reared and slashed the fresh air with his hooves.

Cordelia's brows rose suspiciously. *What a showman! He did that intentionally, knowing what a handsome sight it was!* she thought as she returned his wave and smiled as if to say, "I'm doing just fine. No problems here. This is easy as pie!" and thought to herself, What arrogance! I bet he's practiced that move—*and* that smile!

"The general is quite a man, ain't he, ma'am?" Bug asked, grinning from ear to ear.

"Oh, yes. He's quite a man all right," Cordelia agreed, but for the life of him, Bug couldn't tell if she was putting him on or not. She smiled innocently at his puzzled glance. They continued on in silence.

~*~

That evening the long procession of soldiers, wagons and Indians broke up into numerous campsites, the soldiers migrating to their own fires and the Indians peeling off some distance to theirs. Cordelia and Minnie were baffled, not knowing where to make their temporary home.

That first evening, they decided to split up. Minnie joined her people, and Cordelia allowed Bug to lead her to the soldiers' campfire. It had been a long day and they hadn't stopped for lunch. Of course, she'd unpacked some cold chicken and Bess's delicious rolls and shared them with Bug and Minnie. She sat on a wooden three-legged stool that Bug snatched from the chuck wagon, and eagerly accepted the tin plate of beans and bacon one of the men passed to her.

Feeling suddenly ravenous, she found the first hurried bites delicious. But she realized after a few minutes that, hungry as she was, she was just too exhausted to finish her dinner. Doodlebug was only too delighted to finish her portion as she bade them goodnight and hobbled back to the wagon.

Taking the canteen from the side of the buckboard, she swallowed a mouthful of the chilled water, then quickly capped it and hung it back. Water was scarce out here. She wanted her supply to last as long as possible.

Just then, a shadowy figure appeared at her elbow, causing her to shy quickly away with a gasp.

"Shhh! It's me," the general whispered to her. "I have to talk to you."

"George, we have nothing to say to each other," she whispered in reply.

"Delia, please!"

She allowed him to walk with her a few steps away from the wagon. Then, in the moonlight he faced her, gently holding her by her arms.

"About last night," he began.

"George. Last night is in the past. We both have to forget it!"

"Would that I could, my dear. Would that I could. I have to explain something to you."

"All right, George," she sighed, dreading what she expected would follow. But he surprised her once again.

"Last night I think we were both just . . . caught up in the moment. I very much regret allowing that to happen. You see, I've never been away from my wife for this long before. And when I'm with you, well, it's almost like being with Libby. You're very much alike in so many ways."

"Please, George, you're not going to say you thought you were with Libby, are you?"

"Of course not. I'm just explaining my admitted attraction to you. But I know it's wrong. And I want you to know that if anything happened between Libby and me, I would be devastated. I love her more than I could ever describe, Cordelia.

"But I'm a man. And as such, I'm certain that if there were no Libby, no Robert, then there would be George and Delia. I have never been so tempted before, and I pray I will never be as tempted in the future. My life and my heart belong solely to my wife. I just wanted you to know that I have prayed for God's forgiveness. And now, I seek yours."

"Then may God forgive us both, George." She looked calmly into his eyes. "You have my forgiveness. Thank you for coming to me tonight. I know you have a lot on your mind out here."

"Thank you for hearing me out. I must go now. Goodnight, Mrs. Lawson."

"General."

With that, he mounted his horse and rode toward his own tent.

She stretched and rubbed her sore muscles for a moment before climbing into the bed of the wagon. With a heavy sigh, she scooted close to Minnie—who was already sleeping—and settled into the narrow space they had cleared for themselves.

Cordelia wasn't about to complain about the sleeping arrangements. At least they were off the hard, frosty ground and after covering themselves with the quilts and comforters Bess insisted they take, they were warm. The last thing Cordelia remembered was replaying, in her head, the conversation with the general, looking up into the starry sky, hearing drumbeats and the singing of Indians at a neighboring campsite, the muffled voices of the men, and the closer crackling sounds of the fire at their own campsite. She could faintly smell the charred wood burning into the night.

Out here under the stars, she felt so close to God. Her prayers seemed strangely . . . unhindered. She smiled to think that a mere ceiling could hinder her prayers, but this broad expanse of sky drew her thoughts ever closer to her Father in heaven. She wondered, again, if it could be possible that Robert could be gazing into the same big sky. She found comfort in that thought.

Just as she closed her eyes, she heard the melancholy sound of an Indian flute cutting through the darkness with the melodic etchings of the musician's soul; making audible the inaudible, making tangible the intangible. The expressive melody lulled her into a deep and lonely sleep.

Thirty-One

The next morning, she woke with a start to the sharp, clear tune of reveille ringing out into the frosty morning. She'd heard it many times from inside their quarters at the fort. This was the first time she'd been awakened from the field and she had to admit it was startling! A person had to be stone deaf or dead not to hear it.

Sitting up, she was surprised to find the members of the camp already about the preparations for their continued journey. As Bug hitched the mules to the buckboard, Indians and soldiers alike scurried around carrying burdens of differing sizes and contents, packing, rattling pans, tearing down camp, shoveling soil into the trenches used to collect the human waste naturally accumulated on such a journey with so many people.

The trench-digging the day before had been fascinating to Cordelia. A company of about a dozen men formed two lines facing each other. At the front of the line, the first four men on each side used picks. The men at the back of the formation had shovels. They worked in rhythm and in perfect time. STRIKE, step, step, step, STRIKE, step, step, step. The men at the front of the line broke up the earth, and those at the end shoveled it out of the trench. In no time, a furrow of at least one-hundred yards had been dug. This teamwork was simply amazing to Cordelia. She admired its efficiency and was, quite honestly, surprised the soldiers had figured out such a feat.

While the men attended to their horses or mules, feeding and grooming them in preparation for the long day ahead, the company cooks, ten to each company, busied themselves with the breakfast preparations for the men. Of course, the high-ranking officers, like General Custer, always brought along their own cook for this task.

After a quick breakfast, Cordelia heard the next bugle call. Robert had explained that this one was called the "General." That was the signal for the tents to be packed and made ready for travel.

Then came Cordelia's favorite, "Boots and saddles." That's when the horses were saddled and the wagons moved into position in the wagon train. Everyone waited with no small amount of excitement for the next command.

Cordelia's burnished locks were in disarray, as she had not bothered to take her hair down the night before. Seeing Minnie at work with her own braids, Cordelia decided to follow suit. Sitting upright, she took the pins from her hair and stored them in one of the carpetbags she'd brought. Fetching her brush, she managed to untangle the worst snarls in her hair. Minnie helped her with the last bit, and then quickly wove it into one long, thick braid that hung down her back.

With that done, Cordelia washed her face and hands and climbed onto the hard seat of the buckboard. In a very few minutes, Bug climbed up beside her with his ever-present grin.

Cordelia nodded in acknowledgement.

When they heard the next bugle blast, Bug explained to her that it was called, "To horse," and Cordelia watched as the men of each company led their horses into line in the appropriate spaces between wagons. Each trooper stood at the head of his horse awaiting the next command.

"Prepare to mount," she heard from the commanding officers up and down the train as the soldiers placed their left foot in the stirrup.

"Mount!" Every man in the cavalry mounted his horse at that command, this simultaneous motion appearing to Cordelia as some kind of giant machine propelled by a single source of power.

Bug grabbed the reins of the buckboard waiting for the bugle to sound the "Advance," the last command of the series. Bug explained that if every man had a mount, they could make twenty to twenty-five miles per day. However, when people were walking, especially women and children, the soldiers had to be satisfied with much slower progress.

Bug slapped the reins and off they went with a jolt, taking their place in the long train of wagons, horses and plodding people, carrying their loads. Some pulled their folded tipis, lodge poles and belongings on a travois, two long poles across which a hide had been stretched. Their packs and bundles were loaded onto the travois, which was pulled either by human effort or by the few dogs that ran with the tribe. This was the first Cordelia had ever seen of a travois, a most efficient way to haul their burdens, she decided.

As sore and stiff as she was, she realized how blessed she was to have the opportunity to ride in a wagon. Her eyes raced across the bent and bowed forms of those less fortunate, those having to walk across this rough terrain. Mostly women, some pulled their travois while others carried their burdens on their backs. Cordelia longed to give them all a rest, longed for enough wagons to carry each of them. But remembering her promise to General Custer that she was to stay in her buckboard along the way, she knew she could do nothing to lighten their loads.

She turned to check on Minnie, who was obviously in a better frame of mind today. She sat in the wagon on her knees, facing forward, as she held onto the back of the seat, humming softly to herself.

"What are they doing?" Cordelia asked her, seeing some women plucking tall, bushy weeds from the prairie as they walked.

"We call the plant 'horsetail.' See how it look like horse tail?"

"Yes, but why? Do you eat it?"

"No. Take it for bleeding. Inside or outside bleeding. Stop it. Very strong medicine. Drink it for that. Or put it on wound. Heal very fast with horsetail."

"Amazing," Cordelia responded, wonderingly. She anticipated learning much more from the Indian people.

Just then, a young Indian boy mounted on a big bay gelding trotted by them. Sunburst began to whinny and fight the lead rope that held him to the wagon. Watching him snort and try to rear, Cordelia was baffled by his behavior until she noticed the young Indian's mount. There was the silhouette she knew by heart—the red-earth color, the three white-stocking feet and long black mane and tail.

"Chief!" she breathed.

"Stop him, stop him!" she cried, standing and pointing toward the young brave. Bug slowed the team, but before he could stop, she had jumped down and was running after the young Indian, who held the rawhide ropes of five other horses trotting behind him.

She held her skirts as she ran, oblivious of her shockingly exposed ankles, of the ruts in the road, of her aching muscles or of the surprised eyes turned in her direction. All she knew was that she had to catch up to that horse, to that young man. Her heart pounded in her throat as she chased after them.

Dimly aware of someone calling her name, she was stopped abruptly by a muscular chestnut ridden by none other than Captain Todd Otis. He stared down at her in disbelief.

"What do you think you're doing, Cordelia? For the love of God, you shouldn't be running in your condition! What's happened?"

"Todd! Look!" she cried, pointing up ahead at the Indian boy and his horses. "Look at the horse he's riding! It's Chief! Chief, Todd!"

Todd's head whipped around as he studied the horse. "It might be, Cordelia, but I'm not positive."

"Well, I am! I rode next to that horse for months, you know. Please stop him, Todd. That boy may know something about Robert! Here, help me up!" she demanded, holding her hand up to Todd.

"You shouldn't . . ." he began. But Cordelia shrieked at him, "Todd! Please!"

One look into those anguished eyes and Todd slid his foot out of the stirrup, allowing her to place hers there and, taking her hand, pulled her up behind him. Together they took off after the boy on horseback. Cordelia arms encircled Todd's waist loosely as they cantered the short distance to the boy.

Todd maneuvered his horse beside the Indian and motioned for him to stop, which he did, searching their faces with worried eyes.

Cordelia had never seen Todd's expression so stern as he demanded the boy tell him where he'd gotten this horse. By now he, too, recognized Robert's horse, Chief.

The boy's puzzled eyes revealed he did not know what was being asked. Cordelia wished with all her heart for Jeremiah before she remembered Minnie. Locating her buckboard, she motioned with excited arms for Bug to hurry to this spot.

He had been following her chase and now pulled the team out of line and moved toward them at a snail's pace, in Cordelia's frustrated opinion. Chief pounded the ground with one hoof as Sunburst strained again at his lead.

"Minnie!" she called. "Minnie, come here! Quickly!" Minnie hopped from the back of the wagon and approached the congregation of horses and people before her.

"Minnie, ask him where he got this horse! Ask him!"

Minnie asked the question and the boy gestured with his arms as he answered her with a lengthy explanation.

"What did he say?" Cordelia wanted to know. She could feel her head pulsing with excitement and anticipation.

"He say he found this horse. This boy is called Andrew Jackson. He is best in our village at getting horses."

"But *where* did he find him? Ask him if he knows anything about Robert."

Minnie began to understand the weight of the situation. She walked to Chief's head and stroked his muzzle, then asked the boy the questions.

The boy answered with a short response, shaking his head vigorously.

"He did not see anyone. He does not know anything about the captain, ma'am. But he knew this was a soldier's horse because of the saddle."

"But does he remember where he found the horse?"

Minnie asked. Cordelia was relieved to see the boy nod his head this time and point again behind them.

"He knows where it was but it was many day from here. Many day from village."

Cordelia spoke quietly, but with firm resolve, to Todd saying, "We must go back and look, Todd. We must go to the place he found Chief. There may be some trace of Robert. Even if it's just . . . well, we just have to go!"

Todd thought about this long and hard. "I don't know, Cordelia."

"What do you mean, you don't know!" she demanded. "We have to go!"

"I'll have to speak to the general about this. He's riding up ahead, I think. I'll find him and talk to him. But I guarantee that even if he grants us permission to investigate the site, he won't allow you to go, Cordelia. Get it through your head that such an excursion would be too difficult. It has to be several days' hard ride from here to the site and then several days back to join the train, if you're not already at the fort by then. In your condition . . ."

"All right, all right! But will you go, Todd? Will you be my eyes?" she interrupted again.

"Yes, Cordelia. I'll go if the general agrees. You'd better tell Andrew Jackson here to stay close to your wagon until I return."

Minnie translated the instructions and Andrew sighed in relief. It didn't seem he was in trouble after all. In fact, he was apparently in a position of importance. He stuck his narrow chest out and held his chin high as he agreed to their request.

Todd rode to the buckboard, where Cordelia transferred back to the hard wooden seat of the wagon. Then he rode forward over successive undulations of earth, like the smooth billows of the sea, until she couldn't see him anymore. Dust clouds and white covered wagons blocked her view of his form.

Though it was a cool day, she wiped her moist palms onto her skirt as she tried to rein in her stampeding thoughts, hopes . . . and wishes. Then she breathed a prayer to God that Robert would be found, and that, Lord willing, he would be alive!

The whole morning was spent in frustration as she awaited

some word from Todd. To release some tension from her weary mind, she told Bug the whole story about her husband, about the search and about the Indian boy on Robert's horse.

To his credit, Bug allowed her to talk, though he knew all about the captain's disappearance. Turning an eye to the Indian's horse, he, too, recognized him as the captain's mount. But what he didn't tell Cordelia was that he was in on the first search for Robert. He knew just how rugged the terrain was and how hard they searched the area for any sign of the young captain. He didn't hold out much hope that Robert had survived the Indian ambush. Still, it was a puzzle as to where the body was. Maybe they could find something after all, he decided. So he said so to Cordelia, whose grateful eyes smiled with all the hope of heaven held in their depths.

Bug silently hoped she would not be disappointed.

As morning turned to afternoon, Cordelia's searching, expectant eyes were finally rewarded as Todd rode back to her. Riding alongside the buckboard, he informed her that the general had approved this mission. He and Andrew Jackson would take a half-dozen soldiers and ride back to the place where Chief had been found.

"He doesn't want you to have any regrets, he said. He wants every possibility exhausted so you'll have peace of mind. Already he's arranged to give us supplies and manpower for this assignment. We'll leave at once."

"Good." Now that she was getting what she wanted, she was suddenly, and unusually, quiet.

"Cordelia, please don't get your hopes up too high. I'm worried about you."

"Don't worry, Todd. I know the odds are poor that you'll find anything that will lead you to Robert. But there *is* a chance, poor or not! And I'm willing to take that chance. I've thought about it lot, as you know, Todd. I know there are hundreds, maybe thousands, of women who watched their husbands go off to war and who never heard from them again. Unfortunately, that's one of the dreadful things about war. It's the not knowing that haunts you. I know there's a likelihood I'll never find out what happened to him. But I still have to hope. Surely you understand that, Todd."

"Yes, I understand. Good-bye, then, my dear. The general will watch over you, he says."

"I'll bet!" she retorted with a teasing smile.

"I advise you to watch *him*!" he replied with a wicked smile. He motioned for the boy to follow him. Needing someone to lead his horses, he allowed Minnie to climb aboard one of his ponies and hold the leads for the others. This number of ponies showed Andrew Jackson's wealth among the tribe. They exchanged several phrases before he rode off with Lieutenant Otis to join the other men and the supply horse.

She craned her neck to watch them as they rode back in the direction from which they'd come. "Go with God, men. Go with God," she whispered.

~*~

Two days later there was still no word. They were almost to Camp Washita at this point. She tried not to think about it, but no matter what she was doing, it was never far from her mind.

The journey south had been more difficult than she'd ever imagined. Though the days became more and more like spring-time, the nights were still cold. But she loved the nights the best. The sounds of the prairie under the canopy of heavenly lights were the backdrop for her dreams.

And in one of those dreams she was riding next to Robert, smiling at him, her heart bursting with love as she watched every graceful motion of his athletic body. The one disturbing element of this dream was that, though she could see him and sense him next to her, he seemed oblivious to her—as if she were beyond his grasp, beyond his awareness. She was riding next to him, but he was riding alone on the prairie. Their horses' pounding hooves became so loud they woke her.

When her eyes fluttered opened, she heard the pounding hooves of a horse approaching the stationary wagon. She sat up in time to watch Custer's flamboyant approach; curls bouncing, white teeth flashing their smile while he took off his hat and nodded to her. Drawing up next to the wagon, he breathlessly greeted her and apologized for not checking on her more frequently in Todd's absence.

"How have you managed the trip so far, Delia?" he asked. "Is there anything you need?"

"I confess it's been harder than I thought it would, but we're fine. Thank you for asking."

It was then that Minnie woke with a start and bolted upright when she saw the general's face looking into the wagon. Wordlessly, her eyes opened wide and her poor, demonic-looking face went pale as she fought hysteria at his sight. This was the first time she'd seen him since the day of her attack last December!

If George Custer was flustered, he didn't show it. Instead, with eyes reflecting God's own kindness, he spoke to her with a voice soft and warm. "No, Minnie, don't be frightened. This gives me the opportunity to apologize to you for that dreadful day so long ago. There is no way I can change what has happened. All I can ask is your forgiveness, though I am not deserving of it in any way."

For a brief moment, this sounded very familiar to Cordelia before she realized this was the wording of his apology to her after his initial impropriety with her. She surmised from this that the general had all too much experience making pretty apologies, yet his face was a study in sincerity at this moment. In fact, were those tears in his blue eyes?

She leaned forward to make sure, but his hat was back on his head now. He stroked his bushy mustache again and bid them both good day. Then he rode off in the direction of the front of the train.

Minnie and Cordelia looked at each other. She placed her arms around Minnie protectively and Minnie seemed to take comfort from this gesture. She cried not a tear but her sorrow was a thing Cordelia felt as her own.

This first contact was over. Cordelia knew that Minnie had dreaded this day but she felt the general had acted most humbly—a monumental feat for him, she thought—and Minnie had maintained more control than she'd ever hoped for.

The memory of Min-nin-ne-wah-hah-ket murderously crouched in the corner of her pantry like a trapped animal flashed through her mind.

"What a long way we've come, the two of us," she said aloud. "Have we only known each other for four months? So much has happened to both of us." She held her close as she continued, "You're going to be all right, Minnie. We both are. I know that now, no matter what happens."

Through the noisy bustle of activity around them, Cordelia again heard the pounding of horses' hooves. Squinting toward the direction of the sound, she spotted the riders approaching at a distance. As they drew closer, she realized Robert was not among them.

"Yes, Minnie," she whispered. "Nothing is the same for us now as it was those months ago. Do you realize that? Both of our lives have completely changed. But we'll be all right. We'll keep fighting for what we love."

Sadly watching the exhausted riders lope towards her, she continued, "Life is precious. And in our lives we will be able to find peace and contentment no matter what adversities we're given. There will be sorrow. I know that. But as long as we continue to trust the Lord and to love Him, He will bring us through everything."

She placed her hand lovingly over her middle. "Every breath we take is a gift from God, Minnie. And as long we have breath, there is . . . hope."

~*~

Later that night, and miles and miles away from where Cordelia camped for the night, another young woman stirred a pot of beans and beef over the open flame of her own campfire. The soft firelight illumined her face and hair, exaggerating her look of concern. Her father sat mending a leather apron he used in his blacksmith work.

"Leona, don't look so worried. He'll either make it or he won't."

"Papa, he's just got to pull through. He's such a good man," she replied, looking toward the wagon where the injured man lay unconscious.

"How can you possibly know that? He was unconscious when we found him and he's still unconscious. You don't know anything about him!"

"I do, too. I can't explain how I know. I just do," she pouted. "Taking care of a man like this just makes a person's heart naturally warm up to him, I guess. I want him to wake up," she said, looking into the starlit sky. "I want him to live, to laugh, to . . . to love."

"Leona, please don't get your hopes up. He's so hurt right now that any minute could be his last. You've done a good job, but don't get your hopes up that he'll wake up and want to marry you. Seems pretty unlikely to me that he'll ever wake up at all."

"No, I told you, this morning he stirred. I thought he was going to wake up then, but instead he just got real still again. I know it's silly, Papa, but yes, I do want him to open his eyes and love me."

His hearty laugh filled the night with warmth.

"I'd better go tend to him before we eat. I need to change that bandage again. The clean ones are probably dry by now," she said.

He watched her snatch the bandages off the line she'd hung them on and step into the confines of the wagon.

Leona held his head up gingerly in one hand while she unwrapped the old dressing with the other one, tugging gently on the last of it—the part that always dried and clung to his scalp. Tossing it next to her in the wagon, she reached for the soft, clean bandages. Starting at that terrible gash in his scalp, she carefully wound the dressing around his head, tucking the end of the bandage underneath the rest to hold it securely.

Admiring her work, she picked up a compress soaked with clear, cool water and bathed his face. Though she wasn't a nurse, she seemed to know how to take care of this man.

He was scarcely breathing when they'd found him just south of Camp Supply lying on a massive rock shelf in a pool of blood with nothing on but his socks and a blood-soaked pair of long johns. Her father wanted no part of it, but Leona insisted on half carrying/half dragging the man to the wagon where she made room for him to lay. The only wound they found on his body was that nasty wound to his head. Leona's father said it looked like a bullet must have grazed his skull. He suspected it was not so much the wound as it was the loss of blood that kept this young man from regaining consciousness.

Her father wanted to take the man back to Camp Supply. Let them take care of him. He had no way of knowing who the man was or where he lived. Leona begged him to let her tend to the handsome young man herself. He finally agreed to take him with them on their long journey to Arkansas.

The wounded man also had a ring on his finger, which Leona quickly removed and tucked into her pocket without her father seeing. She glanced at the chest where she stored it, unseen and almost forgotten.

She wished she really could forget it. Did this man really belong to someone else? Feeling the chill in the air, she pulled the blanket over him and tucked it under his thin body. Once more, she squeezed a little of the clear water between his parched lips, then bathed his face again. She thought she detected the slightest movement of his head. Yes, his eyelids twitched and squinted. Then, with a little flutter, he finally opened his eyes. Unfocused and bleary, at first, he blinked a few times and it seemed to Leona as if the world became clear to him again. He sought her face and studied it, though still hovering somewhere between sleep and waking.

She found herself looking into the softest brown eyes she'd ever seen.

Other Books by Deborah Howard

Sunsets: Reflections for Life's Final Journey

Where is God in All of This?

It's Not Fair! with Dr. Wayne Mack

Help! Someone I Love has Cancer

Help! Someone I love has Alzheimer's with Judy Howe

Help! I'm So Lonely

Salvation is of the Lord: An Exploration of God's Saving Work

Jonathan Edwards and The Christian Pilgrim

About the Author

Deborah Howard writes from her home outside Little Rock, Arkansas. Usually writing in the area of theodicy, she departed from her "serious" nonfiction to this "entertaining" fiction—her first historical fiction series. Not only has she previously published books of her own, but has been instrumental in editing and ghosting books for others.

www.deborahhoward.net